WARRIOR FAE
TRAPPED

Also by K.F. Breene

DDVN WORLD:

FIRE AND ICE TRILOGY
Born in Fire
Raised in Fire
Fused in Fire

MAGICAL MAYHEM SERIES
Natural Witch
Natural Mage
Natural Dual-Mage

WARRIOR FAE SERIES
Warrior Fae Trapped
Warrior Fae Princess (Coming Soon)

———————

FINDING PARADISE SERIES
Fate of Perfection
Fate of Devotion

DARKNESS SERIES
Into the Darkness, Novella 1
Braving the Elements, Novella 2
On a Razor's Edge, Novella 3
Demons, Novella 4
The Council, Novella 5
Shadow Watcher, Novella 6
Jonas, Novella 7
Charles, Novella 8
Jameson, Novella 9
Darkness Series Boxed Set, Books 1-4

WARRIOR CHRONICLES
Chosen, Book 1
Hunted, Book 2
Shadow Lands, Book 3
Invasion, Book 4
Siege, Book 5
Overtaken, Book 6

WARRIOR FAE TRAPPED

BY K.F. BREENE

Contact info:
www.kfbreene.com
books@kfbreene.com

CHAPTER 1

CHARITY LOOKED UP in time to catch the rusty red metal door before it slammed into her face. Someone bumped into her backpack from behind before offering a murmured apology.

Grimacing at the near miss with a busted nose and public ridicule, she pushed out of the lecture hall and peeled off to the side. Students poured out around her into the dark of night, half-asleep and happy to be done with the late class and on their way home.

They had no idea how good they had it. None of them did.

She stilled in the moment, inhaling the crisp ocean air. Santa Cruz was heaven. The mild climate, the cool city buzz, and the thick nature in the surrounding hills. That she attended college here was beyond fantastic—it was a dream come true. One she feared she'd wake from.

"Night," Donnie muttered as he passed by. One single look at his perfectly styled hair, uber-trendy clothes, and perfect face quick-started her heart.

"Nuuun." What the heck was that? Had she suddenly started speaking in Wookiee?

She shook her head, desperate to be cool at least *once* when speaking to this guy.

"Nine—t. Night!" she finally got out.

He didn't glance back as he walked away, his friend Mason falling in step. Together they were like a shining beacon of prestige and designer clothes. She would never earn a place in their super-trendy and wealthy social circle, but that didn't hinder her from watching their nice backsides.

She grinned at the thought and swept her gaze out toward the trees, taking one more moment to savor the lush natural surroundings. A soft itch between her shoulder blades invaded her thoughts. Someone was watching her.

An unobtrusive figure caught her notice out of the corner of her eye. She glanced that way.

A dark-haired man stood just off the pavement beside a large redwood tree, mostly bathed in shadow except for a slice of light that cut across his lips, showing a grin.

He stepped forward, the movement strangely blurred, too fast for the nonchalance of his poise. His weight was perfectly balanced with a fighter's grace, as though he were ready to spring forward.

Tingles of apprehension worked up Charity's spine. Growing up in a low-income area with a lot of crime, she knew the signs of an attacker. She knew that her five-foot-five frame, small demeanor, and dainty features practically screamed: *I'm vulnerable, take my money.* Usually a hard stare backed with her fighter's confidence could make a cracked-out thug think twice.

This wasn't a cracked-out thug. This man was dangerous—she could read it in the loose readiness of his body, in the lean muscle gained from violence, in the predatory stare meant just for her.

Skin crawling in a way she hadn't experienced before, she turned away from the trees and headed across campus, making for a bright patch of light from a lamppost. A muffled roar from the distant surf merged with her soft pants, her breath speeding up as something primal coiled within her, urging her faster. She glanced back, wondering if this character was as quiet as he was abnormally quick.

The space near the tree lay empty. The man was nowhere to be seen.

She ripped her gaze forward again, half expecting him to be waiting in front of her with open arms and a smile.

Nothing.

The concrete walkway ahead of her, which led down some steps and wove between buildings, lay dark but for that lamppost, and mostly empty. He'd vanished without a sound.

Laughter rang out to the right. Her heart skipped a beat. Two people her age, a man and a woman, sauntered out from a building, arm in arm.

She let out a shaky breath and kept her fast pace.

The soft itch between her shoulder blades turned into a burn. Not only was the watcher still out there somewhere, monitoring her progress, but now he had company. She could feel it.

Adrenaline fueled her body, boosting her senses. She reached another set of stairs and took them two at a time.

"I agree," she heard not far away.

Charity jumped and swung that way. A patch of trees sat in a large gap between buildings, collecting shadows and secrets. Nothing moved. No more voices drifted on the wind. Someone had been there two seconds ago, and now the area was deserted.

"What the hell?" Charity breathed out, moving again. She felt like prey. Like something being toyed with.

She increased her speed, intent on getting the hell out of there. She hadn't survived one of the worst neighborhoods in America to get taken out here, just as her dreams were unfolding. To hell with that.

Around the last bend, before the walkway emptied out into the busier thoroughfare near the parking lot, a familiar smell greeted her. Designer fragrance heavily applied, mixed with lilac lotion.

Samantha!

A surge of protectiveness stole Charity's breath. Her roommate was somewhere nearby, likely clueless to the danger pressing in on her.

Charity rounded the bend and, as expected, found

Samantha sitting on an otherwise empty bench, so focused on her phone that she was oblivious to the night around her.

"Sam, what are you—"

"Oh my God!" Sam jolted and clutched her phone to her chest. Upon seeing who it was, she let out a deep breath and sagged. "Charity! You scared me!"

"What are you doing sitting out here by yourself?" Charity asked, stepping closer. She glanced around, her skin still crawling. The watchers were out there, somewhere, in viewing distance yet still hidden.

What did they want with Charity? Couldn't they tell that she didn't have anything worth taking?

A low laugh drifted on the night air, filled with sex and heels and wicked daggers.

Charity reached for Sam's hand without thinking, grabbed her wrist instead, and yanked her to standing. "Did you hear that?"

"Hear what—are you serious right now? With the grabbing?" Samantha twisted away. "Why are you being so pushy? It's really unflattering, Charity."

Charity recoiled, strong and efficient when in combat mode, but completely out of her element when dealing with her elite classmates, Sam included. If making people feel small were a superpower, her roommate would be wearing spandex.

"Come on," Charity urged, *sans* touching. "You shouldn't be sitting out here by yourself. It's dangerous."

Sam crinkled her nose and shook out her wrist, though she started to walk. "Are you kidding? This campus has, like, zero crime. I'm fine. There were a ton of people walking by before you came."

"Something is out here tonight," Charity murmured, peering into the darkness surrounding them.

Sam flicked her long blonde hair over her dainty, bare shoulder. It wasn't exactly off-the-shoulder sweater season, but Sam made it work. "Honestly, if you'd been in this much of a hurry after class, I wouldn't have been waiting here all night." Her right three-inch designer heel hit a divot and her ankle wobbled, but she continued her strut like a champ. "It's been forever. What kept you?"

"My class only ends a half-hour after yours," Charity said, feeling the burn between her shoulder blades lessen to an itch. That man and his crew had dialed back their attention. Good news.

"Yes. At ten." Sam checked her watch. Diamonds glittered in the light of a lamppost. "It's ten twenty. Where have you been?"

The path opened up, revealing a two-lane road flanked by sidewalks and backed by forest. Cars slowly passed by, pausing at crosswalks for pedestrians heading for the parking lots or the bus. Many of the students on campus dressed like Charity—jeans or leggings paired with sweaters and shirts. Only a small group wore the kind of wealth donned by the likes of Samantha and Donnie. They were the out-of-towners, mostly.

The people not rich enough to buy their way into Yale, but plenty rich to deck themselves out in hundreds if not thousands of dollars of clothes and apparel.

Charity had no idea how she'd ended up riding the edges of their circle. It was madness. Plenty of people would kill to be in her shoes.

Well…not in her shoes exactly, since each had more than a couple of holes—the sole was coming off the right one, and the left one was always mysteriously damp. But people would line up to get the scraps Charity didn't mind accepting, like random rides, a cheap room off campus, and leftover food (Sam thought leftovers were beneath her). A little attitude was a small price to pay for the perks and benefits of being Samantha Kent's friend.

"I didn't realize you'd be giving me a ride," Charity said distractedly. The itch of the watcher continued to fade the closer they got to the street. She sighed, releasing the tension in her shoulders. Her new friend didn't plan to follow them home. Maybe he hadn't been interested in her, as such, but the school's expensive equipment. A high-level thief would probably be that stealthy and intense. She'd only known the low-level kind, jerky and drug-addled.

"Jet and I are taking a break," Sam said, her sashaying hips catching the attention of two different guys. "The passenger seat is free. I mean, honestly, what guy trades his car for a new surfboard?" She huffed and shook her head, glancing at the people in their vicinity and giving each a dismissive once-over. "He was insanely hot, but clearly his priorities were completely off. Daddy would throw him out of the house if I brought him home."

Of course, *Daddy* would never meet any of the guys Sam saw. She'd have to be with them for longer than a couple weeks for that.

"Jet was a stupid name," Charity said, pausing on the sidewalk for a car to pass. Sam was already stepping onto the crosswalk. Tires chirped on concrete as the guy behind the wheel slammed on his brakes.

"I know, right?" Sam said, flicking her hair again. "I mean, at first I was like—that's kind of cool"—she made a line in the air with her hand—"*Jet*. He calls himself"—she did the line again—"*Jet*. Not many people can give themselves names and make it work."

"There's a reason for that."

"Totally. *Ugh*." She lugged her purse to her other shoulder. "I hate how heavy my handbag is."

"That's why backpacks have two padded straps—"

"Anyway. Finally, I realized that he was a total dweeb. He wasn't even good in bed. I'd been totally fooling myself."

"Dweeb? How very eighties of you."

"I know. Eighties trends are coming back. I'm using the words to go with them. Rad, right?"

"Not really."

"Hurry up. I need to get home and go through my closet. There is this totally fetch party tomorrow night and I need to wear something great. It's exclusive. They actually *mailed* invitations. Not email, but *mail*-mail."

"Snail mail, they call that."

She stopped by her sleek, champagne-colored Porsche and swished her hair over her bare shoulder before opening her door. "The words were in this old-fashioned cursive font, but all loopy. It looked hand-written. Like someone actually used a fountain pen and wrote on the paper." She pushed the seat up and dropped her handbag into the back before jabbing the button to open Charity's door. "Only a handful of people were invited." She preened as she sat in the car. "I am on a very short list, and I'm only a freshman."

"Awesome." Charity got into the front passenger seat, touching as little as possible so as not to dirty anything, dropped her bag between her legs, and closed the door after her.

"It totally is." Sam's voice rang with excitement. She absolutely lived for parties and status. This sounded like both rolled up into one. "Jessica got invited too, *thank God*. We're going to go together so we don't look like losers showing up alone."

"Good call." Charity draped the seatbelt over her middle, adding just enough to the conversation to fly under the radar. It was what kept her so firmly at the edge of the social group. "Power in numbers."

"God you're weird."

Or maybe not.

Besides the weird maybe-thief she'd seen on campus, it felt like a normal night, with a normal amount of awkwardness. Charity certainly didn't expect her life was about to change forever.

CHAPTER 2

"HURRY UP, CHARITY!"

"Sam, no way. I am not going to that thing." Charity put a hand on the open textbook in front of her. "I'm busy tonight."

Samantha stalked into the room like a runway model, her shimmery metallic dress flowing over her curves and stopping just below her crotch. Her Underoos were going to get some breeze this evening. Black straps from her four-inch stilettos crisscrossed over her ankles, and spangled bracelets tinkled as she irritably placed her hand on her hip. The woman could be tenacious when she wanted something, and she *really* wanted Charity to go to the exclusive party with her.

Jessica had called to cancel. She hadn't wanted to, but she'd gotten food poisoning and could barely get off the bathroom floor. Sam was devastated. The party was invite-only, she couldn't do the inviting, and now she'd have to go alone, since she'd die before missing such a swank gathering.

Unfortunately, not ten minutes later, Sam had received a phone call inviting Charity to the party in

Jessica's place.

"Charity, no normal student sits in their room on a Friday night. Not even the biggest dweebs. You're coming. And hurry, because Richard said we should come earlier than the invite said." She popped out a hip. "Something about the caterer."

"Richard?"

"The guy offering you the chance of your lifetime." She paused. Charity offered her a blank look. Sam rolled her eyes. "The guy on the phone? Inviting you to the party?"

Charity schooled her expression into one of defiance. "Sam, I have a test coming up, and this book isn't going to read itself."

Sam's perfectly sculpted eyebrows dipped low. "Firstly, if you download text-to-speech, it will absolutely read itself."

Charity paused in her rebuttal. "Really?"

"Second, you're getting straight A's, you're an overachiever, and everyone hates how you make them look bad. You don't need to study tonight. You need to go to this party."

"Yes, let's talk about that." Charity leaned an elbow on her ramshackle desk. "Doesn't it seem odd to you that a rich dude who sends out fancy invitations with incorrect times would allow you to bring your roommate? I mean, I'm not exactly keeping up with the Joneses."

Sam scoffed. "Clearly they knew I'd hate to go

alone, and they're making things right. It's a smooth move, if you ask me. They're letting me take my little project." She gave Charity a sarcastically sweet smile that received a glower in return.

"Who are *they*, anyway? I know plenty of dicks, but not one Richard." Charity grinned at her joke.

Sam didn't get it. "They"—she drew out the word—"are influential and important, and *they* think I am worthy of their time."

"You've managed to answer my question while simultaneously ignoring it—"

"And *they* invited you, which means you are coming. I will not go to this party by myself, Charity. I simply will not."

"Well, you're going to have to because—"

Sam's voice lowered an octave as she said, "Charity, I did not beg my parents to move you in here so you could sit in your room like a librarian and piss your life away."

Damn it. She was bringing out the big guns.

"I'm studying for a test, though," Charity whined. "That's the opposite of pissing—"

"I could've left you in that tiny dorm room. Remember that place? Peeling paint, weird smell, probably mold in the closets. I could've let you huddle up in the corner, with all the other nerds, and listen to someone snoring all night. I could've, but I didn't. Do you know why?"

"You secretly loathe me?"

13

"Because you can be cool. That's why. You need to have friends, Charity. You need to be reminded to file your nails. And you need to get your ass to a few parties once in a while. Let me help you. Get up, get dressed, and let's go!"

Samantha stomped from the room with hips and breasts flying, making a counterargument impossible.

Charity blew out her breath and leaned heavily against the desk. When Sam had decided the dorm rooms were too filthy, noisy, and cramped for her to contemplate staying there, not to mention the horror of the communal bathroom, she'd cried to her daddy to fix the situation. He had rented this modest house in downtown Santa Cruz. He could've afforded something much nicer, but the low-budget accommodations were supposed to teach his daughter a little humility.

Yeah, right. She'd used his credit card to deck out most of the place with quality and trendy furniture the likes of which Charity had never even touched before, let alone used.

Surprise of surprises, Sam had asked her assigned roommate, Charity, if she wanted to move with her. And while Charity hadn't minded the size of the dorm room, its faded and peeling paint, or even the communal shower, she had minded the incessant buzz of conversation and drunken laughter, which had proven a distraction from her studies. Charity had promised her mother that she'd make something of herself, and by God, she would fulfill that promise if she did nothing else in the world.

Too bad the good fortune came with a price tag.

Samantha hadn't only wanted Charity along because she thought she was cool. Not even because she was quiet, respectful, and cooked and cleaned like she was hired help. No, Sam had insisted on Charity's tenancy because she was fascinated by a poor kid from the wrong side of the tracks. "Ethiopian poor," Samantha had said as she glanced over Charity's belongings, contained neatly in two thirteen-gallon garbage bags. Samantha just could not believe someone could live with empty closets, empty cupboards, a couple of pens, and a computer she got out of the lost and found.

Ultimately, how she'd gotten here didn't matter. Charity was in bliss with her luck. She had a bedroom mostly to herself (guests used it, too), a big backyard to practice martial arts (which she'd always been strangely great at), and a clean kitchen.

Samantha knew all this, of course, and used it as her secret weapon when she really wanted something.

Damned foul play!

"Seriously, though," Charity shouted, picking at her threadbare jeans and putting in a last-ditch effort to get Sam to relent, "I do actually have a test on Thursday. Plus, I don't drink. How fun could I possibly be?" Into the ensuing silence, she yelled, "Spoiler alert: not fun at all!"

"There are plenty of other things to do besides drink…" came the disembodied reply.

"Like what?" Then it dawned on her. "I don't do drugs, either. Super not fun. Happy with a pocket protector. Best left at home."

"Donnie's going to be there."

Charity's shaking head jerked to a stop. Fizzy excitement she couldn't help bubbled up her middle.

First the big guns, then the low blow. That crush was so stupid, too. She couldn't even talk to the guy. She stammered with a red face every time he said two words to her. God forbid he try for a conversation. He was too pretty for his own good. Too suave by half.

So why was she now contemplating going to a party she wouldn't have any fun at, with a girl who would ignore her as soon as they got there, just to see him? She might as well pour paint on her head and label herself a social pariah.

Sam's head popped into the doorway. "And he always looks good when he goes to parties," she said with a mischievous grin.

"Fine, I'll go," Charity grumbled, hating herself for uttering the words. Hating Sam for making her.

She looked down at herself. One knee looked back up through the hole in her jeans. It wasn't a trendy hole, either. It was a Kmart special hole in a pair of jeans so old they should've been shot and buried in the yard.

"What am I going to wear?" Charity called as Sam ducked away again. "Earlier tonight you called me a hobo tramp."

Metallic black material flew into the room. It shimmered and sparkled before landing on Charity's desk, washing across the surface, and then slinking down to the floor. Samantha popped her head back in, shooting Charity a pointed stare. "Don't you dare spill anything on it."

"Why do all of your going out clothes resemble something a cross-dressing rock star would wear?" Charity mumbled, picking up the dress. "Besides, I can't wear your clothes. What if I do spill something? I can't…"

She cut the sentence short, not wanting to admit that she could barely afford her hoodies, let alone an extravagant, fashionable dress. Some things were too awkward to voice, especially around people who didn't understand the value of money, or how lucky they were to have it.

"Hurry up," Sam called. "We need to be fashionably late, not late-late."

Knowing a losing battle when she saw one, Charity lugged herself out of her chair and faced the smudged closet mirror. The shimmery fabric twinkled, light reflecting off the disco-ball material. She put the dress to her body, the fabric cascading over her baggy clothes, and took in her appearance.

A little color in her pale face would make her look like less of a vampire. A wider set to her flat brown eyes would definitely give her more wow factor. Maybe a curl to her mop of brown hair, or a highlight or two. Did they have time for a nose job?

She smirked at herself, moving away. Plain but perky. It could certainly be worse.

A shoe torpedoed into the room, smacking off the edge of the bed. Another shot in as the first was bouncing around the floor.

"Hurry up!" Sam shouted.

Charity fingered the dress and sighed. "How bad can this party be?"

CHAPTER 3

"**O**H MY GOD, *he's* here?" Sam stomped on the brake, making the seatbelt dig into Charity's pronounced cleavage.

"I already regret this dress," Charity mumbled, pushing back in her seat.

"That is who I think it is, right?" Sam sounded giddy as she leaned heavily over the steering wheel to see through the darkness.

The one-lane dirt road surrounded by thick redwoods flared out for several feet before a private road branched off to the left. Two cars were parked before the turn-off—a Range Rover and another SUV. Dim light spilled out from the open car doors, illuminating a few people standing around the vehicles. Other lights peeked through the branches of trees beyond. The house clearly sat at some distance.

"Is that the driveway? Because there's no more room to park down here. Jeez, why would someone live this far out?" Charity looked through the rear window of the Porsche. They'd traveled a half-hour to Scott's Valley, a place generally known for wealth, only for GPS to guide them off the two-lane road onto this deathtrap. "I mean, if someone is coming in, and someone else is going out, one of them has to back down this skinny freaking driveway to let the other pass. That's crazy. Fire season must make these people awfully nervous."

"Shh," Sam said, her gaze rooted to a guy with his foot on the bumper of the expensive SUV. A few people stood around him, all of them looking up at the ladies' approach.

"That guy has no respect for fancy cars," Charity whispered, trying to pick out their various appearances in the moonlight. "I like that."

"That *is* him. That's Devon!" The lights from the dash highlighted Sam's smile as she inched along, the Porsche moving impossibly slow. "When I showed him the invite earlier, he didn't say anything. It makes sense that he'd be invited given…who he is, but he never goes to parties. I mean, obviously he couldn't say no to this, right? I wonder why he didn't say anything, though? He is so incredibly hot. Mm, I love bad boys."

Charity leaned forward to try to get a better look at the guy who had so completely captured her room-mate's attention. He projected lazy boredom in a stylized sort of way, as if he'd rolled out of bed, taken a shower, primped, and then used gel and hairspray to emulate the look of someone who'd rolled out of bed. But it was clear from the ripped jeans, raven stubble, and tight white shirt that he was definitely going for a badass vibe. James Dean of the modern age.

If he'd wandered through Charity's neighborhood growing up, he'd have gotten his wallet *and* his shoes stolen.

"I take back what I said earlier," she said, her mouth twisting in distaste. "I don't like anything this guy is selling."

Samantha leaned back in her seat, and her boobs popped, cut through with the seatbelt. She didn't seem to notice.

"He's a junior, I think." She eye-goosed him. "Or maybe a sophomore. He is *the* available bachelor. Well, you know, if you like the dangerous type…"

She said it like she might've said, "If you like *gold*…"

"What sort of danger? Does his dad's secretary wave a sharp pen around?"

Sam *tsked*. "He carries a *gun* for one, smarty, and so do his friends. For two, he's in a gang. He's the leader."

"A gang?" Charity couldn't help the disbelieving smirk.

She'd seen gang members. Guys so hard their eyes screamed murderer from twenty yards away. Brutal killers with the smarts to stay out of jail. They'd gun down a kid to get even on a drug score.

This guy was not in a gang.

Except…

Her gaze frisked the crew as they drew closer. There weren't any telltale bulges in the usual places street thugs hid weapons, at least none she could see in the dim light, but the way these guys (and one girl) held themselves, with their shoulders pointed her way, loose and easy, their posture screaming readiness, it was clear they could handle themselves. There'd be one helluva tussle if she met one of them in a dark alley.

Or a dark, one-lane road deep in the trees…

"We should keep going, probably," Charity said.

Samantha stopped just before the rear end of the Range Rover and rolled down her window, her chest still pushed out prominently, which looked really awkward in the car.

"This is the opposite of what I said you should do," Charity murmured.

"Hey," Samantha said as Devon straightened up.

He walked closer with a swagger born of infallible confidence. Broad shoulders sported lean muscle, and his white T-shirt stretched over a flat stomach. He stopped by the car but didn't lean down toward Sam, something not many men would have passed up, given all the boobage on display.

"Why are you guys down here?" Samantha said in her sex-kitten voice. "Isn't the house up there a ways?" She pointed to the private road ahead.

"It is, yeah," he replied, sounding unimpressed. "We're not going. I hear those parties can be pretty dangerous. You should head back."

Sam laughed, breathy and overdramatic. She was laying it on a little thick. "Dangerous?" she asked, "For you?" She laughed again. "I don't believe that for a minute."

His large hand touched down on the side of the door as he finally bent toward the open window. His intense gaze came into view, banging into Samantha. "Dangerous, even for me. I hear those guys spike drinks. If you go, you should stay away from the punch. I'd get out of here, if I were you."

Sam leaned toward him, her lips curling in pleasure. "Don't you want to come and keep me safe?"

"Good Lord," Charity murmured, half wanting to cover her face so it was clear she wanted no part of this.

That was when his gaze darted toward her, as hard as steel and just as ruthless. Wildness lurked in those eyes, coiled and ready to be unleashed.

Charity's chest tightened, and a cold trickle worked up her spine. For the second time that day, one word slithered through her thoughts.

Predator.

Pretty boy had teeth.

"You should turn back," he told Charity directly, his voice rough. "That party is no place for you." His eyes darted from her clothes to her shoes, which should've been hidden by the darkness, then to her wrists and her neck. Her face. A furrow creased his brow as he took in her lack of jewelry and her dusting of makeup. All Sam had lent her was the dress and shoes, asserting that no one would notice or care that Charity didn't have bling. Given that Charity preferred not to be frosted like a cake, she hadn't pressed.

But Samantha had been wrong—this guy noticed,

and with his not-so-subtle gaze, he was telling her that she didn't belong. She was a hobo tramp in an expensive outfit.

Usually she didn't care what douchey rich kids thought. She laughed it off. Why not? She was proud of how far she'd come. But for some reason she didn't understand, his intelligent gaze poked her uncomfortably. It cut through her defenses and jabbed at the core of her. The real her, where she hid her secrets and vulnerabilities. The place without any armor.

"You should go," he said again, his tone commanding. Urgent. "Turn around. Trust me. Go home."

"Oh my gosh." Sam brushed his fingers with her own. He flinched back. "You're so silly." She pouted, complete with a protruding lower lip. "I RSVPd that I'd go. They're counting on me." The pout turned into a sexy smile, and Charity had to applaud Sam's facial gymnastics. "But I promise I'll be careful."

"They're not going to change their minds," one of the guys near the Range Rover said.

Devon bent once more, looking at Charity. Appealing to her. He must've known, hell or high water, Samantha would go to that party, but he clearly thought Charity might heed his warning.

She didn't understand why he cared.

"Why are you skulking around down here if you're not going?" Charity asked him.

His stare intensified, and he shifted his weight as though he had something to say.

"Exactly. He'll go." Sam swept her hair from around her shoulders and set it to draping down her right side, giving him a better view for one last look at her breasts. "Won't you?"

When he didn't comment, Sam smiled and wiggled her fingers.

"See you inside," she said, and rolled up the window.

"Maybe we should listen to him," Charity said as the Porsche passed the small gathering of people. "I mean, he's camped out down here on Killer's Highway, warning people away. Clearly he thinks this is a bad scene."

Samantha scoffed. "He's just hanging out with his boys before heading to the party the rest of them weren't invited to. He'll go. Anyone invited to this party would be stupid to decline. The host is an internet mogul or something. He's really well-to-do."

That meant insanely rich.

"Okay, but does this internet mogul have a basement he likes to chain people in? Because swank party or not, that's not an awesome way to spend a few months, you know?"

"You are so weird," Sam said, her gaze flicking to the rearview mirror as she pulled up the drive. "Devon's probably trying to manipulate us. But you can't shit a bullshitter."

"I don't think that's a saying."

"He'll show up, don't worry. He'll hang out with his

guys, like I said, then bounce and hit the party to pick up the drunk girls."

"There's so much wrong with that statement…"

"I'm ready for this moment. I will go home with him tonight."

"Okay…but you're my ride."

"It's fine," Sam said, although Charity wasn't sure *how* it was fine.

Around another blind bend that must've resulted in more than a few accidents, Sam rolled to a stop next to a keypad. She reached out of the window and entered the code.

"You had it memorized?"

"Of course," Sam said.

A large gate decorated with what looked like arrows shooting into the sky shuddered to a start, swinging open. The road went a ways further, down an incline, before it opened up into a large driveway. High-dollar vehicles were parked along the side, and the house, glowing excessively, lazily stretched out fifty yards in front of them. The house looked so modern that it might pass for a spaceship. A path dotted with flowers wound toward the impressive front entrance nestled between columns, welcoming the wayward traveler—if that traveler happened to own an island and a sweatshop.

Charity tried to melt into the Porsche's bucket seat. She resented agreeing with that clown with the Range Rover, but it was clear that she didn't belong here. This was a dozen steps above Sam, and Sam was a marathon above Charity. Charity would stick out in a very bad way. She said as much.

"C'mon, you look great," Sam said, getting out of the car.

"What millionaire wants to live at the end of that death road, anyway?" Charity climbed out of the car. Her dress pulled down, nearly exposing her breasts, before cinching up, not far from giving a crotch peep show. "Why do guys get to wear clothes that cover their bodies, and fashion tells women to basically go nude? I mean, don't guys usually have to pay for that pleasure?"

"You're so weird," Sam said again—it was her favorite observation of Charity—and her hips swayed as she made it to the front of the car. "To answer your question, a millionaire that wants privacy."

Devon's urgent tone resurfaced in Charity's memory. He'd been so adamant that they should turn around.

"Or maybe a millionaire with a lot of secrets," she murmured, looking back the way they'd come.

CHAPTER 4

D EVON STARED AFTER the Porsche as it disappeared around the bend. He should've tried harder to get his message across. Samantha never would've turned away, but he'd seen the wariness and intelligence in the other lady's eyes. She had street smarts, he could tell. She might've listened. She might've let one of his guys take her back to the main road so she could get a cab.

"Who was that chick?" Dillon asked.

"The one on the right, the pretty blonde, was invited. Samantha Kent," Devon said without inflection, hiding his unease. "Her daddy is some big-shot CEO. She has a trust, I think, but Vlad isn't after her. He wants her dad. He's going to try to use the daughter to get what he wants from the old man."

Vlad was a cunning, ruthless elder vampire who thought nothing of breaking magical law in the Brink, what magical people called the human world. Vampires were prohibited from changing humans, but the elder didn't intend to ask for permission, either from the humans he planned to change or the shifters who regulated magical law in the Brink.

"I meant the other one. She doesn't belong," Dillon said.

"No, she doesn't." Devon leaned against his SUV and kept from clenching his jaw. "Jessica Young was invited. That was not Jessica Young."

"Was she a last-minute change?" Jimmy asked, easily their least prepared and most immature pack member. "Or is she in the way wrong place at the absolutely worst time?"

Devon directed his gaze back toward the private road. "I don't know."

"I recognize that chick." Andy scratched his nose, expression troubled. His dirty-blond hair stuck up at all angles, the result of using his fingers for a comb after his surf earlier. "She's in my physics class. Damn smart. Dresses like a poor street kid. Smells funny."

Devon remembered the way the gal had scowled when he'd noticed her lack of jewelry, something none of Samantha's friends would leave the house without. They wore bling like it was an art form. Instead of inviting scrutiny, as Samantha always did, this woman shied away from it. If her eyes could've literally shot knives, he would've had to change to his wolf form to heal from the wounds.

"Why would Vlad be interested in a poor street kid?" Dillon asked.

"He wouldn't, unless there is something we don't know." Devon bit back the annoyance in his voice. Surprises were liable to get his whole pack killed. He turned back to Andy. "Smells funny how?"

Andy shrugged and ran his fingers through his hair. "Dunno. She just…doesn't smell right."

Devon pushed away from the bumper of his car. "Is it something we've got to worry about tonight? Or is the smell because she doesn't shower?"

"She smells good. Tantalizing. She's that Sammie girl's roommate. Maybe she got sucked into this gig. The girl is dirt poor, I hear. White trash or something." Andy scratched his chest, catching a hole in his T-shirt and ripping it a little bigger. He didn't seem to notice. "I definitely tried to hit that. You can tell she's feisty, ya know? She wasn't havin' none of it. Hah! She ignored me. She's jonesing after that Donnie kid that got an invite. It's obvious."

Dillon snorted, throwing his arm around his girl-friend Macy's shoulders. "This surprises you?"

"Hey, man! I can usually get the girls. Not as good as Devon, okay sure, but I'm freaking hot, yo. Girls like me."

"Not all girls, apparently." Dillon chortled.

Devon hit each of them with a hard stare. Nerves were to be expected in these situations. Hell, they were going up against the baddest vamp he knew. He'd question his pack if they weren't a little squirrelly. But there was a difference between nervous jitters and acting the fool. They were currently skirting the line.

As expected, their smiles withered.

"I don't think we have to worry about her," Andy

said. "She can't have anything a vamp like Vlad would want. Except blood. Maybe she's the blood bank for after."

That wasn't any better.

"Can't save 'em if they don't want to be saved," Rod, the largest of the pack, said as he glanced up the dark drive.

Rod was right. The chick had made her choice. Devon couldn't do anything about it now. They'd set up shop dangerously close, and if he approached the house too soon, he'd alert the vampires. They had to wait a couple of hours, and by then, everyone who'd drunk the turning potion would be as good as gone.

"When's this going to go down, again?" Rod asked, digging his hands into his pockets and turning away.

Anticipation ran through Devon. This was his first big changing party. His first real chance to prove himself to Roger, the alpha of the North American region. Devon needed everything to go perfectly. He needed his pack to be on top of their game.

"I was told two or three," Devon answered, breathing through the flip-flopping of his belly. He had to stop thinking about the stakes. It was messing with his head. "Roger doesn't think Vlad knows we're on to him. Vlad apparently hopes this party will go like the one he threw in Europe two months ago."

The European pack had recently lost their alpha when a powerful mage had up and ripped the shifter out of him. No one had even known that was possible, but from that time onward, Europe had been scrambling to place someone new. Powerful shifters from across the region kept trying to fight their way to the top, disturbing the lesser packs and sending everything into disarray.

Despite a short-lived truce between the shifters and vampires, formed for a collective storming of the Mages' Guild's compound, Vlad hadn't hesitated to take advantage of the upheaval in Europe. He'd waltzed in, changed twenty people right under the shifters' noses, and then waltzed back out, unscathed.

But this was the North American region, and Santa Cruz was Devon's territory. Despite being part of the team that had collaborated with Vlad for the Mages' Guild compound, he wasn't about to stand back so their former ally could waltz into his territory and make new vamps. Finding out about the party had been a stroke of luck—the bastard had been cocky enough to send out paper invitations to girls that couldn't help bragging. Alerting Roger of it had earned Devon this emergency detail. His pack's job was to stand guard until Roger arrived with his crew. The more experienced shifters would then take out the middle-tier vamps and go head to head with Vlad, while Devon and his pack headed off and discharged any newbie vamps. They'd make sure Vlad's attempts to increase his numbers failed.

A pity they had to wait until the changing process was underway, but Devon knew his limitations. He couldn't take on the elder without Roger. Even Roger would be hard-pressed to take on Vlad with his last-minute, thrown-together team. They had to wait until the vamps were at their weakest. Besides which, making new vampires was a crime, but hosting a party was not. They had to catch Vlad in the act.

He checked his phone for the umpteenth time. No service. They'd have no way of communicating with Roger. Vlad had found a perfect spot to turn new vamps. No cell service, a long private drive attached to a one-way road, no neighbors for miles. He was trapping his victims until they became his allies.

Devon's mind drifted back to that gal. Soon she'd be cut off, too. She'd be trapped in a house with a host of hungry vampires.

CHAPTER 5

S AMANTHA'S DAINTY FINGERS curled around an ornate knocker resting on the wide double door. Apparently the invitation had said to use the knocker rather than the doorbell.

"I have to say, despite the remote location, this house is pretty sweet," Charity whispered, breathing in the fresh floral scent from the many flowers lining the walkway behind them. She rubbed her arms, trying to shake off the strange tingling that had started once they passed through the perimeter gates. It had only gotten worse as they approached the house. "Feels a bit creepy, though, doesn't it?"

"*Shh.* Don't embarrass me." Sam banged the knocker against the solid wood.

"You're using a gargoyle door knocker on a state-of-the-art, modern house, and you're worried about me embarrassing you?"

Samantha banged the knocker a second time before stepping away and fussing with the hem of her dress. It wasn't going to get any lower.

Metal tinkled before the door swung open, revealing

a young man in his twenties with a pale, handsome face and a flawless complexion. His acute gaze hit Samantha first, then stalled on Charity.

"You smell ravishing," he said, hunger lighting his eyes.

Charity frowned. She hadn't put on any perfume, mostly because she didn't own any, and she hadn't showered since morning. She had no idea what this guy might be smelling on her, especially since Sam smelled like a perfume factory after an earthquake. Surely one whiff of Sam would deaden his senses.

"Thanks," she said in a doubtful tone.

"Please." He stepped to the side and swung his arm toward the interior. "Come in."

"Thank you." Samantha gave the man a winning smile and brushed her hair to her back as she passed him, her shiny blonde tresses adding movement to her slow saunter. He didn't notice.

"Your house is absolutely lovely." Sam half turned back, her eyes glittering suggestively. "I'm Samantha, by the way. You can call me Sam."

"I know." He closed the door, and his dark eyes lingered on Charity. "This isn't my house. I am but the greeter. Did you find us okay?" He waved them forward.

"Oh." A small frown bent Sam's features as the group crossed the grand entranceway and started down a wide hallway decked out in wood and marble, with vaulted ceilings and interesting abstract paintings adorning the light gray walls. "We did, yes."

Off to the left, a sitting room opened up. A woman stood in the center, wearing a long leather duster over a ribbed black and red lacy corset. Tight leather pants tucked into leather boots with four-inch stilettos. Her outfit was as sexy as it was strange, and she looked like an absolute badass, even though she wouldn't be running very fast in those shoes. Then again, given Charity was teetering around like a clown on stilts, she wouldn't go very fast, either. If the zombie apocalypse happened later on, they were sunk.

The woman's head turned slowly from the window she'd been focused on, revealing an angelic face with flawless, radiant skin not unlike that of their still-unnamed greeter. The woman's smile didn't reach her eyes.

"Welcome," she said in a sultry, feminine hum. Tingles of apprehension filtered through Charity. There was something familiar about her tone. The pleasing quality of the word.

Charity shivered. Murmurs drifted out of a room up the way, and light spilled across the shiny hardwood floor.

"Follow me," the man said, before darting around them, his movements faster than they should've been, considering his previous pace. More shivers arrested Charity as her mind flashed back to the man she'd noticed at school the previous night. His speed. His fighter's grace and balance.

"What is wrong with you?" Samantha said out of the side of her mouth. "Stop rubbing yourself. It's not cold in here."

Charity took her hands off her arms as the man turned the corner into a large dining room with a crystal chandelier hanging over a dark wood table that could comfortably seat at least twelve. China and crystal peeked out of cabinets against the wall, and a leafy plant on a pedestal in the corner gave the space a comforting splash of green.

The room was empty, but she could hear the hum of conversation. The other guests were nearby.

"It feels a little…" Charity paused when the man looked back, that focused gaze clamming her up. For some reason, she didn't want him to know she thought the environment felt…*off.*

Dangerous.

Or was that Devon guy in her head? She had excellent instincts, but she had to be able to listen to them.

"Why was that woman standing in that room by herself?" Charity asked as they crossed the space.

"She is making sure no unwanted…guests attempt to sneak in," the man said, pausing by a closed door.

Sam nodded, as if it were perfectly normal for a woman to stand sentinel in the middle of a dim room, staring out a window at the side yard in case party crashers planned to traipse in through the bushes.

Charity couldn't help but grip Sam's wrist, the urge to turn back and run strengthening. Sam swore under her breath when she shook her off, then said, "Don't make me regret bringing you."

"I already regret you bringing me."

They stepped just beyond the door and into a large kitchen awash with light and littered with pretty and trendy people holding what looked like shimmering crystal goblets. All maintained artfully bored expressions despite the price of the drinkware in their hands.

"Enjoy." The man turned and moved off in the direction they'd come, apparently off to greet more partiers.

"Why use the door knocker if someone has to stand close by to hear it?" Charity asked.

"He's welcoming the guests, hello? Did you see his suit? It was top quality and tailored. It must've cost a fortune."

Charity hadn't even noticed he was wearing a suit. She'd been too distracted by his hungry gaze. Every time she'd glanced at him, his eyes had been on her.

Serial killers didn't congregate together at parties, did they? They were more lone-wolf types?

Though even if they did, it wouldn't be the best move to target wealthy kids for a massacre. Their parents would hire the best lawyers, and the press and public interest would ensure the cops stayed on the job and found the killers.

She shook her head. Sam was probably right about that guy Devon. Hot guys played girls for sport. What could possibly be dangerous about this setup?

And yet...

"If anyone says anything about a basement, I'm out," Charity murmured.

"He was my age, too. I wonder if he's single," Sam whispered, running her lip through her blindingly white teeth. Her line of thinking had clearly gone a completely different direction.

"I think you should aim higher than the door-knocker guy. He wouldn't be much fun to hang around with, standing in the front, staring at the door, waiting for someone new to come knocking..."

"God you're weird. This is why you get A's in creative writing."

"I get A's in creative writing because I do my homework and study for tests."

"That too. Hmm." Sam tossed her hair before slinking down into a sexy pose, pushing out her breasts and jutting her hip to the side. "Look at all the hotties."

Charity followed her gaze, taking in the room. Guys and gals, all of them close in age to Charity and Samantha, gathered around an island in a sea of granite. An elegant crystal bowl of punch rested in the middle of the counter. Five or so people hovered around with their goblets, laughing nervously while shooting furtive glances at the beautiful people around them.

"Well, I'll be. Devon was right. Punch? What are we, at a high school dance in 1982?" Charity asked, also glancing at the devastatingly handsome and beautiful people around the periphery of the room. Their suits and dresses fit their fantastic bodies perfectly, and each had glittering accessories to match—jewelry for the women and cufflinks for the men. They stood at ease in groups of two or three, chatting with one another but often not facing one another. Their attention was instead fixed on the slightly younger and definitely less polished group around the punch bowl. It was like they were at a dance and awkwardly waiting for members of the opposite sex to ask them for a dance.

"It *is* like high school," Charity said. "I hated high school."

"That's because you were a nerd."

"Nope. It was because I was labeled a poor, stinky kid who ate garbage and lived on the other side of the tracks."

"Gross. T-M-I."

"Awesome. I knew you'd lend a compassionate ear. I did shower, by the way. Anyway, why doesn't anyone on the perimeter of the room have a drink?" Dropping her voice to a whisper, she added, "Do you think Devon was right about it being spiked? Also, isn't it odd that we're standing here, staring at everyone?"

"You're staring. I'm taking it all in."

"Yes, right. Clearly different."

"The punch is obviously just spiked with alcohol or people would already be acting weird," Sam said to herself, chuckling a little. "Devon was a little too dramatic in his scare tactics. I need to start mingling before he gets here. He'll want me more if someone else has my interest."

"Aren't these parties supposed to have kegs and cans of beer and shots of tequila? I mean…*punch*?"

"It's classy. Come on." Samantha started forward, graceful despite those huge heels.

Charity clattered after her like a newborn colt just learning to walk. "*Why* do people wear shoes this tall? They are horribly uncomfortable."

Samantha smiled at a decent-looking guy with a slouch and an expensive watch. He nodded in hello and scooted to the side, making room for the new additions.

"Hi," Sam said to a girl with airbrushed makeup as she grabbed a goblet from a silver platter. She shifted her gaze back to the people arrayed around the edges of the room. They all had flawless skin, like the other two people Charity had seen upon entering the mansion. Their unblinking stares focused on the kids with the punch. It was like they were waiting for something.

The shrooms to kick in, perhaps? Maybe their next line of coke?

With their effortless perfection and mannequin-like poise, they had to be models. At least, most of them did. They'd clearly been brought in to give the party some flare. There was no other explanation. Given punch was full of sugar, and these people were all slim and muscular, perfectly defined, Charity would bet they were seeing purple elephants and short men with green hair. No wonder they weren't revolting over the lack of drink options—the drugs were keeping them plenty busy.

Charity started as crystal was thrust at her. She glanced at the thruster, a platinum-blonde girl in her mid-twenties with a fierce scowl.

"No, I'm okay," Charity said. "I think the side effect to punch might be scowling a lot…"

The scowl strengthened.

Don't tease the rich people, Charity.

The girl shifted her scowl to Sam, who was just realizing something was amiss.

"Charity!" Samantha whispered. "You need to drink or you'll look ridiculous."

"Nice attempt at peer pressure, Sam, but I will look ridiculous regardless. How is an expensive glass going to help?" She took the goblet anyway. As soon as possible, she'd pour out the contents and refill it with water. It would be the fastest way to keep Sam off her back.

"So this is cool, right?" Samantha asked, stepping away from the others to put herself on display. Two of the pretty lurkers zeroed in on her. "Kind of a small, elite group. I haven't seen most of these people before—they're *hot,* though. Speaking of hot…"

Charity followed her gaze across the huge space. A guy with a half-filled goblet stood near the sliding glass door. His powder-blue shirt, collar popped, went perfectly with his Euro-style jeans. His runners were bright red to match his watch.

Her heart clattered around in her ribs.

Donnie!

His gaze was attached to the ruby-red, pouty lips belonging to a beautiful dirty-blonde woman.

"Hmmm, this is *good*!" Sam whispered in rapture, looking down at her drink.

Charity glanced down at her own beverage, finding an ice cube swimming tranquilly within the pink punch. Ignoring it, she said, "Doesn't everyone here seem almost...*too* attractive? Like, all of their skin is...poreless."

"*Too attractive*?" Samantha scoffed before taking a huge, and not very ladylike, gulp of her drink. She dabbed the moisture off her lips with a dainty finger. "Are you serious right now? As if there is such a thing. No flaws are *good*, Charity. Probably plastic surgery."

Charity opened her mouth to argue. Closed it. Donnie was on the move! He threw a shrug at the incredible beauty and then exited through the sliding glass door.

Immediately, Charity's brain buzzed with three excuses to leave Sam and follow him. Granted, a sprained ankle didn't make much sense, but that was the beauty of being the token poor girl—Sam assumed all poor people were crazy.

She opened her mouth to excuse herself when she heard, "Hello."

A man whose approach she'd neither seen nor heard stood mere inches from her side. She flinched, startled. Liquid sloshed out of her goblet and over her wrist. Drops *plunked* onto the floor as her eyes rounded and her jaw went slack.

The man was, quite possibly, the most handsome guy she'd ever seen in her life. Literally, her entire life. High cheekbones and a straight nose adorned a gut-clenchingly beautiful face with noble features straight out of a storybook. Shapely lips pulled up into a heart-throbbing smile below velvety brown, sparkling eyes that surveyed her in rapture. It was as though she were the only thing that existed on this plane, and nothing would tear his attention away. Charisma oozed from him in heady waves, deliciously sexy and sinfully suggestive. Her body tightened up and a burst of sweat drenched her armpits.

Clearly she was not as sexy as this man. Why was he talking to her?

"I don't believe I've had the pleasure of your acquaintance," he said in a musical though somehow still unbelievably sultry voice.

Her lady parts burst into flame. His proximity seared her body, begging her to step closer. To touch him. To let him touch her, intimately. A desperate need to be alone with this man overwhelmed her. She wanted his body pressed up against hers, skin on skin. Him inside her, thrusting.

CHAPTER 6

"I… I…" SHE heard herself say, a world away.

"I… I…" she tried again, somehow not able to form any sort of coherent thought.

"Maybe you would like some more punch? I see you have spilled yours. Such a travesty. Here, let me assist you, if I may…" His voice set her heart to hammering. Warning tingles spread across her skin, like fire ants biting down. The contrast didn't make sense. The way he'd singled her out didn't make sense.

She fell into his entrancing stare as the crystal goblet disappeared from her hand. Her arm dropped, suddenly bereft of strength, to hang limp at her side. His sweltering gaze left hers as he walked toward the island and punch bowl, unnaturally slow.

"Maybe just one," she murmured, fighting the impulse to hurry after him. She didn't want to let him get too far away. She needed to be with him in a way she'd never needed anything in her life.

She watched in ravenous fascination as his muscular arm, sleek and delicious, spooned some punch into her glass. He turned toward her, a smile flirting with his mouth-watering lips, so extremely kissable and inviting.

Suddenly he was right next to her, as though time had skipped a beat. As though he'd teleported.

She shook her groggy head, dizzied with lust. "How did…?" Her words drifted away as the goblet was gently placed into her hand. Such a gentleman, this man. Such a handsome, suave gentlemen.

They don't make them like this anymore.

Numb fingers wrapped around the chilled crystal. A stranger's fingers. Rough and clumsy compared with that delicate touch wrapped around her wrist, sending waves of sensation through her body.

"Drink—it is delicious," he said.

"What's in it?" she asked, looking down at the liquid, suddenly parched.

His laugh melted her panties. "Why, unicorn blood, of course."

She chuckled at his joke, contemplating alcohol for the first time in her life. Really contemplating it. What harm would one drink do? He'd gone to the trouble of getting it for her, after all.

The itch across her skin grew stronger, turning violent. A strange, musky smell tickled her nose, somehow detracting from the beauty of the man. Pricks of pain spread out from where his hand touched her skin—a sharp contrast to the raging lust. A warning pulsed in her brain, combating the searing heat of his proximity.

"Drink," he whispered, his breath rustling her hair.

She groaned, needing his touch. The pain intensified, begging her to step away. Her hand rose to her mouth, in someone else's control.

"But I don't…" The goblet brushed her lips. Her gaze dipped down, to the pink liquid inching up the crystal interior. Memories of Walt, the man she refused to call her father, flashed through her mind. Fear somersaulted her stomach.

She took a step back and forced the goblet away.

She didn't drink. That wasn't about to change because of a pretty creep with a penchant for peer-pressuring strangers.

"Where are you going?" he asked. "I wish to get more closely acquainted. I am in rapture. You are *exquisite*."

She ripped her gaze away from his mouth. A blast of cold air assaulted her, hitting the sheen of sweat coating her body and flash-freezing her. Logic rushed in and stole her breath. It was as if she'd awoken from a weird haze. She couldn't remember the stolen minutes properly, but she did know one thing: she'd wanted to have sex with a complete stranger. Really nasty sex. The kind you didn't tell people about.

Acting on the siren blaring at the back of her head, she about-faced without a word and haphazardly stalked across the room and out through the sliding glass door. She'd always been a little antisocial, but…well, that guy was weird. Her reaction to him was weird.

And what was he, thirty? What was he doing messing around with an almost twenty-year-old?

She dumped the contents of her goblet on the grass outside. "I've been to some parties with pushers, but that guy was ridiculous."

"What's that?"

Charity froze. *Donnie!*

He lounged against the wall looking all hot and trendy. Butterflies filled her stomach.

"Oh. Nothing." Charity pushed her hair away from her face. "Hi."

"Hey," he replied, and glanced off toward the yard, where the still waters of a large pool glowed from within. He could play cool in his sleep.

Charity nodded with her whole body like the dweeb Sam called her and tried to tuck a thumb through a belt loop. Her hand went skittering off her hip.

She didn't have a belt loop.

Grabbing for something, *anything* to talk about, she said, "So pretty, ah, good party, right? Nice house."

Donnie shrugged, watching a woman peel off her clothes and jump into the pool. His words were drowned out by the splash and ensuing shriek of laughter. Her friend stood watching her, clearly on the fence about joining. The alcohol was working harder on one than the other.

"Sorry, what was that?" Charity asked, stepping closer.

He turned his slightly-less-handsome-than-usual face toward her—attractive men were ruined for the moment in the face of Mr. Holy Crap He's Creepy But Hawt. Donnie's gaze took her in. "You clean up well."

"Oh, um…" She tucked a lock of hair behind her ear. She'd take that backhanded compliment, no problem. Hell, she'd frame it if she could. "Thanks."

He nonchalantly returned to scanning the backyard.

"So, uh…you got an invite, too, huh?"

One of Donnie's shoulders jerked up in a lopsided shrug. "I go to a lot of these things."

"Right, yeah. No big deal." She shrugged too, then grimaced at herself.

"Who'd you come with?"

"Sam. Samantha." Charity stepped even closer, desperately trying to emulate Sam's gracefulness. "You know Samantha Kent? I came with her. Earlier. She drove."

"Oh, right."

"Yeah. Right." Charity clenched her jaw, then her whole body, to stop herself from saying or doing anything else embarrassing.

They both looked out at the pool, where the woman floated lazily in the middle, beckoning to an intense-looking, pretty man now standing at the edge. His fashionable clothes were firmly in place—it didn't seem like he was keen on the idea of swimming. The skinny dipper's friend stood close by his side, clearly happy with the decision she'd made.

"So…" Charity racked her brain for more conversation. Now that she could speak intelligibly around him, it struck her that she wasn't sure what to say. He only talked a lot around other guys, and that was usually about sports. Charity knew next to nothing on that topic. "How long do you think you're going to stay?"

"I dunno. All right, I'll see you in a while." He turned to her for a moment, showering her with his full attention. He smiled and squeezed her upper arm. "Find me later."

Fireworks went off in her middle. She wrestled to control an elated smile dripping with doe-eyed devotion.

"Sure, yeah," she said, trying to play it cool and refrain from squealing. "No problem."

He pushed off the wall and sauntered back toward the house, draining the remnants of his glass and probably going for more. Charity checked her wrist, remembered she wasn't wearing a watch, and debated.

She couldn't very well go back inside right now because Donnie would think she was following him. Too clingy. But the only other person she knew at the party was Sam, who was also inside.

Charity took a few steps and glanced through the sliding glass door. Donnie stood at the counter, refilling his cup, as she'd suspected, surrounded by a few drinkers with serene expressions. The gorgeous models had drifted closer to the punch bowl, two of them clearly having worked up the courage and presence of mind to chat. No Sam.

That made things easy. Charity could kill some time

by looking for Sam. Then she could force Sam to wander close to Donnie and hopefully go for Awkward Talk round two.

Decision made, Charity began to turn when the dark-haired man from earlier turned to look at her. Deep eyes shocked into her, devouring. Her skin tingled furiously as warmth spread through her middle. Thoughts of sticky sex and panting breath filled her mind.

She yanked her gaze away. "What is up with that guy?" she murmured, painfully aroused and a little freaked out by it. She didn't understand the effect he had on her, nor did she understand the full-body itch warning her away from him.

Breathing heavily, she stumbled away. Was a quiet night of studying too much to ask?

She passed the pool and curved toward the front yard. A side door caught her attention, however, and she let herself in, figuring she'd give the greeter a break. She wandered through a stale room with no obvious personal effects, equipped with its own bathroom and sitting room. A guest suite larger than her house growing up. She shook her head as she surveyed the enormous TV mounted on the wall near the open door.

Lo and behold, Sam's voice floated in on the scented air from the hallway!

"—I don't know," she was saying.

Charity ambled closer—the high heels were completely useless for walking. She heard another woman say, "I definitely think you have a shot with Donnie."

Charity slowed.

"I'll put in a good word for you," the stranger said. "I know him really well."

"Are you sure about Devon, though?" Sam asked. "I'd much rather go for him."

"He's not even coming," the other girl said. "He wasn't invited."

"Are you sure? I saw him down the road."

"You did?" Silence filled a pause before someone *tsk*ed. "I don't know. But regardless, I wouldn't bother with Devon. I've never seen someone successfully land him. As soon as he bangs a girl, he completely loses interest. He's notorious for it. I definitely think Donnie's your best bet."

A sigh wafted in to Charity, who was currently holding her breath, waiting for the verdict.

"Okay, then. Talk to Donnie for me. But, like, don't make me sound eager or anything. Just, like, see if he's interested or whatever. Totally back off if he's not, you know?"

"Obviously, yeah. Maybe see if he's into something casual at first…"

"And, you know, if he wants to…hook up tonight or whatever, I'd be down for that." Sam paused for a minute, giving Charity time to wonder if her heart was trying to break her ribs. "Or do you think that's too slutty?"

"No, definitely not. That's the way you kinda have

to play it with people like Donnie. You've got a lot of competition, you know? Make sure he knows you're for real and not some tease."

"Yeah, that's what I was thinking. But…don't mention it to anyone, all right? Let's keep it quiet. I don't want to hurt anyone's feelings or anything…"

The other girl snorted. "Yeah, right! Hurt feelings? Everyone will be jealous!"

"I know, but…still," Samantha said, tempering her snobby voice. She used that voice when she was uncomfortable but didn't want to show it.

"I mean, sure. Whatever," the other girl acquiesced.

"Cool."

"Cool."

"I gotta pee," Samantha announced.

"Yeah, me too. I'll go with."

As the footsteps receded, Charity exhaled and fell back against the wall. Disappointment tugged at her. In reality, she knew she didn't have a shot in hell with Donnie. She'd always known that. Sure, maybe she could bang him, like Sam was thinking, but that wasn't her style. She wasn't into casual flings. But man, it sucked that Sam was blasé about going for him, knowing Charity was seriously crushing on him. Sam wouldn't even stick with him, either. She'd get tired of him in a couple of weeks, and that would be the end of it. Meanwhile, Charity would have to hear them having sex through the thin walls.

She blew out a breath, sinking into her sadness. She

wanted to stamp her foot and yell about life being unfair. To throw a tantrum and maybe go give Sam a piece of her mind. But what would that solve? The world worked how the world worked—there was no point in getting all twisted up about the inevitable. A lot of things in her life had been unfair. A girl had to celebrate her wins instead of dwell on her losses. Maybe she wouldn't get the guy she liked; so what? She was working her way through school in a great city, and she was at a party so elite they had a guard dressed in leather watching for crashers. She had it pretty good.

As far as Donnie went? Let Sam try to make conversation with him. She'd pull her hair out.

Smirking, Charity headed out and down the hall with a painful shamble. Her mind drifted to other matters, like why would someone pay four hundred dollars to be this uncomfortable? Was a severed toe fashionable? Because Charity saw no other use for the heels.

Wincing, she turned left at the end of the hall and found herself in the foyer. Relieved to recognize her surroundings, and even more so to discover the greeter was gone, she hobbled out into the evening air. Sam had been right about the punch. It didn't seem dangerous. Everyone but her was guzzling it, and only the skinny dipper was acting on the crazy side of drunk. She'd give Sam a couple of hours to mack on her eye candy before she wandered back in to check on her.

A horrible thought struck her—Sam was drinking,

and this place was a cab driver's nightmare. Charity didn't know how to drive very well, and Sam wouldn't risk her Porsche.

Did her roommate plan to spend the night?

Dread rolled over Charity. It wouldn't be a big deal to spend a few hours here, but all night? Anything could happen during the vulnerabilities of sleep.

CHAPTER 7

C HARITY SLOWLY BLINKED her eyes open. A sea of shimmering dots swam within the black sky overhead. The tops of trees peered down at her, still in the calm night.

It took her a moment to orient herself. The last thing she remembered was staring up at the stars, tracing the constellations with her eyes. It was a slow, boring business, tracing constellations. After about the fifth time, she'd switched to thinking about schoolwork, which was probably about the time she'd fallen asleep.

She rubbed her eyes and pushed up to sitting. Moisture clung to her legs and nestled in the grass around her. Silence had settled on the property, broken occasionally by a night bird calling out. A glance up at the large house twenty yards away and she realized with a start that all the windows were blackened or dimmed, upstairs and down.

How long had she been asleep? When she'd first lain here, an occasional shout floating across the backyard, most of the downstairs windows were blaring with light, and two bedrooms upstairs glowed, too. By the look of it, the party had shut down and everyone had retired.

"Crap," she muttered, hurrying to stand. All the blood rushed to her head and she wobbled forward.

Sam would absolutely leave her, especially if she'd hooked up with someone. Granted, she'd be an enormous fool to drive drunk, especially on the small, winding road out of this place, but if she'd sobered up and taken off, Charity would be screwed.

She peered in a window as she passed. No one waited in the darkened room. No shapes writhed in the corners or on the couch. But there were a ton of rooms in that house—hopefully the rest weren't deserted.

She rounded the house, but instead of heading for the front door, she hobbled down the driveway to the line of parked cars, thankfully about as full as when they'd first shown up. A bird blared out a warning, this one from the poolside of the house. Either it sensed her, or someone else was wandering around the area. She hoped for the latter. People awake meant a chance at a ride out of here. A couple of them went to the same school, after all. They'd probably live in a similar area.

Halfway down the line of cars and the bumper of Sam's Porsche peeked out around an Audi. Charity's sigh of relief felt like it came up from her toes. Sam wouldn't leave her car behind. She was still here.

"Where do you think you're going?"

Charity jumped and slapped a hand to her chest, where her heart was trying to break free and sprint away. A guy drifted out of the darkness. Graceful and covered in lean muscle, he reminded her of the guys hanging out with Devon. She didn't remember seeing his face, but then, she'd barely glanced at anyone but Devon.

"Once you go in, you don't come out," he said, his voice low and rough and full of menace. Danger radiated from him, that predatory essence she'd been encountering a lot lately.

Her small hairs stood on end and warning vibrated through her body.

"Wh-what?" she asked. She minutely shook her head, trying to get her thoughts back on track. "Look, bud, I don't want any trouble. I'm only out here to check on my ride situation."

"You haven't completed the change yet, have you?" He continued to stroll closer, his energy advertising his vicious intent.

"I don't know what you're talking about." She ambled backward, pissed that she didn't have a change of footwear. She'd never fought in heels before, especially unforgiving, abnormally uncomfortable heels, but she'd do what she had to.

"No?" He increased his pace, not about to let her get away. His button-up shirt drifted to the sides of his defined chest, but his advance wasn't sexual. "How many cups of elixir did you drink?"

"I don't drink," she said. Moving backward was slowing her down, but she wasn't about to turn her back on this guy.

He cocked his head, and in the dim lighting, she could just see his eyes narrow. "Now, now, you don't need to lie to me. You already smell different."

"Now you're talking crazy." She gritted her teeth against the pain of blisters forming from the shoes and pushed faster, twenty yards from the house and ten from him. Except he kept gaining on her.

"You should've stayed in the nest until you mor-phed. You would've had a better chance. But it's better this way. I'll kill you quick and easy. It'll be painful for you, I won't lie, but at least it won't be prolonged, right? I don't even need to change to do it."

Her heart quickened, which was amazing, because it was already beating a mile a minute. She took long strides just short of a run, knowing he'd probably spring into action as soon as she tried to book it. She needed to distract him until she could make a fast hobble-sprint into the house and scream for help.

"Why are you loitering outside, anyway?" she asked, turning for a few fast steps before glancing back. Sure enough, he'd jogged a couple of steps forward. Her breathing harried, she nearly wanted to stop and strip off the heels, but she didn't have time. He'd be on her before the first buckle was through the loop.

His thin lips pulled up into a sneer. "Waiting for you, of course."

She shook her head. Fifteen yards to the house, five from him. She'd never make it. She'd need to stand her ground, get in a hard shot to a vulnerable area—eye, throat, or groin—and *then* hobble-sprint.

She stopped and faced him, her feet planted and her hands out, pretending to ward off his advance. He'd think she was helpless, lose his wary edge, and give her an easy in.

She hoped.

"I don't even know you," she said, allowing fear to ride in her voice. Playing into her role as a helpless damsel in distress.

"Did you even ask what was in that drink?" he asked, his energy becoming eager. He sensed blood about to be spilled and it excited him.

Cold washed through her body. Fear pulsed deep inside.

She maintained her calm. She was trained for this. Ready.

"He said it was unicorn blood," she said.

The guy sneered. "I didn't know vampires told jokes."

"Dude, you need to lay off the drugs. They are having a bad effect on you."

Three yards away and the guy stopped, facing her. The lights from the front porch gleamed in his manic eyes. He leaned forward, all eager anticipation.

"Not me. You." His muscles coiled and he sprang, his hands out and reaching for her throat.

She swung her hand up as she turned, pushing his reaching hands to the side, fast-stepped to him, as much as she could manage in the shoes, and punched him in the middle, hard and fast. The breath gushed out of his mouth. She turned, wobbling, and sharp pain cut through her heel. She ignored it and slammed her other fist into the side of the guy's neck, losing some force because of her unsure footing.

"What the hell—" The guy's body shivered. A strange green mist drifted around him.

"Stop!"

The voice rang out, deep and full of command she couldn't help but heed. The guy in front of her froze just as she did, the manic light in his eyes drying up and alertness taking over.

Devon strode up the driveway, his face hard, an air of command pumping out of every pore in his body. Now was the time to run. To yell for help. But all she could do was stand and stare, caught in his influence.

"What's going on here?" he asked, barking each word.

A new fear trembled through Charity, one she didn't understand. Something within her didn't want to disappoint him. Didn't want him to be angry with her.

She took a step back, remembering the fog of lust from the unbelievably attractive man in the house. This was similar, but not sexual. This was like seeing her battle commander stalk up and feeling the need to fall in line.

"What is happening to me tonight?" she asked in a daze.

"You drank an elixir that will change you," Devon said, stepping between her and the other guy. "Did you take blood?"

"I…" His strong presence felt like a blow to her middle. "I didn't drink—The punch, you mean? I didn't drink any. I don't drink." She shook within the power of his proximity.

"She's lying," the maniac guy said, his eyes narrowing at her. "She hasn't changed, but she is on the way. You can smell it."

Devon bristled and half turned. He didn't need to say a word. The other guy visibly backed down, his back bowing and his eyes drifting toward the ground. It was clear who held social status here. Good news for her.

Devon turned back toward her. His commanding presence locked her up again, keeping her feet solidly planted on the ground. She had no idea how. It was starting to rankle.

"You didn't drink the elixir?" he demanded.

"Why do you keep calling it an elixir? Seriously, it was just punch." She stared up into his classically handsome face. Not perfect, like the beauty of the guy inside, but with a rugged flair she much preferred. "What do you mean, change me? What the hell is going on here?"

He leaned forward a bit, transferring his weight to the balls of his feet. A fighter's move.

A flare of fire tickled her middle.

I will rock your world, mama's boy. And throw your

shoes on the nearest telephone wire.

And she definitely could've…in her runners.

Damn you, Sam, and your stupid fashion.

"It was not just punch. It was a special elixir to pre-pare your body for the transformation into a vampire. Taking a vampire's blood will complete the change. If you do not take blood, you won't be transformed, but you'll be vulnerable to them for the rest of your life. So this is very important, did you drink that…punch?"

The crazy words were delivered in such an earnest tone that she almost believed him.

She huffed out a laugh and edged backward.

"Did you drink some of the punch?" he demanded, moving into her personal space. His size dominated her. Body bristling, muscles tense, he waited for something. It almost seemed like he was daring her to defy his unspoken command to stay put.

Like a breeze gently worrying a single leaf on the autumn ground, something tickled the roots of her being. An ember flared to life deep within her chest, kick-starting a trickle of pure adrenaline, like a natural spring. Electricity poured into her arms and legs as she sucked in a sweet shock of cool air.

Her chin lifted of its own accord; she was defiant within his hard stare. Yet strangely excited to meet it. She couldn't help the start of a smile. Like when she was sparring with her old martial arts instructor, she felt gloriously alive.

"I get it." She nodded in understanding, taking another step away. "You guys were down there doing acid or something, and you've come to crash the party, like Sam said you would. You're seeing things, right? Alternate universes." She nodded again, wondering if Devon would turn on a dime and start talking about killing her, just like the first guy had. Maybe they were on bath salts. "Cool. No, I didn't drink the secret elixir or vampire blood. I came out here to get away from everyone, and now I'm going to go check on my roommate. You can probably come in. I don't think the door-knocker watcher will be there."

"She smells, boss," the first guy said.

"I think that's her natural smell," Devon responded. "The one Andy talked about."

Charity didn't wait for them to finish their discussion about her stench. She lurched into a hobble-sprint—better late than never—pumping her arms and taking big strides, trying to cover as much ground as possible. Her ankles wobbled.

"I got her," the first guy yelled out.

"No, wait—"

Feet slapped the ground behind Charity. A hand wrapped around her upper arm and whipped her around.

"Let her go!"

But the guy didn't listen. His other hand was already closing around her throat.

She jabbed his eyes with her fingers and slammed her fist into his throat. Although he'd already lost his grip, she swung her whole arm up to knock him away faster, shoving him toward an advancing Devon with all her might.

The two guys grappled with each other to find their feet, but Charity was already sprint-hobbling again, heart in her throat and nearly at the door.

"No, wait," Devon said again.

This time she didn't hear the footsteps. She was already at the door, shoving it open, when a larger hand, stronger, closed around her wrist. He yanked her back, but she turned and kicked, using the doorframe to steady herself. Faster than lightning, he dodged and reached for her with his second hand.

She ripped free, slapping at his hands, and ran through the door. Her heel slipped and she was falling, the yell for help caught in her throat. She expected his body to slam into her. His hands to wrap around her and drag her back. But nothing happened.

He stood in the threshold. His gaze darted around like a pinball—past her, down to the ground in front of him, up to the doorframe—before finally settling on her. He shook his head slowly, his intelligent gaze sparkling with warning.

"Come out," he whispered, as though the house were a sleeping dragon and he didn't want to wake it. "It is incredibly dangerous for you in there. They'll kill you. Come out. Come back to me. I can protect you."

She scrambled to her feet, pain shooting through her toes and heels. The clack of the heels was loud in the quiet house.

"You're crazy," she said, her heart still beating frantically. "Do you hear yourself? You need to go sleep it off."

He gripped the frame. "You don't understand. You're in their territory now. Please come back out. I *will* protect you."

She edged away, not wanting to turn her back on his furtive stare and drugged-out mind. He was in a fairytale right now, and she didn't want to wake the beasties and turn his trip into the nightmare his friend was living.

"Please," he said again, but she was already turning the corner. Although she had no idea why he wouldn't come inside, she was thankful for it.

She pushed through the cavernous house, her heart ringing in her ears even more loudly for the silence. The kitchen waited, dimly lit and deserted, the crystal goblets sitting empty on the countertops.

Where was everyone?

She glanced at the clock over the microwave. It was much later than she had suspected, but still, it was only one o'clock. And most, if not all, of the cars were still there...

Charity peeped through the sliding glass door into the empty backyard. Two piles of clothes lay forgotten on the dewy grass near the pool. The blue water shimmered from its subterranean light. The peace and tranquility of deep night had descended, laying a thick blanket over the party scene.

But still…where was everyone?

She glanced back the way she'd come, making sure Devon hadn't followed. It was empty. Quiet.

"This has got to be the strangest party I've ever heard about. Ever," she murmured, finally slipping out of the shoes. "This can't be a normal college deal."

Confused, she grabbed a glass from a cupboard and filled it with water. Leaning back against the sink, she went over her options. She could walk thirty miles home with bare feet, she could call a cab with no money to pay for it, or she could wait around until someone agreed to give her a ride home.

"Hmm, I guess I'll take door number three, Jimmy," she said quietly, immediately regretting that she'd spoken out loud. Her voice was way too small for the huge, empty space.

After finishing her water in a few glugs, Charity made her way deeper into the house, checking the many gaping rooms for any people. When she found no one, she continued toward the stairs. As she continued her search, another thought occurred to her. Donnie's Charger was still here. Done up sporty, black on black, it was hard to miss. She hadn't been thinking clearly when she'd glanced at it earlier, but now…

Lead filled her chest. If he hadn't gone for Sam, he'd found someone else. The last thing she wanted to do was walk in on him and some lady.

Doesn't matter. I'm lucky to be where I am.

A wide hallway dotted with closed doors greeted her at the top of the stairs. She stood next to the first door and listened. A quiet house listened back.

Pursing her lips, she reached for the gleaming handle before turning gently to see if it was locked. It wasn't.

The door swung inward slowly, revealing a dark room. Light from the window spilled across the floor and the bed. The *occupied* bed. She froze.

Two bodies writhed on top of the sheets, the man's mouth locked in a fervent kiss on the girl's neck. His bare backside repeatedly pushed toward her body, met by the upward swing of her hips. A feminine moan curled through the air.

Oh my God!

Charity yanked the door shut and then winced at the *thud* of wood banging off wood. She stood rigid in the hallway for a moment, half in shock. She wasn't a virgin or a prude or anything, but…*yikes!*

Moving down the hallway, she tried another room, equally unlocked. Rather than swing the door open, she opened it a crack and listened. A feminine moan teamed with masculine grunts had her backing out quickly.

Did no one lock doors in this place?

Thankfully, the house had a crap-load of rooms. Not all were bedrooms, no, but based on the chorus of grunts she heard from what looked to be a bathroom, that didn't matter.

Had the whole party retired to the bedrooms? Was that what it was, a big hookup party?

Sam's conversation with the other girl blinked through her thoughts. The explanation of a hookup party fit. Devon wasn't going to work, so Sam went for the next available bachelor in her age range. Everyone so far looked and sounded like willing participants, so they were definitely on board. The few who weren't into the notion had probably already taken off.

Dang it, I could've gotten a ride.

After the fifth try and some furious blinking—the naked gymnastics on the pool table were a marvel—she finally stumbled into an empty bedroom. Two twin beds were stationed on opposite sides of a room organized with bins and toy boxes. Being that she was, apparently, the only one with a G-rated sleeping agenda, she figured she was doing the kids a favor by choosing their room as a crash pad.

After locking the door firmly behind her, then checking it just to make sure, she placed Sam's heels by the bed and fell onto a pink duvet. Judging by the duplicates of everything, the occupants were probably young twins—the only scenario by which two kids were likely to share a room in a house with countless bedrooms.

Charity took her millionth deep breath for the night. Waiting out a sex party hadn't been on her list of to-dos for the weekend. All she wanted to do was go home without being waylaid by the hot psychopath out front.

CHAPTER 8

"EXPLAIN YOURSELF," DEVON demanded, anger spiking his pulse.

Jimmy's face paled, but the rigidity didn't completely leave his spine. "She was trying to get away. It's our job to stop that."

"It's your job to follow orders," Devon said, leaning into Jimmy. "She didn't drink the elixir. You heard her yourself."

"And you believe her?" Jimmy mumbled, looking at his feet.

"You saw how confused she was. Nothing we were saying computed. She thought we were drugged up."

"But her smell—"

"Was not the smell of a human in transition. Not even remotely. In the absolute simplest of terms, she smelled…" Amazing. Out-of-this-world fantastic. So great it had made his mouth water. "…good. Vampires smell bad. See the issue?"

"Yes, sir," Jimmy murmured.

"You scared her into that house. She wasn't even supposed to *be* here, for all we know, and now her death warrant is signed. She'll be food, without question, and very few food sources brought to these things make it out. You all but guaranteed that we'll have one more to clean up."

Jimmy looked up with round eyes, his body shaking. "Sorry, sir," he bleated, finally submitting. "It's just—she seemed so sure of herself, you know? Usually dames are either half scared or half turned on by us. And she'd come from the house, and I—"

Devon let the rage infuse his eyes, cutting off the yammering. "You screwed up on this one. You'll face the consequences."

Jimmy gulped. He nodded mutely and resumed staring at the ground.

Devon bit back a curse. He wanted to send Jimmy home, but he couldn't. He needed every last member of his pack to take on the newbies. Roger and his pack would be wrapped up in combat with the elder and the upper-middle-level vamps.

"Get into position and change forms," Devon barked. "Roger is moving into position as we speak. The vampires have pulled back their territory presence to the house, which means they're preparing a fierce defense. We should assume they know we're in the area. We'll strike in an hour, two tops. We aim to get them while they're at their most vulnerable."

"Sorry, boss," Jimmy said again.

Devon clenched his teeth. It didn't sound like Jimmy meant it.

Oh yes, he'd be dealt with.

"Go," Devon said, turning his back on the lesser male.

The memory of the girl's smell resurfaced. He recalled the strange light that had kindled in her eyes, making them glow, when he'd advanced on her. It had sparked something, that light. The perfume of her had oozed a little thicker, tantalizing. Mouth-watering. He'd never smelled anything like it. He wanted to bottle it up and spray it on everything around him. It was intriguing and irritating at the same time.

She had a fighting background. She'd moved fast and efficiently. Regardless, she wasn't fast enough to take on a vamp. And that smell, whatever it was, would attract them in droves. They'd overcome her in moments.

Guilt and regret pinched his gut as he turned and jogged down the hill, returning to check on the rest of his pack. There was nothing he could do about it now. Her only chance was to hunker down until help arrived. Best-case scenario, she found a closet to barricade herself in until Roger and crew could make it in there.

As he moved away, one thought floated up: *I should've warned her that vampires can magically open locks.*

CHAPTER 9

CHARITY STARTLED AWAKE. She jolted in the narrow bed before pushing to sitting and wiping her eyes. She shouldn't have given in to the urge to lie down. The late hour and the boredom had lulled her to sleep.

The tiny pink clock on the white, lollipop-looking bedside table read 2:47. She held in her sigh of relief. Given the level of effort in the horizontal gymnastics she'd witnessed earlier, everyone's stamina should've given out 'by now. Their fatigue would be wearing off, and those not accustomed to sharing a bed would be ready to slink away.

She got to her feet and tiptoed to the door. A patrol of the hallway would give her a good indication of the state of affairs. If a few rooms were empty, she'd try to find a window that looked down on the driveway. She didn't dare wander out there again—who knew where Devon and his homicidal friend would be in their acid trip. They might be rigging booby traps out there for all she knew. The crazy made a point of doing crazy things.

She grabbed the lock to flip it, and a blast of apprehension ran her through.

The door was unlocked.

Waves of adrenaline pumped into her blood.

She'd locked it when she'd come in. She knew she had. She'd stood here, fumbled for a second to grab it, and cranked it over. She vividly remembered feeling the tiny bit of assurance a lock could give.

Why was it now unlocked?

Barely able to stand still for the sudden anxiety throbbing in her chest and the blood pounding in her ears, she backed up a couple of steps to the middle of the room. Turning slowly, afraid of what she'd find, she looked at the other bed.

The soft sound caught her attention first. So soft she hadn't heard it until now, when she was *really* listening. Panting, almost, like a dog in the hot sun. Shallow, quick breathing, barely audible.

Gritting her teeth and peering through the heavy darkness, she could barely make out a shape, something like a miniature mountain range, in the glow from the clock on the other nightstand. Moving closer, her skin crawling and her insides dancing with unease, she narrowed her eyes to see who had picked the lock, or perhaps found the key.

Some of the mountains rose and fell, and it took Charity a moment to see that the tempo of the movements matched the panting. Large breasts, their nipples erect. A woman, then, her hands at her sides and the rest of her body still.

A thread of worry wormed through Charity. Was

the woman in trouble? Was she suffering from post-traumatic stress? Or had Charity been wrong about the stamina of the partiers running out, and they'd simply changed rooms?

The thread of worry changed to a rush of anger. If this woman was in trouble, Charity would help in any way she could. If nothing else, she'd beat the offender senseless. If it was the other…well, maybe they needed a good thump for breaking into her chosen room. She was tired and grumpy and about done with the insanity.

She took another couple of steps and grabbed the glowing clock radio before turning it toward the bed. Platinum-blonde hair caught her notice. The scowler! Just as Charity had thought, she lay nude on top of the covers, her hands at her sides and legs straight. Her eyelids flickered and her eyeballs moved under the skin, as though she were in an intense REM cycle.

Beside her lay an equally nude man with an incredibly defined body and a great set of arms crossed over his chest. He was trying to make himself smaller so the woman would fit in the bed. On his neck, nearly lost to the shadows, was a trickle of liquid seeping from a gash.

Was that…?

Charity leaned in a little.

That was blood. The woman had gone for an over-zealous hickey and actually drawn blood.

It was not just punch. It was a special elixir to prepare your body for the transformation into a vampire. Taking a vampire's blood will complete the change.

75

Charity's disbelieving though incredibly uncomfortable chuckle disturbed the near silence of the room. She shook her head, flicking her glance down the bed. Between strong thighs stood a large erection.

Charity jerked back, and her face flamed in the darkness. The man's eyes snapped open. His head fell to the side and his gaze landed on her.

"Hmm. You smell delicious," he said, sexy and sinful and sensual. "I am ready for you."

"Good God." Charity staggered backward. "No, no. Ha! Ha. No. I'm just… I was in here, see?" Why did she suddenly sound like a nineteen-thirties gangster? "I was sleeping on that other bed, and you came in…"

"I can handle one more. The previous specimens were fairly weak in their need." He rose like a mummy in an old-timey movie, his torso lifting up with no turning or help from his hands. "But you… I can feel the strength in you. The power. Are you human? What are you?"

"Grossed out, mostly." She took another step back. "Honestly, this is a simple matter of being in the wrong place at the wrong time. I didn't mean to spy. I was just wondering why someone broke into my room."

"It is not your room. It is Vlad's room, and he has given leave for his children to use it. You are not ready to cross over. Did he put you here as a refreshing snack? He is a thoughtful master."

"Good God," Charity said again, reaching down to grab Sam's shoes. "You're talking crazy. Everyone at this damn party is talking crazy. This is no place for a person like me. I have no sense of humor."

"I can lick the humor into you."

"That's...not...flattering for you." She hurried toward the door. She could fight him off, sure, but his dick's standing ovation was disconcerting. It'd be best if she got the hell out of there.

He bounced off the bed like he'd been ejected and landed on the floor next to it, his knees bent to absorb the impact. He straightened up slowly, and the soft glow of the clock revealed the smile curling his lips. "You're gorgeous. A refined, pixie-like beauty. All natural. I love it. I hope you taste as good as you smell."

"Nope." She reached for the handle, hardly believing what she'd just seen. This guy should be in the naked Olympics or something. "Jesus, man, put that thing away."

He surged forward, a little jerky but incredibly fast despite it. She ripped the door open, her body in *flee* mode. She'd never fought a naked guy coated in sex, and she really didn't want to start now.

His reaching fingers grabbed the side of the door. She stopped, planted a foot, and side-kicked with the other. Her foot hit the man's chest center mass. The sound of material ripping competed with his grunt as the loudest thing in the room. She'd ripped Sam's dress.

"Damn it," she said as he flew back. "Look what you made me do!"

She plunged into the hall, the scuffling behind her

77

electrifying her body. She started jogging as pounding feet ran behind her. The kick hadn't deterred him. He was coming after her!

Before she could decide to run faster, yell, or turn and confront her fear of bodily fluids smeared on a naked man, a door swung open ahead, emitting a ghastly creature born in a nightmare. Long, matted hair fell over bony shoulders. Breasts like deflated balloons drooped from a skeletal, greenish chest, the skin hollowed between a xylophone of ribs. A ghastly face hissed, showing two huge fangs protruding from black gums.

"Holy fuck-tarts, what the fuck?" Charity said, dodging a reaching claw-like hand, its nails ending in sharp points. Horror blocked out her thoughts. The discomfort from a moment before turned into full-fledged panic.

More doors swung open, strange howls ripping at the night. Charity ran so fast that she could barely feel her legs. She hit the stairs, taking them two at a time, hearing animal-like thumping behind her.

Faster!

She jumped down the last four steps, stumbling on the marble floor, and sprinted for the front door. For a way out. Maybe even for Devon. He'd been interested in her safety, hadn't he? Maybe he wasn't crazy or high after all. Besides, he was strong. Powerful. Allying with him was the best chance she had.

If she could get to him.

Her bare feet slapped the marble before she jumped down two steps into a den. A shape appeared in the far archway. A flaccid penis waggled between bowed legs, swampy skin nearly white. The thing was cutting off her exit.

A burst of fear exploded deep in her gut. That ember within her, which she'd first felt outside, flared to life again, but this time the heat started to burn through her middle. Electricity zapped down her arms and legs, filling her body. Clearing her mind.

She spun and barely zipped past the creature that had been chasing her. Its clawed hands reached for her, flicking her hair as she passed. A horrible, inhuman screech filled the room.

Mind buzzing with barely contained panic, she thundered down a hallway and burst into some sort of sitting room. Veering right, hearing the breathing behind her, she sprinted toward the next doorway and around a corner.

A claw came out of nowhere, reaching for her face. She screamed in surprise, batting it away and ducking under the other hand, never losing speed as she bolted into the kitchen.

The sliding glass door! Up ahead and thankfully open. All she had to do was get through that door. She was sure of it.

The *click-click-click* didn't make sense at first. Until she saw one of the creatures running, trying to head her off.

Faster!

With a burst of speed she didn't realize she had in her, she raced that thing to the exit.

It reached the opening in the glass at the same moment she did. Claws raked down her arm. Crying out, she veered and bounced off the doorjamb. She staggered, but caught herself, and pushed her way into the night air.

Another creature came at her from just outside. Claws swung at her face. She screamed and dodged out of reflex. Fangs glistening in the moonlight, the thing screeched like a bird of prey. Black saliva dripped from equally black gums.

"Oh God!" she cried, pivoting. A claw raked across her back. Pain made her adrenaline throb.

She jumped off the two steps beyond the door and landed awkwardly on the stone walkway. Her weight took her to the ground, the fall too awkward for her to turn it into a roll. She glanced up with her heart in her mouth, seeing a claw slashing down.

Lightning surged through her body, responding to her fear. A strange power throbbed deep inside her gut. Sweet effulgence flooded her, electricity sizzling down her limbs as she threw her arms up to protect her face.

Like a strobe light with the wattage of the sun, radiance rained down on the swampy creature. It howled in pain and rage, shrinking from the intense glow.

Not knowing what was happening, but knowing she'd gained an advantage, no matter how short-lived,

Charity hopped up and surged forward, sprinting down the stone path toward the front yard, desperately hoping that safety was close at hand.

When she was halfway down the path, exhaustion creeping into her limbs, the light blinked off behind her. The night washed back in, cutting down her visibility. Her toe hit a divot and her body lurched toward the side of the house. Bouncing off the siding, she staggered forward, desperate to keep her momentum.

Another screech sounded, the hunter sighting its prey.

Please no!

The door of the fence surrounding the backyard loomed ten feet in front of her, tears of panic and fear making it swim and jiggle in her vision. She was almost there!

Pushing past the fatigue, hellbent on getting through that gate, Charity put on another burst of speed, and then screamed. A fanged face had stepped through the side door she'd used earlier in the night, arms out to grab her.

She threw up her hands again, blocking her face. Her body flooded with hot spice, a crackling sound drowning out the screeches from all around her. Sunlight, weaker now, once again rained down. The sizzle of flesh competed with the bug zapper sound of the light. *She* had done this, she realized, although she didn't understand how. There was no time to consider the implications—although the creature ahead of her stumbled back into the house, howling, the one behind her pushed through the light, its hiss trailing her up the walk.

She willed herself onward, trying to ignore the fatigue. Her dragging limbs.

A fierce growl dragged her gaze left.

Loping across the sparkling grass, hair bristling and teeth bared, ran the largest wolf she had ever seen. Adrenaline sharpened her senses as the bright moonlight fell across the beast. Bigger than a Great Dane, it watched her with humanlike intelligence, cataloguing her movements with dual-colored eyes, one pale blue, one dirty green.

Oh no! Oh, God. Oh no!

Its growl competed with the hiss of the thing behind her, two huge beasts bearing down on her. The gate swam into focus, five feet away. Three.

The wolf lunged. Graceful death.

Time slowed down.

She reached for that electricity. For that flare of light she had somehow caused.

Nothing happened.

Canine teeth were bared, paws spread wide as the wolf flew through the air. Her heart rang through her ears.

The next growl ended in a sickening crunch of bone. The wolf had slammed into the creature behind her.

More wolves followed the first—huge, agile animals

running through the yard. Their fierce growls filled the night air, interspersed with angry screeches. Charity didn't know if they were fighting each other or not, but the distraction gave her a little cover.

Staggering like a drunk trying to pass a sobriety test, she lurched through the door and into the front yard, turning to her right. Hope filled every inch of her being, fighting the desperation. But instead of finding Devon, all she found was another large wolf.

A cry wrestled with her newest scream. The beast snarled, its lips pulling back from large canines. It loped forward, on the attack.

She turned toward the cars.

A giant black wolf blocked her way.

Its lips pulled back from its teeth in a silent snarl. It took a quick step-jump, ready to attack, only to hesitate at the last moment. Its head dropped, assessing her in that way predators sussed out their prey. A soft bark and it circled wide.

She didn't stop to wonder what was going on. She ran. What else could she do? Blood freezing in dread, she kept going, willing her feet to carry her a little further. If only she could find cover.

No, if only she'd wake up!

Another wolf approached from the right. One more, from the left and slightly in front. They were closing in on her, operating on silent commands. Working together like dancers in a show. She didn't have much energy left. Lead filled her limbs.

Please wake up...

The gray wolf on the right was the first to lunge. Mouth open, it chomped toward her outstretched arm. She pulled her arm away and swung the other around to punch it in the side. Her fist connected with fur. A blast without fire concussed the air. Light shimmered. The wolf yelped and flew away.

She stared for one beat, unsure what had happened. But another beast was already jumping at her. She dropped Sam's shoes, still, miraculously, in her hand. She hit this one the same as the first. Once again, the air concussed and the wolf flew away, rolling across the ground like it was caught in a windstorm.

A hole opened up in the circle. Not thinking, she ran at it.

Her moment of relief was short-lived.

Coming at her, mid-leap, was the huge black wolf, graceful and effortless as it barreled into her. Paws hit her shoulders. The weight knocked her backward. Her head smacked the cement. Blackness took over.

CHAPTER 10

A BLUISH GLOW bathed Charity's face. Soft material hugged her body. Her mind swam, sleep hanging on, distorting her perception. She blinked in confusion at the rough stone wall rising to her right. It met an equally pockmarked stone ceiling.

She did not like that waking up in odd situations was starting to become a norm.

A rustic light fixture hung on the far wall. A bluish-purple flame, almost like one from a Bunsen burner, danced within the metal casing. But this flame didn't look controlled. It flickered and moved, alive, like a flame from a torch.

Am I dreaming?

She palmed her forehead, trying to contain the pounding headache, and thought back to her last memory.

A kid's room. Two twin beds. A nightstand...

Flashes of matted hair and black gums ruined the quaint image.

Enormous wolves.

Fear seeped through her as she envisioned the massive black wolf bearing down on her.

Breathing heavily, she wiped her face and glanced around. Whatever those creatures were, they weren't here now. There was no screeching or growling—no noise of any kind. It was as silent as a tomb.

Vampires.

She shoved that ridiculous thought away.

Werewolves.

And that one. Those thoughts were absurd. There had to be a logical explanation for what had happened. If vampires and werewolves were real, the human race would know about it. That was a secret too big to keep. Besides, there were about a million stories about vampires, and never once had she heard them described as swampy monsters.

Had it been close to Halloween, there would have been some explanation for the insanity. Unfortunately, it was nearly March. The Easter Bunny wasn't this messed up.

So. What next?

She glanced around the stone room lit by the strange, flickering flame, then lifted the cushy comforter. Someone had dressed her in sports sweatpants secured with snap buttons and a large T-shirt, probably a man's. The shirt was clean and white and smelled like cotton. It was a comforting smell and a comforting setup in a non-comforting room.

She gritted her teeth. She had *better* not be in some rich guy's basement. Boy would he rue the day he'd made such a mistake. And whoever had taken Sam's dress *better* have kept it and treated it right. And, you know, they better have grabbed Sam's shoes, too, while they were wrestling her body away from the enormous, couldn't-be-real wolves.

Funny, this inability to feel fear at the moment. Her flight out of the nightmare house had apparently numbed her to this current predicament.

That was handy.

She pushed back the comforter and swung her feet off the narrow bed. A soft rug embraced them, but the movement made her newly aware of half a dozen aches and pains. She reached around and fingered her back, feeling the padding of bandages. More covered her arm. A bruise discolored her shoulder where she'd rammed the doorjamb in her haste to get outside. Various scratches and bruises marred other areas.

She blew out a slow breath. The numbness wobbled.

It wasn't real, what she'd seen. It wasn't. Maybe the partiers who had broken into her chosen room had dropped a tab of acid into her mouth. That would explain it.

She hoped that explained it.

The bed groaned as she pushed off it. Standing, feeling better on her feet despite her throbbing head and aching back, she took in her surroundings. A simple wood table sat next to the bed, holding a glass of water. An equally simple couple of chairs occupied the corner at the far end of the square room, next to a dilapidated dresser holding a porcelain basin filled with water. A mirror hung over a bare wooden shelf, and flip-flops lay next to the bed.

Absently, she scratched her chest, then paused. An electric heat pounded through her middle, a feeling similar to what she'd experienced last night but amplified. Energy zipped through her, invigorating despite her soreness. Excitement—was it excitement?—coiled in her gut, urging her to spar, or fight, or pick up a sword and start hacking at limbs. She just felt so...*good*. Really good.

Fucking amazing, actually.

"What the hell is happening to me?" she whispered, padding to the door. "Seriously, this had better not be a rich man's basement."

At the door, she looked down at the oblong handle and belatedly saw the rusty key sticking out of the keyhole beneath it. A relieved sigh exited her mouth.

If it *was* a rich man's basement, he either wasn't trying to imprison her or he was really, *really* forgetful. And therefore really, *really* stupid.

With a last glance at the dancing blue flame, she wrenched the handle and pulled it. Hinges groaned as the heavy wood door swung inward.

Charity grimaced and peered out into the darkened room beyond, ready to slam it shut and turn the key should any of those creatures rush her. A soft rustle drew her eyes to a couch in the middle of the room. It sat opposite two modern recliners with a cozy coffee table between them, sporting a doily trapped beneath a fruit bowl.

The blue light from behind her washed over a bare torso. Movement made Charity brace…and then the man sat up and blinked. He quickly wiped the sleep out of his eyes and stood.

Relief flooded her at the sight of this remnant of her frantic escape from the mansion. Devon.

Shirtless and with black hair sticking out in all directions, he walked toward her with the grace of a dancer. His upper body was lean but solid, his muscles defined. A tattoo covered his shoulder with elegant and artistic scrollwork, wrapping halfway down his bicep. Asian calligraphy cut down the side of his stomach, weaving between his six-pack and sculpted obliques.

Scowling so hard that she absently wondered if she'd kicked his puppy in her sleep, he stopped a little too close, imposing on her with his size, easily half a foot taller than her.

"Out to cause more havoc?" he asked.

She matched his scowl, having no rebuttal for his vague accusation. Shouldn't he be explaining things rather than bandying about insults and threats?

"Where am I?"

He scoffed. "Don't play dumb. Do you know what you did last night?"

She blinked as an answer.

"You single-handedly allowed all but three of the newbies to escape from that house," he went on. "While we were dealing with you, we missed a mass exodus. You made me look incompetent!"

The heat in her middle flared in the face of his anger. Adrenaline pooled in her body, demanding action of some sort. To run or fight or laugh or dance—to get moving.

She shook out her sizzling limbs. "Look. I don't know what you're talking about. I was running for my life last night! I just need to get home…"

Footsteps pounded down wooden steps across the vast space. Charity squinted through the darkness. A large shape hit the bottom step and moved in their direction. The soft light from the open bedroom door highlighted firm, broad features. The man was…large. Not tall so much—shorter than Devon—but massive. Huge barrel chest, tree-trunk arms, thick, solid legs. The man was power and strength in an imposing package.

"I see our guest is awake," the newcomer said as he walked up, his voice masculine in a way Charity hadn't realized a voice could be. The light fell across his features as he neared them. A wide nose adorned his square face, sporting scruff from a couple of days without shaving. His gaze zeroed in on Charity.

She registered his eye color. One pale blue, one faded green, like a beat-up dollar bill.

A memory jogged to the forefront of her brain. A wolf lunging at her. Barely missing. Crashing into the strange creature behind.

The numbness pulled away again, and this time, a

thousand images flooded her. The way he moved. How he stood. Graceful death. "No. *No!*"

Electricity flooded her like she'd been hit by a snapped power line in a storm. Before she knew what she was doing, she surged forward and slammed her fist into the big man's stomach. The air around her fist solidified then exploded outward, as if she'd physically shoved him. He flew backward, surprise lighting up his face.

Another memory started to surface, but Charity took off running. The itch in her chest blossomed out until it encompassed her whole body, giving her speed and power she'd wait until later to question. She rounded a rustic table and jumped onto the base of the stairs. Devon's light steps followed directly behind her. Stronger and with longer legs, he was gaining.

She burst through the dense, heavy door at the top, the effort costing her precious seconds. A hand closed around her borrowed sweatpants, trying to yank her back. The snap buttons resisted for a moment, then popped open, the pants ripping away from her body like she was a basketball star about to take the court.

Devon stumbled and fell behind her, loud thuds against wood.

She burst into a living room. Ten or so people stopped what they were doing and turned her way. Puzzled expressions followed her senseless flight through another door and into a large kitchen. More shocked faces turned. Eyes dipped, surveying her lack of pants. Not stopping, she barreled through the far door and flung herself outside. The word "Help!" died on her lips.

She stumbled to a stop and her jaw went slack.

Devon's solid body slammed into her from behind, knocking out her breath and taking her to the ground. She was rolled over and pinned. Devon stared down into her face.

"What's wrong with you?" he asked, his breath ruffling her eyelashes.

"Where am I?" Panic threatened to overcome her. "What's happening to me?"

She felt his pressure ease up as he shifted then stood. He reached down a hand. She ignored it, watching the gold filaments swirl around his fingers.

"Am I hallucinating?" she asked, tongue thick in her mouth. "Am I still hallucinating?"

Strong hands hooked under her arms and hauled her up. Devon steadied her, leaning in close. "You've really never been here?"

Blinking excessively, Charity shook her head slowly. "The sky is orange." A tear leaked out of her eye, the first time she'd almost cried in four years. "This isn't real. None of this is real…"

Small granules of gold drifted by like dust motes, swirling playfully in the soft breeze. The sky was a soft orange, horribly surreal yet strangely beautiful. In fact, everything around them had a surreal quality, like they stood within a children's painting of Fairy Land. A cobblestone lane ran under her feet, leading away from the gigantic castle from which she'd emerged, a medieval behemoth with rough stone walls and arrow slits made for violent defense.

Devon's intense gaze softened. "This is the Realm. We brought you here to ask some questions."

She scrubbed at her chest, that crazy feeling of euphoria pulsing within her. She wanted to laugh so hard that she couldn't speak. And then stab someone with a gilded knife.

"I think I'm going crazy," she said in a wispy voice. Her legs wobbled.

Devon stepped closer and wrapped a solid arm around her waist, keeping her upright. "I thought I was hallucinating the first time I stepped through, too. But you get used to it."

Small dwellings made out of clay, like rounded huts, with straw roofs dotted the lane opposite the formidable castle. Flowers decorated the front yards, many of which were encircled by white picket fences. Flourishing trees and bushes gave the folksy area a wooded feeling, closing the homes in with natural comfort and privacy.

She looked back at the huge medieval castle. "One of these things is not like the others…"

"C'mon," Devon said. "Roger wants to talk to you. This may be your first time here, but we need answers for what happened in the Brink."

"The Brink?" She resisted his tug urging her back to

the castle.

"The human world. Non-magical."

"Non…magical." A laugh bubbled up as she noticed a person walking toward them. She blinked. Then wiped her eyes and blinked again. "Is that…"

"Don't point!" Devon ripped her hand out of the air.

"Okay, but just to be clear. That. Woman. Is. Blue. That should not be possible."

"She's a sprite. Would you come *on*?"

Charity pushed him away so she could stand on her own. Ignoring the wobbles from numb legs, she tried, and failed, not to stare at the petite *blue* woman wearing a bikini top made of leaves.

The woman's luminous green eyes darted up, connecting with Charity's. A wrinkle wormed into her brow before her narrow face cocked to the right. They continued to stare at each other as the sprite passed, the sprite looking as confused and bewildered as Charity felt.

"Is a human in this world as weird as…what I'm seeing?" Charity asked quietly.

"You're not human." Devon gripped her upper arm, as though her words had suddenly reminded him of his purpose, which had, in turn, spoiled his mood. "You got in here, so you have magic in your blood. I have no idea what you are, but the smell and feel of you is different than anything I've ever encountered. You better stop playing me for a fool."

CHAPTER 11

HER TEMPER FLARED. "Here's something that's *not* a secret: you're a dick."

"Nice."

"I'm in the Twilight Zone, and you make this about you?" She pulled up her hands, analyzing the tingling sensation. For some reason she couldn't begin to explain, she yearned to hold a sword. A sword! What good was a sword in the age of guns, drones, and missiles?

As she blinked at her digits, the throb in her middle turned into a manic pounding. The sensation ran up and down her body and back in fantastic vibrations, singing in her blood. It welled in her chest, fizzing and sputtering. Some of it branched out, traveling through her shoulder and connecting with Devon's touch on her arm.

Confusion stealing over her, she let her gaze travel up his round bicep, over his tattooed shoulder, and to his intelligent brown eyes, beautifully speckled with green and gold flecks. Their gazes locked. The humming between them, while completely foreign, felt absolutely *divine*. He flexed and his muscles popped, the effect somehow heightening the vibration between them, throwing her into a weird trance.

Slowly, she put her tingling palm on his pec. The singing in her blood intensified. The prickling increased, stopping her breath.

"Magic," Devon whispered, clearly feeling it too. "You have a lot of it. It's…flirting with mine. Somehow." He tilted his head to the side, analyzing. "You're not normal."

"Oh, well, thank you for your expert analysis."

"It's also not the time to cop a feel." His lips tweaked into a lopsided grin, as if he weren't used to smiling.

"It's always time to cop a feel," she replied absently, pulling back her hand. She stared at her palm as she took a step away from him. Although she missed the feel of him, the warmth in her chest remained, supplying electricity. It was starting to get annoying.

"Why don't you invite our guest back inside?"

The guy with the dual-colored eyes stood in the doorway of the castle. His pose said he was trying for patience, but the intense energy crouched within him, straining at his skin, said he could just as easily spring and kill them all.

"You were a wolf," she said dumbly, backing away. Might as well get it all out there. Insanity was more fun when you shared it. "I saw your eyes. You were a… You attacked a strange creature. I don't understand any of this."

"We won't harm you." The man held up his hands. "You are in no danger here. Maybe we should start from the beginning, and then someone can give you a tour of the Realm. Please." The man gestured her inside.

"He saved your life," Devon said. Then, as if he were a male stripper, he ripped off his sweats with one powerful tug, revealing a pair of fire-engine-red boxer briefs. Bending down, he began fastening his sweats around Charity's bare legs to cover her up. It was a sweet gesture ruined by his attitude problem. "If he'd wanted to kill you, you'd be dead ten times over."

Devon's challenging tone, though certainly justified if he were telling her the truth, fanned the fire in her gut. Her fingers curled into fists, unbidden.

Once he finished his task, Devon straightened. "So are you coming or what?" He lightly touched her arm again. Electricity crackled between them.

"I'm coming," she said through clenched teeth, clinging to calm with everything she had. Another tear leaked out. She batted it away.

A few minutes later, she found herself seated at a worn table in the biggest kitchen she'd ever seen. Devon, who'd disappeared and then reappeared in another pair of sweats and a shirt—the castle clearly had a large supply—sat beside her, and the man with the dual-colored eyes, who had to be Roger, sat opposite her. He clasped his hands in front of him. "Let's start with what happened at the party, shall we?"

"Give the girl a minute to get her bearings." A plump woman with curly brown hair turned from the counter. She set a steaming cup of brownish liquid in front of Charity and patted her on the shoulder. "I'm Beazie, dear." The middle-aged woman smiled. "I run the domestic affairs here in the castle. That includes the kitchens and sleeping quarters. So if you need anything—anything at all—you come see me and I'll sort you out. All righty?"

"Am I stuck here? In this world?" Charity asked.

"Oh my, no." Beazie laughed and patted Charity's shoulder again. "Of course not, dear. You'll get to go home as soon as everything is straightened out, don't you worry."

"That hasn't been decided yet," Devon stated, the gold specks in his eyes dancing dangerously.

Beazie *tsked* at him. "Mind your manners, young man. This is your pretty guest. Be courteous."

The broad-faced man smiled good-naturedly, his attention never far from Charity's face. "I'm Roger," he said. The rest of what he said was gibberish. "I'm the alpha of the North American region. In other words, I oversee all the various packs within North America, and each of their pack leaders, my sub-alphas, report to me. I'm like a CEO in a large company. This is one of seven regions spanning the world."

"Uh-huh." Charity dipped her finger into the steaming brew. Heat bit her skin. The expected sensory result was welcome. At least hot things in this place steamed. Her world and theirs had one thing in common.

"We're known as shape shifters. We have magic that allows us to change into an animal form," Roger continued. "We use our animal form, and the inherent magical properties therein, to help police the human world from magical species—like vampires, for example, or corrupt mages. We're supernatural police, if you will. Our goal is to keep the secret of magic from the non-magical. Does this make sense?"

"Mmm. Mhm…" Charity tapped the table. It felt and sounded like real wood.

"This is Devon, whom you've met previously, I think. He's the sub-alpha of the Forest Clan, but we call him an alpha for the sake of simplicity."

"Sure, yeah. Simplicity." Charity nodded and tapped her chair—also like real wood.

"Primarily, Devon's team is responsible for taking out all newly formed vampires in his area," Roger said.

"She must know all this, sir," Devon said, obviously trying to keep his aggravation at bay. "She repeatedly ignored my warnings about going into the house with those creatures. She played innocent well, I grant you, but her timetable isn't believable." He ticked off a finger. "She disappears when the elixir is being consumed, somehow without alerting them." He ticked off another finger. "She returns after they are engaged in creating the new vampires." A third finger. "She alerts the whole house right before we strike." He dropped his hand. "This has to be part of Vlad's plan. There's no way she could've snuck around his people, or escaped him, for that matter. It's not possible. She must have been on their side all along."

Charity's hand stopped mid-reach, the material of the mug forgotten. "Are you serious?" she asked, rather calmly given the circumstances. "You not only want me to buy in to all this...insanity, but you think I'm somehow a part of those freaks' circus? Have you completely lost your mind? None of this can be real..." She blinked at the guys in front of her, then the castle around her, then the gold filaments lazily drifting past the castle windows.

"Vampires are also shifters, in a way," Roger said, still somehow patient. "They have two forms—a human form, which tends to be more beautiful and faster and stronger than the average human, and a creature form that is stronger and faster still. Someone I know calls that their 'swamp creature' form. I'm sure you can see why. You met them in their human form at the beginning of the night, and their swamp creature form toward the end. They were as real as you or me. As real as the chair under your butt, and the table under your arms."

"That's all still questionable," Charity mumbled, tapping the mug. It felt like ceramic.

Charity shook her head and held up her hand. "Seriously, am I in a coma or something?"

"The sooner you admit to your ruse, the faster we

can move on," Devon growled.

"Why? You seem pretty convinced by your little theories," she spat.

"Enough," Roger said quietly, nearly under his breath, but Charity's small hairs stood on end and her skin prickled, as if danger were running directly at her with a grin and red glowing eyes.

Devon's ordinarily lush lips pressed into a tight white line.

And that was why Roger was an alpha over a large area. He was intensely scary. That made sense.

"Charity, why don't you walk us through how you got to the party?" Roger said, back to good-natured, as if he hadn't just scared the room silent.

Charity wasn't fooled. She still had unpleasant shivers and an insane urge to flee.

Calming herself, she explained how Sam had peer-pressured her into going to that party. Thunder clouds peeked through Roger's calm eyes when she got to the part about Devon's goon threatening to kill her. Cocky McCockerson at least had the sense to appear mollified. Finally, her words tapered away as one horrific thought slammed into her.

"What happened to Samantha? And Donnie?"

"While not everyone who was invited to the turning party was actually meant to be turned—some were there for food supply, and thanks to you and us, they'll mostly be fine and will remember little—Samantha and Donnie were not so fortunate. We believe they were turned."

"No." Charity furrowed her brow and shifted in her seat. "No, that can't be…"

Roger and Devon shared a look that stopped Charity's heart. Neither commented.

Anger pulsed through her. "If you knew what would happen, why did you let them go to the party?" Charity asked, her voice rising in pitch. "Devon and his friends were just hanging out in the road. They warned us, sure, but it was vague at best. Why didn't they block the road off? Get more specific?"

"You don't believe us now, after you've seen them," Devon said. "Do you really think you would've turned back if I'd told you not to go because you'd be turned into a vampire?"

"So you let those things kill innocent people? Change them into those, those *creatures*?"

"We wanted to take out the vampires before they could distribute the drink, but there wasn't time," Roger said, compassion sparking in his eyes. He felt for the lost, she could see it. It eased the tightness in her middle, if only a little. "We only found out about the party hours before it started. I couldn't organize a big enough crew on such short notice, something Vlad, the elder vampire who organized all this, surely knew. We had to go for plan B and try to take out the host when they were at their weakest. You see, when an established vampire gives blood to a new vamp, they have to give it in large quantities. It severely weakens them. Slows them. Unfortunately, by then it was too late for the humans to be saved."

Unease churned Charity's gut. That incredibly handsome man had pressured her to drink the punch for a reason. If not for her past, she would've taken him up on it. She'd wanted to. She'd barely turned away.

What if she hadn't? What if she'd stayed?

Images rolled through her mind, of bodies writhing in the dark, of terrible creatures chasing her through the house.

She shivered. "Why them, specifically?" she asked quietly, bile rising in her throat.

"I can't say exactly," Roger replied. "It varies, the people they choose. Some are wealthy and some poor, some have outstanding business connections and some have nothing at all. This particular situation was intended as a statement, I believe. To Devon and myself."

Devon's head snapped Roger's way. He hadn't known this information.

"Recently, I was forced to work side by side with Vlad to eradicate a larger evil," Roger told Charity. "The effort was led by a woman that Vlad is respectfully at odds with. This woman is maybe the only person—or creature—that makes him nervous, as far as I can tell. He keeps his distance from her and her natural dual-mage friends." Fire glinted in Roger's gaze. "He is making a statement that I will not garner the same respect from him. Given that my crew ran into vampires who, based on their strength and speed, had clearly not participated in the turning, I suspect this was an elaborate plan to strike a blow to my forces. To bring me down." Roger's smile froze Charity's blood. "But Vlad did not realize another wild card was in his midst."

A sickening feeling gnawed at Charity's guts. She shook her head.

Roger nodded. "He did not foresee you throwing a stick in his bicycle spokes. He was completely disorganized when we descended, his plans frayed. He had no choice but to run rather than fight, and in so doing, he lost a few of his own."

"Wait…" Devon's voice drifted away. He seemed to be struggling with the destruction of his theory. His gaze darted from Charity to Roger, then back.

"I have one question, however," Roger went on as though they were all on the same page. "Without knowing why you were there, why didn't you drink the punch?"

She ran her hand over her face, hoping it would help her addled brain. "I don't drink."

"Why not?" Devon pushed.

Charity shrugged, uncomfortable. "Walt, my…dad…" The words were like a knife in her gut. "He was an abusive alcoholic. I never want to turn out like him. I heard alcoholism runs in the genes."

Devon leaned back in his chair.

Roger nodded with a sympathetic expression. "I'm sorry to hear that, although it saved your life in this instance. And who are your parents, if I may ask? Are they magical?"

Manic laughter bubbled out of Charity before she could clamp a hand over her mouth. "Sorry. No, Walt is not magical, unless you count his ability to clear a room with a fart. He had his mouth on a bottle constantly. He didn't work much, and when he did get a job, he got fired almost immediately. My mom had to support us. Her dad was a deadbeat—she dropped out of college to take care of him—and then she married a guy just like him. I'll never understand why. I don't think she did, either. Anyway, she didn't have the credentials for a good job, so she worked all the time. Very mundane situation—no magic from either of them."

"And where are your parents now? Do they live near you?" Roger asked, and Charity could tell he had his kid gloves on. He was dialing down his scary power so she wouldn't bolt. She appreciated it, but if the outside world weren't orange and filled with gold dust and blue people, she would've run long before now.

"Walt lives in a bad part of Chicago," she said. "He's mooching off the state."

"And your mother?"

Charity shrugged, picking at the table edge. "She took off when I was sixteen. Left a note, apologizing. It pleaded with me to graduate college and make something of myself. To turn out better than she did." Charity shrugged again, pain wobbling within her like kernels of popcorn, ready to explode. She hated thinking about it. It was the only thing that could really make her cry anymore. The only thing that could spear down through the thick crust she'd built up since that day.

"Wait," Devon said. "Your mother left you with an alcoholic father? Just...left? Did you have anyone to take care of you?"

"I was sixteen. I'd had plenty of experience taking care of myself by then. And I had John."

"Who's John?" Roger asked.

"He was my boyfriend. He had two normal parents that trusted him. Still poor, but they had enough. They treated me like a stray, but I didn't care because I got hot meals and a warm house. I pretended to go home after they fed me, but really I climbed through John's window after they went to bed. Going home with Walt drunk... It wasn't the best place for me."

"And where's John now?" Devon leaned forward and put his elbows on the table.

"Texas. We parted ways after high school. I came here and he went there. It didn't make sense to stay together long distance."

"His decision?" Devon asked knowingly.

Charity narrowed her eyes at him, remembering the things she'd overheard about him. He certainly wouldn't do long distance, if any of those things were true. Or a second date.

A familiar pain tightened her throat. The split with John had shattered her heart, but it had been for the best. He'd needed to get out on his own and live his life, and her path lay in a different direction.

She took a deep breath and struggled out of the pain. She'd promised herself, after her mother had left, that she wouldn't let bitterness eat away at her. That she would embrace life, hang-ups and all. Sometimes it was a struggle, but she'd always pushed through before, and she didn't intend to stop now. No matter how hard the road got, or what stood in her way—including whatever *this* was—she would keep going until she realized her dreams, one way or another.

She sighed. Easier said than done.

"And you haven't heard from your mother?" Roger's voice dripped sympathy, thawing her a little more toward him.

Charity shook her head, so close to tears that she was fidgeting frantically to stop them. "She walked away and never looked back. I don't blame her—Walt is big, dumb, strong, and mean. She didn't have it easy. Sometimes the bruises looked like permanent marker. I had somewhere to go. She…well, she left to save her life. I can't begrudge her, or any woman, that." She wiped away a stray tear and bent her head so her hair would cover some of the pain on her face.

"But she walked away from her daughter." Anger slashed through Devon's previously controlled expression. "Why didn't she take you with her?"

"That isn't our business," Roger chided softly. "I'm sure this is a tender subject."

Charity shrugged.

"And that's why you're in college? For her?" Devon

made it sound like an accusation.

Charity was about to tell him where he could shove his judgments, but Roger got there first.

Only Roger didn't need words.

One *look* had the air turning brittle with unspeakable menace. Devon jerked ramrod straight, as if he'd received a verbal command.

Charity hunched, nerves dancing like skeletons.

"I slipped into some dark days after that, I'll admit it," she said. "It was a dark year, but I'm a fighter. Always have been, both physically and emotionally. I'm smart on my feet, have martial arts training, and push through life's crap. She knew that. After a while, I made peace with it." She wasn't sure if her babbling was a defense against Devon's words, or merely a way to keep herself from sprinting out the door like a rabbit from a fox. Either way, the words kept burbling out. "I hope she's doing well. I hope she found a guy that treats her well. Or maybe no one at all. Maybe she'll be happier with only one mouth to feed. With only one person to look after, finally. I hope I see her again, though. Someday."

Devon's fists clenched. "No *way* are you this magnanimous. Your mom walked out on you, and you're *happy* for her? I call bullshit!"

"Just because you chose not to forgive, doesn't mean others need to make the same choice," Roger replied in the same soft tone.

Devon's eyes hardened, but it didn't hide the raw,

aching pain hidden beneath the anger. She knew that look—she'd worn it consistently for that dark year. Probably still did, from time to time.

She wasn't the only one with a past.

Charity dropped her head. "Anyway, she got out a few years before I did. Now I'm here—at school, I mean, not *here*. With the orange-ness and blue people and… Speaking of here, when can I go home? How do I even…get home…"

"We'll come back to that," Roger said, getting up. "How about you get a tour, eat some breakfast, and settle in a little bit. When all of this"—Roger waved his hand around the kitchen, implicating the great wide world outside the walls—"sinks in a little, we'll come up with a plan. Sound good?"

Charity gave him a vague smile, because saying no to a man like Roger wasn't something she could stomach at the moment, but no, that didn't sound good. Tour be damned—she'd find the quickest way out of here and take it. She hadn't been on the vampires' chosen list—her mind still stuttered at the idea that those fabled creatures were real—which meant she wasn't in danger. She could hitch a ride out of here, no problem.

But as she sat idle, thinking, little bits of information stitched themselves together. The handsome man outside of her classroom. The watchers, stalking her and Sam out to the street. The laugh.

Roger thought she was an unplanned wild card, but

could he be wrong? While she hadn't gotten an invite, she'd been approved as a sub for Jessica. Was she now a hunted woman?

CHAPTER 12

ROGER GLANCED DOWN at Devon. "Send two people with her. Then meet me in my office."

"Yes, sir." Devon stood with grim determination. He watched Roger's back disappear through a door leading deeper into the castle before turning back to Charity.

He took a deep breath to keep a leash on his temper. Despite what Roger had said, he had a hard time believing Charity hadn't had a deeper purpose in that house. How could a girl who oozed magic not realize she had any? Granted, last night he'd only smelled her—this throbbing electric pulse she gave off was something new—but her magic was too potent to have just started to mature. Much too potent. And even if she hadn't known about it, no random girl off the street, whether she had fighting training or not, could get past an elder vampire.

She'd taken on a whole house of vampires! It wasn't just luck and raw power that had gotten her out of there alive. Nor did he believe the vamps had spent the night around her without realizing she was special. Not with that smell. Not with the strange, ethereal quality of her skin, which seemed to glow from within. She was keeping something to herself, he knew it.

Or maybe you're pissed that she's in Roger's favor for some reason, and you walked away nearly empty-handed…

He gritted his teeth and worked on another steadying breath. Last night had been his big chance to prove himself to the best alpha in the world. Probably his only chance, and he was lucky to have even gotten one. All that work for nothing. He'd botched it. He'd only gotten three newbies of nine.

All because he'd needed to guard one girl.

Sure, Roger seemed to think she'd saved them rather than screwed them, but Devon couldn't help feeling like a failure.

He stared down at the girl's heart-shaped face and dainty features. Her eyes were almost the same brownish-red as her hair. Her beauty was offset by the firm set to her jaw, the attack readiness of her pose, and the defiant sparkle to her eyes. Her magic poked and prodded him, goading him to violence, drawing out his raw aggression. Her silent challenge was clear, as it had been since she'd woken up. But being that she wasn't pack, he wasn't allowed to establish the pecking order.

Could this situation get any worse?

"I don't speak scoff," she said.

Yet another deep breath.

"As you heard, I'll hook you up with two escorts,"

Devon said coolly, tamping down the desire to upend the table. "They'll take you around this area. Try not to stare—some species think that's a challenge. You don't want to provoke a Jorogumo or a Hellhound."

Charity stared at him with squinted eyes and shook her head. Her brain was trying to shut down. He knew exactly how she felt.

"They'll be in shortly," Devon finished.

Before she could ask a question, he was striding through the interior of the castle. He found his pack a moment later. They'd gathered in one of the sitting rooms, waiting for Devon. As he walked in, they all looked up, ready for instructions. Probably wondering what came next.

So did he.

"Andy, Macy, you're on tour duty," he barked. "Take Charity around a few of the safer parts of the Realm. Stay close. Keep her out of trouble."

"You want *us* to keep her out of trouble?" Macy said, her light brown hair pulled back into a tight ponytail.

"That lady seems good in a tight spot," Dillon reflected. "Give her the rules and she should be fine."

"You've seen her in action for a total of fifteen minutes, bro. What makes you an expert?" Andy asked.

"Great question," Macy said, crossing her arms over her chest.

Jimmy smirked. "Jealous much, Macy?"

"Irritating much, Jimmy?" she shot back.

"She got out of a house full of vamps," Dillon said. He scratched his hooked nose and looked up through his lashes at Macy. "Then she somehow got past Roger and ran out of the castle. Doesn't take a genius to notice the obvious."

"She shouldn't have been scared back into the house in the first place." Devon's eyes flayed Jimmy. "Roger's probably wondering why I have such a poor handle on my pack. We screwed up, starting with you, Jimmy."

Jimmy shrank down in his chair.

"You'll be disciplined after I talk to Roger," Devon continued. "Until then, Andy and Macy, ease Charity into this world. Roger wants her acclimated, and I won't let him down again. Rod and Dillon, start tracking the new vamps. If, by some miracle, Roger doesn't pull me off this detail, I want to go after them immediately. A lot of the vamps that turned them are dead, which means they'll be out of control. If we don't get to them fast, the innocent bodies will pile up."

"Yes, alpha," the room chorused.

"And Dillon is right: Charity seems to have a penchant for survival. She not only reacts quickly and effectively, she knows something about fighting. I'm not sure how much, but she knocked Roger out of the way like he weighed nothing. If she's to be believed, she grew up in an extremely dodgy part of Chicago. Problem is, she isn't in a dodgy part of *her* world. She's in *ours*, and she doesn't have a clue." Devon gave Macy, and then Andy, a poignant stare. "Watch her constantly. She's going to gawk, and point, and do other potentially awkward things that might lead to a confrontation. Don't let it happen. She starts throwing people around with her magic, the elves will get involved. I'm counting on you two to keep that from happening."

"Yes, alpha," Macy and Andy said in tandem.

Devon nodded and barely hid a sigh. He didn't look forward to what came next.

Strapping on an expressionless mask of rank, Devon found his way to Roger's office before knocking on the polished wood door, one of the many new additions the alpha had made to render the castle livable.

There was a muffled "Come in," and he pushed through.

Roger sat at a large oak desk with neat stacks of paper pushed off to the sides, leaving most of the surface bare. His elbows rested on the arms of his chair as he waited for Devon to take a seat.

"So, you had a small hiccup in your mission," Roger began. His tone was even. Not accusatory. Not yet.

Devon nodded. "When Charity went into the house for the last time, she hadn't consumed any of the elixir. When she came back out, she seemed wild. In human form, but not exactly human. She didn't smell like a newbie vamp, though, so I signaled for my people to subdue and not kill. That proved...more difficult than I had anticipated, wasting valuable time. By the time we returned to the mission, we could only extinguish three newbies. Three we watched get away—too far out of reach—and the others must've left in the pandemonium Charity created."

Roger studied Devon with an expressionless mask. Devon hated that stare. It was impossible to tell what the alpha was thinking.

Finally, Roger said, "I find it commendable that you had the foresight to subdue and not kill. Many men your age would not have had that presence of mind within the circumstances."

Devon nodded once, wary of the compliment. The next moment proved why.

"You made a grave error, of course," Roger went on.

"Yes, sir. I tried to physically keep her from going back into the house, but she proved...elusive. By the time I got to her, she'd already crossed the threshold into their domain."

"It seems you underestimated her twice in one night."

"Yes, sir." Devon's jaw clenched.

"You're young. Mistakes are to be expected. What do you plan to do with Jimmy?"

"Disciplinary action. I thought I would talk to you before I came to any decisions."

"Good, yes. I need you to start taking out those newbies as soon as possible. They're already out there gaining strength with feedings. For that, you need your whole pack."

Devon's spirits lifted. He wasn't being taken off the hunt! Roger was giving him a second chance.

"But I think I promoted Jimmy too soon," Roger said. "He is a little too immature for your pack. I'm going to transfer a new wolf to you. She comes from a southern region. She's had some experience and is ready for the next level, I think. She'll replace Jimmy for now."

Surprised, Devon just nodded. He hadn't seen that coming. It meant he'd have to train a new member, which took time and effort, but it also meant he wouldn't have to worry about Jimmy. It would probably amount to an even trade.

Roger tossed a file in front of Devon. "That's the new wolf's file. You can review it later. We have more important matters to discuss. Charity."

Devon slid the file to the side. Here it came.

"In a way, Jimmy's incompetence was a huge stroke of luck. If he hadn't chased Charity back into that house, she wouldn't have had to escape. If she hadn't escaped, I wouldn't have seen, firsthand, what she is capable of.

"As you know, vampires aren't the only creatures capable of wreaking havoc in the human world. Something is drawing demons to the Brink in record numbers. If the two groups are working together, there will be hell to pay. The elves are calling Lucifer in for a chat, but we can't wait to step in. The elves and the Underworld forget how quickly things move in the Brink. It'll be overrun if we don't act. It is well within our right."

"Excuse me for asking, but what does this have to do with Charity?"

Roger entwined his fingers on the desk. "Just as vampires aren't the only nuisance in the Brink, shape shifters aren't the only beings suited for peacekeeping and hiding the magical world."

"You mean the Magical Law Enforcement offices?"

The MLE did a similar job to that which Roger's pack performed, but they were connected with a secret branch of the Brink government and often got waylaid in red tape. Not to mention that vampires had been known to bribe the MLE officers, while other magical peoples, like the Mages' Guild, downright scared them into inactivity. The Brink shouldn't have needed two organizations to police the supernatural, but here they were.

"No," Roger replied, and his tone could've turned water into ice. It was clear he didn't appreciate the interruption. "In earlier times, shifters fought beside other magical creatures. For whatever reason, the shape shifters have seen growth, but other magical beings are in decline. Many have retreated deep into the Realm to regrow their numbers. Unfortunately, they haven't ventured back into the Brink. Not even toward the edge of the Realm, where we are.

"One of the creatures we used to fight beside was a subset of the fae, gifted with enhanced strength, speed and fighting prowess. Their people called them *custodes,* or guardians. But outside of their people, they were referred to as the warrior fae, because they were fearsome fighters—strong, quick, and brutal. Their magic could turn the tide in a fierce battle. Their numbers aren't large compared with fae as a whole, even going back centuries, but if you were lucky enough to have one on your side, you did everything in your power to use that weapon to its full potential."

Devon had heard something of the warrior fae. Everyone had. They lived deep in the Realm and kept to themselves. He'd never seen one. In fact, he'd never spoken to anyone who had.

"Now, the warrior fae guard their children like we do," Roger said. "Like humans do. And since this type of fae haven't ventured out of the Realm for some time, that we know of, it is very unlikely we'd run across one of them."

"Sorry, sir. I'm still not sure how Charity fits in."

Roger's stare zeroed in on Devon. "She seems mild-mannered, doesn't she? To me she does, anyway. Listens, engages…she's polite. But with you—when you assert your dominance, she pulls back her sweet exterior and shows her iron core. She won't put up with you pushing her around. Her magic doesn't flirt with yours; it entices yours. It challenges yours, doesn't it? She senses her magical equal in you, I'd wager. Something in her rises to the occasion."

Devon shifted uncomfortably. "Her magic isn't as strong as mine."

"Not yet." Roger leaned back in his chair. "But as I

understand it, the warrior fae don't come into their magic all at once. It's gradual, usually guided by their kind. Charity's magic has been kept at bay throughout her adolescence. I'm not sure if it's because she's been in the Brink, hidden away from other magical users, or that's just how it goes for her kind, but her magic is seeping out. Soon it'll start to gush."

Devon leaned forward and gripped the arms of his chair. "Wait. What are you saying?"

Roger put both hands on his desk. "I have no idea how it happened, or why she is in the Brink, but it seems you've found us a warrior fae, Devon. One that we must keep safe at all costs."

CHAPTER 13

CHARITY HEARD MACY snicker as Andy swept his hand toward the castle.

"Here we have our headquarters," he said in a lofty tone. "This castle once existed in the Brink in Europe. We have no idea how it came to stand within the gnome village, but it is estimated that it made the shift hundreds of years ago. The non-magical human inhabitants died in the crossing."

Charity stared at her tour guide, trying to place his face. She was sure she'd seen him somewhere before, probably around campus. Who would have thought that a few of her fellow students had magical alter egos? The sandy-blond hair and button nose gave him a boy-next-door feel, and his laidback demeanor and easy smile set her at ease. He would fit into Santa Cruz perfectly.

Macy, whom Charity didn't recognize, seemed more on point. Intelligence shone through her brown eyes, and she held herself with confidence. Her brown hair fell to her mid-back, and a kind smile surfaced anytime Charity screwed up her features in bewilderment at what she was seeing. They both seemed like good people.

"Now, the thing with the Realm is, there aren't definable rules," Andy went on, motioning them forward. "Not all the time, anyway."

"Yes, there are. The elves create the rules, and violently enforce them." Macy half turned to Charity. "They're the government. We basically work for them to keep order in the Brink. Why they concern themselves with the Brink, I don't know, since they never go there. But…" She shrugged. Clearly she wasn't too curious of a person.

"I meant rules regarding the elements, Macy." Andy ran his fingers through his messy hair, making parts stand on end. He didn't bother patting it down after. "Sure, we have *laws*. Everywhere has laws. But take the weather, for example. It's always perfect. If I want to wear a sweater, I'll be comfortable. What if I'm naked in the middle of the night and need to go for a stroll? No problem. I'll be just as comfortable as if I were in that sweater."

"Why would you need to go for a stroll in the middle of the night while naked? Is it a medical condition?" Macy asked.

Andy frowned at her. "Maybe I have a leg cramp and it can't wait until I get dressed."

"But why aren't you dressed in the first place?"

He blinked at her. "Because I'm sleeping."

Charity lost the thread of their argument at the sight

of huge horns jutting out from an inhuman head. The protruding nose with flaring nostrils, surrounded by fuzzy skin, gave the distinct impression of a bull's head. Below that, a bare chest, thick with muscle, sported savage-looking arms. Ragged white scars crisscrossed deeply tanned skin. The creature's torso ended in legs that seemed half-man and half-bull, clomping the ground with hooves.

"Oh my God, you guys," Charity said. She belatedly remembered not to point and ripped her hand out of the air. Too late.

The bull's eyes, already pointed in Charity's direction, homed in on her. The creature slowed to a stop twenty yards away, staring.

"It's staring. So that's rude, right? I'm off the hook?" Charity asked out of the side of her mouth.

"Oh crap. Look down!" Andy lowered his gaze. With a squeak, Macy did the same.

Charity thought briefly of looking down. It would be the smart thing, surely. But that danged heat inside of her flared brightly, taking over. She leaned forward, just a fraction, and stared into the creature's round, beady little eyes. Excitement fluttered her stomach. Sweat broke out on her brow, logic not completely on hiatus.

"Charity, *look down*," Andy said through gritted teeth.

"Half of me really wants to," she murmured, her muscles firing with adrenaline.

"Then why aren't you doing it?"

Charity flexed and relaxed her right hand, feeling that strange itch for a sword. Feeling the sweet breath of battle against her face. "Because the other half has gone insane."

Andy ripped off his shirt and stepped forward. Macy pushed Charity behind her, the second wall of defense.

"That's a minotaur," Macy said quietly. "They're mean bastards. If you look them in the eyes, they take offense. If it's Roger or someone strong enough, usually they'll ignore the challenge. That's because they know they can't win. They're not stupid. But us..." Macy shook her head as Andy ripped off his basketball-style sweats with snaps for seams. The same sweats they all wore.

A loud huff preceded the minotaur's stamped hoof.

"This is happening." Andy pushed down his boxer briefs, completely nude now. "This is definitely happening."

"Why is he stripping?" Charity asked in a furious whisper, bouncing in place, trying to shake out the adrenaline buzzing through her. "What if we run away? My pride will be fine if we run away."

"Andy's getting ready to change. And that thing is faster than it looks." Macy ripped off her own pants. "Stay right there, okay? Don't move."

"But..."

The minotaur stamped its hoof again. It bent, pointing its dirty, dull horns their way. Dull or not, with enough force, they'd spear through their middles handily enough.

"Here we go," Andy said. Green swirled around him like smoke. Fur rolled and boiled, a wolf erupting from his skin.

Charity's mouth dropped open. She'd known what they could do, theoretically, but she doubted she'd ever get used to seeing them shift.

The minotaur started forward, its jog quickly becoming a run.

Macy's shirt drifted to the ground.

Fear shocked through Charity's body as she watched the huge creature barreling toward them. And then the fire in her middle pulsed hot. Electricity zinged through her limbs and rolled within her body.

Without realizing what she was doing, she stepped out from behind her protection. Standing on her own, she stared at the charging minotaur.

A fierce growl ripped the air. Andy, or the large gray wolf that had been Andy, crouched as the beast neared.

"Get back!" Macy yelled. Green began to swirl around her.

A surge of spicy heat pumped into Charity's bloodstream from that deep source in her body. A manic grin lit up her face. She locked eyes with the beast, and *dared* it to keep coming. She didn't know what she'd fight with, but it didn't matter—she'd rock that thing's world and send it limping home.

A *rrrraaaahhhh* sound rumbled through the beast's thick chest. It shook its shaggy head. Then slowed. A hoof clattered against the ground as it stopped its advance. It huffed at her, clearly debating.

"C'mon, you bastard. Show me what you've got." Charity held eye contact. The wild thing within her flared. Pulsed higher. Hotter. She heard the song of battle calling to her. And wanted to answer.

The minotaur huffed again, its muscles relaxing somewhat. Charity heard Macy suck in a sharp inhale. The beast proceeded to cross to the other side of the line and amble past as if nothing had happened.

"It's leaving!" Macy whispered. She straightened up with wide eyes. "Holy crap, Charity—you have a ton of magic. But why can I only feel it sometimes, I wonder…"

Fur boiled and shivered before disappearing back to skin. Andy sprawled on patchy grass.

"Jesus, Charity," he said, panting as he crawled to his feet. "Please tell me you've learned your lesson. Those things are not fun to rumble with. I am relieved I didn't have to."

Charity scratched at her chest. Her heart pounded in her ears. She couldn't get enough air all of a sudden. "What is going on with me?"

Macy's excitement turned into confusion. "What's up?"

"Just…" Charity shook out her arms, trying to dislodge that electricity. "I don't know. I…"

"Out with it," Andy said, standing and then putting his hands on his hips and bending at the waist, looking like he'd just run a mile. In the nude. "We're all friends here."

"Does it take a bunch of energy to change into a wolf or something?" Charity said, not able to explain the intense feeling.

"Yes. I'm tired. What's up with that scratching at your chest? Your boobs falling off? Because that would be awful."

Charity couldn't help a smile at Andy's jest. "My chest… It's like there's this fire trying to get out, or something. I don't know. It's been like this since last night, and it's way worse today. It feels weird."

"Magic," Macy said as she refastened her pants. "Your body is trying to grow into its magic. It must be. It feels kind of like that when we go through the *summons*."

"The *summons*?" Charity asked.

"Yeah," Andy continued. "We're shape shifters, right?" Charity nodded. As ludicrous as it sounded, she'd come to accept that. Mostly. "Right, okay. So we get to a certain stage in our lives where our bodies start to change. Like puberty, but for shape shifters. Mine came after human puberty, but a lot of people, like Devon, hit them both at the same time."

"I did." Macy raised her hand. "I got *summoned* the day after I got my period."

"Anyway…" Andy steered Charity around a molehill. "Watch out for those." He pointed at the small opening. "They're not like Brink moles. They bite when you step on their front porch, and it itches for weeks. Right, so when you get *summoned*, your body gets all hot and feverish and *strong*. Way strong. You almost feel invincible. But your skin crawls, too, like it's on too tight. Itchy, yo."

Charity rubbed her chest. That sounded about right.

"I thought I had some sort of rash, even though I didn't see any actual skin irritation," Macy said.

"It's uncomfortable." Andy nodded. "But so is puberty in general, you know? So half the time you think everyone else is going through it, too. But then you get a, like, superhuman sense of smell. And bionic hearing. That's not normal, right?"

"Don't stare at that guy, Charity, he's a jerk at the best of times." Macy bumped Charity, knocking her stare off a being with green-tinged skin and fiery red hair.

"So then it's up to our parents to talk us through our first change," Andy said. "And if your parents didn't get the gene or hate that they change and refuse to do it, like Devon's mom—then another family member."

"Devon's mom?" Charity asked, remembering his look of soul-crunching loss.

"Shut up, Andy, that's pack business." Macy gave him a hard shove.

"It's not like she won't be pack soon. Or else why is

Roger bothering to—"

Macy *thwapped* him upside the head. "Don't get involved in whatever Roger's got going on. Let Devon handle it."

Andy rubbed his head, expression sour. "Let's get this tour over with. Charity, do me a favor. If you see something that surprises you, stare at the ground."

CHAPTER 14

"SERIOUSLY, DEVON, I know how to walk." Charity ripped her arm out of Devon's grip as they scaled the mountain of steep, twisty stone steps on the way to Roger's office in one of the castle towers. Apparently they needed another powwow before she could go.

"You've stumbled twice," Devon groused. "I can't have you falling and braining yourself."

Charity rolled her eyes as she reached the landing, tired of his attitude. "You should be more worried about me braining *you*." Devon pushed her out of the way so he could shove the door open for her. "Oh yeah, real gentlemanly—abuse a girl so you can open the door."

"Just get in, would you? I'm exhausted, and I can't finish my mission until I get you off my plate. Sooner the better. Your magic and your attitude need a serious adjustment."

Crazy heat flared within her, as if fanned by his words, and a smile tweaked her lips. Her hand itched for that sword.

"Yes. That." Devon shoved her through the door

and directed her down the hall. "Knock it off. It's pissing me off."

"Need to get me off your plate? I don't want to be *on your plate* any more than you want me there, trust me," she muttered. She entered the office, then hesitated, causing Devon to bump into her backside.

The barrel-chested alpha, Roger, stood behind a massive wood desk, tracking her movement with his different-colored eyes. A wave of shivers washed over her, her reaction to a predator in her midst. Any flare of defiance she had toward Devon dwindled as her flight reflex kicked into high gear. The whole situation was disconcerting.

"Please, sit," Roger said, indicating one of two large leather chairs in front of the desk.

"How did you get leather in here?" Charity did as he said, lowering into the cushy chair. "I can't imagine you kill cows in this place. Although that minotaur would probably deserve it."

"We got the furniture here the same way we got you in here. Carried it," Devon muttered as he sat in the chair beside her.

"Charity," Roger began, ignoring Devon's comment. "We need to discuss what comes next with you. Your presence at the house may have helped us derail Vlad's plan, but as you are aware, it also created a problem. Six new vampires are now hunting humans. Given that we were able to extinguish some of their creators, they'll have limited guidance and control.

They'll drain their food sources dry. Bodies will pile up. This is a very dangerous situation for the non-magical in the area."

"Sorry about that," she mumbled, because it felt like she should say something.

"I would like to employ you," he went on. Devon shifted uncomfortably next to her. "I would like to use you to help clean up the overspill from that party. I think you could be an asset to our organization."

Charity shook her head and pushed to the end of her seat. "Look, I'm really sorry that I got in the way, but I have a life I worked hard for. I don't know what the status is with my roommate, but I do know I need to get back to my regularly scheduled program tomorrow. Right? Tomorrow's Monday? Or does time move differently here?"

Roger clasped his hands on the desk. His biceps jutted out. "Time moves at the same pace, but travel time within the Realm fluctuates depending on the path. Getting from here to, say, the other side of the world could take merely an afternoon if the right paths were traveled. It could also take ten years if they weren't."

"I see. Okay, well, tomorrow I work in the admin office, and then Tuesday I have classes. So…I gotta go. It's been…great, but I think it's time for you to show me the way home."

"You think you can just move on from this place and go back to a normal life?" Roger asked, and Charity couldn't tell if it was a genuine question or a threat.

Magic clearly existed in the world, and Roger's job was to keep normal people from knowing about it. He'd done a bang-up job so far, since Charity still couldn't wrap her head around any of this, but did what she'd seen incriminate her? Was knowing about the magic like seeing your kidnapper's face?

"He wasn't threatening you," Devon said, as if reading her mind.

Charity didn't mask her sigh. "Oh, good. Well, then…I think I can. I mean, I'll always look harder—and probably avoid—the shadows, and I'll certainly wonder about people's secrets, but this is just one more speed bump on my life's nightmare journey to dreamland. I can't derail now when I'm three years away from graduating. I'll never get another opportunity like this again. I have to move on, and so…I will."

"I'm not asking you to give up your life," Roger said with a glimmer in his eyes she didn't much like. Her flight reflex kicked up a notch. "I am asking if you want to work for me."

Roger's stare beat into Charity's skull and then bounced around in there for a while, turning her defenses into jelly. Her body shivered from the strain of holding that ferocious, predatory gaze. Violent energy coiled within his skin, threatening to break free.

Devon sat unnaturally still, probably to keep from drawing that intense, commanding stare. Good Lord, Roger was terrifying.

"There are a few reasons why I don't think that

would work," she began slowly, working through what felt like lockjaw. "First, I don't turn into anything besides grumpy—"

Devon snorted.

"Second, I barely got out of that house. I would constantly be a hindrance. And third, I don't have any spare time. I'm working and studying constantly. That party was a rare occurrence."

"Quit your job at the administrative office," Roger said. "You can't be making much there."

"It's a cushy job that lets me study while I work. I need it. My scholarship won't cover all my expenses."

"You have a scholarship?" Roger leaned back with a quirked eyebrow. "Impressive. How much does it cover?"

"It was a full ride, but that's just for school, books, and a meager stipend for rent. I still have to come up with money for food, clothes, and other supplies."

Roger's eyebrows nearly brushed his hairline now. "Wow. You must be extremely intelligent and hard-working."

Heat filled Charity's cheeks, and she squirmed in embarrassment. Although he was clearly trying to butter her up, it was nice to get recognition. Only her mother had ever praised her for doing so well in school.

"I did what I had to, plain and simple," she mumbled as she picked at her nail. "But you can see now why I need to treat my education like a gold bar."

Roger leaned forward against the desk. It almost

looked like he was ready to pounce.

She gulped audibly, her whole face hot now.

"My organization pays more than your job at that school," he said. "Much more. Quit the admin job and work for me. Devon and his men will keep you out of harm's way"—Devon jolted, clearly hearing that news for the first time—"and I'll make sure your balance of school and work is perfect. All you have to do is help extinguish a few vampires. Your life will only change for the better."

He wanted to send her into battle against those nightmare creatures, and her life would change for the better? Was he joking?

She scrubbed her stupid palm against her leg, trying to quell that insufferable itching.

"Any day," Devon grumbled under his breath.

Devon wanted her to say no. Desperately. She could see it in the tightness around his eyes, in his sagging lean against the elbow he'd planted on the chair arm, feel it in his magic beating on her, trying to subdue her. To put her in her place—beneath him.

She gritted her teeth and turned away, fighting that flame within her. This was crazy. All of it. She didn't care about the pack social structure and where she fit within it. She didn't care about pretty-boy jackasses with a dominance complex. And she certainly didn't have a problem saying no when it went against everything she was working so hard for in her life.

So why couldn't she get the words out? Why did she

want to take the job just to shove it in Devon's face?

"I want to go back to normal," she told no one in particular. "I want to go back to when my life made sense."

"You can get back there, you just have to accept a new normal," Roger said. It wasn't helpful. "Devon's team has to work out the location of the new vampires, anyway. How about I give you a day to think about it?"

No.

It was there, right on the tip of her tongue. So easy to say, normally. Easy to say to anyone but the alpha staring at her, that was.

Then another thought occurred to her. "If all this really happened, then my roommate is a…" She couldn't get the word out. Her voice rose in panic. "Where am I going to stay?"

"You'll stay with Devon."

"What?" the two cried at once.

"No," she said, finding it easy to deny Roger this time. "No, that'll never work. This kid has a temper problem that I don't want any part of."

"If you'd stop getting in my way and assaulting me with your magic, I'd—"

"I didn't even know I had magic until today. I still don't believe it. So clearly it is your—"

"Enough," Roger said.

Charity's mouth snapped shut, but not even the sudden chill freezing the air could disengage her glare from Devon. He stared back just as intently, the green and gold specks in his beautiful eyes dancing. Fire blazed between them, demanding action.

The silence lengthened.

"You have a lot of power locked up inside of you," Roger said calmly. His eyes glinted with humor. "It lightly stings my skin when you let it out. It also calls to us—shifters, I mean. Our magic complements each other, yours and Devon's and mine. Our style of fighting does, too. Or, at least, it once did."

She pushed Roger's words away. She'd had enough. "So…I have some studying to do…"

"I know this isn't ideal for you," Roger said, "but if your roommate has been turned, that house is no longer safe for you. Eventually she'll return, if only because she's hungry—"

"Hungry?" Charity squeaked.

"You're human. You have blood. Hence, you are food," Devon said.

"But I thought you said I was magical. Macy and Andy said—Oh my god, *Andy*! He's in one of my classes. Jesus, I'm tired. I wonder why he didn't say anything."

"Stay on topic, please," Devon muttered, his face pale.

"Vampires can feed off most anything," Roger said, "but you are a human with magic. And let's not forget that you were invited to that party. Or, at least, you were allowed to go. You could very well be in their sights. Even if Samantha doesn't return, that doesn't mean you're out of danger."

Charity's heart sank. She'd known that, of course. They were interested in her, the vampires. That fear had been in the back of her mind the whole time; she just hadn't wanted to bring it out and into the light.

She dropped her head into her hands, not sure where to go from here. "What kind of magic do I have? Andy and Macy seemed to think you'd know."

"For simplicity, magical people call you a warrior fae," Roger said.

"A warrior fae," Charity repeated slowly. "Like a fairy?"

"A fairy is a type of fae. Warrior fae is another type," Roger said.

"I see. Aren't I supposed to have wings? And be short?"

"You are short," Devon replied.

"Five-five is not—" Charity breathed through her nose for a moment, trying to ignore him. She dared not meet his eyes again. She didn't trust herself not to flip his chair back and kick him somewhere soft.

"We'll go over all that in time," Roger said softly. "For now, you two need to get back to the Brink and get a good sleep. After that, Devon will create a plan that will, hopefully, include Charity."

"You want us to go back *now*?" Devon jerked upright. "Not stay here until it's time to act?"

"I think Charity has had enough excitement. Why don't you grab some of her things from her old house, help her get comfortable?"

The vein in the Devon's jaw pulsed. Oh no, he did not like this any more than she did. Which soothed her. At least he wouldn't hit on her or demand constant homage to his glossy good looks.

"Charity," Roger said, giving her a smile that seemed out of practice. "I hope to work with you soon. You are an extraordinary woman."

The embarrassment was back. Charity tucked a lock behind her ear.

Devon stared at Roger like he'd never seen him before. In a moment, he shook himself out of his astonishment and turned to Charity. His frustrated scowl came back immediately. Charity couldn't help but laugh.

They wouldn't get along, that much was obvious. She wondered how long it would take for one of them to punch the other in the mouth, and who would break first.

CHAPTER 15

"CHARITY, WAIT!"

Devon must've been a serial killer in a past life. Karma was really screwing with him. He had six newbie vamps to hunt, school to attend, a pack to lead, and somehow he had to host, protect, and keep tabs on a chick who wouldn't stop arguing with him. The woman constantly shot him scowls barely masking her desire to clock him.

He wanted to reciprocate with all he had. But he wasn't allowed to. Roger had made that clear. He was to be her protector—it was on him to keep her alive.

"Wait for me," he said through gritted teeth, running across the plush green grass of Samantha Kent's small front yard. He held his Glock low and close so as not to alarm any neighbors who might be peeking out of their windows. The last thing he needed was for someone to call the cops on him. His usual recourse—changing into a wolf and fleeing—wouldn't be possible now that he was on protective duty. Charity would never be able to keep up on foot.

On second thought, a serial killer wouldn't have

been bad enough for karma to land him in this detail.

"It's fine. I'll be real quick," she said as she reached the door.

Shadows draped across the dilapidated front porch. They'd spent far too long at the crossing between Sector Eight and the Brink thanks to Charity's damn questions.

"Why do they call it Sector Eight?" she'd asked as they stood in front of the crossing. "And why the Brink?"

"The Realm is divided into eight sectors. Our head-quarters are in Sector Eight. The Brink…just *is*. I don't know. Will you come on?"

She pointed at the portal, refusing to walk right up to it. "What is this fuzzy line in the air? And is that a bench circle over there? Do people come to the border and hang out, like teenagers at a 7-Eleven?"

"It's the tear in the fabric of the worlds that allows us to pass from one to the other. And yes, if they get tired or are waiting for someone, they hang out and rest for a while. Will you *please* come on?"

After they finally crossed, she asked, "Did you buy that Range Rover new?"

"Yes. *Get in*."

She scoured him with condescension before she said, "Must be nice."

He'd nearly strangled her.

She lived with a rich person. She hung around her roommate's rich friends. She occasionally went to rich-people parties. She was jonesing after a rich person. To

all of that, Andy said she was sweet, smiley, and extremely blasé. Nothing bothered this girl when it came
to money.

Except for Devon, apparently, even though he'd
earned it all. Growing up, his mother hadn't even told
him about his shifter genes. Then, when they'd materi-
alized, she'd given him an ultimatum: ignore the
summons or be cut off. She'd wrongly assumed the
threat would scare him into staying with his family. It
hadn't. He didn't respond to bullying, even from his
own mother. He'd made his money by working hard
and rising in the ranks, not to mention investing well.
He'd gotten into that school on his own, too.

Which he'd screamed at Charity after losing his
temper yet again.

Her response?

Snorting and looking out the window. As if she
didn't believe him. As if he wasn't living up to her
expectations.

For some reason, he alone ticked her off. Now he
had to live with her, work with her—thank God he had
different classes, or he'd quit his job altogether.

Part of him wanted to scream at her. Or wrap his
fingers around her neck and shake. But as the hideaway
key turned in the lock, those thoughts fled.

He snatched her back from the door and thrust her
behind him.

"*Wait,*" he seethed. "Anything could be in there."

"I thought you said they couldn't go out in daylight?"

He felt her palm press to the center of his back, keeping tabs on his body movement. She wanted to feel his intentions so she'd know which way to dive. *Smart.*

"They sleep during the day, but it doesn't mean they won't go active if their territory is invaded. This is Samantha's residence. She'll define it as her territory, and if she's inside, as soon as it's breached, she'll rise to defend it. And any other vamp with her."

Charity sucked in a breath. In a shaky voice, she asked, "How do you kill them?"

He took in the smells—the stale whiff of vampire, a pungent, musty scent that clashed with the sweetness of Charity—and lowered the gun as a car drove past. "With a gun, you shoot them in the heart. You can also rip off their heads or expose them to sunlight. The problem is, these bloodsuckers are beyond fast. If there are more than one or two in here, we need to get out. No fighting, no trying to defend yourself—get out."

"I know."

Yes, she did. Probably better than he.

He nodded and put his shoulder to the door. It was the first time he might have to confront one of these creatures without fur.

"Keep your wits," he whispered. "We need to stick together. We need to have each other's backs."

"Like a pack."

Dillon was right—give her the rules, and get out of the way. This all might be new to her, but she had street

143

smarts in spades. "Exactly. Like a pack."

He took a deep, steadying breath. He needed to trust her like he would his pack mates, but it was hard, given everything she didn't know about her own magic.

"If anyone's here, I'm banking on it just being Samantha," he said, grabbing the handle. "New vamps are solitary beings. They're hunters. Only when their appetite is sated will they fall back into their previous lives as humans. They'll remember schedules and clutch on to their failing humanity. For a while, anyway. Until that erodes away."

"I know what you and the others think, but Samantha isn't one of these creatures," Charity murmured, defiance in her voice. "She made it out. She did. She would've seen through it—she's smarter than people give her credit for."

Devon stayed silent, letting her keep that fantasy for a while longer.

He peered into the gloom without crossing the threshold. The vampire stench thickened. He could only pick out one signature, though, and it lacked the subtle aroma of lingering decay, something common with the older ones.

A young vamp had blown through. It had probably come here to escape the mayhem at the party. It hadn't known to seek refuge in the Realm, so it had gone home. But it was starving. It would have had to leave to find food.

Unless...

Had the vamp come for solace, or dinner?

He turned slowly to glance down at Charity's fearful yet determined features. She knew the truth—he could see it in those velvet-brown eyes—she just didn't want to believe it. Samantha probably pissed on her constantly, but Charity thought of her as a friend. She was preparing herself to see a friend die.

Devon's stomach twisted in sympathy.

"I don't think anything's in here," he said softly.

Charity met his eyes, a plea not far from the surface.

"I'll still go in with you, just in case," he continued after a pause.

"A vampire has been in here, hasn't it?" Charity asked. Her chin raised a fraction, but the action didn't hide the worry in her eyes.

He nodded slowly, staying connected with her gaze. Trying to keep her rooted.

"And a different one wouldn't have come here unless it was looking for me," she said.

"Correct. But only an older one would be looking for you. An older one hasn't come through here."

Her face fell. She lowered her chin.

He turned back to the door and glanced at the threshold. He was about to find out if he was wrong.

He stepped through the door.

All that awaited him was silence and the stale air of a closed-up house. He reached back for Charity and felt her palm connect with his. It was extremely unlikely that a demon would creep up behind them and rip

Charity away, but weirder things had happened. He wanted to make sure she stayed with him.

Pop.

A thrill ran through his body. He looked to the right, waiting. Four smaller pops followed before silence regained its dominance.

"The house makes sounds all the time," Charity whispered, pushing her side up against his backside. She must've been watching their six. She might've been a novice to magic, but thank God she wasn't a novice to danger. "It's old. Solid, but it shifts, I guess. Settles."

Devon took another step into the stuffy space. Charity stepped with him, their movements perfectly in sync.

"Done some burglary?" he asked despite himself, his lips lifting in a grin. Only those up to mischief could move like this. He should know.

"Where I grew up, there was nothing to steal except drugs, and that would get someone dead real quick." She paused as they stepped again. "The bedrooms are at the back."

They walked with unneeded stealth through an entryway that opened up into a modest living room with brand-new furniture. A side hallway led back to a kitchen.

"This place seems small for someone like Samantha," Devon said quietly, not wanting to disturb the static of the house. "You still watching our six?"

"Yeah. We're clear. Her parents were trying to teach

her humility."

Devon snorted as they reached the kitchen and kept edging down the hallway. Two rooms branched off, one large, a master suite, and a smallish bedroom. As expected, Charity walked past him into the smaller room. Once inside, she snatched a duffel bag from the back of her closet and dropped it in front of a particle-board dresser.

Devon stepped into Samantha's room. A whirlwind of clothes and jewelry littered the various surfaces, representing thousands of dollars' worth of fashion. A whiff of vamp lingered in the stagnant air. In contrast, the moment he stepped into Charity's sparse, orderly room, he received a punch of vamp smell.

It had definitely come back for Charity. When it couldn't find its easy prey, it had left for other attractions.

Not good.

"Why not leave her in the dorm?" Devon asked, picking up their conversation.

"Apparently some things cannot be tolerated."

Devon thought he heard a little snark in that statement. Was she judging Samantha?

He leaned forward to get a glimpse of Charity's face. Passive as always.

Why the hell was she giving him such a hard time when she'd let Samantha off so easily? He nearly asked, but a part of him feared the answer. For some reason, he didn't want this woman to stand in judgment of him.

Any more than she already had, that was.

But he couldn't let it go. "Why'd you move with her? Why didn't you stay in the dorms?"

Charity looked up at him with a furrowed brow. "Are you kidding? Why did I leave the *dorms*...for a house?" She laughed softly and opened her top dresser drawer. "Samantha's okay. When she isn't trying to live up to other people's expectations for snobbery, she's mostly down-to-earth. I pay the same rent for a lot more space. I'd be a freaking dummy not to tag along."

Devon had to agree. He'd hated the dorms.

He crossed the room and peeked through the curtain. "Your luck, you'd probably get another yup-yup anyway."

"Exactly. One without any redeeming qualities. Like you." Charity laughed, a carefree sound that bespoke of green fields and blooming flowers.

Devon shook his head, but he felt himself thawing. He wiped the pad of his finger across the desk and then rubbed it against his thumb. No dust. He shook the desk, and then stopped when it wobbled fiercely. She'd probably found it on the street. No frame held her full-sized bed, and besides a random marble and a few crystals, her one decorative item was a porcelain statue of a ballerina. The pink paint on the tutu was worn and faded. Cracks lined the legs and arms.

"Where'd you get the ballerina?" He touched it gently, feeling the cool surface, before glancing at the deserted hallway, just in case.

Charity shrugged. "It was my mom's when she was a kid. She left it to me."

Devon didn't miss the tightness around her eyes and the tension in her shoulders. She was trying to hide some sort of vulnerability, he'd bet his life on it. Her mother hadn't given it to her at all. That old statue was something her mother had left behind, much like Charity. Whereas Devon would've thrown the thing against the wall, followed by anything else within grabbing distance, Charity had clutched it to her heart in remembrance. She savored the memory of the woman who'd walked away.

Devon's fists clenched and he ground his teeth. He turned toward the door. "Hurry up. The sun's starting to set."

"Jesus, don't flip moods all that quickly, do you? Pretty even-keeled, then?"

Devon ignored her as she crossed to the closet, taking out three sweaters that looked old, faded, and moth-eaten. The way she delicately removed them, she might've been handling evening dresses. She folded them with care and tucked them into her duffel bag over the top of worn jeans and faded T-shirts. After that, the only thing left in the room was an ancient laptop.

It was then he realized what Andy had meant about being poor. Dirt poor. Those sweaters were her *nice* clothes. When she went out somewhere respectable, she wore faded jeans and one of those tatty sweaters.

Devon ran his hand through his hair, blindsided by sympathy.

She'd been left by her mother, then her first love, and still she trudged on. With nothing but her intelligence and determination.

It was commendable, which was probably why Roger had given her that weird smile.

Devon blew out an aggressive sigh and nearly punched the wall. He didn't like when crap like this pushed past his barricades. It messed with his focus, which might get him thrown out of Roger's pack. Why the hell had he been saddled with this detail? He was a greenie sub-alpha in a pack of college kids. He didn't know the first thing about protecting someone, and he wasn't great at keeping women happy, either. This sort of thing wasn't in his wheelhouse, and even if it had been, someone as important as Charity apparently was needed a heavy hitter. Someone who had been in the trenches for a while. Someone who could throw down if Vlad came calling.

"You have a whole language made up of scoffs and grunts," Charity said as she checked under her bed. "I can't decide if it's good or bad that I don't speak it."

"How much longer?" he asked.

The only thing left in sight was a picture in a cheap, fake silver frame. A haggard and worn woman looked out from a round, sun-damaged face. Her thin eyebrows hung low over her dark brown eyes. Pronounced crow's-feet etched her skin and stress lines marred her forehead. For all that, her smile was large and radiant, with a sparkle in her eyes for the picture taker.

"I took that a year before she left," Charity said, noticing his gaze. She sighed. "We snuck into the county fair and spent the day looking and watching."

"Looking and watching?"

"Yeah. At cows, pigs, crafts, people, kids—we went from place to place within the fair and looked at everything. I found a few tickets and rode a ride. It twirled me, spun me, flipped me upside down—oh man, it was *awesome!*"

Charity's eyes sparkled in pleasure, and her smile lit up her face, radiating a beauty that pumped up from somewhere hidden. All too soon, her bearing tensed and she sobered, her gaze finding the picture again. Pain flashed across her dainty features before she turned back to her duffel.

"My dad got worse after that," she went on in a soft voice. She carefully picked up the frame. "More violent. She had never smiled much, and after that day, I don't remember her smiling at all. But that one day, we both laughed like children. It was the best day I can remember."

Charity hurriedly swiped a tear off her face. "She was forty-five in that picture."

Devon tore his eyes away from Charity's face in surprise. The woman looked at least ten years older. Life had unabashedly ripped away her vitality. It was too bad.

"Anyway." The picture was placed on top of the clothes. The duffel had room to spare. "I'm ready."

"You won't be back here for a while; it's too dangerous. Take everything."

"I got it," Charity said, glancing down at her bag.

"What about shoes?" She'd only grabbed one holey pair. He looked in her completely bare closet.

Charity's face closed down, a hint of embarrassment showing in a flush. She squared her body to him, and her magic slammed into his, almost knocking the breath out of him.

Ah. Right. She didn't have anything else. He let it go.

He jerked his head toward her dinosaur laptop. "You gonna leave that?"

She scowled. "I was going to grab it on the way out."

"All right, then let's go." Devon scooped up her laptop, let her grab the ballerina, and motioned her out of the room.

"Yes, I know it's old," Charity said with a stiff back as she led the way, "but it works."

Devon didn't look down at the computer. "At least you have one."

He barely heard her sigh. "Exactly."

As they passed the kitchen, Charity dipped in toward the cabinets.

"What are you doing?" he asked, peering out the windows.

When he glanced back, she was ripping food out of

one of the cupboards, piling it into a brown paper bag.

"Are you kidding me? The vamps will be waking up shortly, and the newbies will be starving. They need a crapload of blood in the first few weeks. Sam might be coming back here. This is not the time for a snack."

He jogged toward her and reached for her arm. She ducked out of the way and grabbed out some more cans.

"I just want to grab a couple things."

"Charity, I have food at the house. Let's *go!*"

She grabbed a box of what looked like granola bars and dashed to the fridge.

"You aren't serious. You aren't." He was losing patience. "Come *on!*"

"Yup." She dropped the last few items into the paper bag, then zipped down the hall and out of the house, emerging into the new night. Alone.

Swallowing back a curse, he launched after her. She was already at the car door by the time he exited the house, too fast for her own good. Shaking his head, blood rushing in his ears, he did a quick glance around before he clicked the fob, unlocking only the driver's-side door. Ducking into the car, he checked it with his nose. Only the regular smells. No trespassers. No vamps.

"Are you dumb, or something?" he yelled across the hood, completely out of control.

She didn't react to his temper like his pack did—she simply frowned. "Why?"

He opened his mouth then closed it. He was completely at a loss for words.

Movements jerky with anger, he unlocked her door. Once she was safely in the car, he climbed into the driver's seat, waited for her attention, and then made a show of looking in the back seat.

"Did you see what I did there?" he asked as he pushed the ignition button. "I *checked the back*."

"I saw that, yes. And you are implying I didn't and should have?"

"Wow, you are astute, Miss Taylor. I can see how you've made it so far."

"Did you think that maybe you could've just told me that, instead of being a dick about it?"

"I shouldn't have to teach you logic."

"I have a different frame of logic than you do, obviously, since the car was locked until you stepped out of the house with your clicker thingy."

Devon gripped the steering wheel so he didn't grip her neck. Her magic poked and prodded him, and her smell threatened to melt him through, making this confrontation a hundred times worse.

Willing himself to be calm, he said, "Okay, fine. Look, you need to let me lead you out of places. You need to always assume things have been left *unlocked*, because many creatures with magic aren't impeded by human electronics. Or deadbolts. Magic is the only key they need. You have to defer to me—"

She huffed.

"—until you know what you are doing. Okay?"

She barely nodded, but she did. Devon took a large breath and shook his head.

He might quit his job after all.

CHAPTER 16

AFTER ABOUT FIFTEEN minutes of driving across town, the shiny Range Rover turned off the highway toward a small shopping center with neon signs and twinkling lights. Charity came out of the stupor induced by Devon's cushy leather seats in time to see him pull into a deserted fast food drive-thru.

"What do ya want?" he asked, eyeing the options.

The bright glow of the menu chased the darkness away. She traced the edge of her fingernail as she remembered the balance of her checking account. It was under twelve dollars, which would need to last her the whole week.

"I'm okay. I brought food." Her stomach growled, punctuating her words.

Devon hung his head. Lines of fatigue had worked around his speckled eyes, making his thick black lashes droop. He leaned back against the seat. "Look," he said. He ran his hand across his face. "I know you're starving. Neither of us want to go home and make something. I also know you're holding out because you don't have the money. It's five dollars, Charity. I'm good for it. You need to learn to pick your battles."

"Number three, please. With a Coke."

"*Thank* you."

When they got their food, Charity reached for a fry.

"No, not yet." Devon scrunched the top of the bag so the heat would stay in.

"What do you mean?" she asked as he turned off the street and onto a dirt road.

"Can't eat until you get there. It'll let all the heat out."

Her mouth dropped open as she watched him expertly handle the vehicle around a sharp turn and a jutting tree. The soft green lights from the dash carved out the structure of his face. His deep-set eyes and high cheekbones almost made him look regal, but that strong jaw and slight cleft in his chin bent him toward core-tighteningly masculine. She could understand why Samantha wanted him over Donnie. He wasn't just a guy with a handsome face or a nice body; he had a certain *raw* quality about him. He was bare and ruthless and unkempt. He might've styled himself *just so*, but that was a façade. Underneath, he was wild. Uncontrollable and untamable. Savage, even.

Charity took a deep breath. He'd be miserable to house-train. Thankfully, all she had to do was somewhat get along with him until she could figure out the next steps.

"Me hungry," she said. "I just want one fry."

"No. The rule is, you have to wait until you get

home."

She stared at him. "Didn't you just say we had to pick our battles?"

"Yes. And this is my chosen battle. You can't open it until you get there."

"It's not a present!"

"It will be when you get there. Fries are delicious." A childlike grin lit up his face.

Charity snorted as they pulled into a driveway lined on one side with a beautiful lawn and flower garden. Yawning trees surrounded the property, offering beauty and privacy. A light clicked on as they neared the garage, bathing the driveway. The residence sprawled out, beckoning them in like wayward travelers.

"Are you the only one that lives here?" Charity asked, fries forgotten.

"Yes. I bought it a couple years ago."

Devon balanced the computer, the food, and her duffel bag, leaving her to bring in her bag of pillaged food and the drinks. As she climbed out of the SUV, her gaze slid to the murky darkness that pooled between the bases of the trees pressing in on the house, turning into an oily black deeper into the foliage. Anything could be hiding in there, ready to surge out at them. But that wasn't why her heart was suddenly rampaging through her chest. She was terrified that the creature who stepped out of the darkness would wear Sam's or Donnie's face.

"You coming?" Devon asked, heading toward the

front door.

Hustling toward the house, she was still looking at the tree line when she bumped into Devon. Normally she would apologize and step back, but the solidity of his body, and the feeling of safety it imparted, shocked into her. She pushed into him, her stuff held out to the sides so her whole front was plastered against his back. She buried her face in the groove between his back muscles like an ostrich at the beach.

"This place is warded. Unless we're sieged, no one is getting through," Devon said tiredly.

"What do you mean, warded? Like with magic?" she mumbled into his shirt.

"Yes. I hired one of the best mages I could find to place protective spells around the property. You'll be safe here. As safe as anywhere, at least."

He waited for a second after opening the door. She waited with him, tempted to fall asleep against his warm, manly-smelling T-shirt. It had been a long day.

"Charity?"

"Devon?"

"What… Can… Seriously?"

She tilted back on her heels, eyes half-open. A quick gaze to the tree line, and…

They were still standing there. Why were they still standing there?

"Go." Charity nudged him with her chin.

He stepped to the side and scowled down at her. "Ladies first! Hurry up. I'm starving."

"Only you are still a jerk when you're being a gentleman." She grinned before trudging into the house.

"At least I *am* being a gentleman. I bet your precious Donnie didn't hold doors for you."

She was about to grudgingly accede when reality slapped her. Donnie was no longer the boy she'd known. He was almost certainly a vampire.

"Sorry," Devon murmured, closing the door behind him. "I wasn't thinking."

Struggling for a cleansing breath, trying not to let fear erode her courage, she glanced around. They'd entered a living room of sorts, with a huge media center off to the side. The furnishings and decorative art were classy but not showy. Everything had been bought for use rather than grandstanding. Down the hallway and to the left was another living area, but without the electronics. Two couches faced each other in front of a fireplace—a sitting room?

The next stop was the kitchen, decked out with high-dollar appliances that looked new and shiny. Also unused.

"How long have you lived here?" Charity asked, putting her stuff to the side and setting the drinks on the small, circular table in the corner, removed somewhat from the island. A formal dining room peeked out through a doorway off the kitchen.

"A little over two years. I got a bonus when I made alpha. I'm the youngest alpha since Roger." Pride rang in his voice as he tore into the bag of greasy delight, somehow not immediately shoving a fry into his face. His control was unreal.

"Everything here looks really new," Charity said, watching in fascination as Devon took out each component of his meal and set it in front of him, just so. He opened his hamburger, but didn't immediately chomp down. Instead, he spread the paper, put his fries—still untested—in the corner diagonally, and his Coke directly in front of him. Only then he did he start to eat.

He also noticed her staring.

"What?" he asked through a full mouth.

"Precise, aren't we?"

He took another bite.

She reached into the bag and extracted three fries from her carton. A body needed a little treat before she unwrapped the burger. As soon as she first saw bun, she went for it.

"Jesus. Savage." He stared at her over his burger.

"You do things your way, and I do them my way. Just because you happen to think this is English tea time…"

He snorted, taking another bite. "I never got fast food as a kid. Or dinners out. My mom always cooked. Not very well, either. My dad was actually a reasonable cook, but he maintained that it was a woman's job. My mom accepted that."

"Only the unpaid cooking seems to be a woman's job to some guys. They don't want to do it themselves, so they push it on their wife and say it's *women's* work,"

Charity said, rolling her eyes. "Given that the top chefs of the world are largely men, they are mistaken. But then, if you can get a good wage for something, men generally assume control." She paused. "No offense to your dad."

"None taken. He was a good example of what not to grow up to be."

"I had one of those, too. And I didn't get fast food, either. We didn't have the money to spend on a meal that runs right through you."

Devon grimaced, the expression melting into a smile. "Gross."

Charity laughed. "I cooked, mostly. Walt didn't eat much, and my mom worked a lot. If you wanna eat, you gotta cook."

"I should've learned, but now I just…hate it. I suck at it."

Charity took a bite. "Marry a pretty girl that loves to wait on her man and you're all set."

Devon snorted but didn't comment.

Lost to their own thoughts, they finished the rest of their meal in silence. After they finished, Devon led Charity down a long hall.

"Yours is here." He motioned to the last door on the left. He dropped her duffel outside the door, already defining the space as hers, with the privacy to go along with it. It was reassuring. "I'm right across the hall in case…whatever. Boogeymen, I don't know. I'll show you the laundry room and whatnot tomorrow."

"Great." She picked up her duffel and walked into the room.

He watched her check it out. "Sheets are fresh. Well, they haven't been slept in, anyway. Bathroom is clean."

A sliding glass door led out to a patio draped in the black night. She peered into the enormous closet, which would probably fit a desk, and then noticed the door at the back of the room. "No way." She pushed through it, and found herself in a bathroom bigger than her room back in Sam's house. "I have my own bathroom?"

Devon grinned, sharing her delight. "I assume that's okay?"

Beaming like a fool, she bobbed her head. "Sorry, but this is a first. Not having to get dressed to pee in the middle of the night will be a rare treat."

His gaze drifted over her body. A spark of male hunger flashed in his eyes and was gone again so fast that she almost thought she'd imagined it. The next second, he wore his familiar scowl. "All right, get some sleep. Tomorrow night we'll meet with the pack and hash out a plan." He hesitated in the doorway, as if belatedly remembering that she wasn't in his pack. "Are you going to work tomorrow? At the college?"

She bit her lip. "I haven't decided. I don't know that I want to get involved in all the stuff you have going on."

His gaze bored into her. "Roger seems to think we need you. For that reason, I hope you'll think about it. If you're on the fence, I'm sure he'll approve a trial period."

"You don't think you need me?"

"So far you've done nothing but cause havoc and get in the way. Call me jaded, but I doubt that'll change."

"Oh yay. Devon the Dick is back. And here I thought I was seeing a whole new you…"

He smirked, something he seemed to immediately regret based on how quickly he wrestled it off his lips. "Get some sleep. See you tomorrow. If you need me, I'm right across the hall."

He closed her door with a soft click. His rotating moods were worse than PMS.

Charity chucked off her borrowed flip-flops and stared at the bed. She wanted to dive in, headfirst, and then sink into oblivion. But those groceries weren't going to put themselves away, and she didn't have the money to replace the perishable items.

Devon's door was already closed. Absolute silence greeted her in the hallway. Stagnant silence, like when it was so quiet that a person's ears made their own white noise.

Stepping lightly, trying not to disturb the deadened sound, she tiptoed down the hall. The darkness pressed on her. Dim moonlight filtered in through the windows, speckling the ground through the leaves outside. Shadows clawed toward her feet. Pools of night lurked in the corners and under furniture. Make-believe eyes watched as she passed.

Knowing this was all her imagination but unable to

chase away the flashes of memory from the nightmare house, she hurried into the vast kitchen. She grabbed her paper bag of food, wincing at what seemed like a veritable shotgun blast of noise.

Ward or not, Charity couldn't help but wonder— did the vampires know where she was? If Roger was right, she'd destroyed their plans. Were they out to get her?

She glanced up at the kitchen window, at the dark, gnarled branches dancing in the wind, laughing at her. The shades had all been left wide open. They, whoever *they* were, could watch her through the bare windows. Breath coming fast, she shoved the stuff that needed to be kept cool into a mostly empty fridge, tossed everything else on the counter, and hurried back down the hall.

She stepped into her room and closed the door. After lowering the shades on those windows, she stared at the large sliding glass door.

Who didn't put curtains on a sliding glass door?

If they came in through that door, Devon would never reach her in time. Sure, she had her own defenses, but her strange magic might fail—she didn't even know how to use it.

Trying to catch her breath and think rationally, she saw movement. A streak across the window. Claws scrabbling on the wood porch.

Sucking in a gasp, she practically dove out of her room and into the hall. That same watchful silence

165

greeted her, the dappled shadows down the hall threatening to suck her in. Bare windows watching her progress.

Memories from the night before flashed through her mind like a strobe light.

Panic rising, she reached for Devon's door like a child going to her parents' room in a thunderstorm. The handle turned, thankfully not locked. She stepped in and shut the door behind her. Then locked it.

Magical creatures could open locks.

She fast-stepped toward the mound of man on one side of the king-sized bed. He was already sleeping soundly.

How can he sleep after what happened last night?

She hesitated. Now what?

But she knew what. As awkward as it was, she needed reassurance. She needed some sort of human comfort. Maybe a few words from him would do the trick. Hopefully, because she didn't know what else to do.

When she lowered her hand onto his bare shoulder, he burst up. A blade came out of nowhere, glinting in the moonlight before it kissed her neck. Both of her wrists were pushed above her head and secured with one of his large hands. He pressed against her, pinning her to the wall. His eyes, nothing but pools of shadow, stared into her.

"What are you doing in here, Charity?" he asked in a low growl.

She stood paralyzed, captured by his much larger body. Trapped by his strength and power. She started to quiver.

"I w-was af-fraid," she stammered, her wrists aching in his grip.

He leaned in close, so close they were breathing the same air. The heat from his body shocked into her, along with the manly perfume of his skin. A moment later, he stepped away, pulling back the blade. It was only then that she realized he wore not a stitch.

"Nightmare?" he asked nonchalantly. It was almost as if he a) wasn't standing nude in front of her, and b) hadn't just trapped her with a knife to her throat.

She didn't have long to think about it. Flashes of sickly green skin, fangs, and claws flickered through her mind. She glanced at his door. In her mind, it all waited out there. In here, she had him. He knew what he was doing and could protect her.

"I... Sorry, I know this is weird, but..." She didn't know how to phrase what she needed to say without sounding completely lame.

Can I sleep at the foot of your bed like a dog because I'm afraid of being alone for the first time in my entire life?

His soft sigh rustled her lashes. As if reading her mind, he bent and scooped her up into his arms. The next moment she was flying, landing on the other side of his bed in a tangle of limbs and hair.

He slipped between the sheets with his back to her

and cuddled into his pillow. "Go to sleep. You're safe here. I sleep soundly, so snore all you want, but don't elbow me if I do. I hate that."

Another flashback of a monster reaching for her, claws outstretched, had her shimmying out of her borrowed sweats and hoodie and climbing into the bed beside him. She was only in a T-shirt and panties, but there was no way she was going back into her room without an armed escort. Not tonight, anyway.

Suddenly she wasn't so confident in what she'd told Roger. Maybe she couldn't move on from this so easily. Her life had changed in every possible way, and she was only now catching up.

CHAPTER 17

"**H**EY!"

Charity felt a hard nudge, shaking the bed. "Hey. Charity."

She cracked a groggy eye open.

Devon stood at the side of the bed—his bed—with his rumpled hair and the scruff on his face accentuating his rugged good looks. It was the exact style he'd worn out the other night, except this one lacked all the polish and product. A bright halo surrounded him from the sunlight streaming in the large windows behind him.

The tightness in her chest from the night before loosened, releasing the tension in her shoulders.

Sunlight. Glorious sunlight.

She sighed. In the safety of the day, she should probably feel a little awkward about how she broke down last night and practically begged to sleep in Devon's bed, like a child. As a rule, she didn't open herself up to people, not even to John. When people knew your weaknesses, they could exploit you. Could wring you out and torment you. She'd seen it firsthand with how Walt had treated her mom. Charity had enough going on in her life without falling into that particular vat of slime.

But at the moment, she was too tired to care.

"What?" she mumbled, fatigue dragging her eyelids back down.

"It's ten o'clock. Are you going to work?"

"Hmmmmmmrrrrrrr."

"I'm the wolf, not you. You sound stupid when you growl."

"I don't feel good."

"Then call in sick. Are you always this helpless?"

She sat up in a grumpy rush, her hair swirling around her head like she'd been caught in a windstorm. "I barely slept last night."

"I know. You're incredibly loud when you toss and turn. Are you going to work or what? I'd like to go back to sleep."

"Then go. I'll find my way there. Why'd you get up if you're just going to go back to bed?"

"Coffee. I planned on staying up, but I'm still exhausted. Quit asking questions and figure yourself out."

She slapped the soft, luxurious down comforter. "Go away." She thumped her head back into the pillow. Awkwardness could definitely wait.

His dark chuckling trailed him out of the room. "If you're going, hurry up. There're no buses this far. I have to drive you."

Charity lay still for a moment. She did really hate that admin job. She'd lied to Roger when she said they let her do her schoolwork. She was kept busy enough to be marginally useful and bored at the same time. It also paid minimum wage in a place where the cost of living was high, which was the pits.

She rolled out of bed and stood with all the energy of a zombie that had been blasted in the chest with a shotgun. Wait…were there zombies?

Trudging out, she heard the TV blaring in the front room.

Devon sat on the leather couch with his feet propped on the coffee table next to a steaming cup of coffee. He flicked his phone with his right thumb while pointing the remote at the TV with his left hand.

"Multitasking, huh?" she asked, flopping down in a recliner at the far end of the room.

He didn't answer.

"So…how often do you work?" Charity asked.

"Until the job's done."

"But you have time for school?"

"Yes. So does Andy, who isn't nearly as smart as you." He dropped his phone, changed a channel randomly, and focused on her. His eyes were intense and businesslike. "Roger makes sure we balance school and our duty. It's in the pack's best interest for us to graduate. It'll provide the organization as a whole with great skills and connections within the Brink. Sometimes it can be…stressful, but it's still doable."

"What's the pay scale like?"

"It depends on rank and involvement. Since

you're…an exceptional case, I'm not sure. What're you making now?"

"Minimum wage, fifteen hours a week."

Devon's jaw dropped at the same time as the remote. "And you wonder why you don't have any money. Why didn't you get a real job?"

Charity could feel her body stiffening defensively. "I don't have any prior experience. Or interview clothes."

"Hell, a fast food chain would've paid better. Anyway, you'll make a lot more than that, I can assure you. With insurance."

"Which I'll probably need."

Devon leveled his gaze on her. "I would like to say you won't, and that I will make sure you're safe, but in our life, there are no guarantees."

Charity waved him away. She'd never had any guarantees.

She chewed her lip—she did really hate that admin job. And being poor. She *hated* being broke all the time.

What was a little danger, really? She'd be with a pack of wolves, not alone like last time. She'd have experienced people to help her. Besides, if those creatures were still looking for her, she'd be sucked back into this mess anyway. She might as well get paid for it. And with a trial period, like Devon said, she could get out of it if she wanted to.

Why is this decision so easy to make? That can't bode well. Nothing in my life comes easily.

"Do you have a house phone?" she asked, not wanting to think any more on the subject. She'd just talk herself out of it.

Confusion crossed his face. "Why would I need a house phone?"

"To make calls, genius."

He held up his cell phone. "That's what this is for, *genius.*"

"Fine. Can I use it?"

His stupid jaw dropped again. "You don't have a cell phone?"

"You know, this is why hanging out with rich people is actually kind of nice. They think everyone who isn't a millionaire is poor. So when they treat me with astonished pity because I don't have an electronic gadget, it's a standard affair. But no, I don't have a cell phone, because I hilariously decided eating and dressing myself was more appropriate. My bad."

"Jesus, how do you stay upright with that giant chip on your shoulder?"

Charity thrust out her hand. "Can I use your damn phone?"

"Ever heard of pay as you go?" He tossed his phone at her.

"Ever heard of shut up?"

"You owe me dinner, too, remember." He aggressively raised the remote at the TV, smirking. "I assume that means you're calling in sick? Or quitting?"

She turned away from him and stared at the picturesque screen of the phone. Tiny squares dotted the image of a cresting wave. While she'd seen an ad or two for these phones, and spied kids in her classes going to town on them, she'd never actually used one. It wasn't as intuitive as she'd heard others claim.

Devon pushed off the couch and headed toward the kitchen. As he passed, he veered in close and tapped a square with a white telephone on a green background.

Oh yeah. Good clue as to which button she was supposed to tap.

"I would say don't quit your day job, but I don't think that would help," Devon said smugly as he moved out of the room.

"Oh, shut it," she muttered.

When she called in sick for the day, she also gave her two weeks, and was told that they didn't really need her to come in anymore. Apparently, the job was only in existence to help kids in need.

She didn't like the feeling that gave her, though she couldn't exactly say why.

She headed back to her room and bed, stopping in the kitchen to return Devon's phone. When she didn't find him, she glanced in the other rooms, coming up empty until she returned to his bedroom. He lay in the middle of a sea of rumpled, pure white covers. His discarded boxers had been thrown onto the floor.

"You always sleep naked, huh? Or is this about to be a rejected invitation?" Charity asked with a grin. The room smelled of musty boy. Not unpleasant, but he could stand to open a window. To that end, she did it for him, letting in a soft but sweet-smelling breeze.

"Ah yes, Andy hinted that you found power in playing impossible-to-get. The guy asked you out, and you didn't even remember him. Don't worry, I like my women pleasant. You don't fit the bill, *Chastity*."

Crap! *That* was why Andy was so familiar. Even with the reminder, though, she only vaguely remembered the dinner invitation. Sam had scoffed at the whole scene and pulled her away quickly. Andy had seemed tickled, she remembered, and hadn't pressed. He'd never approached again, nor had he shot her scowls like other guys she'd rebuffed (she had nothing to wear on a date and didn't need the distraction anyway—something men didn't seem to understand or accept).

She placed his phone on the nightstand, and then lingered. "Listen…" She cleared her throat. "Thanks for last night, by the way. I was… I just…"

"Stop talking. I'm trying to sleep."

She huffed her annoyance, though she didn't really feel it. Biting her lip, she nodded into the silence. He wasn't going to let her admit out loud that she'd been afraid. It was appreciated.

"Meeting is at eight o'clock tonight," Devon mumbled with his eyes closed. "Wear something nice. Oh, that's right, you don't have anything."

She picked up one of his shoes and threw it at his head. She shut the door as he yelled, "Ow!"

Sometimes, violence was extremely gratifying.

CHAPTER 18

"**Y**OU'RE UP," DEVON said as he strolled into the kitchen.

Charity looked up from her red wine reduction sauce.

He sauntered over, rolling up the sleeves on a snug white button-up that hugged his well-defined chest and popping biceps. The bottom was tucked into a pair of Euro-style trousers, hugging his trim waist and accenting his muscular thighs. He'd gelled his hair into that bad-boy, styled-yet-messy look, and the hint of side-burns set off his strong jaw. The way he carried himself bespoke money and prestige. His cultivated demeanor overlaid that raw physical power. Power that didn't flirt with the fire in her middle now as much as it had in that strange other world.

She said as much.

"The Realm is magical, and so it brings out your magic," he said, stopping next to her. "It heightens it. When you're fully into your magic, it'll probably still be easier to use in the Realm, but you'll feel it just as strongly in both places."

She nodded, although it would take a while to get used to talking of magic, she had no doubt.

"You hungry?" she asked, returning to her sauce.

He leaned on the counter, assessing her with a heavy stare. His eyes roved over her, taking in her stained hoodie before drifting down her unfashionably ripped jeans. Just like when he'd stared at her before the party, she felt completely exposed. Laid bare, like he had ripped away all her defenses and could see the girl underneath. The vulnerable, sometimes scared girl who needed a warm body to lie next to when things got out of hand.

Face heating in embarrassment—he'd spotted the holes in her sneakers—she concentrated on stirring the sauce and fervently hoped he'd go away.

"Where'd you get all this food?" he asked.

No such luck on him buggering off, then.

"Brought most of it," she said, "but found some of it in the cabinets. The wine is old, but I can compensate for that. I threw away half the stuff you had in your fridge. Not that there was much to begin with. It looked like a petri dish in there."

Still he stared. Was he hoping for a magic trick or something?

"Look, if I'd known you wanted a staring contest, I would've brushed my teeth," she groused.

"Looks like you're making a gourmet meal." His gaze roamed her ingredients. "How'd you learn to cook like this off food stamps?"

She gritted her teeth at his suspicious tone, feeling that fire she'd thought had dulled kindle in her middle. Apparently, it had been waiting for him to get on her nerves.

She tried to keep the aggression and defensiveness out of her voice. It was his house and she was a guest— she'd best remember that or she'd get kicked out on her butt.

"I had to get creative. When you have three ingredients, most of which have passed their expiration date, you need an imagination."

He leaned more heavily on the counter, now able to peer directly at her face. "I can tell when you evade questions because you're uncomfortable. What's the real reason?"

"Know me that well already, do you?"

"You're not that hard to read, Charity. Why?"

"Why is this a big deal?" She sighed like a teenager who'd been told to clean her room. "I imagined I was in a top restaurant in New York, okay? I'd retreat into my head, envisioning myself somewhere else, in someone else's life, and make a dish out of whatever was lying around. As I got older, it became my happy place. We were poor, yes, but if I could help it, I didn't eat that way. Happy now?"

He grunted, apparently satisfied. "Make some for me. I'm starving."

As he moved away, he adjusted his shirt and smoothed his pants, surely trying to perfect his already immaculate appearance.

"Oh hey"—she snapped her fingers—"I forgot to tell you. I put your runway out back. It was getting in the way. You'll have to practice your Zoolander poses out there."

He stopped smoothing his pants. A slight red hue colored his cheeks. "Cute," he said with a scowl. He strode toward the front room.

Smirking, she went back to her task. She couldn't beat 'em, or join 'em, but she could surely make fun of 'em!

A HALF-HOUR LATER, she feigned nonchalance as she placed his plate on the coffee table in front of him. The ingredients were simple, but she'd made sure the taste and presentation were elevated. Given all she'd done wrong since she'd met him, she wanted to impress him with one thing she could do right.

Without saying a word, she retreated to the recliner in the corner, desperately trying not to be obvious as she peeked at his face. She'd cooked for Samantha a time or two, and that had gone over well, but Devon was so exacting that she was afraid he'd pick out each flaw.

He lowered his phone to the side and studied the contents of the plate. "Where's the meat?"

So then, more of a broad strokes kind of guy when it came to food.

She huffed out a laugh and settled down with her

meal.

"I didn't have any. A portabella is similar, though. Kinda."

He scowled before sawing into the mushroom, his movements coarse and unrefined compared with her former roommate's. It meant, unlike Samantha, he hadn't spent his life in fine restaurants across the country.

A stress knot eased out of Charity's shoulders.

Devon popped the bite into his mouth as he surveyed the TV. His head jerked down to his plate. "Mmmm." He leaned back and closed his eyes. "Jesus, Chastity, this is *good*. I had no idea vegetables could taste this good. Weird."

Apparently that nickname would stick. Great.

Except she found she really didn't mind all that much. A smile wrestled with her lips as a thread of pride wormed through her.

A knock sounded at the door.

"Come in," Devon shouted, back to bending over his plate.

Andy sauntered into the room with wild, windswept hair, a T-shirt with little holes running along the seams on his shoulders, and the smell of the sea.

He plopped down on the couch opposite Devon, the closest seat to her. "Charity, my Charity, how goes it?"

"Hi, Andy. Hey, I didn't mention the other day, but I recognize you from—"

"Whatcha eatin'?" His head swiveled to Devon and

then back to her. "Did you cook?" He leaned closer. "Did you make any for me?"

"Oh. Sorry, I didn't realize I should've." She also didn't have enough money to feed other people.

As if hearing her thoughts, Devon said, "I haven't gone shopping yet. She whipped this up from what she brought over last night. Get something frozen or order pizza." His voice dropped an octave. "And give her a little room to eat."

"She's got room." Andy barely leaned away. "I'm sick of pizza and frozen food. It's all I ever eat anymore."

"Not my problem." Devon scraped his plate and then licked the prongs of his fork.

Definitely not the refinement of Samantha or her friends. It was refreshing.

Another knock. At Devon's call, in walked the guy named Rod, a giant with hulking shoulders and surprisingly graceful footsteps. His dark eyes flashed around the room, touching each person before settling on Charity's plate. "What's that?"

"Dude. She cooks. Looks good, too." Andy's gaze followed the fork up to Charity's mouth.

"Did you make any for me?" Rod asked, bending to get a better look.

"This is getting awkward," Charity mumbled.

Dillon and Macy filed in next, fingers entwined. Macy beamed at Charity. "Hi! You decided to join us, huh? I could use another girl."

Andy leaned toward Charity again. It didn't seem like he could help himself. "Bite?" He opened his mouth like a little baby bird.

"Back off, Andy," Devon growled.

"You'd think I had drugs or something." She handed her loaded fork to Andy, who bit it so eagerly that he almost dented the metal.

"Oh my God," Andy said, falling back against the back of the couch. "Charity!"

"Why? What?" Rod took a step closer. "Is it good? Is it that good?"

"It's *ah*-mazing. A-*may*-zing!" Andy's eyes rolled back in his head, and Charity let her smile blossom at his antics. She supplied Rod with a bite.

"Good God, woman." Rod shook his head at her. "You're a rock star. I mean, my dad is a pretty good cook, but he ain't got nothing on you."

"All your dad knows how to do is grill," Andy said. "She'd whoop his ass."

"I just said she was better, didn't I?" Rod replied angrily.

"You said she was better—you didn't say she'd stomp on him, slap his ass, and call him Susan."

"All right, all right, let her finish her food," Devon said, and a burst of power rolled through the air.

Like leaves stirring on the forest floor, Charity felt her magic respond to his. Heat pulsed in her middle, and she quickly finished off the rest of her plate so she could escape into the kitchen.

Macy grabbed Devon's plate. "I'll help."

"Since when do you clean up?" Rod asked skeptically.

"Since I want to get away from your ugly mug."

He snorted. "I feel sorry for Dillon, having to deal with you."

"You shouldn't. At least he gets laid."

Rod nodded and shrugged at the same time. Point to Macy.

"How goes it?" Macy asked Charity a moment later. The plate clinked against the countertop next to the sink. "Did it go okay with Roger? He was acting kinda strange…"

"Oh, good. So he normally isn't that intense?" Charity rinsed her plate and tucked it into the empty dishwasher.

"No, he isn't normally that calm. I heard he smiled."

Charity rinsed the other plate. "If that was nice Roger, I do not want to see mean Roger."

"Like I told Andy, it's best to steer clear. Let Devon be the middleman on that one. He's able. I am not."

Charity smirked. She filled a glass with water and drank it as the doorbell rang.

"That must be the new wolf," Macy said, waiting for Charity to finish. "Jimmy got reassigned. I heard what he did to you. That must've freaked you out."

Charity sniffed. "It sure wasn't what I was expecting, I'll say that much."

Macy took a few steps with her back to the front

room. "Well, don't worry about it. He got reassigned. This is a new girl. Thank God! Seriously. Being the only girl with a bunch of stinky, rude guys is the—"

The words died on her lips as she turned around.

In the living room, it was like someone had pushed the pause button. All the guys stood motionless, staring at the newcomer like a pirate would a treasure map. Macy's mouth dropped open slowly, fear washing over her features.

The newcomer had arrived. And holy crap, she was freaking gorgeous.

Charity had seen pretty girls in her day. Hell, she went to school with a bunch of them. But few of them had achieved this caliber of perfection. Long blonde hair streamed down the girl's back, curling at the ends. Light brown, shapely eyebrows arched glamorously, setting off smooth but defined cheekbones and pale blue eyes surrounded by long, thick black lashes. Her full, pouty lips smiled as she surveyed the men. She was clearly used to being the object of attention.

"Hello," she said in a sultry voice, matching her smile. "I'm Yasmine."

Devon rose from the couch slowly, his spine rigid, his eyes riveted. "I'm Devon, the alpha of this pack. Welcome."

Yasmine's eyes sparkled as she looked him over. A coy grin pulled at her lips and she slinked down into a pose that blasted *sex!*

Silence settled onto the room. No one moved.

What was everyone waiting for, the theme of *The Bachelorette* to start playing?

"Right," Charity said, "Shall I do the introductions? Otherwise, this is getting awkward."

Yasmine's lovely eyes turned Charity's way. A shapely hip jutted out. Another sexy pose ensued.

"I'm Charity." She touched her fingers to her chest. "I'm new here, too, although we still aren't sure what I'm good for. You've met Devon…"

Devon started, coming out of his trance. He probably should've worn boxer briefs, because he was creating an embarrassing moment for himself.

"Yes. Hello." His tough façade settled over him. Yasmine smiled appreciatively. "Let's take a seat in the sitting room, and we'll go over details."

All the male eyes followed Yasmine as she followed Devon out of the front room.

"Really?" Macy elbowed Dillon. "With the staring?"

Dillon started. His face flared red. Macy huffed and walked out of the room without him.

"You got a little wine reduction drool there, bro." Andy used his pointer to flick Rod's chin. "I don't think girls dig blank stares, by the way. You look like a caveman."

"Yeah, like you weren't looking," Rod said, shouldering in front of Andy.

"Already over it, bro. Girls like that take too much work. I prefer the mute ones."

"Yikes." Charity rolled her eyes. "Jokes like that are

why you're still single."

"Probably," Andy conceded with a grin.

After everyone was settled in the sitting room, where the furniture was decidedly less comfortable but arranged in a sort of circle, Devon leaned forward and braced his forearms on his knees. Thankfully, his lustful haze seemed to have dissipated a little.

"Okay," he said, and snatched a notepad off the table at the center of the group. "Ten recruit vampires were originally at the party. Three were taken down and one is on my love seat. That leaves six active newbie vamps." He glanced at Yasmine. "We need to start taking them out ASAP. There've already been two deaths, which have the police baffled, of course. It won't be long before the MLE office steps in. I would like to avoid that. This was my mission, and I want to complete it. Based on the information Dillon and Rod have collected, we already have one accessible target. We can take that one out after this meeting. I know of a home base for another, so we'll need to plan out how to approach that one."

Charity shifted as something heavy and ugly settled in her stomach. She knew whom he was talking about. They were plotting how to kill people Charity knew. She wasn't sure she was up for this.

"I need suggestions on finding the rest." Devon looked around with a quirked eyebrow.

"Isn't that Donnie guy in a couple of your classes?" Andy asked Charity.

She clasped her shaking hands. "Yes."

"Day or night classes?" Rod asked as he leaned forward.

"One class, two evenings a week." Charity yanked on her ponytail for movement of some kind.

"What time?" Dillon asked.

"Eight thirty to ten, Tuesday and Thursday."

"Tuesday and Thursday?" Devon wrote a note. "Who is free at that time?"

Rod and Macy raised their hands.

"I guess I am, too." Yasmine laughed, a surprisingly high-pitched sound.

"All right, Charity, you'll go to the Tuesday class like normal." Devon pointed at Macy with the end of his pen. "You'll hang around outside. Call if anything strange comes up. We obviously can't take it out in a public place, so we need to follow it. Find its home base."

"Why would it go to class?" Charity asked.

Devon finished writing something and then settled back. "When a person first changes, they're in chaos. A lot of their human traits still remain, but now they have these other needs and wants. The urge to bite necks and take blood can really shock a person. The creators usually shepherd the young vampires through this phase, but because of how this turning party ended"— Devon glanced at Charity—"these newbies will be in chaos. We are trying to get to them before any older vampires step in to guide them. If we get lucky, some of the newbies might fall back into their old routines to bring order to the chaos."

Charity sank deeper into her chair. She noticed Devon's look of sympathy. It helped a little.

"What's my task?" Yasmine said in a loud, clear voice.

Devon shifted his attention. "You'll shadow me. I have a class around the same time as one of the other newbies. You'll post up nearby to keep watch. I'll meet you afterward, and we'll tail that one. Rod, you'll head to…"

"My house," Charity said quietly. "Samantha was there after the party. She was hungry—famished, actually. She plans to track me down. She sees me as easy prey, and if what you say is true, she doesn't have to try to quell the hunger. No one'll miss me."

"We'll miss you," Andy said. She expected a grin or a sarcastic smile. Instead, his expression was serious, almost imploring.

She bit her lip and picked at her nail. It wasn't much, but it helped.

Devon stood abruptly. "How did you know that? Any of that?"

Charity started and blinked to clear away the sudden heat prickling her eyes. "I felt it," she blurted, remembering the strange, crawling feeling that had settled over her skin. She'd almost been able to pick out the path Sam had chosen through the house. In the moment, it hadn't occurred to her that that was strange.

"I could tell a vampire had been there. I also noticed that your body language went from savage to pitying as soon as you got outside my bedroom and had a big sniff. As for tracking me down…" Charity shrugged, dropping her hands to her lap. "That's just logic, right? I've got nobody."

"Had nobody," Devon said firmly.

"I'm sorry, what is it you do? I haven't smelled magic like yours before," Yasmine said in a light voice.

Macy gave Yasmine a look of death. Andy noticed, and his seriousness melted away, replaced by a huge grin. Charity had no idea why.

She shrugged again. "You can talk to Devon about that. I'm still not sure I wholly believe it."

"All right, well…we'll table that for now," Devon said, still staring at Charity. "We need to plan for tonight. We've got a novice and a new wolf. Anything could go wrong."

"And probably will," Charity mumbled. Something told her she'd made a huge mistake.

CHAPTER 19

THE TIRES ON Devon's Range Rover crunched to a stop at the corner of a long, wide driveway. Up ahead, light spilled from every window in the large house, illuminating the porch and rooftop. College kids lingered in clusters, holding beers or cups, jeering and laughing. Occasional screams of mirth pierced the night.

By the look of it, this party had been in full swing for a while, most of the attendees half lit and pushing harder for oblivion. The sweet smell of weed mixed with the sting of tobacco, masking other, more important, scents. Devon would take it; drunk and high was better than suspicious and nosey. These kids wouldn't care what happened in their midst, as long as their indiscretions didn't go public.

They'd taken three cars, and once they'd all parked, he gathered the crew near the trees in a loose circle. The distance they were from the house should ensure none of the partygoers could see them, but if someone drove up or left, at least the crew could quickly find cover. They each held a red plastic cup in case someone wandered past. The interior lights from the cars showered everyone's faces, all confident and ready, except one.

Charity stared off at the house with a fearful expression, picking at her sweater. If Devon wasn't mistaken, she regretted coming along. Her fear would hinder her decision-making, possibly getting her—and everyone else—into more danger.

He kept from blowing out a breath in annoyance. Roger usually had unassailable judgment, but in this, Devon couldn't help but wonder if the alpha had missed the mark.

The other new member of their team, Yasmine, stood poised and ready—eager, almost. Her eyes shone with the excitement of the hunt, her posture firm and fearless. She met his gaze, and he felt the mutual fire of arousal. His insides sparked and his groin tightened in anticipation, both for her and the hunt.

"All right," he said, taking a step closer to her. "This should be a simple extraction. For the new people, our plan of attack is usually to use someone as bait. He or she will lure the subject into a dark corner somewhere in the yard, and then we'll attack. Our subject was a straight male—vamps usually hang on to their human sexual orientation for a few decades, so we'll send in a woman. Yasmine, think you can handle it?"

Yasmine gave him a smile that singed his boxers. "Yes, alpha."

"Good. The rest of us will be in wolf form, waiting

in the shadows," Devon went on. "Lure him out to us, Yasmine. Keep up the act until you see us running."

"Easy," Yasmine answered with a smug smile. She wasn't a novice, he could see that. Better and better.

"What do I do?" Charity asked with a tremble in her voice.

"Hang out for now," he said as he met her velvet-brown eyes. "There's only one, and Yasmine should lure him out easily. I think we'll be good. You'll be safer out here. If something happens and you get in trouble, use the gun."

She sagged against the car, clearly relieved. "Cool."

Rod changed first, a flux of bone and blur of skin, a quick but painful process. A burst of magic flowered, bright green, until his body sank down into his wolf form. The rest of them followed suit, fur and teeth ripping out of human skin.

Smells and colors whirled around Devon as he completed the change, the thrill of the night singing in his blood. He gave a few excited huffs, calling to the others. Even Yasmine, in human form, smiled in elation, sensing the thrill of her new pack.

He gave a soft growl, taking a step toward his intended destination. Picking up on the subtle nuances of his body language and sounds, the rest of the pack filed in quickly, ready to follow. Yasmine started off toward the house, sultry and sensual, rocking her body erotically. Devon watched her for a moment, half wishing she was in wolf form so they could run and hunt together, but that had to wait for later. It was time for business.

A glance back at Charity had him hesitating for a moment. The light glow he'd noticed the other night when she'd run from the mansion had intensified to a soft golden halo. It fell off her in lazy waves, shimmering and moving as if it were alive. Its radiance matched the pulse of power he could feel pumping in her middle.

Too bad that power couldn't translate to something useful in this hunt.

He gave a low, deep growl, yanking the others' attention away from the nervous girl and back to him. Ready for battle.

"All right, then. Good luck. Or whatever," Charity said with tremors in her voice.

Devon took off at a lope. Charity would be fine out here, tucked away from the action. If any humans meandered her way, she could take care of them herself. It was just vampires she had to worry about, and the pack would handle the newbie without a problem.

CHAPTER 20

AN HOUR LATER, Charity had nearly picked her nail down to the nub waiting for the others. Nothing at all had happened. No cars had come or left. No one had stumbled down the driveway, lost and needing to pee. Still, Charity couldn't shake the feeling that danger was coming, drifting ever closer, like a black cloud on a sunny day.

She glanced at the discarded clothes that she'd folded and stacked in neat piles on the hood of Devon's SUV. Atop each was a weapon—a bunch of knives and one nine-millimeter.

Heat pulsed through her chest suddenly, surging up like a fountain of lava. She gasped, sucking in the sweet night air. Electricity filled her limbs and tingled her fingertips.

Movement caught her eye. Halfway up the long driveway, leaves fluttered in a sudden breeze. They calmed for a moment, and then came the distinct sound of a footstep crunching down on them.

Charity held her breath as a man stepped into sight. Someone who was drunk or high, she told herself—not a threat. Still, if it came down to it, she had weapons. The guy took one step, then another, walking with an effortless grace that screamed sobriety. In the middle of the driveway, he stopped, facing the house. An inhuman stillness settled over him.

Shivers settled over Charity.

Breath barely getting past the huge lump in her throat, she stared at the man as he watched the screeching and jeering drunks littering the front of the house. She had no idea what he was pondering, but she knew what she was—

Please go toward the house. Please go toward the house. Please go toward the house!

He turned slowly, as though he wasn't sure why he was moving at all. He stopped halfway around, facing the trees. His head kept turning until...he stared directly at her.

She didn't fool herself into thinking this was some wayward traveler. Or a partier strangely in tune with his surroundings. She didn't fool herself at all, just accepted the situation for what it was.

One of those creatures from the other night was standing in the middle of the driveway, and Devon and the other shifters weren't hot on its trail.

A thrill shot through her body. Her limbs started to tingle and her fingers itched to grab the gun. She had excellent aim and hours of practice, but it was dark and he was way too far away. Besides, she'd seen how fast those things could move. He would see her reach for the weapon and immediately go on the defensive.

Shit.

She stayed frozen. So did he.

What the hell was he waiting for? Was he like a T-Rex; he could only see movement? Because if so, things were looking good for her—except for the sweat tracking down her forehead.

The breeze stirred her hair and somewhat cooled her cheeks. Her stomach flip-flopped as she realized what direction the breeze was coming from.

She was upwind, and she bet those things smelled really well.

Double shit!

The rest of the guy's body swung around.

Charity started to pant with fear. Her instincts went haywire, insisting she do several things at once: run, fight, shoot, scream. She didn't know which command to follow. So she stayed frozen, watching it, hoping Devon—or anyone!—would burst through the trees and save her.

He took a step toward her. And then another. He'd chosen his direction.

Shiiiit!

"Hello," he called from ten yards away in a distinctly familiar, musical voice.

No way. It couldn't be.

"I thought I recognized the smell. And look, so beautiful. Yes, I remember you perfectly. *Exquisite.*"

This wasn't happening.

As he got closer, the moonlight draped over his flawless, perfect face. It was the most handsome man she'd ever seen in her life, for the second time in her life. She couldn't make out his deep, dark eyes from this distance, but she could feel them, entrancing her. Unfurling unspeakable desires.

Her skin crawled as if fire ants were breeding on her body. His perfect smile flashed those even white teeth she remembered from the party. She had no idea how she could see them through the darkness, but the impression registered perfectly, almost a feeling more than a visual.

But underneath that incredibly handsome exterior was an unbelievably dangerous, not to mention ugly, fanged monster.

"What happened to you the other night? I had so looked forward to making your acquaintance," he said as he moved toward her like a poltergeist.

"How do you do that sashaying thing? Are you hovering?" she asked, her voice firm despite her terror. She needed a plan. Any plan.

She really wanted to run.

"Oh no, my exquisite lady. I am graceful, like a dancer. I am gentle, too, like a lover should be. Let me show you."

"No, I'm good."

He stopped five yards from her, softening his predatory gaze (a gaze she could still feel more than see). "You are frightened. You know what I am. So rare, for a human to meet the eyes of one my age and not succumb. I am intrigued. And delighted. But please, let us chat amicably." He gave her a small smile and clasped his hands in front of his body, the model of patience.

Silence stretched between them. Apparently, she was supposed to start their amicable chat…

"What are you doing here?" she asked.

"I have a child here. He is learning control, under my guidance. I have great plans for him. I am paying a visit to check on his progress."

"Uh-huh. Well, don't let me keep you."

"But how can I pass up such a treat as you? Impossible." He scoffed lightly. "You must realize that I do not wish to harm you. On the contrary, I'm glad you did not change. The smell of you is…divine. Too delicious to go to waste. You remind me of something…" His musical voice turned wispy. "I cannot place it, but I have the impression of a pleasant memory. A savory memory." Stews were savory. Not good. His attention returned to her. "My lovely, I can give you everything you could possibly desire—riches, power, cars, servants." He put out his manicured hand. "Come to me."

So strong was the allure of his eyes that it nearly took her breath away.

She barely shook her head, shattering the vertigo that had swept over her.

"Knowledge," she said. "All I want is knowledge, and to make my own way. And look, I'm already doing that. So…yay me!"

"You have strength in you. Power. I feel it. Rich but delicate, like a handblown glass vase. It's unique. Exquisite in every way. I must have you." He took a step forward. "I can give you knowledge; I have much of it. Or I can pay for your schooling—it is expensive for you, is it not? You do not look wealthy. Do you wish to travel? I can have the best tutors in the world attend you and a private jet take you anywhere you wish to go. Whatever you can possibly need, I can provide. Lovers? Doting men? Easily done. I will share you; I am not possessive."

"You are, quite possibly, the most out-of-touch guy I've ever spoken to. This come-on is an epic fail."

He took another step closer, which seemed more like five, given how close it brought him. "I will have you for my own. Resistance is futile."

"Now you're showing your true colors. Well, I'm not the kind of girl to roll over and play dead because some rich, handsome jackass has a dominance complex."

A smile spread across his perfect face. Her gut told her this was his version of coiling. An attack would come soon.

Charity gritted her teeth—although fear still boiled in her gut, it had been overridden by the need to survive. She reached for the weapons.

"A lovers' spat. How engaging. I will win."

He moved so fast that she lost sight of him. One moment he was standing a few yards away, and the next his delicate fingers had turned into bands wrapped around her upper arm, preparing to drag her away.

Fear rolled. Power surged. She snatched a knife, the closer weapon, turned, and stabbed all in one fluid movement. The blade plunged deep into his chest.

She missed his heart by three inches.

He sucked in a breath that sounded like a backward hiss and plucked the knife from his chest. With a flick, he threw it away. Mist hazed the air, and for one moment, his face of inhuman perfection turned to that of a monstrous beast.

She twisted and gouged. Her fist hit his throat. He barely moved.

Beneath his feral smile, his irises began expanding to fill his eyes. He bent to her, reaching for her body.

Her flash of dread turned into a gush of electricity.

She slapped her hand to his chest and let the inner power pour out. A *zap* turned into a *sizzle.* The air concussed. His body sailed up and back in an arc, his limbs weirdly still for a guy catapulting through the air. At the last second, he flipped and twisted...and landed perfectly on his feet, crouched and ready.

"Holy crap," Charity breathed, blinking stupidly.

That perfect smile burned brighter as he straightened.

"What a rare treat," he said, and slowly ran his hand down his chest. "I have underestimated you. You are not what you seem, yet..." He cocked head. "Why are you familiar to me? So sweet. So soft. So brutal. I am in rapture. What are you? You are certainly not human…"

Charity dove for the gun, clutching it and pointing it at her target in a stance born of years of practice. He was moving again, straight at her. His human skin melted away like hot wax, revealing that disgusting thing beneath with huge white fangs and black lips.

Charity sighted, and *breathed*.

The gun jerked in her hand. The creature jerked as the bullet slammed into the center of its chest, an inch or two off target.

It kept coming.

She opened fire, squeezing over and over, aiming, re-aiming, keeping focus. He reached her a moment later, lifted her up, and tossed her across the SUV. She knew a second of weightlessness, the gun clutched tightly, before she was falling again. Her shoulder slammed off the hood and she toppled over the side, landing in a heap.

He was on her a second later, scooping her up like a child.

"I will have you as mine," the creature hissed in her ear. The sound was like a hundred snakes slithering across a dirty wooden floor.

She twisted her body and shoved the gun against its heart. There was no way this bullet would miss.

Click.

The magazine was empty.

CHAPTER 21

"**N**O FUCKING WAY!" she screamed.

Her head hit off the SUV again as the vampire snatched her up. Electricity welled within her. Dizzied but frantic, she *pushed*, and power surged out through her arms and into the creature's body. The creature started to scream, a sizzling sound as her electricity ate away at its exposed, swampy skin.

She shoved back and opened herself up to the current, letting it run through her. The sky lit up overhead, the darkness cracking open, and light beat down on the writhing, squealing vampire. Steam, then smoke, billowed up from the being's nasty skin as its mouth gaped open unnaturally wide.

She put more energy into it, hoping for more juice. The light flickered brighter. The buzzing of the faux-sun competed with the sizzle of flesh.

The vampire stumbled, its arms raised in defense, its skin turning red and black. Through a squint, it met her eyes for a moment before zipping past the tree line, almost too fast to follow.

The light blinked off as she fell to her knees, so

drained that she could barely lift her head. It felt like she'd run ten miles in cement shoes. Distantly she heard sirens. She didn't have much time to get out of there.

Struggling to climb up the side of the car, she heard panting. A massive black wolf sprinted into the middle of the driveway. It did a visual sweep before its nose went to the ground. Another giant wolf emerged behind Devon, breathing raggedly. Two more to the right, followed by a snow-white wolf she'd never seen before.

Must be Yasmine.

They were missing one, though.

Then she saw it, trotting down from the house, blood all over its muzzle. In fact, they all had blood on them, splattered or sprayed, evidence of their exploits.

And the police were on their way.

"We gotta get outta here!" Charity said as Devon approached. "At least me and the cars do." She lowered her voice in case any partygoers were close enough to hear. "If they know someone died here tonight, they'll want to question the owners of all these cars."

He raised his head and stared at her, standing in exactly the place her new BFF had casually chatted about sexual slavery.

One quick bark and deep green magic swirled around him, fur rolling and boiling until a naked man crouched on the ground. He stood, and his gaze shot to a new dent in his SUV. He noticed the gun in her hand, and finally the knife that had been thrown to the side.

"What the hell happened?" Devon asked, striding

toward her.

"I ran out of freaking bullets, that's what happened! Why didn't you load the whole magazine? I could've had him!" She leaned heavily against the SUV. "Did you get the one in the house?"

Devon's eyebrows lowered dramatically. "We got the younger one."

"Okay, well, great, can we go now?" she said, strangely uncomfortable in that unwavering stare.

"Yeah, we need to head out. The cops are close," Rod said as he started doling out clothes.

"Should we leave someone behind to deal with the other vamp?" Dillon asked before he put on his shirt.

Devon's eyes bored into Charity. "We could never handle him. It's an elder." He paused, and with the way Devon was looking at her, the small hairs rose along Charity's arms. "It's Vlad."

"It was Vlad?" Andy asked, incredulous.

"Who's Vlad?" Charity said as Rod swore.

"Not someone you want interested in you," Devon said. "Come on, we need to go."

"Why would Vlad be interested in Charity?" Macy asked, hurrying into her clothes.

Devon, still staring at Charity, shook his head slowly, but he didn't respond. Charity's heart kicked up a notch. Whoever this Vlad was, it was clear he was really bad news. It was also clear that he had an unhealthy interest in her. Them not knowing why made it ten times scarier.

The whine of the sirens increased in volume, echoing through the trees.

"We gotta go, man," Rod said, jingling his keys.

With one last fierce look, Devon started for the driver's side of his SUV. "Charity, with me."

Yasmine's perfect features twisted with confusion for a moment before she turned to Andy. "Ride?"

Andy shrugged, jogging to his car.

Charity sagged against the hood. Even the short distance to her door seemed like an impossible feat.

"Magic is really tiring, it turns out," she muttered, trying to shoulder her resolve and get moving. The sirens weren't far off now. At the top of the driveway, people were running or staggering for their cars or the trees. Everyone wanted out of there before the cops showed up. "Or maybe I'm bad at it."

"I'll get her," Rod said, hurriedly donning a shirt and starting over.

Devon froze as he got into his seat, Rod clearly cutting through his whirling thoughts. He stared at Charity over the hood for a beat before a look of confusion crossed his face. Anger came next.

He stepped away from his car and threw out a hand, catching Rod in the chest. "I got her. Load up."

"You sure?" Rod gave him a confused look. "I'm right here—"

"I got her, I said." Devon's angry gaze pinned Charity to the SUV.

She didn't care who helped; she just wanted to sit

down.

A moment later, muscles bunched and extended, faster than thought. Suddenly she was in Devon's arms, hugged tightly against his chest. It wasn't a romantic hold—he bumped and jostled her to the passenger door, angry about something and clearly unsure how to express it. Once there, he crushed her to him with one hand as he yanked the door open with the other. Then he heaved her in with an inelegant push.

Like she was a skeleton on Halloween, her limbs fell in a tangle across the seat. A hand pushed her butt so she was completely in before slamming the door.

"What the hell is your problem?" she yelled at him as he came around the driver's side. "I didn't mess this night up for you, Devon. I didn't do anything wrong. Why are you being such a dick?"

His eyes flashed to her, boiling with anger. But right under that, it seemed like he was uncertain about something. Uncomfortable, maybe.

And guess what? So was she. She was tired, drained, and terrified. She didn't deserve this treatment. So when he slammed his own door, jabbed the push-button ignition, and finally stomped on the gas, every movement leaking rage, she couldn't help but feel a small trickle of vindictiveness.

"You don't like being a gentleman? Too in love with your image as a bad boy?" she badgered, not sure why.

He held up a flexed arm, his finger and thumb indicating an inch. "I am this close to tossing you out of this car, Charity. Keep it up."

"Alas, but then Roger would kick your ass." The fear and uncertainty from the vamp's attack was like an acid bath to her nerves. She didn't know why, but she wanted—*needed*—to take it out on him. "Can't do much of your own thinking on this one. But that suits—"

Tires screeched as he swiveled the wheel and slammed on the brakes. She smacked off the dashboard. Her face pressed painfully against the windshield.

Parked on the side of the road, he turned on her in a rush. Red lights flared in front of them as Andy stepped on his brakes.

"I don't give a shit what Roger will do," he said. "Shut. The. Fuck. Up."

His fury shriveled her vindictiveness, leaving only uncertainty and vulnerability. Tears welled up, the fear threatening to drown her. She dropped her face, trying to hide the sudden gush of emotion as she crawled back into the seat.

"Sorry," she whispered. "You're right."

She heard a long sigh. He leaned forward, bracing his forearms on the wheel. Sirens wailed as three police cars zipped by.

"Please don't cry," he murmured. "I was too rough. I didn't mean that. I'm sorry."

She quickly wiped away a tear and strapped herself into the seat. "It was my fault. I shouldn't have pushed. I was so scared with that vamp. I keep protecting myself, but I don't know how anymore. I just… I feel…"

"Like you have no control," he said softly. "Your life is on the line, and you have no control over the outcome."

She hugged her arms around her body.

"I felt that way in the beginning," he said. "Like I was slipping through by the skin of my teeth. I barely knew how to turn into a wolf. I had nothing else to fall back on... I was a disgrace during our first battle. I had to get saved by my alpha at the time. I was as embarrassed as all hell. Took it out on the punching bag after."

He leaned back, his eyes still trained on her face. "I can't imagine going up against an elder my first time. Or what it must've been like to wake up in that house. I forget you're new to all this. I forget that you're as green as they come—without any real control over your magic. I just...fly off the handle sometimes. I apologize for how I handled that. I should've known why you were trying to get my goat."

"What a weird saying," she said dismally, feeling a little awkward now that she was regaining control over her emotions. "'Get my goat.'"

Devon snorted, his soft and intent gaze not allowing her to rebuild her walls. "Yeah. But, you know, goats are worth money. For the milk and cheese and stuff."

"I should invest in a goat." She tried to laugh.

"I'm always around for talking, you know. If you need to hash stuff out. I don't know anything about your magic, but I can maybe tell you about mine, and you can learn that way."

"It's okay. I got it." She straightened herself up.

Finally, he nodded, straightening up too. "It's out there, if you need it. We men don't like to talk about our own feelings, but we can sure fix up other people's lives."

Laughter came a little easier this time as she settled back into the seat. She wanted to reach out and touch him, to feel his solidity and ease her fear and uncertainty, but she gathered he wasn't a man that bent to intimacy all that well—at least, the non-sexual kind. She didn't want to trade her uncomfortableness for his. It wasn't fair.

She settled for leaning her head on the back of her seat and crossing her arms over her chest.

Devon had his hand on the gear selector, ready to put them back in drive, when Andy walked over.

"What're you doing?" Devon said, rolling down the window. He'd wrapped his alpha rage back around him like a favored coat. Poor Andy.

"She okay?"

"She's fine. Let's go!"

Andy threw his hands up. "Drop a man a line once in a while." He started jogging back to his car.

"Tonight would've been a success if that elder hadn't shown up," Devon said softly, watching Andy get into his car. "I mean, it's still a success, because everyone is okay, but…"

"I take it the other one wasn't a problem?"

"Yasmine lured it out of the house easily. Led it

right to us, then helped us finish it. She's a strong addition."

Charity turned toward the window. It wasn't a surprise Yasmine had pulled off her task—she seemed competent and capable—but Charity hated being the weak link.

As if hearing her thoughts, like he always managed to do, Devon asked, "What happened tonight?"

"I got beaten up by a vampire."

"Yes. Before that."

Charity relayed the events as Devon drove home. When she got to the part about the vamp's offer, he held up a hand. "Wait." He pulled into his driveway and threw the SUV into park. "He wanted to set you up like a mistress?"

"I guess. He said he'd share me. That he wasn't possessive."

A crease formed between Devon's eyebrows. "I see. Go on."

At the end of the story, Devon's mouth had worked into a tight line. "He remembers you from the party," he summarized. "He wants to keep you as some sort of pet. He offered to give you whatever you want, including men. And then he tried to take you by force? Take you, not bite you?"

Charity brushed her hair out of her face. "That about sums it up. The guy is Froot Loops."

"You stared him right in the eye and said no?"

"Obviously. Otherwise I would be wearing a gold

collar, asking for another doting boy to serve me grapes."

Devon glanced out his window as the rest of his crew walked past the SUV and up to the house, everyone glancing at them as they passed. "I have to speak to Roger. This might be something the elders do. I have no idea. Sounds…"

"Froot Loops."

A handsome smile flashed across Devon's face. It was the first full smile, however fleeting, she'd seen from him. And it was a thing of beauty, so much more real than that vampire's.

Too soon, he was back to serious and brooding. "I wasn't angry at you earlier; I was angry at myself. I left you alone tonight. That was a stupid move."

"You couldn't have known that vampire would find me."

"It is my duty to protect you, Charity, and I failed. It won't happen again."

She crinkled her nose. "You should apply to be one of the doting boys, because that almost made my heart squish."

"Can you be serious for a moment?"

"No. I stabbed and shot a guy tonight. Technically, he might be a creature, but my mind is still trying to agree with my eyes on that one. I emptied a gun into a living body. As if that weren't bad enough, I did it at point-blank range and somehow missed its heart. How bad of a shot does that make me? My brain, as we speak, is trying to unravel in half a dozen ways. So no, serious is not in me right now. Maybe later."

Devon deflated. Charity had finally defeated him, and she wasn't even trying.

He climbed out slowly before walking around the SUV and lifting her out, gentle despite his earlier freak-out. "In that case, let me point out that you scratched and dented my Range Rover."

"Wrong, sir. Your Range Rover scratched and dented my head. And I hold a grudge."

"I have a Red Bull in the fridge. You might drink that. It'll help. There's some stuff in the freezer, plus we always get pizza after a mission. Food always helps when I change too often, or need a boost of energy."

"Genius," she said sarcastically. "You know so much."

Devon gave her a lighthearted squeeze as they entered the house. A moment later, he deposited her in the recliner as the whole pack watched.

She froze while trying to get comfortable. "What?"

"They also apologize for leaving you on your own, even though it was on my orders," Devon said.

"Oh. Well, let's not mention it to Roger. He'll just call me in, and then I'll have to sit in his presence. No thanks."

"Roger's okay," Andy commented, patting the couch next to him.

She laughed at him. "I had a vampire proposition me with money and unearthly pleasures, and you think

I said no to him so I could snuggle up to you?"

Andy shot her an award-winning grin. "I'm just that awesome." He patted the couch again.

Charity rolled her eyes. She did get up, nearly laughing at Andy's flash of astonishment, before hobbling off to the kitchen, using the walls to stay upright. "I'm hungry."

CHAPTER 22

DEVON GLANCED AT Macy as Charity made her way out of the room.

"Follow her," he said. "She's weak, though she won't admit it."

"Admitting it would be overkill," Macy muttered as she got up.

Dillon balanced his elbows on his knees. Quietly, he asked, "Is she for real? Did she really chase off an elder?"

Devon gave a condensed version of the story, not leaving out Charity's heroics. Or the fact that the vampire had propositioned her. When he'd finished, Dillon leaned back in his seat. Andy blew out a breath as Rod stood and started to pace.

"What's the big deal?" Yasmine asked. "I get propositioned by vamps all the time. Tonight, for example."

Devon ran his hand over his face, biting back a harsh reprimand for the juvenile question. Some alphas didn't share details with their subordinates.

"Newbies and lower-level vamps easily give in to their baser desires. They need blood more often, and blood and sex go hand in hand. A pretty girl is extremely pleasing to a new vamp, if he used to be a straight male. Anything that bleeds becomes pretty to a mid-level vamp. But an elder doesn't feed often. It doesn't need to. Which means it doesn't care as much about sex. They live for politics and business. Making money in the Brink and navigating around the elves in the Realm. It eases their boredom.

"But Vlad's actions tonight were strange. He recognized her, which means she made a lasting impression on him the first time they met. He must've smelled us, yet he left his child unchecked and in danger so he could frolic with a human. That isn't done."

"He doesn't think she's human anymore, I guarantee it," Rod muttered, looking out the window, probably in hopes the pizza man had snuck up on them.

"Good or bad?" Devon whispered.

"Way bad, bro," Andy answered. "Way bad. She made sunlight…stuff in the middle of the night. That has got to be abnormal, right? I've never even *heard* of that!"

"You wouldn't have heard of cutting your toenails, either, if Macy didn't harp on you about it." Rod snickered.

"Think Roger knows she can do that?" Dillon asked Devon.

"Knows I can do what?" Charity entered the living room, holding a steaming plate. The simple task looked to be too much for her. Macy trailed her with a concerned expression, carrying two more plates. "Or were you talking about another freak of nature?"

"Make sunlight at night," Dillon answered.

Charity wobbled as she set her food on the coffee table. Andy hopped up and steadied her.

"I'm good." She waved him away, and then sighed as he helped her into the recliner. "I'm not sure if Roger knows," she answered once she was settled. "I did it when I came out of the mansion in a blind panic. He was charging me…or maybe the creature behind me, so he must've seen it then. I know it was him because of the eyes. He might not have realized I was the one throwing the magical sunshine, though."

"He knows," Devon said. "He doesn't miss much. If he didn't understand it at the time, he's figured it out since."

"What have we here?" Rod asked, surveying the plates. Andy was doing the same thing.

"Frozen food delight." Charity closed her eyes and leaned back against the leather. "I just heated up a few things and put them on plates. It tastes like ass, but it's better than moldy bread and cheese."

"Anything at all is good for me." Andy snatched a frozen burrito off the plate. "This'll be a nice little snack until the pizza comes. I'm famished!"

"Are you going to call Roger tonight?" Dillon asked.

Devon didn't need to ask him what was on his mind. That elder wasn't acting normally, and if Charity had thwarted him twice, he'd want to settle the score. Devon's pack would see him again. It was only a question of when.

CHAPTER 23

"**S**IR, WE'VE GOT a visitor."

Roger glanced up from his desk in the castle, finding Beazie in the doorway with a concerned expression.

"Who is it?" he asked.

She twisted her apron. "Lycus, sir. He's on official business."

Roger tensed. Did Lycus ever stop by when it wasn't official business? The centaur wasn't known for his friendliness with other magical races. "Did he say what it was regarding?"

"No, sir. But…there's been some talk about a strange woman that was roaming around here the other day. Bain, that surly minotaur, said he's never felt so much power from a human. Thinks something is fishy. Like maybe we are engineering magical people somehow." Beazie huffed. "He was drinking, of course. But he isn't the only one asking questions."

"I'll be right down," he told her.

"Yes, alpha."

Roger ran his fingers through his hair. After hearing

Devon's report from the night before, it was clear they wouldn't keep Charity's magic undercover for long. If the most cunning elder vampire in known existence was interested in her, he must've recognized the same things Roger had from the turning party. He must know what her magic meant. But Roger had hoped to keep knowledge of her away from the Realm and the elves, something Vlad could be counted on to do as well. He didn't want any more interest from the elves than Roger did.

Roger stared at his papers without seeing them. If the elves had sent Lycus to investigate, it meant they suspected a kernel of truth lay within whatever rumors they'd heard.

He made his way to the courtyard. Lycus waited near the gate with his arms crossed and his rear hoof occasionally stamping in irritation. While some centaurs chose to roam free, Lycus had given up the wilder attributes of his magical race in favor of a life of investigation for the elves. He took great care to maintain his domestic appearance, even going so far as to shoe his hooves for longer travels. He wasn't a favorite among his people, it was rumored, but the elves used him for all their important issues.

His involvement did not bode well for Roger's intentions for Charity.

"Lycus. Good to see you. How may I be of service?" Roger stuck out his hand for a shake. Lycus had to bend to take it. Being half horse, he had height aplenty.

"We've heard some reports that you entertained a non-shifter a few days ago."

"Yes. One of our missions was interrupted by a magical human. We brought her here for questioning. Turned out, she was in the wrong place at the wrong time. She wasn't involved in the vampire turning. We let her go."

"And who was this magical human?"

"A citizen of the Brink. She had no knowledge of her magical ancestry. Her mother left without mentioning it. This was her first visit to the Realm."

"I see." A scowl creased Lycus's flat face. He knew Roger was intentionally being vague, but there wasn't a damn thing he could do about it. Being on a trial period meant Charity wasn't officially Roger's subject—for now, she wasn't registered in the Realm, and she wasn't in the Realm at present. As far Lycus was concerned, she was a rumor. Roger would make sure she stayed that way until they had a better handle on this whole situation. The last thing Charity needed was for the elves to roll in and swoop her up. If that happened, she could kiss her dreams in the Brink goodbye. So could Roger.

"Did you ascertain what magic she had?" Lycus asked, stamping his back hoof again. He wasn't great at hiding his impatience.

"As of now, unknown." Technically, it was true. Roger didn't have any proof, only a suspicion. "She smelled spicy sweet, but her magic only functioned in spits and gushes. She had no real handle on it."

"And how did you know she was magical?"

Roger hid his uncertainty behind a stone mask. This was a time to tread lightly and speak in half-truths without getting caught.

"I guessed," he said, keeping body movement to a minimum. "She was able to escape a house full of vampires without becoming one. I suspected there was something more to her. Teamed with her not-quite-human smell, I decided to chance a crossing into the Realm. We were monitoring her closely in case she didn't have the magic. She was in no permanent danger."

"And you said she had magical ancestry. This was also a guess?" Lycus asked, clearly seeing the cracks in Roger's explanations.

"She claimed both her parents were non-magical humans. It's clear she has magical ancestry, but she knew nothing of magic or the Realm. I had no way of knowing whether one of her parents intentionally hid their magic." And he still didn't. That was the million-dollar question. "Given that she had not intentionally interfered with my duty, that's where it ended. She was released back to the Brink to get on with her life."

"I see," Lycus said, frown lines etching into his dark face. "Yet she had enough magic to get into the Realm."

"Yes."

"And thwart the charge of a minotaur without raising a weapon."

Roger hesitated. "I had two of my wolves with her. One had changed, and the other was ready to. Bain was probably trying to save face by saying it was the girl. He wasn't drunk at the time. I'm sure sobriety changed his perception of acceptable risk."

A hoof stamped again. "I see." Lycus stared for a moment. Roger met the centaur's eyes easily. Pleasantly. There was no sense in riling anyone up. "Bain's report was not the only one we received."

"Oh?" Roger asked. "And what else have you heard?"

Lycus's expression closed down. "That is classified. When do you expect her back?"

"I don't, unfortunately." Roger spread his hands. "Her absence the other night was noticed by loved ones. Brink police were informed. She agreed to give us a pass, since we pulled her out of a dangerous situation, but kidnapping her will get us chased from the Brink. Without us, the vampires will be let off their leash. That would work out badly for everyone."

"I do not care about what goes on in the Brink. Let them handle their own affairs. I would like to question the girl."

The way he said it, with tense shoulders and a hard glint in his eye, meant bad things. Roger suspected Lycus's interest in this matter was a symptom of a larger issue. The elves were worked up in a way that suggested danger was afoot. Roger wondered if this had anything to do with the whispers he'd heard about Lucifer's planned visit. Lucifer hadn't walked the golden halls in…decades. Only something major would bring him here now. Roger doubted this was solely about the demons' failure to stay put.

Roger let condescension slip into his tone. "You realize, of course, that the Brink is a vampire's breeding ground. If they were allowed to grow their numbers without hindrance, they would be unstoppable should they decide to expand their presence in the Realm. Or don't you read history scrolls?"

Silence descended between them. Roger increased the menace in his stare.

Lycus dropped his hands. "If she returns, let me know."

"Just so we're by the book—on whose authority?"

"The Relations branch sent me. Officially."

"Noted." Roger took a step back and then nodded as Lycus trotted out of the gate.

Relations was the faction of the elves who kept their friends close and their enemies under constant threat. They wouldn't have sent someone as high-caliber as Lycus if it were a simple question of unchecked power. Something was brewing, all right, and Charity had sparked the elves' watchful eye.

A shiver coated Roger's skin, something that hadn't happened in years. One thing was imminently clear: for the time being, they had to keep Charity out of the Realm at all costs.

CHAPTER 24

D READ CONSUMED CHARITY, turning into acid and rising up the back of her throat. She stood with Devon, Yasmine, and Macy in a quiet, grassy outcropping on the college campus.

"Okay, Charity, you ready?" Devon bent to catch Charity's eye.

She picked at the frayed material outlining the sleeve of her worn hoodie. If she didn't answer, did that mean she could skip the class where she might see a creature who used to be Donnie?

"Charity?" Devon asked.

"Yes, Devon. I'm as ready as I'll ever be." She brushed a stray piece of hair away from her cheek.

He straightened and took a step toward Yasmine, who would be shadowing him tonight. He held up his phone. "You have my number?"

She nodded and placed her hand on her rear jeans pocket, feeling the sleek new smartphone trapped there. Normal people would've taken pleasure in surprising her with something as exciting as a girl's first cell phone. Instead, Devon had walked into the kitchen in his boxers, adjusted his junk like a Neanderthal, and tossed the package at her.

He'd said, "You needed a phone. Now you have one. You have a new computer, too. It's in the office. Don't break them. What is this, *oatmeal*? You couldn't make something edible?"

She hitched her backpack a little higher on her shoulders, the weight greatly reduced thanks to the thin and light computer she'd unpacked earlier in the office. She should've been over the moon now that she was firmly in the modern age with everyone around her. Unfortunately, all she could think about was whether the cute boy she'd been crushing on all year would be in class tonight—and whether he'd been turned into a walking nightmare.

"That's a work phone," Devon said, professional and confident. "You need to keep it on at all times tonight. Keep it on vibrate, and respond if any of us contact you. Got it?"

"Yes," she responded, brushing the hard outline with her fingertips again.

"If it doesn't show up, wait in the class until one of us texts you with an all-clear. That'll mean we're waiting for you outside."

"Okay." They'd gone over the plan before leaving Devon's house, but clearly Devon didn't think any of it had sunk in. She wondered herself.

His voice hardened. "If it does show up, don't let it get you alone. Vampires naturally beguile their prey.

You'll be attracted to it. Maybe even crave it. But *don't* act on that, got it? That's a trick. You have to remember that those feelings aren't real."

"I know."

"Keep your eye on it, but keep your distance, too. If it follows you, stay around other people until you can lead it to Macy or me. We'll handle it from there. Okay?"

"I know."

Devon looked out over the grass for a silent moment. His sigh was so soft that she barely heard it. Then he stepped closer and put his large hand on her shoulder. The comforting heat of his touch seeped down into her.

"It's not really Donnie, Charity, okay?" he murmured, for her ears alone. "It is a creature wearing a mask that looks like Donnie. It won't care about you; it'll care about your blood. This is a war. Donnie was a casualty of that war. Understand?"

With a sinking feeling in her gut, Charity pulled away. "I know," she whispered again, acid sharp in her throat. She blew out a breath and tried to keep her composure.

"Be safe," Devon said. "Be strong. Macy will be waiting nearby if you need anything." And then he was striding away, Yasmine at his side, the two of them crossing the grass like a couple of beautiful celebrities.

Macy stepped up next to Charity. "How are you doing?"

"If I said 'fine,' would you believe me?"

"If I said 'yes,' would you believe me?"

Charity gripped the strap of her backpack. "I don't want to do this. What if I end up being the bait that lures Donnie to his death? I get that he's...changed, but..."

"This sucks. There's no two ways about it. One day you should talk to Roger about it. Shortly after he became alpha and started cleaning up the Brink, an elder turned one of his good friends as a personal FU. Roger chose to be the one that disbanded the newbie. He felt responsible for killing his friend. Or so I heard. So he knows what you're going through. He'd talk to you about it. He's good like that." Macy patted Charity's shoulder. "At least you had no part in Donnie's change. It could easily have been you. I mean...if vamps can change fae. And, you know, if that's really what you are."

The pep talk was going downhill.

With a deep breath, Charity shouldered her courage and gave a resolute nod. If she waited any longer she'd lose her nerve entirely.

"Good luck," Macy said, drifting toward the shadows.

Luck would be on her side if Donnie strolled in as a regular, hot, hard-to-talk-to guy. Maybe he was used solely for blood? That would be gross, but at least it would still be him.

Each step a trial in courage, Charity made her way

to her class. Once there, she forced herself to walk through the door. An expansive lecture hall greeted her, with a podium set up on a small stage in front of a white screen, and stadium-style steps covered in seats going up to the back of the room. Students sat in front of their laptops, bored expressions on their faces. A few groups murmured, waiting for the professor to start his dull lecture.

She checked her watch. Two minutes to go. Class would start anytime.

As she scanned the faces a second time, relief flooded her. One more time for good measure, and then she climbed the steps to her usual spot in the back.

No Donnie.

Thank God.

She pulled the clunky wooden desk up and over her lap. Maybe he had escaped after all. For all she knew, he was having a long chat with his father's attorney about his next steps. That conversation would likely result in a psych evaluation, given how absurd it would sound. Such things took time, so it was reasonable to expect him to take a week off. Maybe longer.

She dropped her backpack to the ground, forcing her thoughts elsewhere. She pulled out the fantastic laptop, top quality, with a price tag to match. Roger was really going the extra mile, trying to butter her up. Getting her a phone made sense, since communication within a company was key, but a laptop was an extravagance. She had a computer and it did the job fine, slowly but surely. Not like she was complaining. She'd barely yelled at Devon as she was ripping into the packaging, and even then, it had only been to thank him.

The buttering up was working.

As the laptop started, she pushed her backpack beneath her feet. Getting comfortable, she glanced at the door, just in case.

Her heart froze solid.

Donnie moved with grace and confidence, drifting in like a dancer. A slightly wrinkled button-up was tucked into the front of his jeans, and his hair was gelled into a spikey do, on par for his usual style and dress choices. Well, except for the wrinkles. Even so, it wasn't immediately obvious he'd changed in any way.

Except for his face.

Almost glossy in appearance, like he was airbrushed in real life, his face lacked the small discolorations and imperfections of a real person. His handsome features seemed amplified. A little too perfect. Like a mask.

Her heart sank and tears came to her eyes.

Devon was right. They'd all been changed. The proof was right in front of her.

Donnie took to the stairs slowly and purposefully, a predatory grin twisting his lips as he looked over the people he passed. His movements were a little too fluid and easy. She could almost read his mind: *Warm bodies.*

Food storage.

Charity's stomach twisted like his grin. Then his

dark eyes met hers.

He didn't notice the smiles of the girls he passed. Nor the nods of his friends. He was not interested in fist bumps or acknowledging the various people who called his name. He didn't plan to sit with his friends. His sole interest…was her.

"No," she whispered as he reached the edge of her row. "Please no. Go away."

She'd barely given voice to the words, but still his lips pulled into a hungry smile.

Adrenaline dumped into her body, and not just from the stare he kept trained on her. For the first time, he greeted her with a delighted smile, like a boyfriend. He was threading between the seats to get to her. To sit with her. Pleasure mingled with fear, the heat of her core messing with the warning in her brain.

What had she been thinking, agreeing to this? She didn't have the right amount of detachment to stay logical!

"Hey, Charity," he said, almost like the normal Donnie, though now his voice sounded strangely musical. He lowered into the seat next to her. "I hoped I'd see you."

She inhaled his scent, like she always did when he strayed close. This time, the sweet cologne mixed with the smell of a particularly pungent soap was overshadowed by a strange sort of funk. Like food gone off.

She crinkled her nose as a pang stabbed her middle.

"Hi, Donnie, how are you?" She rested her hand

against her phone.

"I'm *good*, Charity. Really *good*. Let's go out after class. I've always wanted to ask, you know. You're hot and smart. Something has always drawn me to you. Your clothes were the reason I held back. I'm not so petty anymore."

Donnie had never put this many non-sports words together at one time. He'd never hit her right in the middle with the things he said.

Down on the ground level, the professor walked toward the podium with his briefcase, her elevated seat giving her the perfect view of his comb-over.

"You've had a change of heart in three days?" she asked, fighting for logic. She touched the keys of her laptop with shaking hands and eyed the glowing exit sign. There was no way she would make it if he moved even a quarter of the speed of that elder. She should've sat near the front.

"Okay, class, let's get started, shall we?" Professor Banks fired up his PowerPoint presentation.

"Sometimes it takes an awakening," Donnie said, his gaze rooted to her face. "I want you. Go out with me." He brought his arm up and gently slid the back of his hand down her cheek.

Fire erupted in the wake of his touch, searing her insides. A strange haze clouded her mind.

She shook her head, trying to clear it.

"I have to focus," Charity murmured.

"Yes. Later, then."

Donnie settled back and swung his arm around her, letting it rest on the back of her seat. He crossed an ankle over his knee. His forgotten backpack tumbled into the space between the chair in front of him and the ground.

Girls glanced back at them with wide eyes, some sparkling with jealousy. His friends looked back, too, snickering or confused. Donnie was claiming her in public, not concerned about PDA.

It was like a dream come true housed in a waking nightmare.

The haze clouding Charity's thoughts deepened, his presence as dangerous as it was electrifying. Twisted sheets and writhing bodies invaded her thoughts. Fingers traced the exposed skin on her neck. Glorious shivers coated her body, sucking her under.

Bing—bing.

Charity swore under her breath.

"How many times do I have to tell this class to *turn off your cell phones*," Professor Banks said, looking right at her.

"Sorry! I just got it."

Trying to clear her head over the pounding of her body, Charity pulled out her phone with trembling fingers. Donnie's warm touch dipped to the collar of her hoodie and then traced her collarbone. God help her, she wanted his hands everywhere.

CHAPTER 25

S NAP OUT OF *it, Charity*, she silently berated herself, trying to pull herself together. Trying to shrug off that fiery touch. The pounding of her core.

A text from Macy swam into view. *Is he there?*

Charity was way too young to be gawking at an electronic device like a hog looking at a wristwatch. "I need to silence this…"

"I'll do it." Donnie's fingers slid across hers as he took the phone, sending raging tingles through her body. He flicked a button on the side. It vibrated once. Then he analyzed the message. His thumbs flew across the screen, too fast to be human.

Why didn't that jog her out of this horribly delicious lust daze?

Yes. Were gonna hang out 2nite, the text read.

"No," Charity whispered, reaching for her phone.

Donnie used her lean to his advantage, dropping his mouth and catching her lower lip between his.

The world burst into color. Her body lit up with desire.

A distant part of her registered the prickled skin,

like red ants biting. It was utterly lost to the moment.

A moan sounded in her throat, long and low. She'd spent all those lonely nights dreaming that he'd kiss her. That he wouldn't care about her lack of money. That he'd choose her over all his other options. And now it had come true.

She couldn't tear herself away. She couldn't dislodge the feeling of worth this moment gave her. Like a dumb girl, she let him angle his head and then open her lips. His tongue flicked in playfully. The hand behind her neck tightened, pulling her in close. The other hand found her thigh. The kiss intensified, her senses lost to the feel of him, to the heady sensation of her dreams meeting reality.

"Excuse me, you two! That is completely inappropriate!"

Donnie backed off, his eyes hungry, his smile triumphant. He turned his head toward the professor, who was two seconds away from telling them to get out.

"Sorry, Professor Banks," Donnie said in his strange, musically hypnotic voice. "Please, continue."

The professor opened his mouth...then closed it. He smiled in a dreamy sort of way. "Yes, of course. Now, let's speak about the indigenous people in Australia."

Donnie turned back to an awestruck Charity. "Take notes, babe. You hate getting behind."

Charity blinked. She held out her hand slowly, not totally in charge of her motor skills. "My phone, please."

He smiled at her and leaned down for another kiss.

She backed away this time, flushed. "Phone. Please."

Her thigh felt cold when he lifted his hand. With a coy smile, he reached into his shirt pocket and extracted her phone. It buzzed as he handed it over, three messages displayed on the screen.

I'll meet you out front after, she sent to Macy.

To Devon's message of *R u fucking stupid???* she replied, *No. I didn't write that message. I'm fine.*

She wasn't fine. The daze wouldn't go away. Desire clutched her tightly and begged her to give in. To claim what she'd always believed she wanted.

Devon: *Leave class NOW!*

"Charity, should I take notes for you?" Donnie asked, like a dream man.

Her fingers flew over the keys, typing words she plucked out of the air without thought. Those lips settled on the hollow next to her shoulder and sucked ever so gently.

"Oh God," she breathed, lost to the fantasy of this moment. Drowning in pleasure.

His hand worked up her thigh, kneading along the inside, nearing her apex. Shivers of delight racked her body. Her eyes closed and her body overheated, desire flooding her. Barely able to keep from spreading her legs, she tried desperately to get herself under control. To claw her way to the surface.

"Don't bite me," she said, her voice wispy.

"You'll like it," he said in her ear, his tongue flicking

out to lick along the ridge. He turned her face with his finger. "I know you've liked me for a while," he murmured against her lips. "This is what you've wanted. I'll give you everything you've wanted, starting now. We'll go to dinner."

Suddenly the class was on the move, standing and putting their stuff away. Her phone was vibrating again. *Where the hell has the time gone?*

"I can't," she said in the same wispy voice. It felt like her brain had detached from her body.

She felt his fingers between her thighs, massaging exactly where she needed it. Her legs spread of their own accord. Their kiss deepened. One hand pulled her into his body, branding her with his heat, while the other massaged in tiny circles, tweaking that little spot that made her speechless. His lips moved lower, down the side of her chin, the classroom suddenly quiet. Empty. Her body wound with tension, his ministrations having taken her to the brink. She moaned and clutched him, needing his touch like she'd never needed anything in her entire life.

The world condensed to his fingers and his heat. Everything else disappeared.

His lips worked down the side of her throat as he pushed her back against the chair, moving around her. Those fingers worked faster, her body responding with an animalistic intensity. His mouth moved low, over her artery.

"*Charity!*"

She heard her name through a wind tunnel. She clutched tighter to Donnie—to the beautiful creature that Donnie had become. She begged him to take her, to take what he needed from her. To claim and consume her.

"Charity!"

It was the fear in Devon's voice that brought her struggling to the surface.

Teeth scraped against her neck as she heard feet pounding up the aisle between the seats. Pressure pushed against her skin, dull and painful.

Alarm finally registered. Those red ants felt like they were tearing her flesh. Pleasure turned into pounding fear so great that she choked from it.

Donnie's face ripped away from her throat. In the next second, he was standing in the aisle, claws elongating from his fingers. A terrible hiss worked around two huge fangs. His lips turned black and his perfect face turned into something inhuman.

Charity flinched back as Devon reached them, a long knife in hand.

Donnie surged toward the attack quickly. Devon, faster still, dodged to the side and struck. The knife plunged toward Donnie.

"No!" Charity screamed.

The blade rammed into Donnie's chest, piercing his heart before he could turn away. His hiss turned into a monstrous squeal, his body writhing, his claws slashing at the air. Devon dodged around him and gripped the back of Charity's hoodie. He yanked, impossible strength dragging her out and over the back of the chair, and threw her into the aisle behind him, shielding her body with his.

But Donnie was done. Her illusion of him shattered. His bony, greenish face howled in misery. He clutched the handle of the knife, black sludge running over his claws. He fell into a pile onto the floor as Devon held a phone to his head.

"Yeah, Dean? Yeah, we need a cleanup. I'll text you the location… Thanks, bro, but it was a close one. All right."

Devon faced her, muscles flexing, face a mask of rage. Their gazes connected for a long moment, the fury in Devon's eyes like hot embers. He didn't say a word.

He didn't have to.

A moment later, he was walking down the aisle, not bothering to tell her to get her crap and get moving. He didn't have to say that, either.

Averting her eyes from Donnie's monstrous form, she reached over the chair and grabbed the laptop, which looked no worse for the mayhem it had witnessed. Charity wished she could say the same for herself.

She stuffed everything in her bag, swallowed a sob at the sight of Donnie's forgotten backpack, no longer needed, and ran to follow Devon. Her first crush after John lay desecrated and destroyed in a pile of sludge. Loss overwhelmed her, followed by desolation. She was out of her league. Although she knew next to nothing about warrior fae, she doubted one would have fallen prey to a baby vampire. A real warrior fae wouldn't need to be saved over and over.

She yanked her phone out of her pocket with a shaking hand. She had three missed text messages.

Devon: *Should I come?*

Macy: *do you need me????*

Devon: *Answer me or Im coming.*

He'd almost been too late. She did not have faith that she would've snapped out of it.

She had never felt so filthy and useless in all her life. She'd also never felt more scared. Samantha was still out there, and so was that elder. How long would it be before they came for Charity?

Would she be able to resist the next time?

CHAPTER 26

WITH HIS HEART still pounding, Devon shoved the door open and took a few steps out, glancing around to make sure nothing waited for them. He stepped to the side, staring straight ahead, and held the door until Charity passed through. He couldn't even look at her. Not without exploding into a blind rage he didn't understand.

A steadying breath filled his chest, the effect not relieving the constriction. Damn it, what had she been thinking? This woman had chased off an elder vamp, yet a newbie had reduced her to a puddle of sex. It didn't make any sense.

And what the hell was with Devon's reactions to the whole mess? He'd never before experienced the overwhelming fear that had choked him on the way to her classroom, not even in battle. Nor had he ever felt the likes of the blind, territorial rage that had ripped through him when he opened the door and saw that thing draped all over her...trying to claim her...

He couldn't...

The sound of his teeth grinding was unnaturally

loud as they stepped off the path toward the nearly deserted parking lot. Charity trudged along in front of him.

Devon flexed his fingers against the stinging regret constricting his ribcage. He was handling this badly, he knew he was. But every time he started to calm down, the image of that vampire touching Charity seared through his head.

"Where's Macy?" Charity asked in a small voice as they came within sight of the SUV. Yasmine leaned gracefully against the door, a splatter of blood on her ample cleavage.

Since Devon had to handle Charity, he'd told Macy to join Yasmine and follow the other vamp. It looked like they'd taken care of it in record time.

"She went home after we took care of business," Yasmine replied in a smug, sultry voice.

The invitation in her eyes didn't stir him tonight. The one thing that could make him feel better, or at least normal and detached, wasn't happening. The overwhelming lust issue he'd been dealing with all week, which he'd hoped to sex away tonight, was completely overshadowed by the weird residual fear pinging manically through his body.

Charity was safe! He'd done his duty. He'd protected her. His obligation was met for the night.

So why the hell did he want to wrap himself around her like bubble wrap and try to soothe her hurt away?

"Get in the car," he barked at Yasmine.

"Hmm, yes, alpha," Yasmine said, clearly loving the show of power. "Your house?"

He didn't bother answering. Nor could he loosen his white-knuckled grip on the steering wheel. When they got to the house, he again shoved the door open, but this time he stared at Charity accusingly as she slithered through it, a shadow of the woman he'd met at the turning party. Broken.

Oh, perfect, now I feel guilty, he thought sarcastically.

Why was he so pissed off?

"Hi, Andy," Yasmine said as they entered the living room. Pizza boxes already covered the coffee table.

"What happened?" Andy asked as Charity curled up into the recliner. "Are you okay?"

Her hair covered her downturned face and she picked at the fraying end of her sleeve. She didn't answer, but then, she didn't have to. It was clear that she was very much *not* okay. Tonight had thrown her for a loop in a way nothing else so far had. Given her recent past, that was really saying something.

Devon's insides churned. He stalked out of the room and punched the wall on the way to the kitchen, desperate to mask his uncomfortable feelings. Reaching for anger to smother the fear and guilt.

The can of beer made a satisfying *pop* as he opened it. Willing himself to calm down and view the situation through a logical lens, like his position demanded, he returned to the living room at a slower pace.

"This is the vamps' fault, Charity," Andy was saying as Devon walked in. Yasmine lowered onto the couch. "The ones who turned him—this is all their fault."

"I barely got there in time," Devon told Andy as he leaned against the doorframe. He was much too keyed up to sit down. "It was about to bite her." He clenched his teeth, not meaning those words to sound so accusatory.

Charity shuddered but remained silent.

"Okay, well, that's not ideal," Andy said, scooting to the far end of the couch to be closer to her. "But the important thing is that it *didn't* bite her, right, Charity? No harm, no foul. I'm sure that thing"—she flinched— "gave you the ol' sexy eyebrow waggle, right? Hell, I have a hard enough time saying no to human ladies, let alone an insanely gorgeous non-human lady who specializes in seduction. Then, bing-bang-boom, you're scraping a vampire off your neck. It's really not your fault." Andy paused and trained his focus on Devon. "You…"

"Dispatched it, yes."

Andy dropped his pizza into the box and leaned back to Charity. "I had a close one, once. Remember that, Devon? It was my first time out. This she-vamp snuck up on me. I was supposed to just be watching, right, so I was still in human form. Then she was breathing all over me, giving me the sex-kitten routine, touching… Yeah, I almost became a donor. Devon had to pull her off. I was a goner, man. So, Charity, it really isn't that big of a deal. Learning curve, you know? It happens to all of us."

"I saw it coming," Charity said softly. "I should've known better."

Andy opened his mouth, but before he could speak, Charity rose. "If you don't mind, I'm going to bed."

"What time is your class tomorrow?" Devon asked.

"I'll get there on my own." She brushed by him.

"Wait." He lightly grabbed her arm so he didn't have to chase her. "What time—"

She yanked out of his grasp, and before he knew what was happening, a solid punch took his breath away. His beer splattered against the wall and the can went rolling.

"Oh shit," Andy said, standing.

Devon barely blocked another punch. He grabbed her arms, trying to subdue and not hurt, but she threw her body to the side and broke the hold before kicking toward his thigh. He intercepted with his knee, blocking.

"Calm down," he said fiercely.

Anger and desperation emanated from her, her brow lowered, her lip pushed out. She was trying to physically fight away the emotional pain. He knew how that felt. So when vulnerability started to shine through her hard mask, he shoved her.

It was the least he could do.

She jabbed at him, a spark flaring in her eyes. He jerked out of the way, surprised at her speed and strength.

Shifting his strategy, trying to exhaust rather than subdue her, he struck at her side. Her hard forearm crashed down on his. He jabbed, hitting her ribs. Her breath gushed out, but she was already moving. Her fist connected with his side and pain welled up. She struck again, but he caught it, then yanked her forward and turned it into a throw.

Charity hit the wall before crashing to the ground. She was up in a flash, charging him like a wild thing. Her shoulder hit his middle. The breath pushed out of his lungs as he staggered back. He rocketed two punches into her midsection, now treating her like a shifter, meeting her on her level so she could fight out her pain.

He hit her again, smiling at her grunt.

She punched him in the face. His head banged off the wall. She stepped back, and then her other foot sped toward his nose, her form perfect. But not fast enough.

He caught her leg against his side before hammering his fist into her upper thigh. Her bruise would be enormous.

She leaned around him and brought an elbow down in the center of his back.

Agony flared. His bruise wouldn't be half bad, either, for the short while it lingered.

"Don't hit the alpha!" Yasmine's voice cut through his fighting haze.

"Not your fight!"

Out of the corner of his eye, Devon barely caught

sight of Andy sticking his arm out in a clothesline to intercept Yasmine. The bottoms of her feet flashed Devon right before she fell flat on her back.

Devon dropped Charity's leg, blocked a punch, and threw a punch of his own. His fist hit Charity square in the chest. She staggered backward, bending over and sucking in agonized breaths.

Possibly that had been a bit too hard…

"I screwed up tonight, all right?" she said, straightening with a red face. "I know I did. I won't ever forget it. But I don't need you hovering over me, rubbing it in my face. I'll take my chances getting to school."

"There are no buses within miles of here. How will you get there?" Devon growled, his whole body poised and tense.

"I've never owned a car. I've always made it. Now is no different. *Back off.*"

Devon took a step toward her, daring her with his eyes to throw another punch. "It is my duty to make sure you stay out of harm's way. I can't have you traipsing around the city with no way to get help. Not with an elder vamp interested in you."

Charity gave him a condescending look, so near breaking that she seemed like she could barely hold herself up. Devon's resolve weakened.

"It'll be daylight," she seethed through clenched teeth. "And I'm not interested in what you feel you can or cannot do. I'm telling you what I *will* do. I don't need—"

Her words cut off and she set her jaw defiantly.

"A babysitter? Is that what you were about to say?" Devon asked.

Charity pulled herself up, tall and proud, her back straight and her chin raised. The effect was ruined by her trembling lips. Without a word, she about-faced and strode away toward her room.

Devon swore under his breath as he watched her go.

"Should I go after her?" Andy asked, ignoring Yasmine's scowl as she got up off the ground. "She probably needs a hug, right?"

Something foreign and uncomfortable squeezed Devon's vitals. He barely stopped himself from issuing a threat to keep Andy at bay.

"Although," Andy went on thoughtfully, "I've always done more harm than good when I try to comfort pretty girls. They heave when they cry, and their breasts are just...right there, you know? I don't mean to, but I get turned on every time. I can't help it! And they can always tell. I have no idea how—it's not like I rub anything against them or whatever—but they always get pissed off. Charity might kick my ass. She's fast. No wonder she was able to get out of that turning party with her skin intact. She's no joke."

"Leave it," Devon finally managed. "She doesn't need you rubbing up against her."

"I said I *don't* rub anything against them. Jesus, bro. You know I'm not that kind of guy. What happened, anyway?"

Devon rubbed his hand over his face as Andy grabbed something to wipe up the spilled beer. When Andy was done, Devon relayed the events as he knew them. He shook his head. "I can't understand why she went for that vamp. She was a rock star with that elder, but this one… It didn't look like she put up any kind of fight. Just gave in to him."

"Bro, she was crushing after him. She probably never thought she'd get him, but always wanted to, you know? And then here he is, all dreamy and stuff, and he's sitting all close, and he's doing that weird googly-eyed thing—she fell into the dream, bro. Sex can mess with the mind."

"Yeah," Devon said in a noncommittal tone. "I didn't want it to go down like that. I didn't want her to see me take him out. But I didn't have much choice."

Andy nodded. "Not much else you could've done."

"Why do we even need her?" Yasmine asked. She lowered gracefully onto the love seat near the window.

"Roger thinks she's valuable. He's entrusted her to me," Devon answered, leaning his head back in the seat and closing his eyes. "Plus, a couple vamps are after her. I have no idea why Roger won't just let her stay nights in the castle."

The ticking of the clock on the wall permeated the following silence. After a while, Andy said, "At least that's another one gone. Two down, four to go."

"Three down," Yasmine said with a smug smile. "When the human had to be saved, the alpha sent Macy and me along to trail the vamp from his class. The vamp went for a trek through the woods, and we jumped her. I figured, why wait, you know? It was only one."

"Why'd she go ambling through the woods?" Andy asked with a furrowed brow.

"I have no idea, but it doesn't matter. We got her."

"But what if it was heading to a meetup area?" Andy trained his gaze on Devon. "A newbie walking through the woods without food doesn't make sense. Maybe we should go back there and check it out."

"There was nothing there," Yasmine said petulantly.

"How do you know?" Andy's eyebrows rose. "Was there a gateway to the Realm around there? Maybe she was meeting her maker. Maybe... I mean, who knows. Taking her out without more info was shortsighted, bro. Er, Yasmine."

Yasmine shrugged, her golden locks tumbling off her shoulder and to her back. "I don't know—Macy suggested it, and I went along with it. It was just the one vamp."

"I'll check into it tomorrow," Devon said as he rubbed his eyes. He couldn't focus on any of this right now. His mind was buzzing.

"I'm going to go freshen up," Yasmine said in a beautiful pout. She *eased* up from her seat, her breasts popping out and her body curving just right.

Devon looked away. "Tonight was a mess," he admitted. Yasmine crossed the room and disappeared down the hall. "I had to take him out in the middle of the classroom. Had I been thinking, I would've gotten Charity out of there before I did it. I'm faster now. More experienced. Taking one of them out, even without shifting, is no problem."

"Number one, that's pretty sweet, bro! No one your age can do that. That's why you made alpha so young, see? Number two, you can't beat yourself up for what happened. Sometimes you gotta react. That vamp needed to be taken down, and I hate to say it, but Charity probably needed that lesson. Especially with an elder sniffing around."

They sat in silence for a moment, reflecting.

"You don't seem like you're in the mood for…shenanigans," Andy said quietly, picking up his slice of pizza.

Devon glanced in the direction Yasmine had gone. "I thought I'd give in to her so she'd stop affecting me. I made those plans before all the crap went down with the vamp."

"Ah. Sex it away." Andy shook his head. "I don't think that works with girls as hot as Yasmine. She's still going to be hot in the morning."

Devon shrugged. "It never lasts. I always lose interest by the morning."

"How is that possible?" Andy asked.

Devon shrugged again. "Don't know. I think a girl is so hot I can barely keep my eyes off her, and then we bang and… I don't know. The magic wears off, I guess. The question has been answered—I've seen behind the curtain and the thrill is gone. The messed-up thing is that it happens the same way even if I've spent weeks dating the girl. Even if I think I really like her. I'm probably going to end up like the Fonz from *Happy Days*."

"You mean an old guy in a leather jacket hanging out with younger kids? That's weird, yo. You need to stay off late night reruns."

"I mean alone with nothing but constant one- or two-night stands."

"Oh. Well, at least you can get laid, I guess. Silver lining."

Devon snorted, closing his eyes. He stayed quiet as Andy finished his pizza.

"All right, bro," Andy said. Was that disapproval in his voice, or was Devon imagining it? "I'm going to head."

"All right, man. Good work."

Devon watched Andy leave the room with a sense of foreboding. A moment later, he heard, "Ready?"

Yasmine turned the corner, her plump lips curved upward in a seductive smile. Once near, she bent to run a hand along his shoulder.

Not able to hide a sigh, he stood and motioned her toward the hall. The sway of her hips held no interest for him. Instead, his thoughts strayed to Charity.

She was probably curled up in her bed, terrified of the darkness caressing her windows. Reliving the night's horror in vivid detail. What might've happened would be constantly jabbing at her. Agonizing her.

He'd been there once. So had Andy. Many shifters had.

Guilt ate away at him. He hadn't been fair to her. She would have no idea that his anger had stemmed from fear rather than judgment or contempt.

Slowing, allowing Yasmine to slip by him, he stood outside of Charity's room, his gaze rooted to the light under her door.

He really should go in to her. He should give her the comfort she needed. New pack members got a year or two to get used to this life. To train and hone their body and mind. Charity had been at it for less than a week. She'd been chased, seduced, propositioned, and attacked. And the things she'd seen… It wasn't fair to make her go through this alone.

"Coming?"

Yasmine was already sprawled out on his bed, completely nude and perfect in every way. She trailed a hand down between her breasts, over her stomach, and then over a parted thigh.

Guilt burned through him.

He felt like his life was coming apart. A week ago, he'd been the master of his own universe, in total control. Only a matter of days, really, yet things had gotten completely messed up. He barely knew what end was up anymore. He certainly had no idea why.

He dropped his head. He felt lost.

CHAPTER 27

CHARITY HICCUPPED OUT a sob from under her covers. She hadn't cried this hard since her mother had left. And if she were honest with herself, she wasn't crying for Donnie. Not for Sam, either, whom she could no longer fool herself about. She was crying because she was afraid. She was crying because, for the first time in a very long time, she didn't feel like she had any control. She'd completely lost it in that lecture hall. Her brain had completely shut off. If Devon hadn't rushed to her aid, she would've let that creature take her. Let it claim her body and then her life.

The thought scared the ever-loving shit out of her.

When you cared about someone, or needed someone, and they walked away, they left an unfillable void in their wake. She'd experienced that with her mother and John; she couldn't bear for it to happen again. But right now, in this screwed-up new life she didn't understand, she needed Devon. She needed his experience and his know-how. Hell, she needed his support. That thought alone terrified her to the core.

A motor revved and then pulled away from the

house. Probably Andy. A moment later, a feminine voice drifted through her door.

She peeked out from under her covers. Two shadows interrupted the light from under her door. Someone was in the hallway. Yasmine?

An uncomfortable feeling churned in Charity's gut. Yasmine would get to cuddle up with the solid warmth of Devon, basking in his protection and strength. Charity didn't begrudge the two their rendezvous—she had no interest in that side of things—but she would miss the innocent intimacy of his presence. He was a moody bastard, but when it really counted, he was a rock. He'd been there for her since the beginning, even when he would've rather been anywhere else.

Miserable, Charity sank deeper into her covers, wishing she had earplugs. She didn't want to hear them and be reminded of how desperate she had been for that creature to touch her. Nor be reminded of who that creature had been.

Before she knew it, Charity was curled into a ball, crying so hard that it felt like her spleen was being ripped out. She didn't hear the car approaching the house, nor the argument that trailed down the hallway. She didn't even hear her door opening and the footsteps to her bed.

Her covers ripped away. A scream died in her throat as Devon bent down in a rush, scooping her up in his strong arms and hugging her tightly to his chest. He flicked off the light as he carried her from the room, crossed the hall, and closed his door behind them.

"But what about—"

"Don't worry about it," Devon answered quietly, depositing her gently onto his bed. He pulled off his shirt and stepped out of his pants, leaving on his boxer briefs, and slipped in beside her. He put out an arm and gathered her up against his warm chest. "Go to sleep. I'm right here. I won't let anything happen to you."

THE NEXT MORNING, Charity moved through her fighting postures, kicking and punching the air with everything she had, trying to forget. Trying to wipe out Donnie's howling face. Trying to scrub away the feeling of being chased through the nightmare house. If she was going to live in a world with those creatures, she needed to push herself harder. She had to get faster, stronger.

Strangely, she wasn't embarrassed about the vulnerability she'd shown the night before. Maybe it was because Devon hadn't shown any pity or asked for anything in return. He'd just...*been there*. The man was a good guy. Extremely loyal. It almost gave him a pass for being a dick half the time.

Breathing out a sigh, drenched in sweat, she slowed. Then stopped. Panting, she headed back into the house. That boring job in the admin office was starting to look better. Especially since she hadn't gotten a paycheck from this new job yet and she needed food.

As she passed through the sliding glass doors and sitting room, she saw Yasmine enter the kitchen in tight, sparkly pink leggings and a tube top that barely covered her large breasts. How the woman wasn't freezing her butt off, Charity did not know.

"Hey," Charity said, wiping her face of sweat.

Yasmine stopped at the edge of the kitchen and popped out a hip. "Well, look who it is." The sneer erased some of her beauty. "The tag-along. I know what game you're playing. It won't work for long, I can assure you."

"I didn't realize staying alive was a game, but I sure hope it keeps working. You want some oatmeal?" Charity measured out some water and dumped it into a pot on the stove.

"He only sees you as his duty, you know," Yasmine continued, undeterred. "He's protecting the damsel in distress because that's his job, and he's damn good at his job."

Charity threw a thumbs-up over her shoulder. "Gold star to you for the worst pep talk ever. Now, about that oatmeal…"

Yasmine huffed and sauntered toward the cabinets. "You're no threat to me." She extracted two coffee cups before filling them. "Watch your back, honey."

"Dude, I'm not even into him," Charity said, exasperated. "We fight, like, most of the time. You're exactly right; there is no threat—Okay, you're walking away. You don't care." She rolled her eyes and snatched up her phone as she waited for the water to boil.

She'd missed calls from both Macy and Andy.

Text from Macy: *I gotta talk to Devon this morning. Need ride to school?*

Text from Andy: *We got class today, yo. Im so gonna sit next to you ;)*

Text from Andy: *I called u. Did u do homework? Need help. Im coming over.*

Charity smiled. Lovable douche, that one.

"Hey."

She jumped as Macy strolled in and took a seat at the island.

Macy grinned. "Scared you?"

"No. I was doing calisthenics." Charity scowled. "Make more noise when you walk around, would you?"

"Sorry. I'm not used to hanging out with deaf humans."

"I'm not a deaf human. I'm a deaf magical being with no real control over her life and said magic." Heaviness filled her chest, stifling her smile. She measured out the oatmeal.

"How are you?" Macy asked, her expression turning serious.

Charity shrugged.

"Do you want a hug, a punch, or a change of subject?" Macy asked, deadpan.

Charity couldn't help but laugh. "Change of subject, please."

"Did you figure out your phone and computer?" Macy asked, bringing out her own phone. "Because I'm happy to make fun of you if you didn't. Help. I mean, I'm happy to help you."

Charity laughed, the dark cloud over her mood quickly lifting. Why couldn't all friendships be this easy?

"I've got all the basics down," Charity said. "I need to steal Devon's CDs and figure out how to load them up. The computer doesn't have a CD drive, though. Also…I haven't seen any CDs lying around."

"No, because it isn't 2001. I thought he said he created a family plan with you when he bought everything. You should have access to his music subscription. I have one if you want to mooch off me—"

"When *he* bought everything?" Charity asked.

Macy paused. "The phone and computer, yeah. Isn't that what you're talking about?"

"He said Roger bought them."

Macy froze with her eyebrows raised. "Oh. Ahuum." She squinted with her eyebrows still raised, a weird expression that clearly implied she'd accidentally outed a secret.

Charity turned back to the pot. "Why would Devon buy me that stuff?" she murmured, warmth filling her chest despite herself. She was cool with him giving her emotional support, since that was his duty as alpha, and as Yasmine had said, he was damned good at his job. But this was…thoughtful. Disguising his kindness by giving someone else credit was even more so. It showed he had a big heart. It showed that he cared about the wellbeing of those around him, even when it wasn't necessary.

"What are you making?" Macy asked, clearly seeing the need for another topic change.

"Oatmeal," Charity said, happy for the continued distraction. "I have enough for you and Andy, if you want some?"

"Ew, no thanks. When's Andy showing up?"

Devon entered the kitchen in sweats and a T-shirt, a coffee cup in hand. He made a beeline for the stove, as was becoming the norm.

"Devon, I need a word with you," Macy said in a low voice, staring at her hands.

He ignored Macy as he glanced into the bubbling pot. "I'm getting tired of this stuff."

"What did you eat before I made oatmeal for you?" Charity asked.

"Nothing. I didn't eat breakfast."

She gave him a blank stare, allowing him to realize for himself how ridiculous he was being.

Instead, he turned back to Macy. "We'll speak after I have my shower and coffee."

Silence filled the kitchen. Devon leaned against the counter, staring at Charity with a familiar expression. This was the way he'd looked at her that first night, when she'd been wearing Samantha's dress. Those beautiful speckled eyes of his had a way of cutting right through her.

She lifted her eyebrows. "Can I help you?"

He didn't so much as blink. It almost seemed like he was trying to solve a riddle.

"Staring is rude," she muttered. "And obnoxious."

"We need groceries," he said as Yasmine walked in and stalled at the edge of the kitchen.

"Fascinating observation, Watson. I shall make a note," Charity said, proud she'd kept the discomfort out of her tone. She wondered if Roger would give her an advance even though she was on a trial period. He had to know she needed it.

"I want to work out a deal," Devon said, ignoring her comment. "I hate cooking. I figured I'd buy groceries if you cooked."

That offer was too generous, especially now that she knew about the phone and computer. She was beyond grateful, but she was already at Code Red in the burden department. She didn't want to put him out any more, not when he was perfectly fine with takeout and his current setup. Roger would definitely be open to an advance. He had to be.

"With school, sometimes I don't have time to cook," she lied, trying to find a polite way out of this. "I don't know that I could hold up my end of the bargain."

"Just make sure we have freezer stuff, then," he replied.

"And then there's the issue that you might not like what I make."

"I'm not picky. I ate a mushroom the other day, remember?"

"Right…" She stirred the pot of oatmeal, which didn't need nearly as much attention as she was giving it. "But I would have no way to get all the groceries."

Devon shifted his stance, his patience drying up. "I'll drive you, obviously."

"It's just…" Charity lowered her voice. "It's not really fair if you help shop, buy, and don't even get all your meals cooked. It's kind of to my benefit, you know? I can't accept that."

Yasmine huffed in disdain. Charity's face flared hot with embarrassment.

Devon didn't notice. He leaned into her space, imposing upon her with his size and the power and energy coiled within him. She could feel his wolf begging to get out, flirting with her. Coaxing her.

"Stop making this complicated," he growled, a command that shocked into her body. He was trying to quell her defiance by dominating her, like the alpha he was.

Fire licked up Charity's middle. The unruly thing within her bloomed heat.

His nostrils flared and his eyes sparked. Electricity crackled between them. His eyes traveled her face before settling on her lips. She could almost feel them tingle.

"Will you do it or not?" His deep, rough voice coated her skin. "And stop trying to challenge me, Charity, or I'm going to answer."

Macy's face went slack. Then pale. Charity barely noticed.

That sweet inferno surged inside her, feeling the call of Devon's magic. The heat boiled higher, filling her. Excited tingles prickled her flesh. She felt wild. Reckless. Damn *good*.

His wolf might want out—but her unnamable power wanted out, too.

She grinned. "Sure. To the groceries."

He bristled, and his power flirted with her senses, strong and heady. His stare burned into her, his wolf scrabbling for a foothold again. The sensation fanned her fire to impossible heights. Her palm itched for a sword.

He shook his head slowly. "Knock it off, Charity. I'm serious."

Excitement swam in his gaze, negating his words. Something deep and hot pounded in her body, begging for fulfillment.

"See? This is why she should be removed," Yasmine said, cutting through the moment. "She doesn't follow orders."

"She's not pack. She has an excuse to defy his orders. You, on the other hand…" Macy muttered.

As if a ruler, bent too far, suddenly snapped, Devon whirled toward the hall, power rolling from him. He pinned Yasmine with the stare he'd just shown Charity. The scowl dripped off her face and she took a step back.

"You need to learn when to speak, and when to remain silent," he said.

"Yes, alpha."

He glanced at Macy. "I'll speak to you in a while."

"Yes, sir," Macy said, back to looking at her hands.

Charity itched her chest as the indescribable euphoria dwindled away. "Well. That was exciting." She turned back to the oatmeal, not able to keep the smile from her face.

"Have you lost your mind?" Macy asked quietly. "You don't challenge him. You just don't. One day he might lose control of his wolf. His wild side will be forced to subdue you."

A thrill arrested Charity. Her body tightened up, most notably in the feminine areas. She blinked at Macy.

"Exactly," Macy said, swiveling her head to watch Yasmine follow Devon out.

Macy had misinterpreted Charity's look, thankfully. Charity wasn't afraid of Devon trying to subdue her.

She was afraid of her excited reaction to the thought that he might try.

CHAPTER 28

L ATER THAT EVENING, Devon pulled into the supermarket parking lot with Charity fidgeting in the
seat next to him. They hadn't spoken since breakfast,
and frankly, he'd been glad for it. She was a distraction
he hadn't needed today. Two more people had been
reported missing, an elderly woman and a teen. Devon
had no illusions about what had happened—they were
food for a newbie that had lost control and drained its
blood source dry. A higher-level vamp had probably
disposed of the body. A newbie wouldn't have had the
presence of mind to do it.

The first newbie they'd taken out had been reported
missing, too. It was only a matter of time before the
others were reported missing. Devon needed to pin
down the rest of those creatures before anyone else paid
the price, and before the MLE office was contacted to
work with the Brink police on the missing persons.
Roger was counting on him.

Unfortunately, none of the surviving newbies had
stayed in the same place for long. Sam hadn't been
attending her classes and had only stopped by her house

to grab some clothes—Rod had checked it out after Devon and Charity's visit but come up dry. The same was true of the others. They weren't acting like normal freshly turned vamps. They seemed more organized. More elusive than even newbies under the guidance of middle-tier or lesser vamps.

Devon wondered if that elder didn't have a hand in things. Usually, an elder would lose interest after the changing party, but none of the typical rules applied lately. Vlad's obvious and extreme interest in Charity seemed to be leaking to all parts of this situation. Devon was no match for someone like Vlad. Roger barely was. Still, until Devon was sure of a connection, he had to keep working on this.

Not an ideal time for chores, but he had to keep his pack fed, and if they didn't get some groceries, Charity would be in a tough spot. He was burning through her food supplies, and Devon knew she didn't have two pennies to rub together to buy more.

"Are you coming in, or what?" Charity asked aggressively, her hand on the door handle. He knew for a fact that this deal skirted her line between pity and fair. It clearly galled her.

He couldn't help a small grin. This was actually a fair trade in his book—the woman could somehow make oatmeal taste good—but her frustration tickled him. It was penance for all the silent challenges she'd made, accompanied by boosts in her mouth-watering scent. They drove him crazy.

"Can I wait out here?" he replied in distaste.

"You aren't driving Miss Daisy. These choices concern you. I don't want to get something you hate."

"You won't. I eat everything."

"Let me rephrase. I don't want to get something you'll bitch about."

Devon sighed and climbed out of the SUV. They had a couple of hours until full night, and he'd chosen an affluent area of town that vampires usually didn't prowl for food. They'd be fine. He hated shopping almost as much as he hated cooking, but eating well was worth this hassle.

She stared down at her list as they entered the store. "Can you grab a cart?" she asked. She glanced back, probably to make sure he'd do it.

The light fell across her delicate features, highlighting her bizarre ethereal quality. She was lovely, extremely pleasing to behold. Everything about her worked in perfect harmony. She caught the eye and held it in such a way that he felt trapped and weightless. Jailed, but not sure if he was panicked or elated by that fact.

"Hello?" she said.

"Yeah, sure."

He met up with her in the most useless area in the store. He told her as much.

"What are you, five? Vegetables are good for you."

"Vitamins are easier to get down."

She smirked and dropped a bag of apples into the

cart. "You liked that portabella."

"Meh."

She chuckled softly. "Right, okay. Do you want to divide and conquer, or take it by aisles together?"

"I hate it here and I don't know where anything is."

A crease formed between her eyebrows. She nodded. "Uh-huh. Yes. I can see you missed my question."

"Together," he growled in mock irritation.

"Don't start with the attitude. It'll just piss me off."

"Oh well, that'll change my whole tune, surely."

She shook her head, another smile lighting up her face.

He cleared his throat, his behavior the night before eating at him. "Sorry about last night. I know it seemed like I was pissed, but I wasn't. Not really. Andy was right—it happens to a lot of people. I was just…you know…worried. It's my duty to look after you, and I did a shit job. I shouldn't have taken that out on you."

"It's fine. And thanks. For helping, I mean. You were justified in the way you acted and the things you said. I completely lost my head. But if it's all the same to you, I'd rather not talk about it anymore."

Understandable, especially for a guy who thought talking things out was the equivalent of a medieval torture device. He'd remember to send Macy her way, though. Women more readily talked to other women. At least, that was what Andy had said.

It was bad when Andy became your expert in dealing with women.

"Also, thanks. You know, for the phone and computer."

Devon gritted his teeth. He hadn't wanted to advertise that he'd been behind those gifts. It was essential to the pack that each of them had a phone, and if he wanted, he was sure he could submit an expense report for reimbursement. But the computer...

In the simplest terms, he was paying it forward. He knew what it was to feel lost, destitute. When he'd answered the *summons*, he hadn't had a dime, a place to stay, anything. If not for Roger and the pack, he would still have nothing. Sure, he'd worked his ass off to earn everything he had, but he couldn't deny he'd been given a boost. So far, no one had done that for Charity. The least Devon could do was give her the right tools to help her achieve success. She was too headstrong and proud to ask for them, so he'd tried to ensure she wouldn't have to.

He rolled his shoulders as Charity crossed something off her shopping list. She'd made one. On paper. Something that had oddly charmed him. "Don't mention it," he growled, hoping she caught on. *Literally, don't mention it again.*

"Should I get more portabellas?" she asked, turning to face him, closer than he'd realized. He caught a whiff of her scent, clean and feminine and not entirely human. Sweet and spicy.

The change of conversation and her sudden proximity froze him up. He started to salivate and stared into her red-brown eyes, sparkling with intelligence.

"What the hell is wrong with you today?" she demanded. "Has Yasmine got your head lost in the clouds or something?"

He grinned while trying to claw his way out of his weird stupor.

"Jealous?" he teased.

"Yeah, right. What've you got that a vibrator can't do better?"

He froze up for the second time, surprised and shocked and holy shit she'd just gotten him hard. That wasn't good.

"Ha!" She grinned at him. "Embarrassed you! Point to me."

He blinked a couple of times, and couldn't help the goofy grin as he looked into her beguiling gaze. An unexpected burst of butterflies filled his stomach.

Still a little flabbergasted, he followed her around the stands of produce, only coming out of his fog when he realized he was shopping with a poor kid who was used to a minimal budget.

"Whoa, wait a minute." He snatched the bag of carrots out of the air. "We're not here to get the cheapest stuff. I want good food. I want organic or whatever. If it costs more, fine."

She surveyed her list. "But…" She cocked her hip. "You don't have much in the house, and we're probably going to have to feed your pack mates."

"So?"

"*So*, it's going to cost a ton to get all this stuff if I don't bargain-hunt."

"No bargains. I want to taste the food."

"You'll taste it either—"

"No bargains," he interrupted, holding up his hand to forestall future arguments. "I'm not telling you what to cook, so don't you tell me what to buy."

Tossing up her hands, she said, "Fine, but don't blame me if you go bankrupt."

"Just so we're clear, I'm definitely going to blame you."

She nudged him with her elbow and smiled. Shaking her head, she headed toward the organic produce.

"I guarantee this will be cheaper than constantly eating out," he said, then stifled a groan when she reached for broccoli.

"True…"

"And easier on the waistline."

"Oh yeah, because you *desperately* need help with that."

"And lots of meat. I eat meat!" Devon flicked her ponytail, the gesture unlike him. But her playfulness was infectious. On that alone he could believe she was fae. When she let herself go, she sparkled with mirth and joy, something that spread like a virus, even to a guy who'd never had a lot of humor in his life.

She led the way to the next aisle, leaving the cart behind.

"Oh, I get to push the cart, then?" he asked, following.

"Obviously. Make yourself useful."

"We get paid at the end of the week, by the way," he said, his gaze snagging on her round, muscular butt. He ripped his eyes away. She'd kick his ass if she caught him looking. "Every other week after that."

"I meant to talk to you about rent." She threw a couple of items into the basket before scratching off more of her list. "We need to work out an amount for that and other bills. I don't know how much I can afford—"

"You're staying as my guest," he said, scanning the boxes on the shelves without really seeing them. "You won't be paying rent."

"I'm staying as your *burden*. Rent is the least I can do."

"Same difference, and no."

She dropped in some olives, and he nearly made her take them back out again. He wasn't a fan. Then again, he'd actually liked a giant mushroom made with old wine. He'd probably enjoy anything she put on a plate. She had a real gift for cooking. And fighting. And annoying the hell out of him. She was a woman of many talents.

"I've never understood that expression," she said. "It's a difference, which by definition means it *can't* be the same. If it were the same, it wouldn't have a difference."

"Leave the philosophical babble for school, please.

Speaking of, how did today go?"

She shrugged as she moved on, stopping in the next aisle to analyze canned soup. "The afternoon class was the one with Andy, so that was actually good. He insisted that I sit with him and his friends. It was nice to be included."

"The guys seem to like you, not to mention Macy."

She turned her face up to his, a smile of gratitude boosting her loveliness. "I've landed in hell, but I'm in the trenches with good people. I didn't have many friends growing up. It's a neat feeling."

"You've lived a pretty lonely life, huh?"

Cans clinked as they fell into the cart. "Yeah. I could never have friends over because of my dad. And when I tested into a preparatory high school, I was the stinky, dirty, poor kid. None of the parents wanted me in their kids' lives. I had one or two school friends, but it's hard to have a lasting thing if you don't see each other after school."

"And when you were older you had that guy John?"

A dreamy, lovesick look crossed her face. She smiled in a serene sort of way.

A way, Devon realized, no woman had ever smiled for him.

Confusion stole over him, followed by a weird clenching in his gut. He waited for the anger to rush in, covering the softness that was growing in his middle. Strangely, nothing came.

"He was my light in the darkness, yes," she said, the

memory softening her face into something absolutely exquisite. Her ethereal quality was practically a beacon. He couldn't understand why people didn't stop and stare at her in rapture.

Then again, now that he was noticing, everyone they passed smiled at her. They might not be magical, but they were affected all the same. He wondered if that was an element of being a fae, or if it was just her.

"We spent every moment we could together from sixteen to nineteen," she answered. "He was a year younger, even though we were in the same grade, so fifteen to eighteen for him. We were together most of high school."

"When did you lose your virginity?"

"Not real nosey, are you?" Charity muttered. "We'd been together a year. I was seventeen."

"And he's been your only one?"

"Yes, and now we can change the subject."

Devon smirked. "Aren't you going to ask me when I lost my virginity?"

"Nope."

"Why?"

"Because I don't care."

He flicked her ponytail again. "I thought women were supposed to be curious?"

"This one minds her own business because she doesn't want a certain beautiful blonde to set her bed on fire while she's sleeping in it."

Devon laughed, picking brownie mix off the shelf

and tossing it into the cart. Charity halted with a frown. She took the box out of the cart and handed it back.

"I like brownies," he said, clasping his hands behind his back so she couldn't take the mix.

She slapped it to his chest. "Yes, I know, but I don't make them from the box. I have the ingredients for brownies on the list."

"You do? Homemade?"

"No, elf-made…"

"I doubt elves eat brownies. But from scratch, I mean?"

"Oh yeah." She scratched her chin as a troubled expression crossed her face. "I forgot elves were real." She applied pressure to the box against his chest. "Yes, from scratch."

He took the box. "How'd you know I like brownies? Are you secretly pining after me? You are, aren't you? You're stalking me."

Charity huffed, but a smile tweaked her lips. "You eat them constantly—how could I *not* know? It's the only snack you have in the cupboards. I find crumbs all over the kitchen. Which is annoying, by the way. You're lucky it's your house, or I'd be all over you to clean up after yourself."

He huffed out a laugh, and warmth glowed in his chest. It was such a small thing, someone noticing his snacks, but he hadn't been looked after in a long time. His mother had lost interest in him as he approached puberty—most likely because she'd suspected what would happen—and his dad had worked all the time. His friends had been tough guys, and the girls in his life had been shallow conquests. No one had really valued him as anything other than a functioning pack mate or a good time. No one had been around to notice what made him tick. It was kind of nice.

A memory wiped the smile off his face.

When she'd curled up into his arms last night, afraid and looking for safety, a deep throb had pulsed through his body. He'd felt powerful in the role of protector, something the alpha in him craved. It was what had made his thoughts stray all day. It was why he might've been avoiding her, just a little.

This morning's unspoken challenge hadn't helped. In her fiery gaze, he'd seen the girl who had taken on an elder and lived to tell the tale. Her magic had pulsed within her, filling the room, singeing his skin. He'd longed to run at it. To take her hand and sprint into battle. This was what Roger had been talking about, Devon knew. Their magic belonged together. He felt it.

He liked it.

He didn't need the distraction of any of this.

"Uh-oh," she said, as though talking to herself. She dropped pasta into the cart, crossed it off her list, and wandered on. "Back to grumpy and brooding, I see. Well…" She sighed and stopped in front of the canned tomatoes. "The fun and easygoing Devon was nice while it lasted." She chewed on her plump lip. "I'm sorry about last night too, by the way."

He froze, half wondering if he'd been muttering out loud.

"I didn't mean to interfere with Yasmine," she finished, and wandered to the next aisle.

He released a breath he hadn't known he'd been holding.

"You didn't ruin anything. Just prolonged the inevitable. Don't worry. It won't last. They never do."

She shrugged, then reached up on tiptoes to the top shelf for her horrible oatmeal. Devon leaned over her to grab the package and toss it in the cart.

"I wasn't worried. I just don't want to step on your toes."

"Well I don't think you have to worry about girls hanging around." He poked a box of cereal, needing a little violence to go with this conversation. "I'm not that kinda guy."

"That's because you go after the wrong type of women."

"Is that right?"

"This must be one of those things that's obvious to everyone else but the person involved. You go after women who are very pretty." She held up her hand. "I'm not blaming you. If I were a guy and Yasmine came on to me, I'd definitely hit that. The girl is freaking hot. But I bet the girls you…date aren't as smart or interesting as you, so you get bored after the sex. Find a girl that has more to offer, one that's looking for more than a hot guy with a hot bod—or in Yasmine's case, an alpha with potential—and you might have more luck."

"I don't want more luck. I'm good with just the sex."

Charity shrugged. "There you go, then. You're all set. But please keep the noise low, because I can't sleep very well these days. *Oh*, I should get earplugs just in case."

Devon stopped in the middle of the aisle and blinked dazedly. "Did you just compliment me on my appearance and body, give me a verbal high five for being a slut, ask me to have quiet sex, and then opt for earplugs assuming I probably wouldn't? Did all that come out of your mouth within the space of thirty seconds?" He narrowed his eyes. "You are a girl, right? Because usually girls are not this cool."

"They are when they have no interest in getting you naked." Charity laughed. "I'm being logical. Like I said, pick different women, and you might enjoy a conversation once in a while."

After venturing up and down another few aisles, they approached the checkout line with a cart full of food.

"Where did you learn martial arts, by the way?" he asked as she stalled in choosing a line.

She looked down her list, her forehead showing worry lines. "I got lessons at a dojo close to my house growing up."

"How'd you pay for it?"

"I didn't. At first I hung around outside the windows and tried to see what was going on. When I got caught, the sensei said I could act as a janitor in exchange for standing in the back. I was about twelve. That was obviously a great deal for me, so I worked hard for them. It turned out I had—have, I guess—a certain affinity for martial arts, so when I started learning faster than anyone else, he paid more attention to me. Eventually he passed me around to others in the community so I could learn different styles." She lowered her list and looked over the heaping cart, her worry growing. "This is too much, Devon."

"You're supposed to be some sort of brutal magical warrior," Devon said without thinking, eyeing the contents of the cart.

She scoffed. "Fat chance." She chewed on that plump lip again, drawing his gaze. "This is going to cost a lot of money, Devon."

He gently moved her out of the way and pushed the cart forward. "Then you had better cook some good stuff."

As the items were slid across the scanner, Charity got increasingly agitated. "We shouldn't have gotten so much."

"It's not like this is an extravagant purchase. It's *food*, Chastity. It won't go to waste."

Her eyes got larger and larger to match the total. He pushed the cart through the lane and took up his position at the credit card machine, watching the bagger organize and bag the items. The total was at $156.78 and climbing rapidly.

Charity lightly grabbed his upper arm. Electricity sliced through his body, sucking his attention to her. She looked like she was on the verge of tears. The total was now at $231.23 and increasing with each slide of the checker's hands.

"What did we do…" she said, nearly whimpering.

"Chastity, it's *food*. I had nothing in the house. This is how much things cost. But don't worry, I haven't put in my club card yet. Savings are just around the corner—I saw you slipping in deals when you thought I wasn't looking."

"I'll help. I'll help pay for it. When I have money from payday, I'll help!"

He pulled her shoulders so she was facing him instead of the mounting total. He placed his palm on her soft cheek, feeling the electricity surge between them. She sucked in a surprised breath, probably from his proximity, or from his touch. Maybe both.

"It's fine," he said softly, ruffling her long lashes with his breath. "This is going to save me money in the long run, I promise. I have the money to buy food; I've just never had the motivation. You're my motivation. Relax."

Her shoulders dropped, just a bit. The knot between her eyebrows smoothed. Her eyes held his, and the intense look in them unexpectedly stiffened his cock for the second time.

He froze. She took a step back, making him drop his hands. Confusion stole through her gaze, something he was sure mirrored his own.

"You're a good alpha," she whispered. "You lead with conviction and confidence. You inspire trust."

"Well, if I can lead someone in the grocery store, I guess I have it made," he said to lighten the mood.

Her grin didn't reach her troubled eyes. She just nodded and moved behind him—without touching—to the bags being placed in the cart.

He turned to the credit card machine, needing to catch his breath. What in the hell was going on with him? Was this her magic somehow?

He tried to push it from his mind as he paid and followed her out of the store. Only a few cars loitered in the large parking lot, a couple up front, probably belonging to patrons, and a couple dotting the far spaces, waiting for employees, no doubt. It belatedly occurred to him that the store had been awfully quiet. It was strange for the early evening hours. Or maybe this supermarket wasn't heavily trafficked; he didn't know.

The early evening embraced them, cool but dry. Lights dotted the open space, showering fuzzy circles on the concrete, barely brighter than the sky.

"Sorry about that, in there," Devon said as he clicked his fob to unlock the SUV. He waited for the rear hatch to lift. "I was trying to get your mind off the total. I didn't mean to invade your space."

A bag crinkled as Charity took it from the cart. "It worked. For a moment, anyway. I wasn't kidding; you're a good alpha. You have this way about you…"

She shrugged. "You inspire trust, like I said in there. You inspire loyalty. I think you're going to go really far. As soon as you get rid of me, anyway."

He laughed as he moved the bags into the car. "My goodness. All these compliments? I scarcely know who I'm talking to."

She joined him in laughter, helping him unload. "Don't get used to it. As soon as I get a good night's sleep, I'll be as surly as ever. I'll get you fighting yet."

He nearly joked about her never getting a good night's sleep, but the memory of her curled up against his body cut the words from his mouth.

He organized the bags in the back of the SUV so nothing would fall over. As he was finishing up, he felt her hand on his arm.

"Devon…"

The smell hit him like a Mack truck. He'd been so distracted by Charity that he hadn't paid attention to their surroundings. It was still early evening, so he'd thought it too early for the vampires to be out. Clearly he'd failed on two counts.

He whirled, keys in hand. Three vamps stood twenty feet away, and he recognized one of them immediately.

Vlad. The most ruthless and cunning elder that haunted the Brink.

He'd come to collect his prize, Charity, and Devon had no backup.

CHAPTER 29

"**I** AM GOING to pass you my keys," Devon whispered, his face inches from Charity's. She must've been correct in her assumption that vampires had excellent hearing.

And then it was confirmed when her new BFF said, "Running is foolish, little puppy. She is the one I want, not you. Running might get her accidentally harmed, and neither of us wants that, do we?"

Cold metal spread across her skin as Devon lowered the keys into her shaking palm. His touch lingered, warm in contrast, before he nudged her behind him.

"Since when do you care about humans?" Raw power laced Devon's words. If he was at all afraid, he didn't show it.

The elder vampire spread his hands in front of him. "I care nothing for humans. But alas, she is not a mere human. I must admit, I have not met her equal in so long, I forgot what her kind smelled like. How they appeared. Like a bonfire among matchsticks; *exquisite*. Truly a work of art, or does not your kind see beauty in the most flawless of magical beings, little wolf pup? I would bet not. You are too busy licking each other's fur and praising your outstanding *duty*."

"I'm going to go out on a limb here and assume you're talking about our mission to protect humans from your kind?" Devon backed up, making her step with him. When she braced a hand on the center of his back, using his movements as unspoken direction, he reached behind and gave her a light shove.

Toward the driver's side of the SUV.

He wanted her to get the motor running while he stalled.

"You are new to the employ of the elves, relatively speaking. You do not have hundreds of years of experience watching their continual decay. As such, I do not fault you for your shortsightedness. Without order, there would be chaos, aren't I correct? Your cause appears noble, I suppose, to the dimwitted. Which shifters largely are, of course. I do, however, fault you for destroying my children. Our numbers have fallen. We cannot wage war in the Realm with so paltry an army. Roger is seeing to his own destruction. But then, I already touched on the dimwitted nature of your race. You need to be led. Blindly, it seems. Luckily, I am an excellent commander."

"You're outgunned," Devon replied with smug assurance. "In this world, and the Realm. You'll have to stick to commanding your dwindling army."

A silky laugh drifted through the air. Charity shivered.

"You forget that I am an excellent negotiator and world-class manipulator," the vampire said. "My allies simply need incentive, and I am providing that. Eventually, I shall provide the Golden Egg to a power capable of rivaling the elves. Children are a great lure, are they not?"

"Right, well, this is fun and all, but what do you want? My ice cream is melting."

"Simple. I want the young woman who is currently trying to slip off toward the vehicle door. Stealth will be the first thing I teach her."

A zing of fear shot through Charity. She froze, halfway to the door. Yes, obviously she'd realized he'd see her slipping away, but still, she had hoped...

"As I recall, she already turned you down." Devon leaned forward with false intimacy. "That's what it means when a girl shoots you."

"You have no idea what you have in her, do you, little puppy?" The vampire's voice dropped an octave, hinting at a wild savagery. Goosebumps joined her uncomfortable shivers. "What lost member of the Royal Arcana you have stumbled upon. I can only say how ardently pleased I am that such a treasure was entrusted to someone so incompetent. More's the pity for your pack of mongrels. Alas—"

One of the side vampires rushed forward. Green magic was already swirling around Devon. Fur and teeth boiled before a huge black wolf wearing the remnants of Devon's clothing lunged to meet the attack.

The vampire hissed as Devon caught it by the throat. He raked the creature's chest with his claws before dragging it to the ground and shaking its head. A fierce *crack* rent the night.

One down.

Short of breath and heart pounding, Charity lurched into action. Two fast steps and she was at the door, yanking it open. Before she could scramble in, the door slammed shut, a manicured hand flat on the surface.

"Now, now," her BFF said, as calm as a spring day. His lips curled in a delighted smile. "Though I do love your spunk." He lowered until his eyes were directly aligned with hers, trying to catch her gaze.

No way! She would never fall for that again!

Anger surged through her, Donnie's memory filling her with pain that boiled into power. The air condensed around her and then exploded outward silently. Her magic flayed his body, scraping some skin off his face. He grimaced, fighting to stand his ground, trying to pit his power against hers.

Clearly he knew more of her magic than she did, including how to withstand it. *Crap!*

Focusing on that heat in her middle, she pushed her palm out. Power exploded from her like a hurricane, this concussion of air greater than the last. He staggered back in jerky movements, losing the fight.

Not wasting any time, she ripped open the door, launched herself in, and slammed the door behind her.

A moment later, he was at the window, looking in. Healing while he did so. He gave her a dazzling smile, thankfully ruined by the bloody cheek. "So much power, but the majority not yet realized. You are truly a diamond in the rough. Darius hasn't found the only treasure in the Brink, it seems."

She didn't know who Darius was, or what this psycho was talking about, but she was glad he'd chosen this moment to ramble on.

She slapped the lock button and jammed the push-button ignition, hoping to hell the vampire didn't break the glass and haul her out before she could get the SUV in action.

A canine squeal/yelp pierced Charity's heart, intense suffering in the sound. A fierce growl came a moment later, Devon hurt but still in the fight.

The vehicle roared to life as she craned her neck to see.

Come on, Devon, let's go!

He was fighting for his life against a vampire in its swampy monster form, so quick that its movements were lost. The thing swiped down, raking its black claws across a blood-soaked, furry shoulder. Devon yelped and turned, ripping a chunk of flesh out of the vampire's leg. The vampire shrieked then slashed. Devon dodged, limping badly. She just barely caught his glance at the car before he redoubled his efforts, lunging, trying to force the vampire further away.

A sick realization turned Charity's stomach. Devon

wasn't trying to get clear and get to the vehicle—he was sacrificing himself to give her more time. He was offering himself as a distraction so she could get away.

He must've known they would kill him for his efforts. He was the enemy even if he wasn't the target—he hadn't a hope of making it through this. Not without her.

Determination and rage welled up.

"No way, Devon. That is not how a team survives. We're getting out of here together."

She glanced to the side for a status update on her BFF. His face filled the window, completely healed and annoyingly perfect. His eyes shocked into her, dark and intense. "Such courage," he said, his words muffled through the window. "You are inexperienced and frightened, but are charging into battle anyway. You are everything your kind should be."

"And you are too fucking weird." She pushed the button to release the parking brake. She hadn't driven a car in a few years, and that one had been John's dilapidated old Honda, but the mechanics had to be similar. Like riding a bike.

The door lock clicked.

Panic bled through her. "What the—"

A manicured hand reached for the door handle.

"Crap—forgot about that!" She slammed her foot against the pedal.

Vlad's muscles went taut, pulling at the door.

She jabbed the button to re-engage the locks, then

focused with that lightning in her chest.

Nothing happened.

She could feel the vampire's magic tingle against her skin. It was like nothing she'd ever felt before.

Another yelp of pain pierced the night.

"No!" She would not lose anyone else to these creatures. She would not lose Devon.

The car lurched aggressively, tires squealing against pavement.

"Whooooaaa shiiit!" This machine had *way* more power than that old Honda.

She yanked the steering wheel to the right, scraping a parked car that had been five spaces away. The smiling face appeared in her window again, the vampire running to keep pace with the SUV.

"Why are you so freaking weird?" she yelled, and yanked the steering wheel again, foot heavy on the gas. The vehicle rocked and then bumped wildly over a cement parking block. "Shiii—Way different. This is way different!" The SUV careened as she tried to straighten it out.

Her BFF appeared in front of the vehicle like a ghost, the lights highlighting his flawless skin. Beyond him fought Devon, liquid glistening within his black coat as he limped then lunged for an incredibly fast vampire. He was slowing rapidly, nearly out of energy.

She slammed on the gas with determination, the Range Rover surging forward like a demon. Her BFF jumped gracefully, his two boots landing with a dull thunk on the hood. She tore the wheel to the right. The creature windmilled but stayed on.

"How the hell…" She ripped the wheel back the other way and slammed on the brakes. The SUV bumped over another cement parking block. The vampire went flying.

"Ha," she yelled. "Try to anticipate me and you get thrown, sucker!"

She ripped the vehicle around and headed straight for Devon. At the last moment, she stomped on the brakes, making the SUV skid to a stop. Impatiently glancing out the passenger side window, she stupidly realized that wolves couldn't open doors.

She threw herself across the seats and opened the door. As Devon leapt into the seat, she straightened up to an enlarging fist within the frame of her window.

She screamed. Shatterproof glass fragments rained down on her as a delicate hand reached through and gripped her arm.

Pain bled into her—nothing delicate about that grip. He would drag her out, and she had no hope of fighting him. The other vamp, bitten to hell but heart and neck still intact, reached for Devon through his open door with his one remaining arm. They were outgunned. The vampires had the advantage.

CHAPTER 30

S HE SCREAMED AGAIN. Electricity surged through her middle as she threw up her hand to ward away her BFF.

Heat and light, an exact mimic of noon, rained down. It shocked into the exposed skin of their attackers. The electric bug zapper noise drowned out the sizzle of vampire skin. Both vamps howled, throwing their hands up to try to protect their faces. As Charity's energy dwindled quickly, she smashed her foot on the gas and the SUV lurched forward. Long screeches sounded as claws tore up the sides of the vehicle.

The sun blinked off like a halogen light, making the car lights seem dim and useless.

"Stay above forty and we're fine," Devon said, his voice weak and hoarse. He was back in human form. Blood oozed from gashes all over his body, a couple of them deep and gruesome. He caught his swinging door in a crimson-covered hand and barely had the strength to pull it closed.

"Are you okay?" she asked, reaching out to touch his shoulder.

He caught her hand and lowered it toward the seat, but he didn't let go. He was shaking just as much as she was. "I will be. Shifters heal fast. I won't bleed out."

"Oh God, Devon, I'm so—" She'd turned the wheel too far. The SUV swerved wildly, nearly dropping them into a ditch. "Crap. This thing is really sensitive. I'm so sorry."

"Keep us above forty, and get us home. We'll be safe as soon as we get past the ward."

"They can run that fast?" She glanced in the rear-view mirror, but no sprinting shapes took up the middle of the road behind them. If the vampires were chasing them, they were taking a different path. "Maybe we should go into the Realm?"

"The fastest of them can run that fast, and I have a feeling your admirer qualifies. Head home. I don't know that my body would survive the crossing just yet." He coughed, shaking with each hacking wheeze of breath. Blood pooled under his leg. Tears obscured Charity's eyes until she could blink them away.

"I need to pass out for a while. The ward will keep out two vamps, no matter how old."

Terror squeezed her heart. His voice was so weak, his body bowed over, as if completely sapped of strength and vitality. "Why do you have to pass out? You can't heal awake?"

"We can, it just takes longer. If I shut down my body for everything but healing, all my energy will go to stitching things back together from the inside out. Take a left here." He coughed again, huge, full-body spasms that had him dipping forward painfully.

"Oh God, Devon… Oh God." Charity was going fifty and dared not go any faster. If she took a corner too fast and hit a tree, those vamps would find them, and then she and Devon would be screwed.

"Almost there. You're doing fine."

"Get my phone. Call…someone. Andy or Dillon or even Yasmine—we should call someone! Do you know Roger's number? Maybe we should call him."

Devon coughed again, his head lolling. "I just need to pass out."

"Okay. Almost…*here*. We're here!"

She skidded to a stop in the driveway, then jumped out and dashed around the hood before pulling at his door. What she saw froze her to the bones.

The overhead light showered Devon's slumped body. It was much worse than she'd thought, and she had thought it was bad. Scores of jagged parallel lines marred his skin. Deep red blood, almost black, dribbled down his back or across his hip, she couldn't tell which, indicating a wide and deep wound that would have a normal human bleeding out quickly. More blood smeared across his stomach, legs, and arms. Very little of his skin was clear, and that was covered in pavement rash and grime.

"Please tell me all that blood isn't yours," Charity said, reaching in for him.

"It's not all mine. I rocked that first vamp. Did you

see it?" His lips quirked up into a painful grin. He coughed and then winced as he spasmed.

"Okay. It's okay. Let's get you inside." She gingerly touched his arm, trying to find a spot to grab with no blood. Slim pickings. "Can you walk?"

"Yeah. Help?"

He basically fell out of the SUV, his larger body leaning heavily on hers. Grunting, she maneuvered her shoulder under his heavy arm and draped him across her body. They hobbled to the front door. Warm wetness soaked into her clothes from his wounds.

"Your bedroom or the couch?" she asked, one arm around his back, the other on his six-pack so he didn't tip forward.

"Bed," he wheezed.

They staggered down the hall, a spot of blood smearing the wall where his shoulder bumped. They barged into his room and hovered near the side of his bed.

"Stand here for a minute and I'll go get...uh, some rags? Do you have rags?"

Devon half climbed, half fell onto his bed. His limbs sprawled out. Red marred the white sheets. His eyes fluttered closed.

"Thanks for coming back for me," he whispered in a rough voice thick with pain.

"Of course I did." She looked over his body. There was so much bleeding! She knew werewolves healed unnaturally fast, had seen evidence of it, but could he really come back from *this*? "I need to clean you up. I have to clean you up."

He didn't answer, and for one heart-stopping moment, she thought he'd died. But his chest rose, then fell, in the rhythmic breathing of deep sleep.

"That's good. Sleep is good." The house listened silently to her words. Branches danced in the moonlight outside the window.

"Why did we spend so long shopping?" Her chest constricted. Hopefully, the vamps didn't know where Devon lived, and if they did, which they probably did, they couldn't get through the ward.

No more time to spare on those thoughts, she dashed to the window and lowered the blinds—his room actually had some. Then she rushed to the bathroom and grabbed a towel. If he wasn't worried about the sheets, he probably wouldn't care if a towel was ruined. Searching through the cabinets, she found a first-aid kit and a stack of large white bandages. He was prepared. Thank God.

Back by his side, she got busy. First she cleaned him off, gently wiping away all the blood so she could get a good look at the damage. Next she bandaged up the larger lacerations, trying to stop the bleeding. She fervently hoped that whatever healing abilities shifters possessed would counteract the need for stitches.

Having seen to his immediate needs, she covered him up with a clean blanket and grabbed his gun from the open safe in his closet—he hadn't wanted to give her his code. She would be damned if all the money Devon had spent would go to waste in the back of the SUV. Not to mention that the house wouldn't save her if the vamps got through the ward protecting the property. That trick with locks was practical for breaking and entering.

She tiptoed out of the house. Although being quiet didn't matter, the action seemed to fit. The still night waited for her, crickets singing from within the folds of darkness. The SUV, scraped and dented, sat in the driveway, alone and forgotten.

No faces or shapes waited at the property line. At least, not yet. But then, her BFF and his buddies had known Charity and Devon would be at that store. No doubt they also knew it would be senseless to hang around outside a warded property.

Still, just in case, she'd decided not to call the rest of the pack. If the vamps were out there, watching and waiting, anyone trying to get in would probably be ambushed. She didn't want to endanger them needless-ly. Devon said he wouldn't bleed out. She had to trust that.

Bag by bag, she brought the groceries into the house and put them away. That done, she trudged back in to check on him, exhaustion dragging down her eyelids. She sucked in a breath of surprise to find the smaller scrapes nearly gone!

Crazy. She wished she healed that fast.

She brushed a strand of hair away from his handsome face and then traced her fingers down his cheek. Sighing, she looked in the direction of her room. She could barely see the sliding glass through the open door. Foliage bowed and waved, no more distinct than plays of shadow in the moonlight. The house sighed around her, quiet and empty except for this room.

Making a decision, she tiptoed to her room and quickly changed into some briefs and a tank top. She returned to his room, put his gun on the nightstand, and lay on the bed. Pulling the blanket under her as protection from the blood-soaked sheets, she slid as close to Devon as she could. His warmth basked her side and his even breathing calmed her anxiety. He'd be okay.

Unable to help herself, she rolled and placed her palm on his forearm, craving the solidity of touch. A tear slid down her cheek. This man would've given his life to protect her. He hadn't expected her to come back for him—he'd *thanked* her, for criminy's sake! It blew her mind. He was so closed off most of the time—so angry whenever he had to feel any sort of emotion—but then he went and did something so selfless.

No one could argue that this man was anything less than exceptional.

Snuggling closer, until their bodies were almost touching, she rubbed his skin with her thumb. She was so lucky he'd been assigned to babysit her. Without him, she would've suffered a horrible fate. Gone mad, or killed by Donnie, or kidnapped and turned into a pampered pet. Dealing with Devon's moods was a small price to pay for her sanity, life, and freedom.

But the fight wasn't over. Clearly the old vampire wanted her something fierce, and now he knew the gamut of what she was capable of. He'd come after her again, and this time he'd surely be better prepared.

So would she.

CHAPTER 31

"**S**IR, WE HAVE a situation."

Roger finished the bench press, his muscles straining under the weight. His beta, Alder, stood in the doorway of the workout room, staring at Roger with the cool eyes of a predator. The white scar cutting from his sharp cheekbone to his neck stood white in his otherwise tanned face.

"What's up?" Roger asked, sitting up and wiping off the rivulets of sweat running down his neck.

"Vampires are gathering near the portals surrounding Santa Cruz. It's rumored the demons are poised to join them. No one has been stopped from entering or exiting yet, but I don't see why they'd station themselves in growing numbers if they didn't plan on blocking the portals in the future."

"Which side are they gathering on—the Brink side?"

"Yes, sir."

Roger rested his forearms on his thighs in consternation. "That order would have to come from someone high up in the vampire hierarchy. What've you heard?"

"I'm looking into it, sir." Alder paused, then added,

"There've been rumors of an Arcana."

Chills ran up Roger's spine. "An Arcana? Have the warrior fae emerged from the Flush?"

Alder shook his head slowly. "Not that we know of. We haven't seen or heard of any movement. I'm also getting reports of a huge release of magic last night. The human papers are calling it a burst transformer. Reports say the sky lit up in the parking lot of a grocery store. It looked like an explosion, but all anyone heard was magnetic buzzing."

Roger held very still. He'd already identified Charity as a *custodes*, based on her ability to summon light and turn a touch into an explosion, but he hadn't seen anything that might mimic a transformer bursting. He hadn't thought her royalty.

But he'd seen her before she'd taken a trip to the Realm. Before she'd spent time with other magical people to coax her out of her shell. Maybe her magic was just waking up, having been mostly dormant in the Brink, unused.

And if that was the case…

Roger stood in a rush and threw down his towel. "Find out everything you can about these rumors." He brushed by Alder and into his main office. "Put someone on Devon's crew. I don't want Devon to know he's being watched—he'll think I don't trust him, and that might affect his judgment—but I want help close, just in case. Vlad knows something, and I want to know what."

"Should we extract the girl?"

"No. If Vlad is sectioning off the Realm, it means he doesn't want to involve the elves. I agree with him. Thankfully, we have more power in the Brink. We don't need to move around in the shadows. It's a stronger play for us to protect her there, not to mention it is her home. Besides…" Roger hesitated in grabbing his computer. "I'm planning to take her to the Flush to get training, but not before she has a strong reason to come back out. She took to Devon's pack easily, and from Devon's reports, she has settled in with them well. I want them to build a sense of family. I'm hoping their connection and her schooling will be a strong enough reason to draw her back out."

"You hope to tie her romantically with Devon?"

Roger chuckled darkly. "If wishes were horses, beggars would ride. No, I wouldn't go so far as that. He shows exceptional promise and ambition—he'll be great someday, I have no doubt—but he's emotionally closed off. I doubt even a beauty like Charity could break through that." Roger headed for the door. He wanted to get to the Brink to check out the situation for himself. "Organize those men. I don't want anything to happen to Charity. If we need to extract her, we'll probably have to fight our way through. And then hide her. That'll take manpower. We're playing chess with a master—we need to up our game."

"Yes, sir. Should I tell Steve to call in his sisters?"

Steve could try the patience of a saint and didn't like being ordered around. Still, get Steve agitated, and step back. The shifter was fierce and extremely competent. Put him with his five lioness sisters, and their pride could tear through the center of the world.

An ideal crew—minus the family squabbles, their unwillingness to work with anyone but each other, the sisters' habit of picking on their baby brother, and the fact that three of the five sisters had just had babies. That family of cats was a nightmare.

"Are they back in commission?" Roger asked, debating. To protect Charity, he'd put up with almost anything.

"Yes, sir. All five were-lionesses expressed their interest in getting back to work. Steve won't be pleased, but…"

"Steve will do what he's told." Hopefully. Steve had gone rogue more than once. What a pain. "Dangle the bait of a pretty warrior fae. He's always had a fascination with the fae. He'll take the job just to check it out. Have Cole ready, too. We might need a were-yeti to cut a path to the portal."

"Yes, sir."

Roger rubbed his temples as Alder left the room. He needed to figure out that girl's lineage, but he also needed the last three newbies taken out. There'd already been too many deaths so far, and if the young vamps were left unchecked, there'd be more. Add to that two new demon sightings reported from a neighboring pack, the vampires' efforts to close off Santa Cruz, the elves' interest in Charity, and the were-cats he was about to unleash, and Roger was in the midst of a high-stakes clusterfuck.

AS THE PALE light of dawn filtered in through the bedroom window, Devon slowly came to consciousness. A soft, warm body pressed against his side, her smell delicate and feminine. Wisps of hair tickled him pleasantly and her hot breath soaked into his neck.

He pulled back the blanket and glanced down at his body. Several bandages were taped to his skin, most soaked through with blood. Peeling one of the larger ones to the side, he revealed a puckered, angry wound, still healing. The bleeding had stopped, though, and only a dull throb remained. The blood smeared across his body from last night was gone. Charity had cleaned him and then patched him up.

He let his head fall to the side until his cheek rested against her forehead.

She'd come back for him. He'd never been so glad to see anyone in all his life. The kicker was that he'd given her no reason for loyalty. A guy couldn't yell at someone constantly, poke fun at her, almost belittle her, and expect her to confront death for him. Yet she had.

Then she'd helped him into the house, tucked him into bed, and fixed him up.

Warmth glowed in his chest. He didn't deserve it, but he'd take it.

He breathed in deeply, savoring her scent, stronger now than he could remember. Tantalizing.

Remembering the look of fierce determination on her face as she'd ushered him into the SUV last night, he smiled and rubbed her smooth arm. The force of her magic had taken his breath away. When he'd seen that flickering light in the sky, raining down pain on Vlad and his minion, Devon had thought he was hallucinating. But there was no denying the sound of their skin sizzling, or the way they'd hissed and shrunk away. She'd magically created enough sunlight to affect an elder. It was…

He shook his head against the pillow and trailed his fingertips across her jaw.

Incredible. There was no other word to describe it. She'd saved their lives.

She sighed softly and shifted with a feminine mew, pressing more firmly to his side. Her leg swung up, her soft thigh covering his so she could hook her calf and foot between his legs. She slid her hand up his stomach to his chest, rubbing his pec before continuing the journey north. She opened her eyes for a moment, connecting with his before closing them again with a sleepy smile. She let her hand flatten on the base of his jaw and angled her lips up to his. Her eyes fluttered.

Without thinking, he dipped his lips to hers, connecting softly. His stomach filled with surprising lightness, rolling and twisting and exploding into a swarm of butterflies. He opened his mouth, feeling her lips respond. He darted his tongue in, sampling. He was instantly rewarded with a complex taste more pleasing than her smell. Sweetness curled around his senses, transfixing him.

He applied more pressure, his tongue now indulgent and insistent. Suddenly, he *needed* her. He couldn't explain it, or even understand it, but a part of him needed to merge his body with hers. It was as if he was half finished, and only she could round him out.

But he wasn't ready to lose this longing for her. This feeling was deep and primal. These urges and desires burrowed down to his roots, and he liked the feel of them. He liked the depth. He liked the...completeness. He wasn't ready to sex that away.

He backed off, smiling when she clung to him. He eased her back down, wincing as he did so. Lord, his body hurt. That was another reason this was a bad idea. She'd probably think he sucked in bed because he could barely move.

As he finished getting comfortable, she shifted as well, staying entwined with him but dropping her head to his chest. She took a deep, satisfied breath. He matched it as he slid his arm around her, hugging her close. He let her proximity and comfort soak into him as he drifted back to sleep.

One thing was infinitely clear: she was his. She belonged in his pack. He would not let any harm come to her. He'd die before that vamp took her.

CHAPTER 32

THE BREAKFAST POTATOES were starting to turn golden brown when Charity caught movement at the edge of the kitchen. Devon lumbered in, nowhere near his usual graceful self. With a wince, he lowered himself into a chair.

"How do you feel?" she asked, glancing at his defined chest. The vivid memory of their sleepy kiss rolled around her brain. It had felt sinfully good. Almost too good. She remembered running her hand up his body, feeling a strange sort of buzz, not to mention his hardness on her thigh as she snuggled closer.

Heat pulsed low, this time not her magic.

She cleared her throat. There was no place in her life, or his, for that sort of nonsense.

"Sore, but good." He rubbed his eyes and yawned.

"I can't believe how fast you heal."

He eyed the steaming pans on the stove. "Thanks again. For coming back for me."

"What was I supposed to do, leave you with those things? They were fast!"

Devon snorted. "Understatement. Did you make

coffee?"

"Don't drink it. Didn't think to make it."

Devon groaned and dropped his head onto his forearms. "That sucks."

Charity leaned across the counter and slid open a window so the steam could get out. When she turned back to her cooking, Devon said, "We need to talk about your class tonight."

She'd suspected this conversation was coming. Normally, she'd agree that only a fool would go to a late class after the events of the previous night. Unfortunately, she had a very important test tonight, and it was too late to make other plans. She couldn't afford to lose her scholarship. Some things were worth the risk, although she doubted Devon would agree.

So she sidetracked him.

"You aren't going to get up and make yourself coffee?" She braced her spatula hand on her hip like a disgruntled housewife talking to a lazy child.

"Please don't badger me right now. I'm not up for it."

Charity rolled her eyes, turned a burner to low, and headed to the coffee pot. If he didn't have his coffee he'd be ten times grumpier, and given how grumpy he was on a good day, the difference could be dramatic.

"I don't think you should go tonight," he said, his head still on his arms.

"I have to. I have a test that counts for a third of my grade."

"Get him to give it to you in his office."

"It's too late for that. He has strict rules about test taking. The only way he'd let me out of it is if I were unconscious in the hospital."

"No problem. As soon as I get some food, I'll knock you out. We're all set."

She huffed out a laugh and grabbed two plates from the cupboard. He must be feeling really sore and tired to be so nonchalant about the situation.

"But seriously," he said, his head back on his arms. "We can figure out a way around it. I'm sure Roger would intervene."

"Roger is very important to your world." Charity dished up two plates. "He doesn't have any clout with the school. He doesn't even have a real job, as far as the normal world is concerned."

"Right, yeah," he said, pushing back against the chair. He winced and scratched a puckered wound on his ribs.

"Do shifters scar?" She set his plate in front of him.

"Charity, this looks delicious." She handed him some flatware. "Not unless the wound is really bad, no. After we get the *summons*, that is. Any scars we get before that are for life."

"Were your wounds bad enough?"

He cut through an egg, paused as the yolk crawled into the potatoes, and looked down at his chest. A small smile graced his lips. "Do you like your men with scars? Or do you prefer them without?"

Her face flamed, and she turned to get them some napkins. "That's not why I asked."

Silence filled the kitchen, and she finally chanced a look at him as she sat down. His smile had enlarged, but that wasn't what captured her attention. He was staring at her in that way of his, analyzing her. Trying to suss her out as if she were a riddle.

"Seriously, staring is rude. How many times do I need to tell you?" she muttered, bending to her meal.

"No, Chastity, they won't scar." Heat filled his voice and her body, and she wondered if he was remembering her stroking his bare chest. She certainly was. She couldn't stop. It was starting to be distracting.

"Oh good, with the nicknames again." She stabbed a potato. His low, dark laugh didn't help her mood.

He sobered quickly, and she wondered if he'd ever had a carefree moment in his life. She wondered if he ever would.

"Joking aside, you can't go tonight. It's too dangerous."

"Look, Devon, I respect your opinion, I really do. And were it any other situation, I'd completely agree with you. But I have to go to this class tonight. I have to."

"We need to get you to the Realm, Charity," he said.

"Vamps are magic. They can get into the Realm, too. They could just as easily snatch me there."

He shook his head, mouth full. After he swallowed, he said, "They wouldn't dare openly flout the laws of the

Realm. The elves would go crazy. The last thing any race wants is to put the elves on a war path to genocide. I've heard stories. They aren't pretty."

"Okay, well…" Charity finished off her eggs. "A vampire isn't going to kidnap or kill me in front of a whole school. They try to stick to the shadows, right? They need to keep their real identities hidden, like you do."

"*Usually* they stick to the shadows, but Vlad came for you in the open last night. Barely after sundown. Elders create the rules as they go, doing whatever suits them best."

"But that parking lot was empty. I didn't see a single person the whole time we were dealing with them. Which seems strange, now that I think about it…"

A line formed between Devon's brows. Clearly her BFF—Vlad—had cleared the area somehow.

"Maybe he had a mage working for him," Devon mumbled, back to his breakfast.

"Great. So if the classroom empties out, I'll leave." Charity shrugged, hating that she had to fight Devon to put herself in danger. If it weren't for that damn test—

Devon issued a hard sigh. "We'll table this for now. I'll ask Roger and see what he says. But don't worry about that scholarship. Roger knows the situation. He won't jeopardize your future. The important thing is making sure you *have* a future." He held her stare for a long time, worry creating small lines around his beautiful eyes. Finally, he lowered his gaze to his plate. "I hope you made a bunch of food. I'm famished."

LATER THAT NIGHT, Charity walked up the path next to Devon. Cars and students littered the road and walkways behind them, many going home for the night and some headed to their last class.

Macy and Yasmine followed closely behind, the girls barely looking at each other, let alone talking. Apparently, whatever Macy had told Devon about the kill they'd made the other night had created more dissent between the girls. Charity got the idea that it had something to do with Yasmine failing to follow orders. Being that it had nothing to do with Charity, she didn't ask any questions. She had enough on her plate.

"I still don't think we should be doing this," Devon said in a low voice. He was mostly healed up and back to his old self—moody and brooding. "This is stupid."

"Roger agreed with me," Charity said, keeping her head down. "You heard him. He wants us to act as normal as possible while he gets people in position. That means you're going to class, too. If my BFF isn't ready with whatever he's planning, then it would be stupid to spook him into acting."

Devon shook his head, veering closer. "I don't agree with him on this point."

"Me neither," Macy murmured behind them.

Their group fell into silence. Whether they agreed or not, it was happening.

Ocean and sea salt hung heavy in the air as they

wove through the buildings. Wind pushed its way through the branches all around them. Usually, she appreciated the beauty of the wooded campus, but now the very trees she'd admired could be concealing nightmares. The edge of Devon's hand brushed against hers as they walked, sparking electricity. She held her breath, almost wondering if he would turn the action into a handhold, wondering what was happening to her that she'd let him.

Finally, however, they reached the lecture hall. He stopped near the door and faced her, waiting for her to meet his eyes.

"You will sit in the front, near the door," he instructed her. "You will be normal—well, your version of normal. When the class is over, you will wait until I text, and then you will meet me at the door. You will not be a hero."

Charity rolled her eyes.

"Understood?"

"Yes."

His gaze intensified. He brought up his arms, as though to hug her close, but at the last moment his eyes flicked to the others waiting to the side. He closed his fingers around her upper arms instead. "I'll see you soon, okay? Be safe."

He about-faced and stalked away, with Yasmine hurrying to catch up.

"Well, that was weird," Macy said as she watched the pair. "What's gotten into him? Since when is he touchy-feely?"

"I think he's being sentimental about almost dying to save me," Charity said.

Macy shook her head. "I don't think he's got a sentimental bone in his body. Or a romantic one. Devon's more of a hit-it-and-quit-it kinda guy."

"Where has Dillon been, by the way?" Andy, Rod, and the girls had stopped in after breakfast to scoop up leftovers and rehash the events of the night before. Dillon had never shown, though, which Charity had thought a little odd, considering it was a pack affair.

Macy shifted uncomfortably.

"Don't tell me he's staying away because of Yasmine," Charity said, eyeing the students entering the lecture hall. Whatever Vlad had done the night before to clear people away was not happening now. She took comfort in that fact. Still, she wasn't in any hurry to go in. Out here, she could still run and call for help. In there, she'd be trapped.

Macy's face reddened. "I told him he didn't have to. I mean, yes, I have a jealousy problem when my boyfriend won't stop ogling another woman—"

"Not to mention that it's not cool to ogle women in general."

"Right. Yes! Why didn't I think of that?" She frowned down at her shoes. "Anyway, he keeps finding other things to do when Yasmine is going to be around. Despite being a shifter, he's strangely non-confrontational."

Charity laughed. "I think he's against choosing sides between you and another pack member."

"Well, yes, I guess there is that." Macy pulled her long hair into a ponytail. "If only she were nice. I mean, look at you. You're gorgeous, and it isn't a problem. She just…" Macy shook her head, watching the dwindling flow of students into the lecture hall. It was almost time. "She rubs me the wrong way, but she's pack. I need to get over it."

After a moment of silence, Charity took a deep breath. "All right, I have to head in. I'll text as soon as I can."

After a welcomed hug from Macy, Charity headed for the door, dread washing through her middle as memories from last night swirled through her thoughts.

She hoped to hell nothing nasty waited inside those doors.

CHAPTER 33

THE ONLY NASTY things that had lain in wait were Donnie's friends. Every time she glanced up to check the time, one of them was looking at her. Some out of suspicion, and some in plain anger. She didn't blame them. The last time they'd seen Donnie, he'd been sitting with her. Now, he was nowhere to be found.

Good thing she was smarter and much more prepared than any of them. She had the test finished with forty minutes left on the clock. She took a quick moment to text Devon on the sly, then hurried to the desk at the side of the stage to drop her test in the basket. The professor barely looked up.

A message awaited her on her phone.

Devon: *I'm here.*

Nervous butterflies erupted in her stomach. She tucked her computer in her backpack and stood, catching a suspicious stare from Donnie's best buddy. It would be a long few weeks until the end of the semester—if she made it that long. She'd probably miraculously escape the elder vamp only to be brought up on murder charges for Donnie's disappearance.

Devon waited just beside the door, his face closed down into a hard mask. Yasmine and Macy stood in front of him, pushed out to the sides like wings. Fierce determination shone on each of their faces.

Full night had descended like a blanket, the soft glow from the light poles splashing the path.

"What's going on?" Charity asked as they started forward, she the only one not in perfect synchronicity.

No one answered her. They didn't need to.

Students ambled toward their cars, clutching books or computers, chatting with their friends or classmates. Every once in a while, a group would look up in surprise, their laughter and chatter dying as they caught sight of one of the still figures amidst the shadows. Eyes widened and mouths gaped as they noticed the unearthly beauty of the visitors.

The vamps had shown up.

"Is this it?" Charity asked quietly, identifying four independent watchers as they headed toward the closest parking lot. "Are we going to have to fight our way to the car?"

"Not with this many people around," Devon answered in a low tone, masking a growl. "You were right about that."

"What about when we get near the car and the parking lot is quiet?"

Devon's fingers closed around hers. "We won't be giving them that opportunity."

His gaze shifted right. Andy jogged in from that side, his eyes pinned to the nearest vampire, who was watching him with a little grin.

Devon squeezed her hand. "We're going to make it, okay? I won't let them take you." Fierce possession rang in his voice.

"You're pack, Charity," Andy growled, something she hadn't expected from him. He fell in on her other side. "We've got you."

Macy and even Yasmine nodded in agreement.

A surge of pure fire lit Charity up from within, exploding electricity out through her limbs. She'd never felt so included in a group of peers. She'd never been this welcomed, and certainly not felt this protected. Something hard and fast took root within her. The song of battle curled through the breeze.

All she could do was nod gratefully. She didn't have a sword, after all. Tearing through campus, chopping off vampires' heads, wouldn't be possible without a sword.

Of all the times to crack up, she was okay with doing it now.

Devon released her hand and drifted further back with Andy. Yasmine and Macy closed ranks, too, the four of them boxing her in. At the bottom of the next set of steps, a beautiful woman stepped out of the trees flanking the path. Her eyes and smile were hungry.

"Why so fast, little puppy?" she asked in a sexy purr. She was talking to Devon.

If only Charity had that sword…

"Mid-level," Devon murmured.

"Left, eleven o'clock," Yasmine said in a brittle voice.

A man lounged against a tree, ignoring the furtive stares of two ladies passing him. He only had eyes for Charity.

"Greetings," he said as she neared. "Nice night, isn't it? Mmm, you smell fantastic."

"Mid-level," Devon muttered.

"Are they going to attack?" Charity asked, electricity crackling from her fingertips.

"Not here," Andy said quietly. "One waited for me outside my classroom. Followed me to you. They know we're young and inexperienced—compared to Roger or Jeffry."

"Who's Jeffry?" Charity asked.

"Jeffry is alpha of the Hunting pack, which goes after higher-level vamps throughout the region," Devon answered.

"Calling everyone alpha is confusing," Charity murmured.

"Leaders like to be called alpha, especially men," Macy said, her words strangely muffled, like she was talking out of the corner of her mouth for secrecy.

It didn't matter. Their admirers heard.

"I agree," a woman said just off to the side, her voice familiar.

One glance was all Charity needed to place her.

There was no mistaking that red lace corset paired with the leather duster and spiked heeled boots. She sat on a park bench, looking ludicrously out of place.

"She was at the turning party," Charity whispered back to Devon.

The woman's ruby-red lips stretched into a smile. "I long to sample you, my sweet. The pleasure I will give you will turn you off that young pup, I assure you."

"I don't swing that way," Charity replied, fire burning her alive from the inside out, fueling her courage. She opened and closed her fist.

"Hmm, that smell. You will, my sweet. You will."

"Vampires are really bad at pick-up lines." Charity shivered.

"Upper mid-level," Devon said in a growl.

"The lovely thing about wolf pups…" The vampire stood slowly from the bench as they passed, her movements languid. She lifted her heel to take a step, and suddenly she was standing in front of them, blocking their way. Someone behind them gasped. "…is that they love the secluded wilderness. Tell me, little pup—how well can you drive those windy roads to your protective ward? Can you maintain speed?"

They planned to ambush the pack where no one could witness the fight.

"Move, or I will move you," Charity said, doing everything she could not to push to the front of the pack. Devon would flip out if she did, and it would jeopardize their whole setup. But man, she wanted to. She wanted to wrangle this fire and direct it at that vamp standing in their way, threatening them. She wanted to light up the sky and burn that creature alive.

"Hold," Devon commanded her, clearly sensing the electricity stretching her skin, begging to be released.

With a lovely laugh, the woman sauntered out of the way, her hips swaying erotically. A younger man off to the side shivered and then bent at the waist before shuffling away in embarrassment. She'd provoked climax without even touching him.

"There's our ride, bro," Andy said, taking a knife out of his belt as they approached the road.

Dillon stood beside the open rear door of a black Suburban in a handicap zone, the only space he could have pulled into that wouldn't block traffic. The front passenger door was open, too, Rod at the wheel with the engine running.

Twenty feet away, lying across a bench like it was a chaise longue, was Charity's BFF.

Cars slowed down as they passed. People around him gawked.

They'd probably never seen anyone so handsome. They had no idea that a monster lurked on the inside.

When he caught her eye, he smirked and winked.

Electricity rolled through her fingertips. Light fizzled along her palms. Fire boiled her blood.

"My own personal stalker," Charity said. The pack pushed in closer. Her butt had gone numb. She had no idea why. "I had such a quiet life. You have no idea how much I miss it."

"I don't mean to take any chances until daylight," Devon said in a rough voice. "We'll go to Rod's. It's well warded and still within town."

"Where's Roger?" Andy asked, helping Charity into the back seat next to Dillon, his eyes never leaving her BFF.

Devon waited until they were all in and the doors closed to answer. "He's getting people together," he murmured, clearly taking no chances with the vampires' hearing. "He's going to try to take down the mid-levelers so the elder doesn't have as many minions in the Brink."

"What a mess," Rod muttered from the driver's seat. "What is it about you, Charity? Do they know you're a good cook?"

"That's it, yes," Charity replied. "They realized I make a mean lasagna."

"You do? When do we get to sample that?" Rod stepped on the gas, cutting off another car.

"I forgot all the food is at my house," Devon said miserably, and she belatedly noticed he was clutching a gun.

"So, how did class go, everyone? Learn anything useful?" Andy asked pleasantly, leaning his arm against her seat. It was like the intense scene outside had never happened.

Charity couldn't help but laugh. She loved the craziness of Devon's pack.

Dillon shook his head. "Rod, you got enough beds at your house for everyone? We should stick together until Roger tells us what's next. If I were that elder, I'd pick us off if I could."

"I got a couple air mattresses, but we probably have to double a couple of people up," Rod replied.

"I call Macy," Andy yelled quickly.

Dillon reached over the seat and flicked him in the head.

"He did call me," Macy said. Charity could hear the strains of humor in her voice. This crew would joke through anything. It was strangely reassuring.

They arrived at a modest three-bedroom house that looked almost exactly the same as the modest three-bedroom houses to either side of it. Also to those across the street.

"Not a lot of originality in this part of the world, huh?" Charity mumbled to Dillon. He snorted.

"I hear better than humans, Charity," Rod said darkly.

Rod pulled into the garage and looked back at Devon. The lights from the dash were reflected in his somber eyes. "If they pool all those vamps together, they might be able to break through this ward."

"They won't chance it in the middle of suburbia. That's why we're here." Devon stepped out and helped Charity after him. "If they were going to make a scene, they would've done it already."

"What were they after, then? Showmanship?" Rod

jabbed a button on his visor. The garage door roared to life.

Charity shook her head into the silence that followed that question. She had no idea. The feelings she sometimes got about approaching danger were absent. Which made it that much more terrifying. She had no idea what would come next.

IT TURNED OUT Rod had a ton of somewhat fresh food in his kitchen—a dream of Charity's before Devon had bought all that food. Unfortunately, Rod didn't have enough of any one thing for their whole group. Charity settled for a tapas kind of dinner. Andy called it a buffet, which was also true. By the time they ate and cleaned up, it was nearing eleven o'clock.

"All right," Rod said, dropping a pile of blankets on the couch as they all gathered in the living room. "I got a king-sized bed in my room. One bedroom has a queen, the office has room on the floor for an air mattress. One full-sized couch—"

"Does it pull out?" Andy asked, eyeing the piece of furniture as though it might have hidden delights.

"It's leather…"

"Yes, Captain Obvious. It sure is. And your head? Is that made of cotton candy and gumballs? Roger bought your way into school. Didn't he—"

"Leather doesn't pull out, you jackass!" Rod punched Andy in the chest.

"I feel like this is a prime time for a dirty joke," Macy intoned.

"You guys," Devon said.

"Anyway, so if we double up, that's six for the beds and one for the couch." Rod glared at Andy.

Andy put up his hands in surrender. "I'm not going to comment on your ability to do simple math. Whoever said you were dense surely didn't know you very well."

Rod puffed up like he was about to lunge.

"Macy and I will take the air mattress. We don't hang on pretension." Dillon grabbed Macy's hand and looked anywhere but at Yasmine.

Macy smiled and stepped closer.

"Charity and I will take the queen," Devon said.

Yasmine's mouth dropped open. She hadn't seen that coming. Neither had Charity.

Into the shocked silence, Andy said, "So, Rod, you and me? I sleep naked and I like to spoon—is that okay?"

Yasmine pouted beautifully as Rod's face turned an angry shade of red.

Andy laughed merrily. "Just kidding, Yasmine. You can have him. I like my men small and mousy."

After a smirk at Andy, Devon took off toward the spare bedroom. Charity stared after him in trepidation before glancing at Andy with wide eyes.

Andy laughed again. "I think I got lucky with the couch, bro. Kind of ball shriveling when you make a woman look like she just swallowed a slug."

"I hope you're talking about Rod," Devon yelled from down the hallway.

"I was talking about Dillon," Andy yelled back.

Charity stared after Devon for a moment, not sure what to do. Although they'd slept in the same bed before, this was a public display. It whispered of a kind of closeness Devon wasn't exactly known for, and screamed of a different kind of closeness he was entirely *too* known for.

But what choice did she have?

Not to mention that a part of her was glad he picked her. That he'd continue to extend the comfort he'd given her the last couple nights. That he'd opted to keep her wrapped up in his safety like a blanket.

Sighing and shoving a smirking Andy out of the way, she trudged to the bedroom. She paused at the threshold, her gaze glued to Devon as he stripped out of his shirt.

"I don't want to…you know," Charity said shyly, tucking a strand of hair behind her ear. "Last night I just needed some comfort. And, you know, those other nights, too."

"And you don't need that tonight?" Devon kept on his boxers as he climbed between the sheets.

"Um…well, tonight you aren't in a self-induced coma."

"I will be soon. Chastity, I won't bite. Unless you ask very nicely."

She shook her head, wondering why she suddenly

felt like a virgin being asked to take off her clothes. She was excited and scared and wound up and eager…

Get a grip, Charity. You're just sleeping in the same bed. It's no different than those other times.

But oh God, something about this time felt different.

With a big sigh, she flicked off the lights but kept the door open. She wanted everyone to know there would be no shenanigans going on in here. She wanted no rumors, and definitely no temptation.

She shed her socks and stepped out of her jeans. After discarding her hoodie, she slipped her bra out from under her loose T-shirt. She climbed into the sheets and huddled in a ball on her side.

"C'mere," he said into the darkness.

"We probably shouldn't, Devon. That's a bit…close."

"Chastity, we did this last night. Nothing happened. I'll keep my hands in safe areas, I promise."

"Do you guys want this door open?" Rod asked from the doorway. Yasmine was behind him, looking into the gloom with squinted eyes. Charity hated that she was living up to what Yasmine suspected of her. She hated that it mattered.

"Yes, please," Charity said before Devon could speak up.

"Afraid you'll fall in lust if people can't see you?" Rod chuckled as he moved away.

"C'mere," Devon said again. "I'll be good. I just

want your warmth. Our shared warmth."

Charity wanted the same thing. However strange she felt about taking their unspoken arrangement public, she knew she wouldn't sleep tonight without Devon beside her. With the night pressing in, he was the only person who could make her feel safe. So far he'd protected her, and she knew he would keep protecting her as long as she needed it. She needed him, plain and simple, like she'd only ever needed her mother and John before this. They were a team, for better or worse.

Sighing in resignation, she scooched closer. "No funny business," she said softly, ducking into his outstretched arm.

He drew her in immediately, dragging her up against his body. His arm held her tight, encouraging her head to find the hollow of his shoulder and her arm to drape across his chest.

"Hook your leg between mine. I like that," he whispered, his breath falling across her forehead.

"We're still just friends, though," she whispered, her face heating with the memory of their kiss. "Or pack mates, if you don't have female friends."

He laughed and squeezed her. "Nope. We are passive-aggressive acquaintances that spoon well together when shit goes sideways."

Laughing softly, she let herself relax and tried to ignore the softness that was working into her core. Affection wasn't what he looked for in a girl. He wasn't that kind of guy.

Though it was really too bad. When he let himself thaw, he was funny, and witty, and loyal. She loved being with him, even when they were fighting. Maybe especially when they were fighting. At those times, the alpha in him exploded out, raw and wild. Uncontrollable. Untamable. If he was in any way similar in the bedroom, he'd be—

She mentally slapped herself.

"Why'd you jump?" he asked tiredly, turning and wrapping his arms around her. "I won't let anything happen to you, Charity, I promise." He kissed her forehead. "So long as you'll come back and save me like last time."

She felt his chuckle through his hard chest and let herself melt into his body, feeling sleep tug at her. She ignored the other thing that was tugging at her, urging her to tilt up her face and taste him again. He'd been an excellent kisser, as good at that as he seemed to be at everything else. Including—

She mentally knifed herself this time.

"Shh, it's okay. I've got you," he said, his lips lingering on her cheek. His hardness pressing against her thigh. "Sorry," he said sleepily, but he didn't move away. She didn't ask him to.

She squeezed her eyes shut and breathed through her nose, trying desperately to ignore the raging fire that was threatening to consume her body and make her do something they'd both regret. Thank God her body couldn't outwardly show what was going on internally. She didn't want him to know how close she was to issuing a green light.

CHAPTER 34

ROGER GLANCED UP. He sat at the desk in his Brink home on the outskirts of town, half a country away from Santa Cruz. Soon he'd move to a remote location closer to Santa Cruz, but first he needed to get his affairs in order.

Alder walked in holding a few fluttering pages in his clutched hand. His face was unusually grim, his heavy eyebrows low over his eyes.

"What is it?" Roger asked.

"Reports have come in about the possible Arcana."

"Possible… So it still has not been confirmed."

"No. There are no guarantees, though it seems like Vlad has no reservations."

It wasn't like Vlad to engage in wishful thinking, but given the magical people that the other vampire Brink power player, Darius, had at his disposal, Vlad might be leaning a little too heavily on outlandish possibilities.

Alder settled into a chair in front of the desk. Soft light filtered in through the many windows in Roger's office, the trees outside swaying gently. Papers crinkled as Alder organized his thoughts. When he was ready, he gave Roger a steady, intelligent gaze. "How aware are you of the *custodes's* practice of questing?"

"You mean, when they come of age and power?"

Alder nodded.

"I know they do it. That's about it."

"When they reach full power, the timing of which varies depending on the individual's power level, a *custodes*—warrior fae—goes on a quest. This quest is self-defined and really could be anything. One person might stay in their home for a moon's turn doing mind-altering drugs. Another might visit each part of the Realm for some purpose. They return, or go back to normal, when they feel they have completed their quest. Once a quest is completed, they are an adult by their reckoning."

"Sounds weak."

Alder huffed, as close to a laugh as he usually came. A shifter's *summons* was an extremely dangerous affair, even with someone to guide the new shifter through their first change. Some were killed attempting to travel to the Realm, and of those who did get in, some lacked the magic to sustain their secondary form for any length of time. They were relegated to a mostly human life, cut off from the more magical members of their faction. Devon's mother had had that affliction. It was why she'd given up on her background and married a non-magical human.

It was also why she'd almost killed Devon. Until his first shift, he'd had no notion he was a shifter. A lesser wolf would've died. Devon had instead struggled through the *summons*, ventured into the Realm on his own, and somehow managed to show up at the castle. It had cemented his incredible potential.

It had put him on Roger's short list of shifters to watch closely.

"Some have more extravagant quests than others," Alder went on. "Regardless, the second Arcana, upon acquiring his full strength, had a dream that he should travel to the Brink and forge a bond linking the warrior fae and humanity. That was apparently it. Just link the two. Reports say that he had no idea how."

"Sounds pretty vague," Roger agreed.

Alder nodded, glancing down at his notes. "So he made the journey through the Realm, largely undisturbed as one of his magic and power level would be, and emerged somewhere near Chicago. There, reportedly, he met a woman, as a handsome man usually does."

"And seduced her, as a fae usually does," Roger added. He already knew where this was going.

"It's said that he loved her greatly. He was apparently convinced that his quest was to sire a child of both bloodlines."

Roger shifted in his seat. "Sounds promising, but I have a hard time believing a fae, let alone an Arcana, would leave a child behind."

"Exactly. They wouldn't. After six months or so, the woman still wasn't pregnant. The Arcana, feeling the pull of home, decided he had misinterpreted his quest. He'd connected with a human, and that was his quest completed. Since he couldn't take his love with him, he had to leave her behind."

"And she was pregnant?"

Alder quirked an eyebrow. "That's where it gets murky. Charity was born about ten months after he left, judging by the reports I have. Nine and a half months, to be precise. She delivered a day before her due date."

"So Charity couldn't be his blood."

"Well, actually, from conception, the doctors count out forty weeks until birth, give or take. Ten months."

Roger sat forward. "So if he gave this woman a farewell lay, then it's possible Charity could be his child."

"It's possible."

"The reports you have can't be all that exact. I wonder how many children were born within that time period, within that city."

Alder grinned, a disturbing sight. "Exactly, on both counts. The Arcana did send someone back to the Brink to make sure a child wasn't formed from that union, and the scout found a run-down house with nobody in it. They searched for the woman in question, but found nothing. Figuring they could sense their own kind, and didn't, they went back to the Flush."

"So…"

"Charity being this child is a shot in the dark. Although it's said only an Arcana can bloom the sun in the darkness."

"I had no idea you were a poet," Roger said dryly.

"I have hidden talents."

"Apparently. Did you visit Charity's parents' house to ask questions?"

Alder grinned again, this time with murder glinting in his eyes. "Of course. Found dear old Dad. He didn't like the look of me. I narrowly dodged a shotgun blast."

"Ah. So we have no idea if this mysterious woman was Charity's mother, and even if she was, we have no idea if the child is the powerful Arcana's. Even if Charity *is* this child, she isn't full fae. She's a half-breed."

"Correct on all points." Alder glanced at his notes again. "But fae scriptures say that a child born of a quest will flourish in power. That his or her power will easily rival an Arcana, if not more."

"If the Arcana's quest was to sire a child at all."

"Yes, that's still up in the air."

Roger stood and stared out the window. "What if she is this child? If she's the missing link and the daughter of the Second, which still remains childless, last I heard."

"Then the Second will move the worlds to get her back. She is heir to the throne. More, she's the product of a quest. Their magical juju people will want to consult with her, and then stars, and then tea leaves or whatever it is they rely on. The elves will want a piece, too, to bend her to their cause. Which is why the vampires—or at least one particular vampire—wants her."

Roger rubbed his eyes, suddenly exhausted. "What does Vlad know that we don't? How is he so sure she's Arcana? There's no way he can effectively verify it until her blood is tested. And even then, he'd need a comparison with the Second. To wave a child at the warrior fae, claiming it's theirs, would probably incite a war if he's wrong."

"Here's where it gets dicey." Alder stared at Roger for a moment. "For you."

Roger steeled himself for the worst.

"Needing more information, I consulted with Reagan Somerset. I hired her to question a lower-tier vampire that was *in the know*."

Reagan was a headcase with a strange magic, bonded to Darius, the other elder playing politics in the Brink. As a rule, Vlad and Darius circled each other. They didn't cross lines, especially in regard to political pursuits. And as a rule, Reagan, magically bonded to Darius, didn't take sides between them and the shifters.

As a rule, Reagan made a huge mess out of any delicate situation she touched.

"What'd she do?" Roger asked.

"She accidentally killed the vampire. Well, actually, he was killed by the little mage she always drags with her, the one with the insane mother I quite like. Penny apparently cut off the vampire's ability to change forms, not realizing Reagan had meant it as a bluff. Unlike with shifters, this killed the vampire."

Roger leaned back, surprised. "Is that right?"

"Yes. She had to hide her involvement in this from Darius, so she incinerated the body. There will be no trace, but she made it very clear she intends to throw you under the bus if she gets in trouble."

Roger rubbed his temples. First Steve, and now this…

"Anyway," Alder went on, "she did discover that Vlad was immediately attracted by Charity's magic, although he didn't make the connection to the warrior fae at first. He had other things on his mind—his preparations for you, to be precise. Reagan mentioned that she was annoyed someone smelled better than she does. Penny rolled her eyes. I'm pretty sure that means Reagan was not serious." He shook his head. "Given that Vlad is over a thousand years old, has certainly met warrior fae before, and likely seen the magic of an Arcana—as soon as he did make the connection…"

Roger let a breath slowly trickle out. "Charity is legit. She's warrior fae—possibly warrior fae royalty. She's one of the most powerful fae in existence, she's heir to the *custodes* throne, and she is in our protection."

"No one can be positive."

Roger laughed humorlessly. "Vlad is going to try to leverage help from the warrior fae by holding the child prisoner. What's his overall plan, though? There is no way he's going to try to out vampires in the human world. Last time that happened, most of them were hunted down and destroyed—and that was before modern weapons."

Alder tapped his notepad. "There're rumors indicating the Realm is his target…and he may have some dangerous allies. It would be easier on the vampires if they didn't have to follow the elves' rules. It would be ideal for the demons if they didn't have to remain banished to their pits. As you know, Lucifer has an appointment to visit the elf royalty. The popular rumor is that the elves called him in due to the increasing numbers of demons in the Brink." Alder quirked a brow. "The whispered rumor is that Lucifer had something of a problem in the Underworld, and is now seeking out the cause. He's searching for a particular type of magical…person. And possibly a vampire accomplice."

A strange unsettlement traveled through Roger. He was the alpha of an entire region, no small feat, but this news raised his small hairs. Something was coming. Something bigger than anything he'd ever experienced. And he knew he'd eventually be pulled into the heart of it.

"All we have is rumors," Alder said. "When I asked Reagan, she punched me in the face."

"She knows the details," Roger said with certainty. "But that isn't essential right now. We'll circle back to it." He blew out his breath. "Vlad's leaked plans would explain the visit from Lycus and also all the newbie vamps that keep springing up. The vampires need bigger numbers to take on the elves. But no magical species has taken on that challenge and won."

"Lucifer has gotten close in the past. If he'd found a few more allies, and the elves hadn't recruited a certain annoying breed of magical shifters, they might've overtaken the elves. The vampires weren't the stars of that show, but Vlad was involved—or at least looking on. He's gotten older and wiser since. He's probably mapped out the weaknesses of everyone involved."

Roger nodded. "If there is a way, he'll go for it. He was trying to up his numbers when he stumbled upon Charity. Now he thinks he's found his golden ticket. In the past, the warrior fae would never have fought against the elves. They were the elves' prized army. But now, after keeping to themselves for so long…"

"The elves would use Charity to bring the warrior fae to heel. The vampires would use her to bring them to their cause. Given how Devon's pack have responded to having a warrior fae in their midst, I have to wonder if we'd follow those enchanting folk wherever they go."

"She is a turning point," Roger whispered.

"I'd like to get her in front of Karen, the little mage's mom."

So would Roger. A *Seer* might shed some light on how important Charity's role would be moving forward. Giving Reagan's recent mess-up, Roger probably had the leverage to make that happen.

"It certainly seems like Charity is the product of the quest," Roger said, thinking of all the elements at play.

"It doesn't change the current situation, though."

"Right now we have Charity," Alder said, his eyes gleaming. "We could harness her the same way. Make our own power play."

Roger leaned back in his seat, analyzing his right-hand man. They'd been through the wringer together, but they'd always guarded each other's back. They approached every new challenge from the same moral foundation. Roger wondered if this would be a rare divergence.

As if reading his thoughts, Alder said, "I'm just putting all our options on the table."

"We aren't kidnappers or mercenaries," Roger replied in a firm tone.

Alder nodded, and Roger realized his old friend had been testing him. He'd wanted to make sure they were still on the same page. Power corrupted, but they had always kept each other balanced. It was good that they still could.

"What now?" Alder asked.

"Vlad is amassing troops. He's pulling them in from everywhere." Roger pushed himself to standing. "Devon is exceptional, but he's not cut out for an elder with an army at his back."

"He survived two mid-level vamps on his own, killing one," Alder said.

Roger hid his smile. He prided himself on finding raw talent. Devon was no exception.

"Even still," Roger said. "Vlad is another ballgame

altogether."

"Charity's ballgame."

"We need to sneak her into the Realm, away from Vlad, and hide her for as long as possible so no one catches wind of where she is until we're positive who she is."

"We need to talk to her mom. Which means we have to *find* her mom."

Roger checked the time on his phone. They needed to organize the extraction before Vlad had enough vamps to bust through Devon's wards. The elder was keeping all his people clustered in groups, knowing it would take more organization on Roger's end to take them down. Organizing to that level took time.

Time they didn't have.

"Get someone else on the newbies. We need to get Devon's pack ready to move her. I don't want to break her away from them. They're her family now. Hopefully."

Alder shook his head. "No need—Devon plans to take out the last three tonight. He's shown himself extremely capable in pressurized situations. I think it's time to move him and his pack up a level."

"Are you sure? He didn't mention this to me."

"I talked with him not long before coming here. He was about to leave Rod's house to transport Charity to the safety of his much stronger ward. He has the last three newbies in his sights and is already working on a plan with his pack. He thinks one night will be more than enough. New vampires no longer pose a threat to his people."

Roger blew out a breath, hating to give his consent under the circumstances. Devon would need all his wolves, which meant leaving Charity within the ward, by herself. Devon had paid good money for that ward. He'd used the best mage in the area. If Charity stayed within its protection, she should be fine. Still, she was new to this life—she might equate invisible walls with vulnerability and run for the trees, leaving herself wide open.

Roger needed to set someone to watch her. There was no other way.

"Fine. Let him take out the last of them. Make sure he impresses upon her the importance of staying within the ward. Post a sentry to watch her, just in case. And give her my private line—tell her to use it for any purpose."

"Yes, alpha."

Roger watched his beta leave the room, his gut churning. This wasn't just about his desire to merge the warrior fae with the shifters anymore, like in times of old. It was about a young woman's life. At present, her freedom was solely safeguarded by Devon, who, regardless of his potential, was the most inexperienced alpha in his pack.

Roger needed to get back to Santa Cruz as soon as possible, or Charity was done for.

CHAPTER 35

"ARE YOU GOING to be okay?" Devon asked, staring intensely at Charity.

She nodded, but the idea of spending the night alone was playing hell on her nerves. She'd always been in danger growing up—her neighborhood had been riddled with break-ins, stray bullets, you name it—yet she'd always slept soundly. But this was different. Maybe the mythical quality of the threat was what had her on edge. Maybe it was the lack of bars on the windows.

Hell, maybe it was that she'd had Devon to lean on since day one.

But given the last couple of outings, she understood why this was the best solution. She wasn't in a hurry to see her BFF again.

"We won't be out all night," Devon said. He put his large, warm hand on her shoulder. "I'll be home before you know it."

She nodded again, hating the prickle of heat behind her eyes. She needed to learn to stand on her own again. She couldn't always rely on him.

That wasn't easy with terror squeezing her chest in tight bands.

"This ward is strong." Devon lowered his voice into a soft whisper. "I had Dean, the mage, check it. It's sound. You'll be safe as long as you don't leave."

Charity nodded. Devon nodded with her, pulling her into a tight hug.

"Just stay in the ward, okay?"

"Okay," she answered, liking the warmth and support of his body. Liking his masculine smell and scratchy stubble. It was all *real*. Being with him helped ground her—it kept her sane through the insanity that was now her life.

He released her with a sigh. The specks of green and gold seemed to sparkle in his warm brown eyes. "I'm looking forward to spooning."

Her face turned warm at his joking grin. She dropped her gaze, shivering hot and cold. "We'll see."

With a chuckle he left the room and, shortly thereafter, the house. She heard his banged-up SUV roar to life, followed by the crunch of the gravel under the tires as he pulled out of the driveway. In another moment, the sound of his motor dimmed and disappeared, a vacant, echoing quiet taking its place.

She was alone.

Charity looked at the window, silently accusing the sun of deserting her as the speckled light in the trees faded. The vamps would be waking up soon. Her BFF's mind would start to drift her way, bent on the challenge of getting beyond the magical ward.

She was so damn alone. It would be a long, *long* night until Devon or one of the pack returned.

CHAPTER 36

"**W**HAT'S THE PLAN, boss?" Rod said, fingering a knife in his pocket.

Devon's hand fell to his own knife. They all had on the customary sweats that could easily be donned or discarded. He stared out of the bushes at the smallish house, the windows dark and door slightly ajar. The grass in the front yard was so long that the weeds had started at the base of the rosebushes. It looked like the place had missed its last gardening appointment, which made sense, since the owner really only cared about sucking on people's necks these days.

"Why are they all in one place?" Devon asked quietly, glancing around the street. "I thought they each had a different resting spot."

Dillon, standing behind everyone else in just his sweatpants, said, "Up until tonight. They're in there with two humans. Blood party, maybe."

Devon shook his head slowly. "Two humans for three new vamps? That's not enough blood. They'll kill the humans. The calculation of it doesn't fit the newbie MO, either."

"Regardless, they're in there," Rod said.

"Why don't we just go in and take them out?" Yasmine asked, standing close to Devon's right.

"We would jeopardize those humans," he answered.

"If we don't go in soon, those humans will probably be jeopardized anyway," Macy said quietly, staring at the house. "Something isn't right. I have a bad feeling about this, Devon."

Everyone but Yasmine shifted in unease. They'd all learned the hard way that Macy's intuition was reliable.

"It does seem like a trap," Dillon whispered.

Devon's heart pumped faster. Battle was near and his wolf was calling.

"Rod and I will change form and do a quick perimeter check," Devon said, staring at the quiet house. "See if anyone is waiting out there. If not, we'll slink in and try to catch them as they feed. Macy is right: if we wait too long, those humans will be as good as gone. We have enough missing persons in the area lately—I want to save lives tonight."

Rod grinned, his eyes bright. Time to shift. Devon stepped out of his clothes, his limbs dancing with contained energy, as Rod did the same. Their burst of magic made everyone step back.

They took off at an easy lope, staying to the shadows, cutting through bushes with skill and practice. Mostly using his sense of smell, Devon searched for signs of other vamps. Elders. After sprinting across the street—hopefully people would think he was just a big dog—he caught a new vamp scent. One he faintly recognized. The vamp had clearly put on the clothes and perfume from its past human life. It had then exited the rear of the house and cut away through the yard.

Why would it leave its house after inviting over the other new vamps and some humans?

Unless this wasn't a trap at all. It was a distraction.

He followed the trail for another five minutes, enough for him to know the newbie had a destination in mind. His hackles rose.

On his way back, he met Rod. Their gazes held for a moment, conveying impressions with the nuances of their body language. It immediately became clear that Rod had come to the same conclusions about the missing vamp.

Charity was in danger.

CHAPTER 37

CHARITY HAD JUST finished reading the assigned chapter in the most boring textbook imaginable when a scream tore through the night. Her head jerked up, the haze of too much studying clearing in an instant. She stumbled to the window, staring out.

Dark trees gently swayed in the breeze and moonlight speckled the ground. Round and jagged shapes squatted within the yard, silent and still. Just rocks. Nothing else moved.

A second scream shattered the quiet. She sprinted through the rooms to the front of the house. Hands pressed against the sides of the window, she leaned forward and looked out.

Her heart stopped.

It was Samantha!

Sam had turned into the long gravel driveway. Her dress flew behind her in tatters. Although it was too dark and far for Charity to be certain, she had the impression Samantha was terrified. Her limbs were jerky with panic and her shoulders hunched.

"Help!" Samantha screamed. She fell to the ground

and skidded along on her knees.

Charity pulled open the door without thinking and ran out, breathing heavily.

She'd never seen a vampire look afraid. Nor had she seen one look as disheveled as Samantha did. Vampires were beings who inspired fear.

Samantha got to her feet, stumbled forward, and staggered. Loud sobs racked her body. She fell again, her bare knees embedded with gravel. "Help!"

Charity stopped at the edge of the grass, just inside the ward. She looked down at the invisible line that meant safety.

Donnie weighed heavily on her mind. She'd made a mistake once, and had nearly paid with her life. She might not survive this time.

"Oh thank God, Charity!" Samantha reached up for her, still five feet away. "Thank God. They're chasing me! *Help!*"

Charity paced at the invisible line, her promise to Devon at the forefront of her mind. Samantha's sobs tore at her heart.

She'd been changed, though! Devon and the others had been so certain of that. Besides, Charity herself had sensed that a vampire had torn through the house she'd once shared with Sam.

But vampires never cried and carried on. They didn't hunch and jerk. Donnie certainly hadn't. Could they have been wrong about Sam?

Indecision eating at her, Charity continued to pace,

not stepping over.

"How'd you get out of the party?" she asked, her voice wavering.

"I woke up when someone bit my neck—they're *vampires*, Charity! How is that possible?" Samantha bowed with a sob. She shuddered, like she was too weak to lift her head.

Charity's throat constricted. She wanted to help Sam so badly that her palms itched.

"But I saw you drink the punch," she shouted, trying to override her need to cross the line. "You turned! They turned you..."

Sam shook her head. "I drank it, but they didn't give me their blood. I ran out when I woke up. There was confusion in the house. Pandemonium. I don't know how, but I got out. They were chasing someone else, I think. And there were wolves. This all sounds crazy, I know." Sam sobbed again, lying on the ground now, unable or unwilling to crawl the few feet to Charity.

Charity paced faster. Obviously it sounded crazy—Charity had thought the same thing, hadn't she? Hearing those words spoken aloud made her feel sane. She'd spent the last several days in the company of people to whom this magic thing was old hat.

"Come across the line," Charity said, searching her friend's face through the speckled moonlight. All she saw was dirt and Sam's usual beauty, pretty enough to give Yasmine a run for her money.

Charity hesitated. Had Sam's looks changed? She'd

always thought her beautiful…but Yasmine beautiful?

Charity turned toward the house and waved her arm over her head in a large arc, trying to trip the sensor. She needed more light.

Nothing happened. She was out of range.

Turning back, she squinted through the moonlight. Was an unnaturally flawless face waiting under all that dirt and shadow?

"Help me!" Samantha cried, pulling Charity's heart strings. "I've been running. They can still change me if they catch me. They've been chasing me, trying to get me. Please, Charity. I need you."

Charity practically danced with the need to walk those five feet. "I can't cross this line, Sam. I'm sorry, I can't go to you. You're going to have to come to me."

A shape appeared down the lane, gliding noiselessly. He smiled pleasantly at Charity.

Her BFF.

"Oh no!" Samantha wailed. "That's *him*!"

She rose and toddled forward like a child, her balance all over the place. She reached out for Charity. At the last moment, her foot struck a rock and she fell.

Charity stepped forward to catch her and then dragged her back across the line.

"It's okay, I've got you! You're safe," Charity said, her eyes fixed on Vlad walking up the lane.

A blur of movement and suddenly he was standing right in front of her.

"Whoa!" Charity staggered backward, half falling

over Samantha.

"Hello, lovely," he said. "You look ravishing today. Please come out. I wish to show you your new palace. I have manservants ready to wait on you. A vampire's bite is intensely erotic, I can assure you. I have excellent control. You would be in no danger. Or you can choose not to be bitten." He spread his hands wide. "You will be in full control, Charity, as befits a princess. You can choose your destiny. I need only your nod of support and your presence. The rest is up to you. I told you, unlike these animals, I am not possessive."

"God, you're creepy." Charity stepped backward, dragging Samantha with her. She didn't dare show her back to Vlad. Just in case.

She felt Samantha straighten up. Charity said, "Let's go inside and wait for Devon."

"Devon. I would love to get my hands on him," Sam said in a silky voice. "He was always out of my reach. Not anymore."

Charity's small hairs stood on end.

Samantha stood poised and elegant. A sly smile drifted up her face as Charity's insides erupted in false desire.

Oh no!

"But you crossed the line! Vampires shouldn't be able to cross the line," Charity exclaimed, backing toward the house.

"You're losing her," Vlad warned. "Don't let her throw her magic. You are not strong enough to survive it."

Samantha ran to Charity's side, only slightly faster than a human, and pulled Charity into a painful bear hug.

"You see," Vlad said pleasantly, "you circumvented the ward by pulling Samantha in of your own free will. I've done my homework. Your little puppy is so young—he forgets that not everyone is privy to these small details. I am endlessly delighted."

"But…"

Samantha started walking toward Vlad, dragging Charity with her.

"No…"

"Careful, Samantha. Her kind tend to become more powerful when agitated," Vlad said.

He had that right.

Charity bucked and twisted, freeing herself from Samantha's arms. Fire exploded through her body as she punched Sam's middle, and then a silent explosion tossed Sam backward. Samantha hit the ground and rolled, stopping just shy of the ward.

"After her," Vlad yelled. Power crackled along the ward, sparks and electricity lighting up a huge dome crouching over the house and yard. Vlad was trying to claw through, and for all she knew, he could do it. He'd clearly had the ward tested, after all.

Charity was already running back to the house. She needed weapons.

CHAPTER 38

CHARITY SLAMMED THE door shut behind her and clicked the lock into place. Maybe Samantha didn't know the lock trick yet. If she had to bust through the window, it would give Charity time.

She sprinted to the office where she'd been studying and scooped the gun off the desk.

The window shattered. Glass tinkled against the hardwood floors.

Charity reached the foyer as Samantha wedged herself into the window. Her pretty face shifted into her other form—a hideous, swampy thing. The creature's head lifted.

Charity bit back a sob and took aim.

"You're going to shoot me, Charity?" Samantha garbled through a mouth full of fangs. "After I begged my parents to let you live with me? I couldn't abandon you to the dorms, and you'd repay me by *shooting* me?"

"But…you're not you anymore," Charity begged, knowing she had to pull the trigger. Willing herself to do so.

Somewhere outside, a snarl tore at the silence.

Charity started and stood on her tiptoes to look out, terrified it was Devon.

Samantha leapt back out of the window, leaving a clump of matted black hair dangling from a shard of glass. Charity stepped closer, gun hand shaking.

A gray wolf, smaller and leaner than Devon, lunged for the elder vampire.

The vamp went blurry, attacking the furry body at a ridiculous speed. Claws extended from its fingers and fangs erupted from its mouth. It dodged left then scraped its claws along the wolf's flank. The animal yelped in pain. Vlad, faster than thought, sliced the other side of the wolf before bodily picking it up and throwing.

Heart in her throat, hoping to all hell Devon hadn't sent one of his pack to check on her, she watched as the elder descended on the wolf and ripped at its body, shredding.

Samantha rushed to the border, only for Vlad to yell, "No! Do not cross that line. This mongrel is nothing. Get the Arcana!"

Arcana?

Samantha turned slowly, eyeing Charity through the broken window. Vlad flicked his hand.

Click.

Charity darted over and manually threw the lock back. When she stepped back to the window, ready to shoot, Samantha caught her by surprise. She was already at the window, her monster face only two inches away.

A hand burst through and grabbed Charity's throat, cutting off her air supply and pulling. Her shoulders hit the window frame. A fierce snarl in the distance cut off in a wet whine.

Dread pierced Charity. She pushed Sam with her palms and then her power, the concussion of air forcing out the rest of the glass in the window and the frame with it. Plaster and paint ripped away with the vamp, though its claws scraped Charity's neck.

Charity got a glimpse of a bloodied wolf lying in a heap. Vlad stared at her from across the invisible divide, his face a terrifying mask of violence.

Without thinking, she fled, sprinting to Devon's bedroom in the back of the house. She slammed the door, locked it, then paused, not sure what to do next. She didn't have long to decide. A moment later, the door thudded. And again. As if a heavy body were slamming into it.

With a loud crack and the splintering of wood, the door burst inward. Samantha stood in the frame, nude and in her human form. Rage marred her beautiful features. "My master is counting on me. Come quietly so I don't have to hurt you."

"Samantha, it's *me*! We're friends. Don't you remember your human side?"

"Friends? Is that why you have a gun?" Fangs elongated from black gums. She was changing again.

Arms shaking, Charity raised the weapon and

aimed. Samantha hissed, moving one second before Charity pulled the trigger. The deafening shot blasted. Sam jerked back, a puncture to the left of her heart. She shifted from beautiful to ghoulish, and she grinned, a ghastly sight.

"Missed me, missed me," she said softly, her horrible singsong sending shivers down Charity's spine.

Sobbing, Charity opened fire. Bullets punched into her former friend. But the vamp kept moving, too fast, the heart hard to hit, even from this close.

Samantha sprang forward and backhanded her. She crashed into the closet doors, her head thumping the glass hard enough that it cracked and spider-webbed. Charity jumped up and then twisted as claws tore through the air. Searing pain bit her shoulder.

She snatched a knife off the nightstand and dodged another claw strike. Not thinking, just reacting, Charity surged forward and slashed downward. The blade burrowed into Samantha's chest.

Samantha's expression melted from rage to shock. She staggered backward and her hands drifted up. Her appearance shifted back to human.

"Charity, what did you do?" Samantha asked, her tone achingly familiar. This was the Sam who'd gotten Charity out of the dorms. The one who'd told her friends that Charity could hang around whenever she wanted to. It hadn't been a great friendship, or an equal one, but it had mattered to Charity.

"I…" Charity sobbed, not knowing what to say. She

stared in horror as her friend's expression sank into a look of hurt.

"Charity, why? I was always good to you."

"I'm sorry, Sam!" Charity cried, stumbling backward against the wall.

Samantha's beautiful face twisted into the visage of a howling, rage-filled monster. The creature she'd become turned, tearing at its ruined chest. Its cries of pain tore at Charity's heart.

Suddenly the vamp was ripped away, the black sludge oozing from its chest cavity dripping all over the wood floor. Devon's handsome face filled her vision.

"Charity, are you okay? Are you hurt?"

"I killed her. I killed Samantha." She sobbed, sickened by what she'd done. By what she'd had to do.

Devon clutched Charity's shoulders, looking hard at the claw marks from the creature Sam had become, before looking down her front and then turning her. He was checking for the severity of her injuries.

"The elder is outside. He...he killed a gray wolf..." Charity forced back the sobs, praying a new friend hadn't died tonight along with an old one.

"I know. It was Sarge. Roger must have sent him to watch you. No one wolf, besides maybe Roger, is a match for Vlad. Sarge gave it everything he had, but..."

"How'd you get in?"

Devon scooped her up and carried her out of the room. She squeezed her eyes shut so she didn't have to see Samantha's ghoulish remains.

Once in her room, he sat with her on the bed, cradling her to his chest. It was only then his nudity soaked into her awareness.

"I left the Range Rover and ran around," he said before she could guess the answer. "The elder was standing in the middle of the driveway. I didn't want to risk pushing him through the ward with my car—if that would even work. He was too focused on you to notice my drive-by."

"I didn't know I could get people inside! I... She was falling. She had dirt on her face—I couldn't tell if she was changed or not."

"Shh, it's okay. You're okay. You did good."

"I killed her, Devon." Charity moaned, tilting her head up to his, wanting him to stop this pain.

"No—vampires killed her when they changed her. That wasn't Samantha anymore. That was a creature. You saved lives tonight."

Charity shook her head as a phone rang in the other room. Devon stared at her for an intense moment. "That is probably one of the pack. I need to go get it."

"Please don't leave me," Charity said, clutching his muscled shoulders.

Devon leaned down slowly, his lips lightly touching the very tip of her nose. "Come with me."

Her entire body tingled. Heat sizzled through his touch. She sank into the feeling.

She barely heard the phone call, as intent as she was on his presence. On his solid body and the ardent need that pumped through her blood. There had been so much violence, so many changes and horrifying new discoveries since that first night at the nightmare house. She'd witnessed the death of her crush, and then she'd had to kill a friend. She needed to forget, if only for a while. She wanted an act of love to push back the despair of soul-crushing loss.

When they were in her room again, she ran her palms up his hard chest and hooked them around his neck. At his confused expression, she pulled his head— his lips—closer.

Apprehension took over his confusion, but he couldn't hide the burning desire in his eyes.

He wanted this too. He *needed* it. But he was an alpha and a gentleman, and so he wanted to do what he thought was right.

"Maybe this isn't a good idea," he whispered. She knew he was also worried that he'd sex away his regard for her. Which meant he felt something too.

She knew about his history, but this felt deeper than lust. Still, she was a realist. She might be wrong, but if…whatever this was…didn't last through the morning, it never would've lasted anyway.

Her gaze trained on his lush, full lips.

Slowly bending forward, she kissed his pec and ran her hands down his defined six-pack. The cool cotton of her shirt rubbed against her face as she pulled it off. Her bra followed it onto the floor a moment later.

"You're so beautiful, Charity," Devon whispered.

"You're…radiant."

She let her eyes drift closed as he kissed down her neck, then sucked in a breath as his hot mouth closed over her taut nipple. Fire consumed her body. "Hmm, Devon."

His velvety hands slid over her hips, pausing to remove her pants. She stepped out and then let him walk her back to the bed.

His kiss deepened. His taste, sweet and exotic, delighted her senses. The world around her dropped away.

He pulled the covers down, then scooped her up and laid her on the sheets. His searing touch trailed fire along her inner thighs as he spread her open. She moaned when he followed his hands with his mouth, licking up her center.

Shivers spread across her body, and her breathing increased. His mouth covered her nub. His fingers worked inside of her. She clutched the sheets and arched as the glorious sensations melted her bones.

"Hmm," she moaned, gyrating up to his mouth. Her body tightened. Her moaning increased in fervency. "Yes, Devon. Almost…" Words fled. Her body flexed as if she held an electric wire. His touch was her sole focus—nothing existed outside of his delicious ministrations.

"Oh!" Powerful shudders rocked her. Fused her teeth together. Pure pleasure vibrated within her. She convulsed from the explosion in her body.

"Holy crap," Charity said, out of breath. She shuddered again with an aftershock of that incredible pleasure. "Wow."

Devon kissed up her stomach. His tricky tongue flicked her nipple before he sucked it in. Intense sensation speared directly through her body.

"You're perfect," he said softly. Almost reverently. When he nibbled her bottom lip and settled his weight on top of her, a strange gravity stole over her. Something about this situation felt so *right*. Like a piece she'd been missing had finally found its place and connected to the whole.

His searing length rested against her hip. When he moved, it dragged along her slick sex. She sighed as her body wound tighter. He rose, resting on his elbows to either side of her face.

"I care about you, Charity," he said. "A lot. But sometimes intimacy breaks me." Sadness consumed his expression, and then it morphed to something else. He almost looked lost. "I want you so bad. You need to know that. But I might shut off if we go through with this. I don't want to hurt you. Knowing what I am—how I deal with things—are you sure you want to take the next step?"

She didn't hesitate. "Yes."

His gaze traveled her face. Longing replaced his earlier emotions. "Okay."

Their kiss increased in intensity, sucking her into a place she'd never been before. Her stomach fluttered with nervousness when she felt his tip prod her opening. She'd only ever been with one man.

"Do we need protection?" he murmured against her lips. "I can't get human diseases. You probably can't either, because of the magic. But I can still get you pregnant."

A strange lightness came over her. She ran her palms along his smooth back, feeling the bulge and play of muscle as he shifted. "I never went off the pill. I'm good. Though nervous."

His lips curled into a smile against hers. "We'll go slow," he whispered. "I'll always protect you, Chastity, regardless of what happens after…"

He didn't finish the sentence, probably not wanting to dampen the mood. Instead, he kissed her, a deep kiss full of a longing that stole her breath as well as her heart. She fell into the moment without any reservations. Gave him everything she had without regret. Without worrying what might come.

Because she knew that he would stay true to his word. Even when they weren't getting along, he always took care of her. She was confident that wouldn't change.

His tip parted her flesh. Her eyes fluttered, and she sighed as he entered her slowly. She squeezed his middle with her legs.

The glorious *fullness* tingled through her. All too soon, it turned into a dull ache. He was *way* bigger than she was used to.

Clearly reading her body's signals, he stopped his

advance and held still. His kiss turned languid as he pulled out and then pushed back in, stretching her slowly. Gloriously. The ache was a little less. On his next slow thrust, less still.

"Hmm." She ran her hands over his back and then moaned again at his advance. "That feels so good."

"Unreal good, yes. God, Charity, this is…" His voice strained as he thrust again, nearly there. He thrust again, a little harder this time, his control obviously fraying. The ache she'd felt turned into pleasure spiraling through her body. The heat surged. Her core tightened.

"More. All the way," she said, squeezing him closer with her legs. Needing all of him. *Right now.*

He complied. His thrust took him to the hilt. He sighed against her lips.

"You'll ruin me, Charity."

She almost didn't hear the words, they were murmured so low. And then all remaining thoughts fled as he moved. The man knew his way around the sheets. He worked her body in such a way that all she could do was cling to his broad shoulders and make unintelligible sounds. He thrust and retreated, clearly as lost in her as she was in him. The rhythmic thump of the bed competed with their frantic breathing.

She scratched his back as pleasure pounded within her, dragging her under. Her body was wound so tight that she thought it was going to crack. The pressure liquefied and condensed, centered in her core. The compression hardened, white-hot. A few more thrusts, expert manipulation of her nipples, and the glorious rubbing of her sex, and—

"Devon…I'm going to… I'm… *Oh… God!*"

She shattered. Pieces of her blew apart. Glorious sensations vibrated through her body. Devon shook over her a moment later, breathing heavily against her lips. He collapsed on top of her and dug his face into her neck.

She soaked in the feel of him. His warmth. His solid body pressing her into the mattress, his hardness still inside her.

She'd never felt so safe.

Her limbs felt heavy, but she kept them draped over him, wanting to remain this close forever. Without bothering to move, she closed her eyes and fell asleep, hoping tomorrow wouldn't end what she'd come to feel for him. Hoping the pain from his inevitable withdrawal wouldn't drown her.

CHAPTER 39

Devon awoke pressed against a warm female body. Irritation stole over him. Waking up touching meant he'd have a harder time disentangling himself. The "I gotta go" conversation was way more awkward when he was still nude.

As he began to disentangle himself, the sweet and spicy smell of her tickled his senses. A surge of warmth rose up, matching the feeling from last night.

Charity.

Sighing in relief, he lowered back down and breathed her in for a moment, hoping he'd get a few more minutes of fulfillment before his desires shifted and boredom crept in.

The soft sunlight streamed through the window. Dust motes swam lazily. He sighed again in utter relaxation. The stress of the last few days softened. Not gone, but hazy in the aftermath of really good sex. In fact, he felt like a puddle of goo, wanting to ooze down over her.

He ran his hand up her bare thigh and over the curve of her soft hip. He lightly kissed her shoulder and let his lips trace down to the curve of her neck. He was so hard he couldn't stand it.

A thought made him pause.

He wanted her again.

It wasn't just sexual desire, either. He longed for the tender devotion he'd allowed himself to express last night. He wanted to revel in her. Make her moan in pleasure and clutch him with her whole person.

Warmth pulsed in his chest, a feeling that had been growing throughout his time with her. One that had only been intensified by last night. Deep and primal, his possession of her burned hot. The thought of anyone else touching her prodded his wolf and sparked his rage. One thought blared through his brain: *She is mine!*

A strange kind of fear washed over him.

He had been prepared to suffer the guilt of hurting her. He was not prepared for this. This—whatever *this* was—was no good. He didn't understand the intensity of it. The crushing need to touch her again. To hold her. To rip someone's face off if they looked at her for too long.

Before he knew what he was doing, he'd launched himself out of bed. Pacing the room, he couldn't help but look at her. Her hair was splayed across the pillow in a brownish-red wave. The strange glow of her ethereal beauty entranced him, urging him closer.

He blew out a breath, resisting. He needed time to think about next steps. He still had a job to do. Everything else had to come later.

"Charity, get up," he barked.

She stirred with a small feminine mew. Her arms stretched upward and she yawned. The sheets fell to her waist.

He gritted his teeth. It took everything in his power not to take two quick steps and taste…

"We have a ton of stuff to do today." Taking a deep breath, he tried to soften the hardness in his voice. "I need to speak to Roger, too. I'd like to move you into the Realm today."

She blinked into the sunlight and her face relaxed slightly. After wiping her eyes, she swung her legs over the edge of the bed and paused for a moment. "Is this the part where we become acquaintances?"

It sounded like a rhetorical question.

"Just… Let's get moving," he said, turning to the door. "I have a lot I need to do before we get you out of here."

"No sweat, daddy-o. I need to take a shower. Oh *wow*. I am sore. I feel like I lost my virginity all over again."

Devon glanced back in time to see her slowly run her hands over the soft curve of her hips. His desire throbbed. He wanted to follow her hands with his mouth.

Why did she sound so nonchalant? Usually girls were all over him the next morning, trying to cuddle and get close. He half wished she'd follow that pattern. But the other half was annoyed that last night had clearly affected him ten times more than it had her. Another first. And probably the most horrifying.

His uncertainty finally morphed into anger, the emotion he had the most experience handling. "Hurry up."

TWO HOURS LATER, Devon shifted from side to side in impatience as they stood in front of an ATM. His pack had taken out the newbies without him, and he'd called in someone to clean up the dead vamp and pick up Sarge's body. Sarge had been practically ripped apart. He hadn't stood a chance against that old vamp.

A sheen of sweat broke out on Devon's face, his body's immediate response to the lingering threat. He would step up and fight that elder to protect Charity. One on one, if need be. Unfortunately, he didn't have high hopes he'd emerge victorious—or at all.

"What's the hold-up?" Devon asked, going over his to-do list. He still had to get supplies to board up the window by the door, not to mention call a body shop about the trashed SUV. Filling out the insurance forms would be interesting. He wasn't sure how he'd explain the claw marks.

"Something's not right."

Devon checked his phone. Still no call from Roger.

Thanks to the efforts of his pack and Charity, all the newbie vamps had been extinguished. That part of his duty had been finished. The other part, protecting Charity, was looking direr. Something bad was brewing, and Vlad was building up to another all-out assault, one that would have a lot more bite. Rod had heard rumors of more demons filtering into the Brink. According to Roger, the closest passageways to the Realm had been blocked off. They had to get Charity out, but he didn't know how.

"Didn't you get paid?" Devon glanced over her shoulder, but he couldn't make out the numbers.

"I mean. I don't know. I think something went screwy." Charity jabbed a button.

"Can I see?" Devon leaned toward her, getting a whiff of her delicious scent. Clenching his jaw, he saw $10,011.53.

"I had eleven fifty-three." She threw a hard look at him, as if he might laugh.

"So?"

"What do you mean, *so*?" She thrust her hand at the monitor. "Unless you guys get ten grand biweekly, something is amiss, genius."

Her irrational anger scraped against his.

Devon pinched the bridge of his nose. "Didn't you read the emails? That's the sign-on bonus. Obviously he gave it to you even though you're on a trial. He probably wants to talk to you about ongoing pay and working full-time or whatever. You'll get back pay, too. Why are you shaking your head?"

"Just…stop babbling for a second." Charity shoved her palm in his face in a *stop* gesture. "I can't hear myself swear."

He ripped her hand away. "What's the problem?"

"What am I going to do with all that money, Devon?" She almost shouted it. Magic oozed from her, something that usually happened when they fought, but more potent.

His wolf soaked it up, loving her unspoken challenge. His desire to subdue her almost had him stepping forward.

"I don't know," he said. "Buy things?"

"Like what? This is *way* too much money. I can't accept this."

Devon rolled his eyes. "Can you hear yourself? Just get some cash. I'm not in the mood."

"You're not in the mood? For what, me talking to you?"

Her magic prickled his skin. Fire burned in her eyes.

Feeding off it, he leaned into her, invading her space with his size. Pulling alpha rank. "You are freaking out over nothing. Everyone gets that starting bonus, because by the time a shifter answers the *summons* and arrives at the castle, they're broke. Yes, many have family backing, but once you're in the pack, you need to stand on your own two feet. Just take it and shut up."

Her eyes flashed. Her jaw set.

But instead of exploding, she seemed to…relax. If not for the burning rage smoldering her gaze, he would've thought she'd backed down.

Shivers started at the base of his balls, usually a sign of imminent danger. The strange smell of her ancestry, spicy sweet, flared. Magic boiled from her, stronger than ever before.

What the hell is happening?

"Is that how you talk to people where you come from?" she asked in a quiet voice. His small hairs stood on end. "Where was that, again? Oh, that's right. Upper-middle-class suburbia. Do rich people not teach respect?"

"Where I came from has nothing to do with anything. What's your problem?"

"I'll tell you what my problem is, Devon. You. *That's* my problem. You prance around with your big house and your nice car and your big paycheck, acting like you came from nothing. Like you're some bad-boy thug with your ripped jeans and the ever-present chip on your shoulder. Well, *I* came from nothing. Yet I have the decency to be nice to people. And your commitment issues? You're just a spoiled little brat who wants to screw every skirt in sight. All guys your age do. But do they? No, because most of them would feel bad if they screwed a girl over to satisfy a craving. You have no morals. No respect for others. You're a scared little poser who's put out because you're being forced to spend time with your latest conquest."

She turned to the ATM, her anger seething around her body like a halo. Magic rolled off her, crackling. Maybe he should have set her straight, told her how he'd really felt this morning—how he felt now—but her magic prodded at his wolf while her words made fury pump into his body.

"You know what?" he spat. "*You're* the scared one, Miss High and Mighty. That's the real problem. Now you have money. You're not poor anymore. You can buy new clothes. And that terrifies you, because now you won't be able to blame all your problems on coming from nothing. Everything you've always identified with is being torn away. *That's* what terrifies you about that number in your bank account. And keep me out of it. I've never lied about what I'm after with women. I don't lead anyone on. You jumped *me* last night, not the other way around. I wasn't preying on—"

He cut off suddenly when her eyes flashed blue, like an overexposed picture. It wasn't a human eye color.

Before he could ask about it, she said, very softly, "If I were you, I would leave now."

Fear wormed through his anger. For the first time in his life, he experienced the flight side of a fight-or-flight response. Her magic was messing with her. Seeping out of her. She was absurdly powerful, and the wild side of him was proud that she'd managed to scare him.

Still, he did step away. He didn't want to get blasted across the sidewalk.

That possibility brought out a bravado he didn't feel and quickly regretted. "I'll be down the street taking care of some things. We'll meet up in a few hours. I'll text you. Why don't you take all your riches and fix yourself up?"

She sucked in a breath, and then her face took on a

frightening mask of rage.

Oops.

She cocked her head to the side, her eyes flashing chalk-blue again. Prickles spread across his skin, like he was being jabbed with a thousand little needles. Magic gushed from her in a flood, the air around her crackling with it.

Before he could apologize, she took her cash, nodded, turned, and strode away.

He let out a shaky breath he hadn't realized he'd been holding.

That hadn't gone well. He'd been a dick—she should've thrown a punch, or tried to kick him in the balls. He deserved it.

But he would not initiate that fight. Instead, he stalked off down the street in the other direction, unnerved by the leap in her magic and disgusted with himself. He dug out his phone, scratched off a clump of dirt from where he'd dropped it last night, and called Roger again. Things were changing with her, fast, and the elder's interest would only increase. They needed to get moving.

CHAPTER 40

S TILL ANGRY, BUT also a little humbled, Charity raised her chin as she strolled down the street. She hated to admit it, but Devon had been right about a lot of things. Her mother would have killed to have so much money. Charity could get a whole new wardrobe. She could eat out and shop at the grocery store without keeping a mental tally of the total.

It was freeing…but it also meant that if the kids at school still scoffed at her, it was because of her personality, not because of an upbringing she couldn't control. If she wasn't liked, it would be because she wasn't likable. It was irritating that in such a short time, Devon had come to know her so well.

He was also right about everything that had gone down between them, the jerk. He had been crystal clear in his stance on dating. She'd known exactly where she stood going in, and she'd been okay with that in the moment.

It wasn't exactly that she had regrets, because she didn't. She'd cherished every second of last night. She just wished it was only about sex for her, as it so clearly was for him.

Well, you live, you learn, Charity.

A FEW HOURS later, Charity had a few bags and was riddled with fatigue. While her shopping efforts had been fruitful, she was really tired of looking at herself in the mirror. Trying on clothes was never fun.

Not having heard from Devon, she found herself wandering down the street, looking in shop windows. She should call him, but the stubborn part of her wasn't going to chase after him like some lovesick puppy.

She glanced into a picture shop selling artistic photographs, art, and frames. The picture of her mother flashed through her mind. If there was one thing Charity wanted that money could buy, besides information on her mother's whereabouts, it was a frame for her mom's picture.

She hesitated in the doorway, looking in, and caught sight of a beautiful blonde standing close to a familiar man.

Heartbeat increasing with each moment, she stepped into the shop, her bags crinkling in her tightening fists. Devon's face pointed down at Yasmine, his body mere inches away from hers. Yasmine laughed and reached forward to play with a button between the swell of Devon's pecs.

A yawning cavern opened up inside Charity, the same sensation she'd experienced earlier with Devon. Molten lava bubbled out of it and filled her entire body to bursting. Electricity rolled and surged, straining within the confines of her skin. Sparks flew off her arms and even her fingers like a cloud of glitter. The desperate need for violence took over her being, urging her to find a sword so she could cut off Yasmine's head in the fastest, most gruesome way possible. Her body brimmed with it, a surging power that threatened to tear loose and bring this whole building to the ground.

Devon and Yasmine startled before looking up with wide eyes.

Logic screamed for Charity to calm down, but her fingers itched for the knife at her belt.

So this is what jealousy feels like. Like teetering on the precipice of a huge killing spree. I need to apologize to Macy.

"Charity, good, I was just about to text you," Devon said, turning toward her.

Too late, Mr. Smooth Operator.

"Time to go," Charity said in a flat tone. Yasmine's stupid gloating face was not helping. Charity wished she could cut that face off and wear it like a mask, Hannibal-style.

"Yes," Devon said, his eyes bearing into her.

"We're going to your house tonight, right, Devon?" Yasmine asked in that dumb, silky voice. She gave him a knowing look.

Charity stepped forward before she could stop herself, her fingers at her belt line.

Cutting out Yasmine's vocal cords was not the right

way to handle this situation. She had to calm down!

"Yes," Devon answered, green mist curling out from around him. His wolf was scrabbling to get out; Charity could feel it. She would rock its world when it did. "Roger is planning a large-scale extraction tomorrow, so we'll all stay at my place tonight. Everyone is heading over in an hour. Charity and I are going to go home and start dinner." Devon stepped beside Charity and reached out to put his hand on the small of her back, probably to guide her out.

"Touching me would be a mistake right now," Charity said in a sweet voice she didn't recognize.

"Are you okay?" he asked, following behind her as she exited the shop.

"I'm great. How about you? Can't be easy to manage all your conquests."

"Charity," he said as he opened the door of the beat-up SUV for her. "She found me in there. She was trying the flirty game, yes, but I wasn't buying. In another moment she would've gotten the message without my having to officially call her down. She's pack—there is a certain way we do things to keep squabbles to a minimum."

"Great, fine. No biggie."

"Can we talk about this?"

It sounded like that request was about as appealing to him as eating a large, juicy grub. His reluctant tone only made her madder.

"Nothing to talk about. You're a free agent, she's

crazy pretty, and I am amaze-ballz. We're all set."

"Charity—" He clenched and unclenched his jaw, then repeated the pattern with his fists on the steering wheel, trying to control his anger. The rest of the ride was tense and quiet. When they got to the house, they saw that the area beside the door was already boarded up. Sarge's remains had been collected before they'd left the house, but the scene of the attack had also been cleaned up. No blood stained the driveway. She only hoped Devon's bedroom had been thoroughly cleaned up as well.

They walked into the house silently, each depositing their bags in their separate rooms—Devon's door had been fixed, but she didn't dare go in to make sure Samantha's remains had been taken away.

"What do you want for dinner?" Charity asked Devon when they met in the kitchen.

"Are you serious? You're not going to say anything about this? I can see that you're mad, Charity. Talk to me."

At the risk of potentially freaking out, and trying to kill him with her bare hands? She was a little unhinged at the moment, so the best thing for everyone was for her to feign calm and relaxed. She had no idea what this strange feeling was that kept surging out of her depths, but it was alive and wild. Best contained until she knew what to do with it.

"I'm fine. Let's just make dinner. Actually, I could probably go faster if you went in and watched sports. Or porn. You know, whatever you lady-killers enjoy." She snapped her mouth shut. That response had gotten away from her a little at the end.

Devon made a masculine sound like a growl but didn't say anything, his handsome face shut down in frustration.

He really was a gorgeous devil. With intelligence, wit, and brilliant prospects. And he was gentle, loyal, and steadfast, too. The woman who finally landed him would be lucky.

Those thoughts weren't helping her get over him any more than her snide remarks were.

She turned to the counter. Her itching palms would have to settle for kitchen knives too dull to be plunged into the resident hot man's chest.

A WHILE LATER, as the shadows were starting to lengthen across the yard, Andy strolled into the kitchen and flopped down into one of the chairs. "What's for dinner? I'm starving."

"Roast chicken, mashed potatoes and gravy, and vegetables." Charity peeked into the oven to check on it.

"Eww, vegetables."

"They're good for you."

"I know, I was kidding. I actually like vegetables. Where's our fearless alpha?"

"Wasn't he in the living room?" Charity glanced out through the archway of the kitchen, not able to see into the living room from that angle, but giving it a try anyway.

"No." Andy scrutinized her. "What's up with you? You in a bad mood?"

Charity shook her head as Devon sauntered in from the direction of his bedroom. He had on his loose sweats, his face grim and determined. When he saw Andy, he said, "Roger set the extraction time for tomorrow, noon. The vampires have a good-sized host of demons watching the portals on the Brink side. We'll probably have to cut through them."

Charity felt her eyebrows crawl to her hairline. *Demons?*

Andy drummed the table, looking unconcerned. "How many are we going up against?"

Devon shook his head as he gave Charity a long, searching look. He lowered into a chair. "Roger isn't sure. Vlad has a lot of resources."

"What about Vlad?" Dillon asked as he entered the kitchen. Macy followed closely behind.

"What's up?" Rod asked, following the others in like a linebacker, all shoulder and muscle. "Oh man, it smells good in here."

"We're smuggling Chastity out tomorrow," Andy said with a grin at Charity.

Her stomach tightened up. Not able to help herself, she glanced at Devon. Who was glaring at Andy.

"What? Is that not funny anymore?" Andy put his hands in the air. "I'm always the last one to know things."

Rod looked back and forth between a silent Charity and the brooding alpha. His gaze fell to the ground when Yasmine walked in. Her blonde hair was done in loose curls, falling to her mid-back. She'd put on light makeup and wore yoga clothes, perfectly outlining that excellent physique.

The scorching look Yasmine gave Devon fired up Charity's craving to kill something.

"Right, I'm going to go…change," Charity said. She needed a long, hot bath and a new place to live.

"You're coming back, right?" Rod whined. "When can we take out the meat?"

"Running away?" Devon asked in a light, unaffected voice, cutting past all her defenses and stabbing her heart.

"I'm not running anywhere," Charity said in a cool tone. "I'm simply going to put on some of the new clothes I bought. You know, to *fix myself up*. Isn't that what you said? Obviously, I look like a dump and you're offended to have me in your sight."

He straightened. "That's not what I meant." His tone was angry. As usual.

"Isn't it? Then, pray tell, what does 'take some of that money and fix yourself up' mean to an intelligent jackass such as yourself?"

"Yikes," Dillon said, shrinking against the far wall. He had a girlfriend, so he was schooled in what *not* to say.

"That's one way to make enemies, I suppose," Andy

murmured.

"Don't you *dare* talk to the alpha like that," Yasmine said, and crossed her arms over her chest.

Charity's red-hot gaze swung that way, her logic on hiatus. "Who's going to stop me? *You?* Let me guess, you're going to shoot lasers out of your mostly exposed tits."

Yasmine's face turned red. Macy's jaw dropped open.

"That would be so sweet," Andy said. "I'd be down for a set of those."

"Enough, all of you," Devon barked. The wolves cowered, the ruthless power and command in Devon's voice enough to remind them of their rank.

Charity waved him away. "You're not my alpha. Stick it up your ass."

She started to walk from the room, but Devon grabbed her arm and swung her back around.

"You need to relax," he said. "You are freaking out over nothing."

Dillon covered his face with his hand. Macy gasped.

Way to work a girl up rather than calm her down.

That yawning chasm inside Charity spilled out more lava. The world went hazy for a moment before it solidified in crystal clarity. Anger and rage seethed inside her, fueled by embarrassment and hurt from the foolish things he kept saying.

Uncertainty and vulnerability curdled into some-thing unspeakably volatile. The strange hum in her body exploded.

She connected a punch to his solar plexus. Surprise spread over his face as he was blasted backward. Clearly he hadn't seen that coming.

That made two of them.

But whatever she'd tapped into felt *great*. It was a high unlike anything she'd ever experienced. Wild and unruly, her hands shot out faster than lightning, connecting blows that would cripple a human.

He wasn't human.

He blocked a kick and then a punch, apparently unsure whether he should engage.

"Fight back, bro, she's on fire," Andy yelled.

Devon blocked another punch but didn't realize it was a decoy, and got a kick to the thigh. He stumbled backward, out of the kitchen and into the sitting room. The failing light from the sliding glass door framed him. And then he took Andy's advice.

He hammered two fists at her midsection, aiming for areas that wouldn't leave lasting damage. He was faster than fast, almost on par with the mid-level vamps. On some level she knew that, yet it seemed like normal speed to her now.

She swiped a strike out of the way, grabbed his wrist, and yanked. His fall forward turned into a large step. She hammered a punch into his kidney. The wind exited his lungs, but he was already moving. He grabbed her and threw, and she went airborne across the room.

"Yield!" Devon yelled, his voice infused with fire

and power.

She hit the wall and fell to the ground. "*You* yield! I like flying." Up a moment later, with elation singing through her blood, she crouched. Ready. She was just getting warmed up.

"I'm serious, Charity, yie—"

Charity kicked, missing. A fist sailed past her face. She blocked the next punch and ducked in, slamming her fist into his side. Then she was airborne again. She hadn't seen that one coming!

A table rolled away as she tumbled to the ground. Why hadn't the fall hurt more?

She got up slowly this time, noticing he didn't advance. He was trying to throw her around to get his point across—*I'm bigger, stronger, and a superior fighter. I am better than you.*

"Yield," he called, standing straight and tall at the other end of the room. "Or I will make you yield."

She cocked her head to the side, the hum of her body so loud that she wondered if anyone else heard it. "Let's see if you like flying, too."

"Charity, *no*—"

She pushed her hands toward him. The air compressed, and electricity surged and then exploded from her. The sliding glass door shattered behind Devon and then he flew out, catching the wind like a tumbleweed. Halfway through the flying arc, he twisted and an aura of magic surrounded him. Fur erupted and his teeth grew. He landed on four feet and then shook off his tattered clothes and bits of glass.

She stared at the huge black wolf, the electricity now crackling between her fingers.

Until she glanced upward.

Shapes moved among the trees in the growing darkness, keeping to the shadows so stray light from the sunset couldn't touch their flawless skin. Predatory eyes stared at her as she stood bare-handed in the ruined doorway. A blur of movement, more perceptible than it ever had been, had her BFF appearing among the dozens of vampires, a small smile curling his shapely lips.

"I see you have found your father's gift, Arcana," he called to her, his musical voice pleasing despite his creepiness. "Let us hope you are still ignorant in all the ways to use it."

She didn't know what that meant. She did know that Vlad wasn't planning on waiting for Roger.

"How many vamps does it take to bring down that ward?" she asked Devon's pack.

Devon now faced the vamps and backed up to stand directly in front of her. He let out a wicked snarl.

"Yes, the puppy has merit, I shall grant you," Vlad said. "He might've made a worthy adversary one day. Alas, I must extinguish him tonight before he can grow into his mantle. Is not that the term he uses for my children? Extinguish? Such a callous word. So unfeeling."

"They have plenty," Rod mumbled from beside her,

his hand on her arm. It was trembling.

"Anyone call Roger?" she asked quietly, not wanting the nosey parkers hovering in the shadows, continuously looking up at the sky, to hear her. For a wonder, she only felt the excitement of the coming battle. Because there would be one. If they'd come back with these numbers, Vlad had figured out a way through the ward.

"I did," Yasmine said in a wavering voice. "He didn't answer."

"I sure hope you left a message." Andy took off his shirt. "'Cause they are coming in soon, and we're outnumbered. By a lot."

"I'm going to light this bitch up like the Fourth of July," Charity said with bubbling anticipation.

"I guess someone better turn off the oven," Rod muttered. "Dinner is canceled."

"What's gotten into you?" Dillon asked Charity.

"Don't know, but I feel great," she replied. "I need some weapons, though. I'm going to do me some killing."

Devon backed up another step and flashed Dillon a look, relaying something.

"Timmy fell down the well?" Charity said as Dillon took off down the hall.

"Have you gone insane?" Macy asked.

"They want her alive—she has nothing to worry about," Yasmine muttered darkly.

"Oh yes, being captured, imprisoned, and sucked on against her will sure sounds like a treat." Andy huffed as he slipped out of his sweats. "Should I change, Devon?"

He got a significant glance. It was apparently a yes.

Dillon jogged out of the house, also shirtless, holding a long, finely worked sword in a glittering scabbard. He pushed it at Charity. "This was hanging in the castle. It was a relic, but Roger said that when the time came, *if* it came, you'd know what to do with it. So...let's hope the time has come."

Charity reached for the artfully crafted blade as Vlad stepped out of the trees. The sun's rays had dried up and ushered in nightfall. Yee-haw.

Her hand closed around the handle. It felt like shaking hands with an old friend. A sharp, shiny, dangerous old friend that stabbed people. Better and better.

"I feel like kicking some ass," Charity said to nobody in particular.

"Shall we just let you handle it, then?" Rod started stripping down.

Vlad had spread his arms wide. A line of vamps stepped up with him along the ward.

"Oh no, we're definitely going down if we don't get help. There are way too many of them, and even though I feel more alive now than I ever have, I have no idea how to kill people. With magic."

"Kill them with the sword, then." Macy joined the boys in nakedness.

"Change, boss?" Rod asked, his eyes on Vlad.

He apparently got a no. How they could tell, Charity had no idea. Only Devon and Andy were in wolf form so far.

Vlad pulled something out of his pocket, though it was too small to see at the distance.

"He's got magic," Rod whispered. "A counter-spell for the ward. It must be. Let's hope it doesn't work."

"With all the power he's amassed, you shouldn't hold your breath," Dillon replied.

Nails grew slowly out of Vlad's hands, nothing else about him shifting. From the awestruck looks on the faces around her, that seemed to be a pretty big deal. The ward dome sparked and more vampires joined Vlad at the periphery, some fully changing to do so. The entire dome lit up, reaching over the house, sizzling and sparking. Magic bowed then arched, a sound like crackling flames ripping along the base. Fissure cracks formed, working their way through the structure.

Devon started to growl. The hair on his back stood on end, his body tense and half crouched, ready for the attack.

"Godspeed, Charity. Give 'em hell," Rod said.

Fur erupted beside her as the rest of the pack changed form. An ear-splitting crack, like thunder, rang through the fresh night. Fire crawled up the invisible wall, erupting into a huge fireball that curled into the sky.

Vlad and his vampires had overcome the ward.

"Kill the wolves; bring me the girl," Vlad shouted as the vampires, far too many of them, whizzed toward the house.

CHAPTER 41

THE WOLVES BRACED for the coming fight, having made a half-circle around her. Charity tore the scabbard off the sword. A bright blue blade glimmered in the moonlight. It sang to her, asking her to play, demanding blood. Something inside her blossomed, happy to fulfill her end of that bargain.

A first wave of vampires descended, monsters all, clearly the youngest and most inexperienced. Devon lunged, grabbing the first by the neck and ripping with his strong jaws. The creature screeched, then gurgled.

One by one, the wolves around her followed suit, attacking the closest vamps, unfortunately opening a hole directly in front of her. As if she'd done this all her life, she posed with the sword. It wasn't something she'd learned in martial arts. Her knowledge was older than that. Ingrained in her somehow.

Two mid-level vamps slowed as they neared the group, eyeing the sword like it was a beast of its own. The one on the right put on another burst of speed. Charity pivoted and then swung the sword. The blade sliced through the neck of her attacker like a knife through cream. The head rolled away and the body fell to the ground.

The other was upon her immediately.

She turned, ready to slash. A streak of black stayed her strike.

Devon rushed in and jumped. He tore a lump out of the throat and then carried the wounded creature to the ground so he could finish his work. Another vampire was already coming, though. And two more to follow.

Charity ran forward, needing more space. A vampire came at her from the left and one from the right, their hands out and their claws extended. Fangs hung from their black gums.

Charity stabbed the first, hitting the heart perfectly, like there had been a target directing her home. The one on the left reached for her, but she dodged and then curled her fingers around its swampy, bony wrist, yanked, spun, and let go. It flew toward Andy.

She pumped a burst of power in that direction. Energy exploded. Two vamps went flying, clearing the way for Andy to grab the vampire that smacked onto the ground and rolled. He pounced on it immediately, ripping through its chest to get to its heart.

A vampire charged her, its fangs flashing. She pivoted and backed down, slicing off its reaching hands. Another came at her from behind. She turned, swung, turned back, and stabbed, dropping the vamp before dancing left to a clear patch of ground. The dance was so easy somehow. So rewarding.

Her blade gouged another vamp, missing its heart. Charity ripped to the side, fixing her mistake. It howled, squirming as it died, creating a temporary blockage for the creature behind it. Charity used the opening she'd created to shove a vamp away from the red-splotched white wolf. Hopefully that wasn't Yasmine's blood.

A fierce growl was followed by a yelp. Fear zipped through Charity's battle high. She slashed the creature in her way so she could see. A gray wolf lay on its side as a vamp descended.

Before Charity could react, Devon was there, ripping the creature away.

A claw raked her arm. Charity spun and punched, the creature too close for her to maneuver the sword. Her magic exploded on impact. The creature's head sailed ten feet further than its body.

She hacked through another's middle. The vampires were attacking more fiercely now—no longer trying to simply catch her, but trying to maim her to make the extraction easier.

Bring it.

Electricity sizzled down her blue blade, almost like the thing was a conductor for her magic. The vampire's guts sizzled as the sword slid deeper into its gut, the creature howling as it staggered backward.

Gracefully dancing to the next vampire, she swung her blade, swiping off a leg, then an arm. She pushed out with her palm, scattering the few creatures clustered in front of her, but the older ones were pushing in on her. The faster vampires with more experience and battle savvy were surrounding her, trying to get at her back. She couldn't turn fast enough, or deliver potent enough cuts with her sword. Combat came naturally to her, but she still was far from experienced.

The beginning of the end.

Charity raised her hand in the air to attempt sunlight. Maybe it would give her and the pack the chance to run. If they made it to the cars, they'd have a chance.

Focusing on her middle, she felt magic surge around her, followed by an earth-shattering roar that shook her bones. Other, smaller roars chorused, followed by the shrieking of a vampire and what sounded like a loud bellow.

Backup had arrived.

Charity shoved her palm forward, exploding the vampires in front of her out of the way. Then froze.

She stared into the gleaming red eyes of some sort of gray-skinned humanoid ram. Two hoofed legs ended in an exposed manhood and the bare torso and arms of a man. Black horns curled out from a bald head. The mouth was too big, filled with fangs, and the creature stood at least eight feet tall. It did not carry a weapon, which made her somewhat nervous. The only time a fighter didn't need a weapon was if he was a weapon himself.

"Not good..." Charity muttered, gripping her sword's hilt with both hands.

The creature stepped toward her, its eyes pulsing

red, its mouth twisted. "Come with me, fae," it rasped.

"So not good…" She back-pedaled.

It came at her. Its big arm swung out, leaving wisps of fire left in its wake. She sliced through its skin, and a gash opened. Slugs and crawlers wriggled out, like she'd lifted a log in a shady part of the woods.

A demon. It had to be.

She screamed—she couldn't help it—and slashed. Another gash opened. Horrible insects squirmed along its skin. Real or an illusion, she couldn't tell, but her skin crawled. The thing grabbed for her. Its claws caught on her sleeve and pulled.

She'd never gotten out of a hoodie so fast in her life.

Dancing back, she swung her sword and then jabbed, sticking it into the stomach. More insects. Its face didn't so much as tweak in discomfort. She lifted her sword for another strike as a huge tan shape streaked through the air.

A lioness landed on the creepy thing's shoulders, hanging on to it with strong paws. Another lioness lunged, ripping into insect-frenzied lateral muscles. Gray wolves of all sizes cut between Charity and the demon, swarming her and forcing her back toward the house.

"No! I am not leaving Devon and his pack," she cried.

One wolf, the biggest, looked up. Intelligent human eyes, one blue, one green, met hers. Roger had come.

He snarled, and the line of wolves advanced on her,

continuing to back her up. Trying to usher her to safety.

Futile effort. Team members didn't leave one another behind. Devon and his pack had sacrificed themselves for her, and now she would do the same for them. Maybe she hadn't been with them long, but they'd accepted her as one of their own. They were the only family she had left, and she would protect them with everything in her.

She shoved a palm out and felt lava surge up within her. Electricity crackled through the air before the concussion. Furry bodies fell backward and kept going, rolling across the hard ground like rocks.

She ran, jumped off the deck, and slashed into a vampire. An arm went flying. She slapped her hand on another vamp's body and exploded it, guts flying everywhere. Whirling, she struck through a chest and got lucky enough to hit the heart. The being convulsed and howled.

The new wolves crowded around her again, this time not trying to force her anywhere. They'd clearly learned their lessons and were now just trying to help.

A teeth-chattering roar announced the arrival of a huge white bear—no, not a bear. Bears didn't have two horns curling from the sides of their heads.

Charity had to pause in bewilderment for a second.

A yeti!

It lumbered in front of her, its chest broader and arms longer than that of a bear. This animal was meant to walk upright, with incredible strength in its upper body. One swipe of its large, claw-tipped hand sent a vampire flying. The yeti crunched another vamp's shoulder with its sharp teeth, and when it shook its shaggy head, the vampire flew apart like an old chew toy.

A chorus of wolves' snarling filled the yard. Roger had brought enough troops to even the playing field.

Charity jogged over a pile of festering insects and then barely ducked in time to miss a limb of fire rocketing at her head. Its spiky-headed owner howled before swinging the arm at her again. Flames licked the creature's body and crawled up its twisted and hideous face. The wolves danced around it, probably nervous their fur would catch fire if they attacked.

"Conundrum," Charity said, wondering the same thing about her hair. "I hope I don't end up looking stupid."

She ran at it, getting inside that arm, before thrusting her sword into its middle. Fire surged around her, kissing her skin. Pain blossomed, and she pumped her magic higher, electrifying the air.

Her magic could fight his demon fire.

She ripped the blade out of its middle and thrust again, and again, hacking like a wild thing and feeling the song of her blade as she did so.

A wolf barreled into the side of the fiery demon. He or she then yelped and rolled away, fur singed and smoking.

She stepped back, spun to get momentum, and

sliced with everything she had. Her blade cut through its neck, nearly sticking on bone halfway through. Her magic crackled around her, fighting the creature's attempt to summon more fire.

The head fell off, but Charity didn't wait to appraise her handiwork.

Panting, getting tired, she looked up at the frenzy of fur and filth in front of her. The battle was alive with teeth and claws. And then, like magic, a path opened up diagonally. Her gaze was sucked in that direction. Her stomach dropped out.

At the edge of the battle stood Vlad, staring at her, clearly waiting for her to notice. With the forces Roger had brought, he knew he couldn't make the grab. How could he not?

He gave her a grin, like a promise, and then point-edly looked down at his feet.

A warthog ran past in a blur. Once the way was clear, a sob of horror caught in Charity's throat.

On its side, trying in vain to get up, lay a large black wolf.

"Oh no," she breathed.

Liquid glistened in Devon's fur, and judging by his weak attempts to get to his feet, it was his blood.

"Take me!" she screamed, staggering forward. "Leave him and take me."

Roger growled and stepped in her way. More of his shifters joined him, cutting her off. She'd not only have to fight the vamps and demons to cross the divide, she'd have to fight her allies, too. To them, she was more valuable than Devon. They'd let him die to save her. She would never get there in time.

As if hearing her thoughts, Vlad smiled and gave her a "naughty, naughty" finger. He was blaming her for so many of his vampires dying, for not coming quietly like he'd wanted. For not giving in days ago.

Claws erupted from his fingers, and he swiped down toward Devon.

Time slowed. Each heartbeat lasted ten minutes. Fear such as she had never known stole her breath. And she erupted.

Sunlight lit up the sky, so bright that even the wolves cringed, but that wicked claw kept going, Vlad undeterred by his smoking skin.

Charity dropped her sword and threw out her hands with a scream.

A jet of pure white light shot from her palms, coalescing to form a thick, buzzing ball. It smashed into the vampire. The razor-sharp claw barely grazed Devon's fur as Vlad jolted back. Devon yelped in pain.

Vlad burst into flame, apparently too old and powerful to explode, as she intuitively knew a lesser vampire would. The flames engulfed him, wild and vicious. Clothes tore as he turned into his monster form. He howled, his body now a bonfire.

The flaming vampire took off running, screeching as he did so. The other vampires followed, their hands held above their heads to ward off Charity's sunlight.

The demons, what was left of them, joined the retreat.

The shifters ran after them, clearly wanting to kill whatever they could.

Charity swayed, feeling like she'd run ten miles in concrete shoes underwater. Her vision started to waver. Large arms caught her and picked her up. Her head lolled on a thick shoulder.

"What about Devon?" she asked hoarsely.

"We'll look after Devon," Roger said softly, carrying her into the house.

She tried to struggle, but everything turned black.

CHAPTER 42

"**H**OW'S THE GIRL?" Steve asked, stalking into the room like he was looking for prey. Wolves always had a light-footed predatory thing going, but the big cats were ridiculous for it. You'd think they were constantly in a game of hide-and-seek.

Roger leaned back from the desk in Devon's sparse office. For a guy who went to school, he didn't seem to use the place much. If Roger hadn't known for a fact the kid was getting excellent grades, he would have stuck his nose in.

"She's fine. She's sleeping it off."

"I hear she threw you through a window."

Roger glared at Steve, not pleased that the story had gotten out. Steve met the stare for a beat before lowering his eyes, just shy of a challenge. It was another irritating thing about cats—always trying to push their independence.

"She woke up as weak as a kitten and demanded to see Devon," Roger explained. "I said no. She listens about as well as you do. It took the last of her resources, but…"

Steve started laughing in big, body-racking guffaws. "The only one to challenge you and win, huh?"

"She's a warrior fae. I can't teach her a lesson unless I want her whole posse on my back. I figured it was easier letting them heal together."

"I hear those two bicker a lot."

Roger snorted. That was an understatement. "They're twenty-somethings—barely adults. Life for them right now is all about fire and passion and wild mood swings. Charity probably doesn't know if she wants to slap him or wrap her legs around him."

Steve bent forward, chortling. "I remember those days. Had a girl that drove me mad. The best was when she slapped me *as* she was wrapping her legs around me."

Roger smiled. The young alpha and the Arcana had formed a tight bond. Charity had proved that today by, yes, using her damned power to toss Roger through a window so she could get to Devon's side.

Devon had proved his devotion, too. He'd gone for Vlad. The young alpha must've known it would be his death. But he had distracted Vlad long enough for the vampires and demons to lose focus as a group. They'd fallen out of sync, allowing Roger to break through the outer barrier and put a crew around Charity. Without a strong leader giving constant, clear orders, lower-tier demons and younger vampires were mindless killing machines, easier to take down. Devon had tried to sacrifice himself to buy her time, something that had surely saved her. In so doing, he'd also created a win for the whole pack.

It was a big day for that sub-alpha. He'd earned a promotion. It would make him the youngest alpha in history to rise so quickly, beating out Roger by ten months. He'd made that leap in part because of Charity.

Steve gazed at Roger thoughtfully. "You're sure, then, huh? That stuff she did, that is normal warrior fae behavior?"

Roger nodded slowly. "Except for that ball of...light? Energy? I couldn't get a good reading on that. No one has heard anything about it. The beta is checking it out."

Steve leaned back and crossed his ankle over his knee. "Whatever she is, she's useful. Hacked through a bunch of vamps. Pretty sleek, too. She knows how to handle that blade."

Roger clasped his fingers together. "That was the first time she's used it. Her control over her magic is largely instinctual, at present. She's had no training, and I would bet she hasn't yet realized her full power."

Steve's eyes widened.

Roger nodded. "Exactly. This is just the beginning. Untrained, brand new, she is worth two experienced shifters in battle. Maybe three. If paired with Devon, constantly bucking his natural tendency to dominate, she'll be even better still."

"Think she killed that elder?"

"Vlad probably isn't dead. Burnt to a crisp, surely,

but his minions will get him blood fast enough to save him. He's too old to be taken down that easily." Roger braced his elbows against the desk.

"Well…" Steve drawled, making a show of twiddling his thumbs. Roger kept his irritation from showing. Barely. "As soon as the warrior fae learn you've got one of theirs, they'll come looking. Luckily, they'll knock. If the elves find out…well, they *don't* knock."

"Thank you, Steven, for this fascinating glimpse at things I already know."

Steve grinned. "You'll have to take her to the warrior fae, eventually. Or else, if you don't care about forming an allegiance with the fae, you could always let the elves take her. They'd give a handsome reward, I imagine, especially if she's really an Arcana."

"If you plan to turn traitor, Steve, I'll kill you before you can make it to the portal."

Steve threw up his hands, still sporting that irritating grin. "That's not what I'm saying, boss. All I'm saying is that the trek from the castle to the Flush can be dangerous. Elves don't police it as closely as they should. Could be you need someone that is excellent in defense turned offense."

Roger snorted. "And I assume you mean you?"

"You don't have anybody better."

"Why would I entrust her safety to a guy that would drop everything for a nap in the sun?"

"I've always wanted to travel the Realm, and I've

always wanted to bed a fae. This is my chance to do both."

"Travel the Realm on my dime?"

"All good things to those who wait."

Roger stared at him for a moment. Steve was right: he was the best in defense turned offense. Male lions, by nature, didn't put themselves in jeopardy if they could help it, but once they decided to engage, they were a force to be reckoned with. Steve would require a powerful alpha to keep him in line, however. Devon had promise, but he wasn't there yet.

"Worst-case scenario," Steve said, "The girl pushes me around, right? She can throw me through a…tree."

Roger shook his head. "It's all up in the air right now. First, she and Devon need to heal. After that, I'll see."

Steve got up slowly, half stretching as he did so. He scratched his stomach with a grin as he said, "All I'm saying is, if you need bodyguard detail, I'm your man."

Roger huffed out a laugh as soon as Steve was out of the room. He was a handful, plain and simple, but he was a good guy. More importantly, he was a pack guy who could navigate the wilds. Tempting.

Roger stared down at his papers, thinking.

There was no way he was going to present Charity to the Flush unless they were a hundred percent sure of her heritage. Right now there weren't many other options, but still. He'd hate to make a fool of himself. That meant taking a trip to Charity's family house and trying to locate her mom.

He had no doubt of what they'd find—he'd seen her fight out there—which led him to his next problem. How would he get her back if they sent her to the Flush to train? She'd suddenly have family, money, and a real sense of community. How many girls turned down a chance to be a princess?

Roger scratched his chin in irritation.

She had the bond with Devon. The best-case scenario would be if that bond turned into love. Given what Roger had heard of the warrior fae and their inclusive community, possibly the only thing that could tear a princess away from her throne was the man who held her heart.

He hoped Devon was up to the task.

CHAPTER 43

D EVON STIRRED, FOLLOWED by a wince. Every part of his body seemed to hurt. That old vamp had beaten the hell out of him. Devon had held his own against a mid-level, but…well, now he knew his own limits.

He flexed his toes, followed by his fingers, making sure everything worked. It was then he felt the small, delicate hand clinging to his.

In a moment of panic, he thought it was Yasmine. She was persistent, and a girl like her would absolutely sit by her alpha's bed to stake her claim and get in good with her desired mate. Marry the same girl, though, and she'd turn distant in a flash, having gotten what she was after.

Devon let his head fall to the side. An ethereal beauty marred with cuts and scrapes lay next to him. Her hair fell around her face in thick brownish-red waves, her lower lip was swollen, and her cheek was black and blue. She was the most beautiful thing he'd ever seen in his life.

He squeezed her hand, willing her awake. Her

breathing was deep and heavy, not like her. Usually, she was an extremely light sleeper who'd stir if he so much as shifted.

"Don't worry. She's fine."

Devon's gaze snapped to the door. His neck protested painfully at the sudden movement.

Roger stood in the frame dressed in a T-shirt that strained at the shoulders and hung loose at the waist. He didn't bother coming further into the room.

"How do you feel?" he asked in his customary calm tone.

"I hurt, for the most part, but I'll be fine. That old vamp was something else. He was… I've never seen anything move so fast and react so savagely."

"Puts hair on your chest."

Devon wheezed out a laugh. "Exactly. I should be as fuzzy as you."

Roger's gaze drifted to Devon and Charity's entwined fingers. "Girls like to know how you feel about them. They like to know where they stand."

Relationship advice from his boss? How'd Devon get so unlucky?

"Got it," Devon said absently. Then, because he didn't know what the hell he was doing, he added, "But she doesn't ever bring that stuff up. I'd feel like an idiot saying anything."

Roger shifted, getting more comfortable. "Well, you're a ladies' man, and she's smart. She probably doesn't want to feel like a fool. You have to suck this one up."

"Nice pep talk, coach."

Roger grinned. "Take it from a failed pro. She'll eat it up."

Devon shook his head and looked back at Charity. "She saved my life."

"You saved hers."

"Nah, I was trying to give her some time to run. Or give you an opening to force her away. But she went and saved me. For the second time."

"I did try to force her away. I also tried to keep her in her room to heal. You're alive, and she's next to you. A smart man knows what that means."

"When have I been a smart man?" Devon whispered, drinking in the sight of her.

"When it counts." Roger straightened up. "I'm keeping her in your pack. I'm also pushing your pack up a level and adding some members. It'll mean you have some older, more experienced, and possibly unruly pack members under your command, but it'll give you a chance to show what you're made of. I wouldn't be giving you this role if you didn't have her by your side. She gives your pack more power, as warrior fae did in times of old. In the event someone stronger than you defies you, remember that fighting is awfully hard when you're being flung through a window."

With a grim face, Roger gave him a slight nod and stepped away.

Apparently Roger had heard about Devon and

Charity's fight. It had been a sliding glass door, though.

He sighed as Charity stirred against him. She issued a little feminine mew before running a hand up his chest and hooking it around his neck. She squeezed a little as her eyes fluttered open.

"Hey," he said softly.

Her eyes darted up to his, and supreme relief crossed her expression, followed by a beautiful smile.

"Hey," she said, and turned a little, covering more of his side. "How are you feeling?"

"Good."

Her smile burned brighter. "Liar."

It hurt to chuckle.

"I hear you saved my life," he said. "Again."

She shrugged and winced. "You tried to sacrifice yourself so that I could get to safety. Again. I think we're even."

He pressed his lips against her forehead. When that wasn't enough, he tilted her chin up and kissed her sweet lips.

"I'd do it again in a heartbeat," he whispered.

Moisture caught in her thick lashes. "Thank you. For everything. I know I haven't made this easy on you, but you never backed down. You've always been there for me. It means more than I can express."

He smiled and kissed her again, rolling just a little so he could feel more of her body. Feeling his ardor rise, and the pain of movement rise with it.

It still hurt to chuckle. "Making love to you is going

to have to wait, but…you're more…than a duty to me, Charity. I care about you." Talking about his feelings hadn't gotten any easier, or less awkward, but in this he would listen to Roger. "So much. I want you to know that. That I have feelings for you."

Her eyes were large and open, inviting him all the way down to her soul.

"I like you too. A lot."

Her smile was just for him, wrapping around his heart and squeezing.

She had a hold on his vitals, and he didn't ever want her to let go.

CHAPTER 44

CHARITY HEAVED A sigh as she lugged her backpack higher on her shoulders. The thing felt like it was full of bricks. She paused in between the buildings, angling her face up toward the blessed sunshine.

It had been two weeks since the battle, and no one had seen hide nor hair of her BFF. In fact, the vampires in the area had made themselves scarce. Word was that they didn't trust a woman who could rain down sunshine on them in the middle of the night.

Charity would take it. She wasn't totally sure how to control her power, but if she had them running scared for the moment, she'd count her blessings.

"What's up, Charity?" Andy walked toward her with a welcoming smile, Rod at his side.

"What's for dinner?" Rod asked by way of hello.

"Really, dude?" Andy put out his hands and frowned at Rod. "It's the middle of the day, you haven't seen her since last night, and the first thing you do is try to get something out of her?"

Rod gestured at Charity angrily as they stopped next to her. "She likes cooking! I'm discussing one of her hobbies."

"Oh sure, yeah. That was your master plan. Discussing hobbies." Andy rolled his eyes for Charity's benefit. "That big blockhead on your shoulders must be hard to lug around."

"Shut up, dick. She knows I'm always around to help." Rod pulled Charity in for a one-armed hug. "Hi. Good to see you again."

Andy stared at him.

"What?" Rod asked.

"I was waiting for you to double down and ask what was for dinner again."

"Shut up." Rod stepped away. "Like you don't want to know."

Charity laughed at their antics, starting forward. "Roger is staying for dinner, I think. He's bringing that crew to fix the ward and read our fortunes or something. I don't know; I stopped listening when Devon started to fuss. Anyway, I'd planned to do a—"

"Ah crap." Andy blew out his breath and stared at Rod for a moment, who stared back. He shook his head. "I forgot all that was happening tonight. I'm out, bro. The joy of eating Charity's food will be totally sucked out of the room with Roger lording over everything. Then there's Alder. Whenever he looks at me, I get the feeling he wants to cut my ear off."

"What?" Charity asked, unexpectedly spitting out laughter. "Why—"

"Yeah, I see that," Rod said, nodding seriously. "Or

some other extremity."

"You guys are crazy." Charity pulled her backpack strap a little higher, trying to stop it from digging into her shoulder.

"Here." Rod grabbed the top strap and peeled it off her back. "I got that."

"First useful thing you've done all day," Andy said.

"You're going to get a thump if you keep it up," Rod shot back.

They took a turn around the path, and the area opened up. Charity spied Devon off to the side, sitting on a bench with his head down over his phone. Her stomach flipped before it filled with butterflies. Her core pooled with heat. Two weeks since they'd told each other they had feelings, and still she got nervous when she saw him. Nervous, and desperate for his touch.

Her chest constricted as they got closer and he looked up. A smile flashed across his handsome face, and two passing gals slowed to gawk their approval.

A rush of jealousy filled Charity with fire. She took a deep breath to quell her raging magic.

Devon's smile burned brighter. He thought her possessiveness was hilarious, mostly because she thought his jealousy absurd. Logically, she knew jealousy stemmed from trust issues, and she didn't have those. At all. But she couldn't control herself. If a girl flirted with Devon, stared too hard, or even stood too close, magic dumped into Charity's body and she wanted to cut a bitch. Then burn her house down. Then pull up her flower bed and plant cactuses. It was ludicrous. Absolutely nuts.

And yet it would not go away.

It wasn't the only thing that wouldn't go away. She flew off the handle a lot. Something triggered her, or nothing triggered her, and suddenly magic flooded her, urging her to reach for the closest sharp thing. It couldn't be natural, something she kept trying to tell Roger. She could regain control with effort, but it was getting harder, the magical surges stronger. Sometimes, the only outlet that helped was sparring with Devon. The furniture had all been broken and glued back together by now. Thankfully, the bed was sturdy, or that would've broken in the naked aftermath of her magic-fueled temper.

"It's weird when he smiles," Rod murmured to Andy. "It makes me think he's about ready to attack me."

"Who, Roger?" Andy asked.

"No—well, him, too, but I meant Devon," Rod answered.

"He might. Even with Charity to even him out a little, he's still a moody SOB."

"You guys—" Charity huffed out more laughter at their absurdity.

"Hey," Devon said, walking toward them.

"Hey," she replied, and she knew she had a goofy smile on her face.

"How was your class?" Devon slipped an arm

around her shoulders.

They talked about nothing much, keeping it light and easy, as they made their way to the loaner Jeep. Devon's SUV was still in the shop, the establishment apparently owned by a shifter who wasn't employed by Roger. He specialized in making up reasons for things like claw marks in the paint.

After Andy and Rod made excuses to get out of dinner that night and parted ways with Charity and Devon, they got in the car and headed home. A moment passed, then Devon cleared his throat.

"Charity, listen," he said. "What we have… What we're… I wanted to tell you—"

"Whoa, whoa, whoa." Charity put out her hand. She'd suspected this was coming, what with Roger breathing down their necks, hinting about opening up and throwing around the L-word. Yeah, right, like that hard-ass alpha ever talked about what made him tick. He certainly hadn't given Devon any advice on how to go about it, because the start of this chat was going as awkwardly as Charity had assumed it would.

This wasn't any of Roger's business. It wasn't anyone's business. Devon didn't have any experience with attachments or relationships. He'd rebuilt his whole life after the *summons*, and he'd done so around the idea of himself as the solitary alpha. Even though that idea might not fit as snugly as it used to, he still had a lot of baggage to unpack. Baggage he had to fold up and put away by himself.

Charity would be damned if she'd hurry him up while he remade the man he was. The process would take time and go through many hiccups. If there were labels slapped on things, and expectations, and hills to climb, it would only take longer. Plus, she had her own issues to sort out.

No, for right now, as she settled into this new life, she liked things exactly as they were. They liked each other, they were dating—they didn't need any L-word complications. They had enough complications with all the times she randomly went crazy and tried to kill him. Luckily, he just viewed it as exercise.

"Look, here's my hang-up," she said, trying not to let the awkwardness of the moment affect her. There was only one thing she did have to insist on. "I'm not much of a player—obviously—and I don't care for the game. If we're sleeping with each other, I'd have a hard time with you seeing anyone else."

A rush of rage and magic swept through her, and she braced against the dash, fighting it into submission. The spicy adrenaline felt so good that she wanted to cry.

Devon chuckled darkly then sobered. "Hey, are you okay? I wouldn't do that to you, Charity. I'm a dick, but I'm not a complete jackass. I've never juggled women. It's always been one at a time. It just never lasted—"

"Stop," she said as he pulled into the driveway, clutching her seat and gritting her teeth. Electricity ran along her skin. Light danced before her eyes. "Don't talk… I need…"

She groped for the door handle and half fell out of the Jeep, staggering toward the trees and taking a big whiff of fresh, forest-rich air. Sometimes it was the only thing that would calm her.

Her magic tore at her, begging to be used. Not able to stand the pressure, she thrust her hands into the sky and let it come.

Sparks and light showered down, brighter than the afternoon sun. Electricity sizzled through the air before it concussed, exploding out toward the trees. Sparks caught in the branches and dried grass. Embers flared. Flames danced.

"Oh God," she said, euphoric and horrified at the same time. "I'll burn the whole—"

Shockingly, the flames shrank then died. The smoke curled then cleared away. Her light show dimmed until it faded.

"Oh," she said, amazingly not weak like she had been after the battle. Still feeling pretty great, actually. Strong. Too powerful. "I guess the magic just…goes away."

"Nope."

Only then did Charity notice the small collection of people standing outside of Devon's house, staring at her. Roger waited among them, standing next to a slouching, pretty brunette who didn't fool Charity. She might look small and fragile, but Charity didn't want to be on the wrong end of whatever she could do. Beside her stood a tall, broad man with a curious expression and hard, ruthless eyes. If he'd been walking toward her in her old neighborhood in Chicago, she would've ducked into an alley, jumped in a dumpster to hide, and hoped for the best.

A blonde woman stepped forward, drawing Charity's gaze with her over-the-top confidence, scuffed leather pants that looked like they'd been through hell and back, combat boots, and beat-up fanny pack.

"I figured I'd lend a hand," the woman said, gesturing at the trees. "You looked like you were having a moment. I didn't want a forest fire to interrupt it."

The way she held herself, rough and loose, spoke of an experienced, nonchalant fighter. Her smile held easy humor and her eyes sparked crazy. This woman had led a hard life of violence. If Charity were in that dumpster, hiding from the man, this woman would find her and fish her out. The gun strapped to her thigh, the throwing knives in the ankle brace, and the sword peeking out behind her were all overkill.

"Who are these people?" she asked Devon, who had caught up to her.

"It's a long story," Devon said. "Basically, we helped them take on an organization called the Mages' Guild, which had gone corrupt." Gesturing to the terrifying blonde, he added, "She's the one Vlad is respectfully wary of, Reagan Somerset. And for good reason—her magic is insane. As is she. She drinks a bunch of whiskey and chases shifters around New Orleans. Anyway, because we helped them, Penny, the brunette, agreed to help us."

"That's not why we agreed." Reagan walked toward a sleek red SUV parked in the driveway. She opened the back, flashing Charity the emblem.

"Since when did Ferrari start making SUVs?" she asked despite herself.

"I know, right?" Reagan huffed. "Sellouts. This one hasn't released to the general public yet. I'm only driving it because it's Moss's new car, and he's going to be *pissed* it was stolen."

"Wait," Penny said, "that's Moss's? Did my mother put you up to this?"

"Yup," Reagan replied with a smirk.

"Who is Mo—"

"Got something for ya," Reagan cut Charity off, pulling out a long parcel wrapped in a burlap sack.

"It's easier if you roll with it," Devon told Charity softly, his hand on her back.

"Roll with what?" Charity asked.

"Us." Reagan strode toward them, holding the parcel out in front of her. "Well, Penny, to be precise. She wears on you at first, but eventually she redeems herself."

"Her jokes never get any better," Penny said.

Reagan laughed. "Why improve upon perfection?" She stopped in front of Charity. "I'm Reagan, the happily insane one. Damn glad to meet you. You have a long, crazy road ahead of you, but what an introduction to your mettle, huh? I was hanging on the edge of my seat, listening to Roger recount the story." She pushed the parcel out a little more. "Dizzy made this for you." Clearly seeing Charity's confused look, she said, "A dual-mage friend of mine. It seems Roger isn't nearly as cheap as we all thought."

Roger shifted his weight, but didn't comment. Charity barely stopped her jaw from dropping open. Was this what Devon meant by rolling with it? She hadn't realized Roger was capable of "rolling" with anything.

"Go ahead," Reagan said, hefting the parcel. "Open it."

Charity gingerly took the package, the core hard and unmoving. She peeled back the burlap, and the sun glinted on deep crimson metal. Removing the rest of the covering, she sucked in a breath.

The sword's finely wrought handle practically glued itself to her palm, finally quelling the itch she'd felt since her power had awakened. Magic flowed out of her and into the metal, a soft hum cutting through the silence. The tip of the deep crimson blade sparked before a sheen of light flowed back over the weapon and soaked into it. She sighed, letting her eyes drift closed. The hilt in her hand felt...divine. Perfect. She didn't even feel the need to sprint at the onlookers and cut off their heads. She was content to hold it in the sunlight, feeling the warmth on her face and in her body.

Reagan stepped back. "Welcome to magic. We have the coolest stuff."

"The magical properties of that blade can be altered,

depending on how your magic grows," Roger said. He gestured Charity closer. "I had the maker—Dizzy—research the types of blades warrior fae used back when they roamed the Brink. He fashioned something in that vein."

"My mother gave it some finishing touches, based on what she *saw*," Penny said.

"What she...saw?" Charity asked, lowering the sword to her side. She didn't want to let it go.

Reagan grimaced. "She's a *Seer*. The worst type of magic, if you ask me."

"Please, Charity, come inside," Roger said, putting out his hand.

Reagan frowned and turned toward him. "Since when do you ask nicely?" She snapped her fingers. "Oh, now I remember. After you get thrown through a window."

Roger's face closed down into a terrifying mask of rage. A thread of anxiety wormed through Charity, and Devon stiffened. Unbelievably, Reagan laughed and turned, falling in beside them.

"By the way, Devon," she said as Devon gently nudged Charity to start walking, "I heard you had a little soiree in your backyard. I'm pissed you didn't invite me. I mean, I wouldn't have been able to participate, what with vampire politics and all, but man, would I have liked to see Vlad's face when Charity barbecued him. I am *so sorry* I missed that."

"The ward was poorly done if a bunch of vampires

could break through." Penny looked out toward the trees. "We can keep it roughly the same size, Roger, but I wouldn't be opposed to adding some booby traps. Charity's magic is fascinating. Bold and electric. It has this"—Penny closed her eyes and tilted her face upward—"lightness to it. Pureness." She smiled and touched her middle. "It feels good. Like the pulse of life. I can see why shifters are drawn to it."

Charity swung the sword, just to feel its weight. "What magic do you have?"

"She's a natural dual-mage with spunk." Reagan winked at Charity. "She stole the spunk from a nasty little goblin."

"I didn't steal it," Penny replied with the annoyance of a woman who was tired of this topic. "I inherited it."

"You ripped it out of its grubby little hands when you killed it," Reagan shot back with an evil grin.

Penny frowned at her then shifted her focus to the driveway. "As I was saying, Charity's magic has less finesse, but that'll actually make it easier for the ward. I can weave elements of her ability into the traps. Now..." She put out a finger, and the rest of the group stopped next to her. "It might blow off someone's leg. That's the downside. But only vampires or demons will set off the trigger, so..."

"You can do that?" Charity asked, swinging her sword again.

"It's a great big world, lady," Reagan said. "You haven't even scratched the surface."

CHAPTER 45

D EVON KEPT A firm hand on Charity, remembering his induction to magic and knowing Charity would need a little support. The team Roger had amassed here included what was probably the most powerful magical talent in the Brink. He didn't even know what Reagan's magic was, just that it had turned the tide in that battle with the mages, and he'd never seen or smelled anything like it. She and her crew collectively possessed a level of experience that was probably boggling Charity's mind.

"Shall we step inside to speak with Karen?" Roger asked, gesturing toward the door.

Devon nudged Charity gently, watching her move that crimson sword in tiny circles. The tip sparked, and occasionally a zagging line of electric magic crisscrossed the blade.

"Who is Karen?" Charity whispered, glancing at Reagan, who nodded and stepped away. She wouldn't be following them into the house. Thank God for small miracles. The woman was unpredictable, and anything might set Charity off right now.

Karen, Penny's mom, an older woman with intelligent blue eyes and an impatient air, waited for them in the dining room. Alder stood at her side, his posture stiff and arms at his back. A crystal ball sat in front of her on a black velvet mat. Next to that was an old and badly worn stack of tarot cards. At the end of the setup, a martini.

"So…you're the—"

"*Seer*, yes," Karen interrupted. "Put your sword…" She squinted at Charity. "Never mind. Sit down."

Charity's brow furrowed, and she looked at Devon for the go-ahead.

"The alpha is looking for you," Alder told Devon, Alder's unwavering stare beating into him, raising Devon's hackles. Charity's magic pulsed into the room, wild and raw and fierce, shocking through Devon's middle. His magic rose to answer the call.

Devon struggled his gaze downward. He had no intention of challenging a superior tonight. "Yes, sir."

"But what if I…?" Charity said, her gaze imploring.

"I'll be right outside," Devon told her, knowing she was worried her magic would surge and she'd have no one around to temper it.

As he was walking out, he heard the snap of the tarot deck and "Well, didn't you find yourself a handsome young man. Congratulations. Just remember, they don't come trained. You have to do that yourself."

Roger waited outside with Reagan, the two of them watching the natural dual-mages standing at the edge of the grass, talking and gesturing as they prepared the new ward. Devon had seen what they were capable of. It was awe-inspiring. That Roger was paying for them to erect a ward around his house showed how serious he was about keeping Charity safe.

"How is she?" Roger asked when Devon joined their powwow.

Devon shook his head. "Her surges of magic are getting stronger. They feel like needles along my skin at this point. Sometimes I have to fight her into submission, and that turns bloody."

"The sword should help a little," Reagan said. "Karen was adamant that she have it sooner rather than later. But it's just a patch. I asked Darius about the warrior fae. He says they typically shepherd their own kind into full magic. At least, the stronger ones do. A warrior fae on her own won't be able to handle the surges when they get too strong. Charity will need guidance. She'll need to be among her own kind."

Roger nodded and turned, looking out at the trees. "We're trying to wait until the end of the school term so we have the whole summer."

Reagan smiled briefly. "You're hoping the start of school will be enough to pull her back out of the Flush?"

"I'm hoping."

"Roger, come on. She's a princess. A *princess*—"

"We're not sure of that," Roger said.

Reagan's eyes widened, and she pointed to where Charity had stood when she'd expelled her magic.

"Really? Not a princess? The backlash of her magic earlier nearly blew my eyebrows off, and thanks to Penny, I just had to have them regrown. That woman is a beast. Besides, do you really think Vlad would be this interested in her if she were any normal magical creature? He got barbecued, man! *Barbecued.* And do you know what he's doing right now? Sitting in the vampire lair in the Realm, all pasty and half charcoaled, drafting plans. He's more intrigued than he ever was. He still means to capture her and use her. If he gets her, then his focus will shift back to me. It's in everyone's best interest if you keep that girl out of his hands. So cut the crap, and start thinking rationally. She needs help, and only her people will give it to her."

Devon held his breath. As a rule, no one spoke to Roger that way. Not unless they wanted a hard lesson in respect.

But Roger just blew out a breath and tucked his hands into his pockets. "We'll see what Karen has to say."

"You guys set too much stock on a silly type of magic," Reagan muttered.

A grin tweaked Roger's lips. "If we were talking about anyone but Ms. Bristol, I'd agree wholeheartedly. Which you know, since you've been on the receiving end of her…fortunes, as well."

Reagan scowled. "Fair enough."

Roger sobered. "I doubt Charity will let us take her out of school unless she's on her death bed."

"Wait as long as you can, sure, but don't wait too long," Reagan said. "Otherwise, you'll have a dead Arcana on your hands, and several very angry live Arcanas at your door."

Roger shook his head and watched Penny and Emery wave their hands in the air, obviously weaving magic. "She was magnificent in that battle. Courageous and brutal, fast and efficient. Everything I've heard warrior fae are supposed to be, and she is completely untrained in her magic. She worked with my wolves perfectly, with the loyalty I'd expect of one of my shifters." He threw a glance at Devon. "If we'd had a host of warrior fae at the Mages' Guild, we would've dominated without question. And Vlad's changing party would have been a nonstarter."

Reagan turned and stared directly into his eyes, a challenge by shifter standards. Roger didn't seem to notice.

"Vlad is planning big things. Huge things. Things that will greatly affect us all. Here. In the Realm. And even in the Underworld. You cannot let him have Charity. He'll know exactly how to use her to manipulate the warrior fae. She needs to be in the protective fold of her kind. I cannot stress that enough."

"I heard you the first time," Roger growled.

The door opened, revealing a grim-faced Alder. "She wishes to speak with Devon."

Roger motioned Devon in before turning back to Reagan.

"I now have a vested interest," Devon heard Reagan say as he headed toward the house. "I shouldn't go too deeply into the Realm, at present, but I'll help in the Brink."

"What about Darius?" Roger asked.

"Darius will have to make a choice—"

Alder closed the door behind Devon, muffling their voices. The chair Charity had sat in was now vacant. Alder moved around the table to take up his previous position, as though Ms. Bristol needed protection.

"Where's Charity?" Devon asked.

Karen tilted the martini glass back, sucking the last bit dry. "Outside." The glass clinked as she set it back on the table. "She needed to go for a walk and get some fresh air."

"What'd you see for her?"

Karen's blue eyes cut through him, her gaze nearly as sharp as Roger's. "That's none of your business, young man. You don't own her. Now, let's see…"

She leaned forward and looked into his eyes. Goosebumps crawled along his skin. Karen nodded and pulled the crystal ball in front of her.

White mist rolled and boiled within the glass. Colors flashed from deep within, and he started. He hadn't expected that. Black threads wove through the white, followed by flashes of green. Then streaks of orange. Devon's small hairs stood on end as tingles swept across his skin. Magic rolled and boiled in the living room like the mists within the glass, potent and powerful. Devon had heard about Ms. Bristol's magic, but he hadn't believed all the hype.

Now he understood why Alder stood by her side, in rapture. Her magic was almost a living thing, stretching out to the limits of the universe while nestled in the confines of that crystal ball. Devon's wolf practically cowered within him, awestruck, sensing something that defied the laws of physics.

In a moment and an eternity both, his ears popped. His heart rate settled down. Alder shifted his stance and took a breath. The carnival ride of the cosmos was complete.

Ms. Bristol nodded and held up her martini glass. "I need another one of these, please."

Alder moved to refill it immediately.

She pushed the ball away and, her eyes a little hazy now, refocused on Devon.

"Sometimes, the things we love the most do us the most harm." She entwined her fingers. "And you do love her." Her brow furrowed. "Or you will. It's hard to tell which from the mists. But the time will come when you need to make a choice. A choice that concerns the rest of your life and, more importantly, her life."

Devon's gut pinched.

"I cannot *see* when this choice will come, but you will know when it is before you. The choice you must make will be against your heart. Against everything you've always wanted. Against your very being. To save Charity's life—to give her a life—you must take the hard road, sacrifice your heart, and let her go."

He shook his head and stood, his middle aching.

Ms. Bristol looked up at him as Alder rounded the corner with a refreshed martini. Her gaze was focused and dominant. Her conviction was unassailable. "When the time comes, Devon, if you truly love her, you must walk away."

Devon shook his head. "She relies on me to have her back. We're a team. We look out for each other. How can walking away from her, leaving her vulnerable, be the best possible plan?"

Ms. Bristol took the martini glass and sipped. She leaned back in her chair. "I have no idea."

Devon tilted his head. "What?"

She shrugged. "I can't *see* that part. I can only see your crossroads, and the choice you must make. Everything else is hazy and unformed. I don't put images in the ball, kid. I just read what it gives me."

"That's bullshit," Devon spat.

"Watch yourself," Alder said quietly, like a whip to Devon's wolf.

Devon's muscles tensed and his body bristled. He stared into Alder's eyes.

Alder returned his stare, and Devon prepared for the older, harder wolf to force him to submit. Instead, Alder said, "She's out back. She could probably use your company."

Devon was moving before he consciously thought to. After a quick detour, he found Charity sitting on the edge of the porch, looking out at the trees. Quietly, he sat down beside her, his gut churning.

"Hey," he said softly.

She glanced his way, and worry crinkled her eyes. She forced a smile. The effort was obvious, and his heart twisted painfully.

"Tarot? Really?" She went back to looking at the trees. "I'm sorry, Devon, but is that really magic? I've had my fortune read plenty of times, and it was all cockamamie. None of it came true."

She stood in a rush and turned his way, her magic rising.

"The Brink is my home. *This* is my home"—she gestured around her—"as long as you'll have me. Finishing school is my dream. Making something of myself is my dream. *This* is my choice, not..." She flung her hand, indicating something in the distance.

He stood with her, wondering what had happened to her sword.

"The woman is a fraud."

He grabbed her shoulders and turned her to him. She looked into his eyes, opening herself to him in a way no other woman had, in a way he cherished, and was eager to reciprocate.

"I love you," he said, feeling it with every ounce of his person. "I will always protect you. This will *always* be your home."

Tears filled her eyes, and she pulled his head down, her kiss sweet but fervent. She clung to him and whispered against his lips, "I love you too. I will always choose you. Over everything."

"I got you something." He grabbed the package off the porch where he'd set it down earlier.

She peeled back the plain brown wrapping, pausing to wipe a tear from her cheek, and then gasped at the picture on the box. A silver frame, simple yet elegant.

"It's engraved." He pointed awkwardly at the top of the box.

Another tear slipped down her cheek from her shining eyes. She opened the flap and pulled out the inscribed frame: *A mother's happiness is like a beacon, lighting up the future but reflected also on the past in the guise of fond memories.*

"The quote is by Honore de Balzac. I thought it fit. We can order a different one, though, if you have something else in mind."

"No." She shook with silent sobs. "It's perfect, Devon." She ran her thumb across the inscription. "It's absolutely perfect."

"That's what I ordered in that shop you saw me in with Yasmine," he explained, resting a hand on her waist so he could touch her. "I thought you might like a nice frame for your mother's picture."

She slipped the frame back in the box carefully, as though it were a priceless relic, and then wrapped her arms around his middle. "I love you. Thank you."

He kissed her again and held her tightly. He'd never felt this way about anyone, and he knew, deep in his gut, that he never would again. He and Charity had traveled a hard road, but he was thankful for it. It had taught him about himself. About what he was capable of. About the ability to love another person.

He'd found the woman of his dreams, and he never wanted to let her go.

Besides, no fortune-teller was right all the time, not even Ms. Bristol.

KAREN WATCHED THE young, headstrong alpha walk away. She sipped her martini again, completely spent. She hated when she had to deliver bad news.

"The Realm will be divided, and that young woman is the key. Her fate—all our fates—will rest on that young man's ability to do the right thing. There aren't many who would be strong enough, not given what he'll be up against."

Alder walked to the window and looked out. "He has amazing potential. Roger has always seen it. When the time is right, Devon will do what needs to be done. Roger has faith in him."

Karen took another sip of her martini, and then turned it into a gulp. "I really wanted to tell him that the only way to get his happily ever after is to do as I said, but the mists forbade it. They're a bunch of awful jackasses."

"They clearly know the way to get the most favorable outcome."

"Oh, don't you take their side." She collected up her cards. "I've done all I can do for them. For their journey. Tell Roger that she can wait until the next quarter ends, but no longer. And *if* she waits that long, Devon must be strong enough to help her balance her magic. If he's not, she'll die on the journey."

"I've made the notes. I'll make sure Roger understands the gravity of the situation."

Karen nodded, then drained her glass. "I hear that woman is a remarkable cook. What's for dinner?"

Printed in Great Britain
by Amazon